# VICTIM OR VILLAIN

## Also by L.T. Ryan

**The Jack Noble Series**

*The First Deception*
*Noble Beginnings*
*A Deadly Distance*
*Thin Line*
*Noble Intentions*
*When Dead in Greece*
*Noble Retribution*
*Noble Betrayal*
*Never Go Home*
*Noble Judgment*
*Never Cry Mercy*
*Deadline*
*End Game*
*Noble Ultimatum*
*Noble Legend*
*Noble Revenge*
*Never Look Back*
*The Devil's Bargain*
*The Recruit*

**The Rachel Hatch Novels**

*Drift*
*Downburst*
*Fever Burn*
*Smoke Signal*
*Firewalk*
*Whitewater*
*Aftershock*
*Whirlwind*
*Tsunami*
*Fastrope*
*Sidewinder*
*Redaction*
*Mirage*
*Faultline*
*Switchback*

**Bear Logan**

*Ripple Effect*
*Blow Back*
*Take Down*
*Deep State*

**The Mitch Tanner Series**

*The Depth of Darkness*
*Into the Darkness*
*Deliver Us from Darkness*

**Maddie Castle Series (with C.R. Gray)**

*The Handler*
*Tracking Injustice*
*Hunting Grounds*
*Vanished Trails*
*Smoldering Lies*
*Field of Bones*
*Beneath the Grove*
*Disappearing Act*
*Silent Witness*

**The Bear & Mandy Logan Novels (with K.M. Rought)**

*Close to Home*
*Under the Surface*
*The Last Stop*
*Over the Edge*
*Between the Lies*
*Caught in the Web*
*The Marked Daughter*
*Beneath the Frozen Sky*

**Cassie Quinn Series (with K.M. Rought)**

*Path of Bones*
*Whisper of Bones*
*Sympathy of Bones*

*Etched in Shadow*

*Concealed in Shadow*

*Betrayed in Shadow*

*Born from Ashes*

*Return to Ashes*

*Risen from Ashes*

*Into the Light*

**The Dalton Savage Mysteries (with Biba Pearce)**

*Savage Grounds*

*Scorched Earth*

*Cold Sky*

*The Frost Killer*

*Crimson Moon*

*Dust Devil*

*Savage Season*

**Avril Dahl (with Biba Pearce)**

*Cold Reckoning*

*Cold Legacy*

*Cold Mercy*

*Cold Witness*

**Savannah Shadows Psychological Thrillers (with Laura Chase)**

*Echoes of Guilt*

*The Silence Before*

*Dead Air*

**The Alex Hayes Legal Thrillers (with Laura Chase)**

*Fractured Verdict*

*11th Hour Witness*

*Buried Testimony*

*The Bishop's Rescue*

*The Silent Gavel*

*Improper Influence*

**Blake Briar (with Gregory Scott)**

*Unmasked*

*Unleashed*

*Uncharted*

*Drawpoint*

*Contrail*

**Jane Cannon (with K.T. Crowe)**

*Blind Trust*

*Collateral*

**Danny Cortez Thrillers (with Andre Gonzalez)**

*Dead Man's List*

*Shadow Directive*

# VICTIM OR VILLAIN

A GWEN KANE THRILLER

L.T. RYAN

AND

C.R. GRAY

Cover design by Momir Borocki

ISBN: 979-8-3470-3557-1

Published in 2026 by Podium Publishing
www.podiumentertainment.com

# VICTIM
# OR
# VILLAIN

# CHAPTER 1

## Gwen

*Girls are just as strong as boys.*

That's what we'd all heard growing up.

And it was a load of bullshit.

Most men didn't have half my emotional or mental endurance. But physically? I'd have to do three times the lifting to get half the strength a male opponent had.

Maybe if someone would've told me that, I wouldn't have wound up in this position. One I knew well.

With my sweaty back suctioned to the mat beneath me, he pinned my wrists at my sides, he pinned my wrists up at my sides. The fluorescent lights hanging from the drop ceiling pulsed around his face, adding a sickly shadow to his strong jaw and creamy cheeks. His expression was blank, minus the periodic eye rolls each time I attempted, and failed, to free my arms from his grasp.

He kneeled between my legs. And where were mine? Spread open around his chest, feet flailing against his unmoving hips. No matter how hard I tried to yank free, that was all I could manage. Flailing my feet around. Only for him to body block my kicks and wedge me further beneath him.

But, as a woman, I was far from Axel's type. It's not like my hands were trembling and my heart was pounding. I was just gritting my teeth at the reminder that, yet again, I stood next to no chance in hand-to-hand combat with a man.

"Fight smarter, not harder, Gwen," Axel said.

Obviously, because if I fought any harder, I was gonna blow some blood vessels.

Exasperated, I released all my tense limbs and grunted my annoyance. "I thought I was supposed to use my legs."

"You are. To kick me in the face once I'm vulnerable." His tone came out just as pointed as my own. "So get me vulnerable."

"If I could remember how, I would, asshole."

He narrowed his eyes.

I narrowed mine.

"Work in reverse," Axel said. "Do the opposite of what you think you should do."

"What the hell is that supposed to mean?"

"Maybe if you paid attention, you'd know."

I paid plenty of attention. The steps were clear. Once his weight was off me, I had to create distance however possible. Kicking, slapping, punching—it didn't matter. Create distance and hit hard enough to disable him long enough to get away.

But I couldn't remember how to create that distance.

It happened every time I was in this position. That was why, even after taking this course half a dozen times, I hadn't managed to pass it.

"Maybe if I had a gun," I said, "I would be just fine right now."

"Too bad you don't."

I grunted and went back to kicking my feet like an angry toddler.

Axel rolled his eyes. "Just tap out."

I didn't want to tap out. I wanted to get this over with.

"What's going on over there?" Rhiannon's voice came from somewhere behind me. "You giving her grief again, Axel?"

I was still kicking, but I couldn't manage to get my feet to the front of his torso. Each time I tried, he swayed his hips one way or the other.

"She's the one who doesn't listen," Axel said.

Rhiannon came into view on my right. The neon pink sports bra popped against her deep brown skin. All her box braids were wound in place at the back of her head. "Well, did you remind her what the next step is?"

"No," he and I said in unison.

I said, "If I don't figure this out on my own, I gotta do this class all over again."

Passing a self-defense course was a requirement to stay at the ranch. Why? Because, in Rhiannon's words, *We're not just here to heal our wounds. We're here to learn how to keep from getting any more.*

Which I appreciated. Most domestic violence shelters just gave women a place to go while they figured things out themselves. Rhiannon's Ranch was different. It revolved around breaking the cycles that brought us here in the first place.

But I was tired of this damn self-defense course. I must have known something about self-defense, or I would've died the day I'd left my husband.

Rhiannon frowned down at me. "But you passed everything else?"

"I wouldn't say with flying colors," Axel said, "but yeah. This is her last hold."

"I'll make you a deal then." Rhiannon perched her hands on her hips. "If I show you how to get out of this, then next time, it's the only hold you've gotta complete. Sound fair?"

"Very." I wiggled my feet some more. "What am I forgetting?"

"Your hips." She pointed to them. "Lift them upward into his groin, and you'll have leverage with your feet."

Damn it. The hips.

I rammed them forward, fast and hard. Axel grunted. Quickly, I slid my arms upward. He released my wrists. The jarring motion gave me enough time to shove a foot into his hip. I slid backward atop the mat. With enough distance between us, I kicked my feet like windmill blades.

He raised his arms at his sides.

Rhiannon laughed and extended a hand.

I took it, using her support to steady me on my feet. The gym door slammed behind one of the other women, leaving just the three of us. The air had cooled without everyone's body heat filling the space. My words echoed off the high ceilings as if through speakers at a concert. "Thank you."

"Don't thank me." Smiling, Rhiannon gave my shoulder a squeeze. "That was all you."

The lack of a completion certificate proved otherwise. "So, next class, I just have to do that hold, and I'm done?"

"Then you're done."

"I can't wait." I grabbed my water bottle off the floor and spun off the lid. "When is it?"

"It's tough to say with the holidays coming up, but probably early next year."

"Ugh."

"You'll be in here for five minutes, and then you can go on your merry way." She glanced at her watch. "Which reminds me. Sebastian's here working on one of my horse's hooves. He said he'd be finishing up right around now though, if you want to meet him at your cabin to get Honey her shot."

To my cabin I went.

As annoyed as I'd been that I failed my self-defense class, I couldn't stay that way for long. Not once I was in my car, driving up the snow-dusted hill to my rent-free abode at the edge of the gravel road. From the gym, it took fifteen minutes of driving past white-doused conifer trees and cabins to make it to mine. My little lemon didn't love the fluffy white that fell from the clouds, forming a blanket on the gravel, but I couldn't complain about this view. So long as I was careful to pump my brakes, I always made it home in one piece.

A green pickup truck was parked half in the snow-covered grass and half in my one-car driveway. The guy sitting in the driver's seat was one of the few men with unrestricted access to the ranch.

I pulled in beside him, offering a smile and wave as I shifted the car into park. Did I get a smile and wave in response? No. Just a curt nod as Sebastian stepped from the driver's seat.

With my purse over my shoulder, I joined him in the driveway. "Sorry I'm late. Rhiannon had me down at the gym. Still taking that damn self-defense course."

"I only pulled in a minute before you." I didn't get a good look at him as he dug around on the floorboards. "Did you pass yet?"

A huff escaped me, forming a cloud against the cold air in front of me. "Nope."

"You'll get it."

Sebastian came around from the front. In one hand, he held his leather bag full of medical supplies. He carried that thing everywhere he went, always prepared to tend to an animal in need. A canvas dangled from the other. The image faced him, but a few smears of color lined the frame.

"How's Honey been?" he asked.

"Still no side effects, still no limping. No one would know she was a senior dog unless I told them." Crossing my arms, I nodded at the canvas. "What's that?"

"Uh." Sebastian trailed his tongue along his teeth, cheeks bright red beneath a bushy brown beard. I couldn't tell if it was the cold wind slapping against his face or just his typical embarrassment at any mention of his work. "I was a little inebriated over the weekend."

"Lucky you." I gave a half smile and cocked my head to the side. "And you want me to admire your wonky, drug-induced creation?"

"No." His breath smoked before his face. "I mean, yeah, it's a little weird, but not the weirdest thing I've made."

"Judging by that look you're giving me, I wouldn't be surprised if it was a lizard giving a lap dance."

Which wouldn't be at all out of Sebastian's artistic style. He had an affinity for animals doing something odd and humanlike. The first time I went to his veterinarian office with Honey, I chuckled at the cigarette-smoking frog and the horse wearing a sombrero proudly displayed in his waiting room.

"No, it's just—I don't know. I guess I had Honey on my mind."

An awkward laugh escaped him as he spun the canvas around. I had to join in on the laughter. Stretched out on the cloth canvas was a perfect rendition of my corgi, dressed as a barista, serving coffee behind a checkout counter. While the backdrop looked a bit cartoonish, the painting of the dog could've been a photographic print.

"I was just playing around," he said, "and this is what came out. I didn't even realize until the next day how much it looked like Honey. She's your baby and everything, so I figured, if you want it, it's yours."

Laughing, I took the painting in my hands and marveled at it a moment longer. He wasn't wrong—it truly was a perfect rendition. Everything from the big, pointy ears half the size of her head to the white stripe descending her little snout.

I told him, "I love it. How much do you want for it?"

The redness in his cheeks receded. A smile I usually knew as crooked reached all the way to his hazel eyes. He waved me off and shook his head. "Nothing. I was just a little tipsy, having some fun, and then I thought, 'Gwen would like this.' So. Here we are."

"I've got to give you *something*." Gazing at it, I slid my finger down the puppy's cheeks, admiring each intricate brushstroke. "What is this—oil paint?" I looked back up at him. "That shit ain't cheap. At least let me pay for the materials."

"It was all stuff I had laying around. I don't know how much they cost." Another dismissive wave of his hand before it found a perch on the back of his neck. "I did have a question for you, though."

"And what's that?"

He opened his mouth to speak, then snapped it shut. His smile returned, cheeks burning bright again. "You think we can get this shot done real quick? It's getting late, and I still gotta pick Lizzie up from school."

"Right. Obviously." I started for the door, glancing at him over my shoulder. "You want me to just bring her out? She's easier to control inside, but if you're in a hurry—"

"No, no. I'll just come in, if that's okay?"

I glanced back at him, assuring him it was fine, and led the way up the steps. Sebastian had come into my cabin a thousand times to give Honey her medicine. What was the apprehension this time?

Honey's barks erupted on the other side of the door once we were closer. The fact that she hadn't heard us talking in the driveway had me curious about her quality of hearing these days. When I opened the door, her barks only got louder. Her nub of a tail wagged hard enough to shake her whole body as she jumped at me, then Sebastian, licking our hands and faces. That didn't stop when we crossed the threshold.

Honey had seen a lot of vets in her life, and even though Sebastian stabbed her with a pain management shot each month for the arthritis in her little legs, she still adored his presence. I couldn't blame her. He wasn't much of a people person, but the way he was with animals could warm any girl's heart. Crouched on the ground beside her, he let her lick him all over.

I gave her head a scratch and kicked off my snow-covered boots. "Guess I'm chopped liver."

"She'd probably like you more if you were," Sebastian said.

Jaw dropped, I shot him a certain hand signal. He only laughed.

Knowing the two of them, this greeting would last a while. Especially after Sebastian told her, "Go get your toy."

So while he sat cross-legged on the floor and gave her all the love and attention she desired, I sank onto the old, floral print sofa.

"Alright, easy." Sebastian shook out his hand at his side and scratched Honey's head up. "You almost drew blood with that one."

Toy bear latched between her jaws, she pressed her front paws to the ground, lifted her butt into the air, and wagged her tail.

"Do you need me to hold her?" I asked.

"Nah, I got it."

He rummaged in his bag and came out with the prefilled syringe in his palm, covered in a handful of treats. Honey rushed over, nose moving like a bee after a flower. He tossed the treats a few feet across the floor. She ran to them. At lightning speed, while she gobbled them down, Sebastian jammed the needle into her flank.

She didn't so much as flinch.

Watching the two of them in awe, I shook my head. "I don't know how you do it."

"Hell of a lot easier with a chunker." He gave her flank one more pet, smoothing down her fur, and rose from his knees. "The dogs who aren't food motivated make everything harder."

"Honey'd eat herself to death if I let her." I stood with him and reached for my purse on the table. "The usual eighty?"

"Yes, ma'am." Hands in his pockets, he pressed his lips together. "Unless you wanna make a barter?"

Slowly, I set my wallet back into my purse. "What kinda barter?"

"Well, you know Lizzie."

"I do know Lizzie," I said.

Lizzie was Sebastian's preteen niece. The whole backstory and how he'd wound up with custody of her? No idea. But she was around the ranch on her days off from school while Sebastian worked with Rhiannon's animals. She was friends with a few of the teens who lived in the apartments in town.

"She sort of—" Sebastian scratched his head and grimaced. "She's not welcome back at her music school."

I choked on a laugh and set my purse down. "What the hell'd she do?"

"Nothing serious. Just some inappropriate verbiage she used with a teacher."

"That checks out."

"Yeah, so I'm looking for someone to help her with her winter piano recital." He nodded out the window. "Rhiannon has her on the solo performance list. But she still needs help with a couple songs, and I know how good you are behind the keys, so I just thought, I don't know. Maybe you'd be down to make some extra cash? I'd rather it go to a teacher she likes anyway. And you guys get along."

*Huh.* I squinted at him. While most of my expenses were covered here at the ranch, my nine-to-five didn't pay the greatest. Like all the other girls here, I was working on building up a nest egg to start a business of my own someday.

"I'm not gonna turn it down." I leaned against the dinette table. "But I'm not really a teacher."

"Yeah, I know. But she already knows how to play." He spoke quickly, hands still jammed into his pockets. Opposed to his usual perfect posture, he slouched the slightest bit. "She's been playing since kindergarten. Just needs a little guidance when she's taking on a new song."

That, I could understand. "In that case, sure. I'm down. What day and time is good for you guys?"

"Her usual lessons were every other Friday at seven, but if that doesn't work for you, we can figure something else out."

"I'm usually off by five on Fridays, so that's perfect."

"Awesome. Great." Nodding quickly, he raked a hand through his shoulder-length brown waves. "I paid the school two hundred a lesson. So I figured I'd just give that to you?"

"Minus Honey's shot." I wasn't one for handouts. The very reason it'd taken me years longer than it should've to wind up in any women's shelter. "That's the barter, right?"

"That's the barter. And uh, I don't know. Maybe we could go get something to eat after? Just, ya know, my way of saying thanks."

I cocked my head to the side. "Me, you, and Lizzie?"

"I, uh—I was thinking just me and you. But sure, yeah. If you want Lizzie to come." He nodded quickly again, throat bobbing with a swallow. "Yeah, that's fine."

My head still cocked, I let the corner of my mouth quirk up.

Sebastian was one of the first people I'd met at the ranch, and our friendship budded somewhere in our frequent proximity. We met each month for Honey's injection. Since he was the vet who cared for all Rhiannon's horses, cows, goats, and chickens, we saw one another around the ranch all the time. I worked four buildings down from his office in the city, and he walked down each day for lunch. Two or three dinners a week, we shared a table at the cafeteria in town for dinner.

Suffice it to say, eating together was far from uncommon.

His visible anxiety though? That was new.

Was it a meal he was asking for? Or something else?

I couldn't say the thought had never crossed my mind. He was handsome in a rough and rugged sort of way, from his six-foot height to his strong jaw and piercing puppy dog eyes. And that beard—my god, I'd fought the desperate urge to run my fingers through it a thousand times.

But I was used to men who made the move. Sebastian never had.

So I pushed any attraction I had for him into a neat little box in the corner of my mind. This last year was about healing. Maybe I'd date again once I had my shit together.

But was he even asking for a date?

"I mean." I raised a shoulder. "I've been dying to try that hibachi place that just opened in Glacier Ridge. But Lizzie's picky, isn't she? I don't think she'd like hibachi."

Shoulders releasing, something glimmered in his eyes. "Yeah, she hates hibachi."

"So just you and me then?"

"Yeah. Yeah, that sounds great." His smile reached his eyes again. "Just you and me."

# CHAPTER 2

## *Sebastian*

". . . And it's just annoying, because I know how to write an essay. Like, I've been in AP English classes since the fourth grade." Lizzie grasped hold of the granite countertop behind her and hoisted herself onto its top. "Literally. I won awards for writing. You remember that, don't you? That short story I submitted in fifth grade?"

If memory served, *I* had submitted that short story. Lizzie kept saying that it wasn't good enough yet. She was nine years old. It wasn't going to win a Pulitzer. But it had won that contest because it *was* good enough.

Wiping my damp hands on my apron, I surveyed the island top for the cherry tomatoes hidden somewhere among the lettuce and onion and cucumbers and peppers. I opened my mouth to respond, but she cut in first.

"Oh my God, are you even listening to me?"

"Yes, I'm listening, and yes, I remember the short story. *The Busy Bear.* Literary excellence. Have you seen the tomatoes? I swear they were—" I spun around and spotted the tomatoes. In Lizzie's lap.

She gave a crooked half smile. "Sorry."

I snatched them and returned to my nearly finished salad in the wooden bowl. "Go on. You're pissed at your English teacher because she gave you a bad grade on your essay?"

"It wasn't a bad grade," she insisted. "It was a C. But it's not about the grade. It's about her feedback. She told me that I need to learn to 'kill my darlings' because I talked too much about my personal views on the subject. Which was the point, right? It was an opinion essay on *Of Mice and Men.* And I know why. Our class is the only class that still reads this book, and it's because she loves it so much. Well, I hated it. And that's what the essay was about, our feelings on the book after having completed it, and I'm sorry—but, wait, you know what? No. I'm not sorry. Maybe in its time, it was an excellent read. But in the modern era, it . . ."

For nearly a decade, this had been my favorite part of every day. Listening to Lizzie rant and rave about school, or drama with her friends, or current events, or pop culture.

At work, the lives of living creatures were in my hands and I had to think fast. I had to make hard calls.

And I guess here, making dinner with my niece, there was still a life in my hands. Lizzie was my responsibility. My responsibility, but also my peace. Following her chaotic train of thought forced my own to a halt.

But I wasn't sure that this was my favorite part of the day anymore. Not because I loved Lizzie and her rants any less. Purely because I had something—some*one*—outside of her now.

With all the time I'd spent at the ranch, I had lots of people. *Community*, Rhiannon always reminded me. *It takes a village, and we'll always be yours.* When I'd taken Lizzie in, those had been the first words out of Rhiannon's mouth.

And they were my village. The staff, the women who came and went. They watched Lizzie when I had to work late, and they brought me their animals when they were sick. I cared for so many people because of that place, and so many of them cared for me.

Gwen was different, though. From the moment I met her, I'd known something was different. She was as quick-witted and smart-assed as I was. We talked, and the rest of the world vanished.

Now, lunch at Maple & Thyme, where Gwen worked, was my favorite part of each day. That, or when our paths would cross at the ranch.

Seeing her, talking to her, breathing in the smell of her perfume, and saying something off-kilter enough to watch her face squish up with confusion, only for her lips to stretch across her cheeks and her eyes to twinkle with amusement, were my favorite parts of every day.

"But I guess one C isn't going to kill me, right?" Propping her elbows on her knees, Lizzie sighed deeply. "I deserve a better grade. I know I do. But it isn't worth the battle."

"Considering you already got fired by one teacher this week?" I dug around in the spice drawer in search of dried dill. "I concur. Not worth the battle."

"Oh yeah. Speaking of which." Lizzie hopped off the counter and came to the island. She dropped a—hopefully clean—hand into the plastic pack of cherry tomatoes and plopped the scoop onto her plate. "Did you talk to Gwen yet? Can she tutor me?"

Dill in hand, I frowned at her. "You know, I really don't like how casual you are about this."

"About Gwen?" She tossed one of the tomatoes into the air and caught it in her mouth. Not bothering to finish chewing before she spoke. "I thought we liked Gwen."

"No, not Gwen. I'm talking about how casual you are over cussing out your piano teacher and getting expelled from the top musical academy in the state."

Lizzie rolled her eyes. "Top musical academy in th—this is Montana. There are probably twenty musical academies in the whole thing. It's not that serious, Seabass."

"Expulsion from any school is that serious, Liz."

"No, that woman was a bitch." Lizzie raised a finger, motioning me to silence before I could scold her. "She called Callie a fat ass because she ripped the leotard that this bullshit company has reused every summer recital for as long as I've been alive. And that's another thing. How much did you pay for those lessons? Because I'm pretty sure they could afford a new leotard that fits a teenage girl of a *normal size*. And I don't even think the teachers were that good. All of mine were snooty, snot-nosed bitches. And that's all I said. The truth. That they are a bunch of snooty, snot-nosed bitches."

A deep breath fell from my nostrils.

They *were* a bunch of snooty, snot-nosed bitches. I only sent her to that school because my parents had already enrolled her before I'd gotten custody. The tuition could cover a small mortgage, the students had their noses so high in the air, I didn't know how they saw where they were going, and the teachers were no better. Old money kind of people. The most obnoxious kind of people.

But Lizzie was my responsibility, which made it my responsibility to correct her. "Language."

She waved me off and reached for the dressing I had just finished making. "You never answered my question."

"Which was?"

"Gwen. Is she going to tutor me now?"

"You're really lucky that she said yes, because if she hadn't, I wouldn't be driving you three hours a week to the second-best musical academy in the state."

She smiled. "Good. Gwen's fun. And she plays better than those snooty, snot-nosed bitches anyway."

"If I have to tell you about your language again—"

Another dismissive hand wave. "So. How are you paying her for my lesson? As good as you paid the *top musical academy in the state*?" She switched to a London accent for that last bit.

"I don't see how that's your business." Bowl of salad in hand, I gestured to the dining area. "Grab that bread off the stove, would you?"

She did, then met me at the antique cherry dining table. The silk-lined seats clunked through the grout lines of the marble tile below. "I mean, are you at least taking her out for a nice dinner as payment?"

"Yeah, we talked about getting something to eat after." My stomach flipped at the words, and I passed Lizzie the bowl of salad. "You've gotta eat some vegetables other than tomatoes, kid. All kinds of nutrients in the leafy greens. Just take them by the fistful if you've got to."

As I instructed, she grabbed a fistful, held it to her mouth, and chewed like a cow eating hay. I wasn't sure if I should roll my eyes or laugh. I did a bit of both. She joined in on the laughter.

When it fell off, she squeezed a piece of chicken between the tongs and laid it on her plate. "Why do you have to be so weird about it?"

"Weird about what?"

"Anytime I bring up that maybe you and Gwen could do something together, or *be* something together, you try to change the subject." Slicing at her chicken, she raised a shoulder. "Why? Why can't you just admit that you like her?"

I didn't like Gwen. I loved her.

I loved how kind she was to animals. How much her friends mattered to her. The gentleness in her demeanor, to not step on any toes at the ranch. And her firmness on almost everything else. Her eye rolls, her sarcasm, her artistry—all of them. From the cake decorating, to the piano, to the simple way she walked through a room.

And that red hair. God, I loved that hair. It was somehow as bright as a fire engine and as deep as a cherry at once. With a color choice like that, you'd think she'd demand attention in every room she walked into. But she was more of a wallflower. Quiet, reserved, almost aloof, surveying every move everyone made in every room.

But get her talking about her dog, or equality, or any man that landed a woman at Rhiannon's Ranch, and then you understood the hair. She didn't have it for attention. It was a warning. Like a venomous animal whose vibrant complexion said, *Stay back. I bite.*

The things I loved about her were the very reason it took so much courage to admit my feelings were more than platonic.

She hadn't even been at the ranch for a year. That meant that less than a year ago, she'd been living in some version of hell.

She never talked about her ex. Never even told me her real name.

So I didn't know her story. Not entirely.

But I knew *the* story.

I didn't want to be a rebound. It could take her far longer to heal, to be ready for what I wanted.

A partner. Someone to move through life with. Someone to come home to, someone to lie beside at night, someone to laugh with.

And I didn't know if she wanted that, let alone if she was ready for it. Never mind if *I* was who she'd want it with.

"I like her very much." I dipped my bread in the garlic-infused olive oil. "She's a great friend, and I'm really lucky to have her in my life."

Sighing deeply, Lizzie rolled her eyes again. "Whatever. I'll shut up and act like I don't have eyes and ears. But all I'm saying is, if you want it to work with her, you gotta be the one to make the move. Gwen spends so much time in her own head, you've got to knock if you want her to let you in."

# CHAPTER 3

## *Gwen*

Honey stayed at the cabin when I went to group. Growls and snaps were a common occurrence in the hours that followed her injection. Better to let her rest in bed while us girls sat around rehashing our trauma.

I started down the gravel path, glancing over my shoulder to check for Simone. Every Wednesday, we went to group together at the rec center and cooked dinner afterwards. Usually, we'd meet on this path. She got off work at five, made it back here around six, drove past me as I was walking into town, and stopped to give me a ride in.

But there'd been no sign of her so far.

With the gloves around my fingers and balaclava pulled up around my nose and head, allowing a few red curls to escape, I wasn't fighting off frostbite. As much as I enjoyed the pine trees all around, the silence of winter, even the snowflakes clumping on my eyelashes, I would've driven myself if I'd known she wouldn't show.

Only a mile remaining of my journey, certain I wouldn't cross Simone's path, anxiety budded in my chest. Was everything alright? Had something happened to her daughter, Junie? I couldn't think of any other reason for her not to be home yet.

Or for her to break our routine. Obviously, I wasn't entitled to her time, but this was what we had done every Wednesday for the last six months. Something had to be wrong.

Descending the hill, I found my phone in my pocket and sent her a message.

**Gwen**
Hey, you coming to group?

Snow crunched under my boots as I glided the rest of the way, nearly jogging from the downhill momentum. I had passed the nursery and was only a few blocks away from the rec center when she finally texted back.

**Simone**

Yeah, sorry. I should've texted you.

It's just been a weird day.

We all had those. I couldn't call anyone at the ranch the pinnacle of perfect mental health.

Simone struggling was a new one though. She was beyond vocal about her anxieties when she was upset. If there was something on her mind, I was usually the first to know about it.

But she respected my space, so I would respect hers.

**Gwen**

It's cool, don't be sorry. Let me know if you need to talk.

My phone dinged again. I expected it to be her, but *Sebastian* lit up the screen instead. My stomach flipped, before nausea flooded it. Why the hell did just his name give me butterflies?

And why did the butterflies make me nauseous? It was like their wings had razor blades on their tips, scratching me up with each flap.

**Sebastian**

Hey, Liz told me to ask you about a song you were playing in the dining hall the other day. Something about rainbows and kittens?

I had to laugh.

**Gwen**

Lmao idk which one she liked, but I've only got two songs by Rainbow Kitten

Surprise on that playlist, so it was either Wasted or Cocaine Jesus.

His response was immediate.

**Sebastian**
. . . that's not what I was expecting.

**Gwen**
Lol you asked

**Sebastian**
When she said rainbows and kittens, I assumed it was for kids.

Another laugh.

**Gwen**
I don't think that's their target audience, no

**Sebastian**
Where tf do you find this shit?

**Gwen**
Reddit, if memory serves. And don't knock 'em til you try 'em. Ela's voice is so dynamic, the lyrics are pure poetry, and they blend rock with EDM beautifully.

**Sebastian**
Hold while I listen.

**Gwen**
Holding.

And there I was, walking down the street, grinning at my phone like a little girl.

What the hell was this?

It was no secret that I adored Sebastian. We were friends. Great friends.

But we'd met the day I got here. I'd literally run here in the middle of the night from my husband with a garbage bag of belongings.

Of course I'd noticed how beautiful the green in his hazel eyes was. I'd smiled at the way he wiggled his brows when he spoke, and each time our fingers brushed, chills swept over my skin. Sometimes I caught myself staring at him a moment too long and had to yank my gaze away.

Because he wasn't interested. Why would he be? He was normal. Stable. He had a career, and a home, and a family.

I worked in a café and lived in a domestic violence shelter.

Why would he be interested in *me*?

No, this wasn't a date. I needed to wrangle in those butterflies, because he hadn't asked me on a date. He'd offered to take me to dinner as payment for teaching his niece piano.

That was all.

My phone dinged again.

**Sebastian**

Wasted's heavier lyrically. Cocaine Jesus is catchier.

**Gwen**

Wasted's one of my favorites. Try Painkillers(:

I could hear his snarky, blunt voice in the next text.

**Sebastian**

Every title involves drug use, Gwen.

**Gwen**

They're not about drug use, Sebastian. It's metaphoric.

He followed up with an eye roll emoji.

The rec center was only a few strides ahead now. I stowed the phone into my pocket, tugged down my balaclava, and did my best to ignore those flapping butterfly wings.

—

I'd never been to therapy before coming to the ranch. Movies always made it look cold and depressing. I wanted to move on from my trauma. Not dwell in it.

But therapy sessions here felt more like a sleepover. A few dozen girls sat around on couches, under fuzzy throws, with steaming mugs of tea or hot cocoa in hand. The pine trees covered in snow outside the window added a level of coziness, rather than cold. And the spread of snacks always got me giddy.

After snatching a couple cookies off the table by the door, I sat in my usual spot on the floral sofa. Legs crossed lotus-style, I smiled and said hello to everyone who walked in. All the faces were familiar at this point.

A couple thousand of us lived here on the ranch. I didn't know each and every name or story, but I could pick out any of these faces from a crowd.

Except for one. She walked in at five 'til seven, only minutes before group started, wearing a pair of baggy sweatpants and a bleach-stained hoodie. I recognized the look, even if not the person wearing it.

Her blonde hair was grown out, brown roots exposed. She wore a bit of makeup, but not enough to mask the dark circle, or the swelling, around her left eye.

Her round cheeks told me she couldn't have been older than twenty.

She stopped at the entrance a moment longer, looking around the room. Most of the other girls gossiped amongst themselves, not realizing she was here. I waved at her, getting her attention.

"You can sit wherever. There's room here if you want." Smiling, I scooched over. Usually Simone sat there, but she wasn't here yet and I knew she'd appreciate me making space for the newcomer. "If you're hungry, grab something to eat, something to drink. Just make yourself at home."

She forced a tight-lipped smile, nodding.

Probably as uncomfortable as I had been my first day here.

She visited the snack table then joined me on the sofa, placing the small paper plate of chips and cookies in her lap. "Thanks."

"No problem. When did you get in?"

"Early this morning." Her voice was soft, shy. Between nibbles on her cookie, she only spared me a glance or two. "How long have you been here?"

"Almost a year." And yet, it seemed like a decade. "What's your name?"

"A—I mean, Delilah. My name's Delilah."

I extended a hand. "Gwen."

Grip soft, she shook it. "Is that the one your parents gave you? Or the one you gave yourself?"

"The latter."

Another smile, this one more genuine than the last. "How long did it take you to get used to using it?"

"A couple weeks. Sometimes I still have the reflex to say my old one, but I was answering to Gwen in the first few days." Settling back in on the sofa, I stifled a yawn. "It's all surreal at first. *Leaving* is surreal at first. This place makes it a lot weirder. A lot better, too."

A humorless laugh escaped her. "Better than where I was yesterday."

Behind Delilah, the metal door to the room clicked open again. This time, a familiar face walked through.

Rhiannon was in her usual: a pair of barn-stained blue jeans and a Carhart hoodie. Tightly braided black curls hung to the center of her back, ending in a rainbow of brightly colored beads, covered with a beige beanie. She wore a bit of makeup, as she always did. Just a pop of pink on her thick lips and a speckle of golden eyeshadow at her inner corner. The only thing out of the ordinary were her white thick-rimmed glasses.

She glanced around the room, her warm brown eyes settling on Delilah. When Rhiannon saw Delilah with me, she smiled. Grabbing a couple of cookies from the table, she said, "Alright, ladies, we're gonna get started."

The room quieted, only dull pop music playing softly from a speaker in the corner.

"Digging the glasses, lady," one of the women in the back said.

Rhiannon cozied into one of the sofas across from me, propped her legs up on the chaise, and covered her mouth between chews on her cookie. "I ran out of contacts, and it's gonna take a couple weeks for new ones to come in. Gotta deal with these damn things sliding off twenty-four-seven 'til then."

"They are cute though," I said.

"They're a damn nuisance," she said. "Anyway. Everybody, this is Delilah." She waved at her. "Just got in this morning. We all know how rough it can be the first few days, so try and help her feel at home."

With bright red cheeks, Delilah waved awkwardly around the room.

"It's been a while since we had a newcomer on a Wednesday," Rhiannon said, "so I thought we'd start out today's session with something I haven't done in a while. I want to talk about our last straws. The ones that broke the camel's back. We all have something, big or small, that was our 'I'm done' moment. I think talking about them might make Delilah feel a little bit more secure in her decision to leave. So. Anyone want to share?"

Not me. Hearing other people talk about what happened to them, the demons they battled every day since, was more therapeutic than talking about my own.

"I will." A girl on the other end of the room raised her hand. When all eyes were on her, she pulled a throw blanket from the back of her sofa and snuggled it around her body. "I'm Eve, by the way. I've only been here a few months, so I'm still adjusting, too, Delilah. If you ever want to talk, I'm around."

Delilah muttered a thanks.

"My last straw probably seems small," Eve said, glancing around the room. "Me and my fiancé were remodeling our basement. We got into a fight one morning. I can't even remember what it was about." Snorting, she shook her head. "I was six months pregnant, and he shoved me.

"He went to work after that. I was upset, so I figured I would go paint some trim down there. Ease my mind, you know?" She twiddled with a fraying string on the fleece blanket over her lap. "Anyway, I started working on it and I dropped my paintbrush. We hadn't put in the floors yet, so it wasn't a huge deal, but I bent down to pick it up, and I saw this hole in the wall."

The door at the far left of the room clicked open again. This time, Simone walked through.

It wasn't her late arrival that had me squinting, though. It was everything else.

Wearing a pair of yoga pants and a black hoodie, she mouthed, "Sorry," as she tiptoed across the room to join me on the sofa. Her long dark hair was tossed up in a messy bun. Not an ounce of makeup rested on her cheeks, nor her eyes. Which wasn't uncommon among the girls here. I wasn't wearing any either. But it was uncommon for Simone.

"The memory hit me like a bomb." Eve's voice grew somber. "I was looking at that hole in the wall, and I remembered when he put it there. I don't remember what that fight was about either, but I remember him kicking that hole in the wall. He tried to punch one first, but he hit a stud and broke his hand, so he started kicking it, over and over and over again."

Tracing her tongue along her teeth, Eve let out a humorless laugh. "And when I told him to stop, that he was gonna break his foot too, he said, 'It's better I hit the wall than you.' He hadn't hit me at that point. But I should've known. I should've known then what it would progress to. Because it did. That's why I'm here. But looking at that hole in the wall? That was the moment I knew I had to get out."

Troy, my ex, had told me that too. That it was better he hit the wall than hit me. Sure enough, one day, he'd decided to hit me too.

"I don't think that's something we talk enough about," Rhiannon said. "Well, not we. The rest of the world. We always hear that boys will be boys, but good men aren't violent. Good men don't punch holes in walls."

I didn't disagree with Rhiannon. But with how I'd grown up, you just couldn't convince me that violence was *never* the answer.

"What are we talking about?" Simone asked, leaning around Delilah. She spared her a smile and a quick wave while she was at it.

"The straws that broke our camels' backs," Rhiannon answered. "The moment we were done. Why we left. You want to share yours?"

It may have sounded presumptuous for Rhiannon to assume that Simone would want to share her experience. But not to anyone who knew Simone. She would tell the most tragic story from her past with a straight face, then shrug and say, "Shit happens. You live, you learn."

Simone and Rhiannon understood one another. The ranch may have been Rhiannon's, but the synergy those two had? I had the feeling Rhiannon was grooming Simone to take over in her place one day.

At that question, Simone tensed. Normally, she would've jumped right in. Hopefully I would find out why at dinner. If she still wanted to have dinner with me, that was.

"I guess I realized he was the villain," Simone said, chewing her lower lip. "It shouldn't have taken me so long to see that. Like when, a week after I gave birth to his daughter, he didn't stop when I said no." Many of us cringed, but Simone only gritted her teeth. "Or like when I was pregnant, and he gave me a black eye. Really, there were a *million* times I should've seen him for the volatile piece of shit that he was.

"But I didn't. Not until I realized that he was worse than me." Pulling in a deep breath, she leaned forward and propped her elbows on her knees. Gaze on the ground, it took her a moment to continue. We all waited.

Eventually, she said, "I get in from work one day, and my daughter's not there. But he is." An annoyed scoff escaped her nostrils. "He's nodded off on the couch. So I wake him up, and I'm screaming, and he tells me to calm down. He just has to wait for a deal to go through later, and then he's going to go pick her up. From his dealer." A humorless laugh. Rubbing her eyes, she shook her head. "I don't know exactly what deal he made. But I know he owed the guy money. And for some reason, our four-year-old seemed like good collateral to him.

"We fought. Probably the worst fight of our relationship. Both of us were covered in blood by the end of it, and he was unconscious. I got his phone out of his pocket, and I called the guy. He wanted five grand." Simone sucked her teeth. "Which was every penny I had saved up to open my salon. But I drained my account, and I ran to his house in the middle of nowhere, and I got my baby.

"And it . . ." Another slow, calming breath. She shut her eyes and took a few more. Her hazel eyes still on the ground, she continued through gritted teeth. "I don't know what those bastards did to Junie. She wouldn't tell me. But she freaked out when I tried to get her undressed to put her in the bath that night. Maybe that means something, maybe it doesn't, but I hope to hell and back that she was too young to remember it. Whatever happened that day, I hope it's buried deep in the back of her mind.

"But what the hell does that matter?" Tossing her hands in the air, her pace picked up. "What the hell do any of my feelings about it matter? What *does* matter is that *I* was stupid. I can say that I was young, and that I was in love, and that it was a cycle of abuse that I was born into because my mom let my dad treat her like shit, but at the end of the day, *I* was an idiot. We spend all this time talking about what *they* did, and yeah, we should hold them accountable for that. But none of us did, right?

"That's why we're here. We ran because they're monsters. They're monsters, and we're fools. They'll never take accountability for what they did. David's never going to feel sorry for what he did to me that day, what he did to Junie, and what the hell does it matter? I can blame him until I'm blue in the face. He's the one who did it, but I'm the one who put up with it. I'm the one who let that happen to my daughter. *I'm* the idiot. We are all—"

"Simone." Rhiannon sat forward too, brows furrowed, voice firm. "A lot of things come up when we talk about this shit, and those feelings are valid. But if you were about to say that we're *all* stupid, that we're to blame for what they did to us, you know that's not gonna fly."

Simone took in one more deep breath, pinching her eyes shut. She shook her head. It took a few long heartbeats for her to say, "I'm sorry."

"You don't have to be." Rhiannon settled back in her seat. "But I just want to make sure we're all clear about how things go in these conversations."

"I know." Simone rubbed her eyes. "It's just been a bad day. I probably shouldn't have come tonight."

"The nights you want to be here the least are the nights you need to be here the most," Rhiannon said. "But I want to talk about that. What you just said, about how you put up with it. How that makes you feel like an idiot." She turned her gaze to the rest of the room. "Now I know we've all felt like that at some point or another. Like we were just as bad as he was. Why do you think that's the case?"

Silence stretched on for a minute. When no one else spoke, I did. "Because they convinced us we were."

Rhiannon's eyes met mine. "And did you know that's the very reason I opened this ranch?"

No, I didn't.

"Not one woman in this room meets the 'perfect victim' criteria." Rhiannon gestured around. "We fought back. We defended ourselves. They convinced us we were just as much at fault as they were. Most of our husbands, or boyfriends, or whatevers, they were decent guys to everyone else. They weren't the stereotypical woman beater you see in movies, were they?"

David was pretty damn close to one. But Troy wasn't. My ex-husband had been many things, but no one, not even the cops, believed he was an abuser.

"And that's the only way the world likes a woman in a situation like ours." Rhiannon tossed an arm onto the back of the sofa. "She never fought back. She had all the bruises, and he didn't have a scratch on him. Except for some bruised knuckles, maybe. Out there, to everyone else, you're only a victim of domestic violence if you never stood up for yourself. But the moment you do, you're the bad guy. You're the idiot if you stay, and you're just as bad if you hit him back. So my point here is, you're right, Gwen. They did convince us we were the problem. But so did the rest of the world. There's nothing the world loves more than hating a woman."

Chills rose over my arms.

Holding Rhiannon's gaze, Simone chewed on her lip.

"You understand me?" Rhiannon asked, eyes wider, surveying her.

Simone nodded slowly. "I do. I'm sorry. I'm just tired. Is it alright if I head home? I need some sleep."

"You're not being held captive." Rhiannon softened her voice, nodding to the door. "Take some cookies for the road."

Another nod, followed by a quiet, "Thanks."

As Simone returned to the door, Rhiannon's eyes settled on me. "Do you want to talk about your last straw, Gwen?"

I could. I could say that it was because he'd hit my dog and broken her tooth.

But that hadn't been my last straw.

My last straw had been the thought that'd circled my mind when I'd seen that gaping hole in my puppy's face.

*If I don't leave him, I'm going to kill him.*

And I'd meant it.

But I couldn't say that out loud.

So I said, "I don't think I'm ready for that."

# CHAPTER 4

## *Gwen*

The nightmare woke me again.

I lay there in bed, staring at the cedar wood ceiling, waiting for my heart rate to settle. Bluish moonlight trickled in from the window on my right. It was the only luminance, just enough to remind me where I was, that I was safe in my bed, in my cabin, hundreds of miles from anyone who would hurt me. Honey snored at my feet, a reminder of that fact.

Eventually, my shaking hands would ease, my heart rate would slow, and I would fall back to sleep. That was the hope. There was a TV on the dresser before me, but no Internet. I could've popped in a DVD, but no guarantee that would put me to sleep either.

I still didn't understand the nightmares. Even from an evolutionary standpoint. I'd gotten out. For almost a year, I had been out. I was safe. I had been safe for all this time.

So why did my brain taunt me with memories I couldn't change? Were they reminders to never go back? Or were they a punishment?

Punishment made the most sense. I deserved it.

When enough time passed, and I was certain I wasn't falling back to sleep on my own, I did what everyone did when they couldn't sleep. Checked my phone.

*New Message: Sebastian 9:52 p.m.*

My stomach swirled, and a smile touched my lips.

Damn it. Damn it, I had to stop this. Last time I swooned at a screen, I was fourteen, and I'd just met Troy.

Clearly, that hadn't turned out well.

**Sebastian**
All's Well that Ends is my favorite.
Counting Cards is a strong second.

Ugh, that damn smile ached my cheeks.

It hadn't been like this with Troy. He never cared about music I showed him.

But Simone listened to songs I sent her too. What the hell made me think this was even the slightest bit romantic?

No, no, no. This was stupid. We were just two friends, talking about a good band. And friends didn't reply in the dead of the night.

I tossed my phone to the pillows and stumbled out of bed. Grabbing my hoodie off the hook by the door, I looked at Honey. Her eyes were open now.

"Do you want to go outside?" I asked her.

She smacked her lips a time or two and looked away.

"Guess not." I gave her a scratch on the head, reached into the drawer below the TV, and came out with a joint.

While I didn't smoke much, Simone had suggested it when I'd first gotten here. I hadn't wanted to, but after that first nightmare, I figured it was worth a shot. It didn't take long to realize she'd been right. Sometimes, it was the only thing that would keep the nightmares at bay. Beyond doubt, it would help me fall back to sleep.

After walking down the hall and through the kitchen, I grabbed my candle lighter off the counter. My attire wasn't ideal for a hike—just a pair of sweatpants, a hoodie, and some snow boots—but it would be fine for a quick smoke on the porch.

The cold wind blasted my cheeks as I stepped outside. Snow trickled from the clouds overhead, adding onto the two feet already covering every inch. The plowed gravel path provided a clear line of how much snow we had gathered in the last two weeks since it came for the mountains.

Autumn in Montana always had a risk of this kind of weather. Back home, there wouldn't be any accumulation for at least another month. Up here though? We could get snow in the summer.

Holding the joint between my lips, I flicked the lighter on. As I held it to the end, something sounded on my left. It was hard to tell with all the pine trees around, especially because my cabin was the most secluded of them all. The first one anyone driving into the ranch would see.

I was in the densest patch of woods, surrounded by them, really. I heard all sorts of things at night. Coyotes howling. Crows screeching. Even a few bears growling. Not to mention the raccoons who loved getting into my garbage.

That's what I thought it was at first. I even glanced around the cabin to look at my cans around back. They still sat there, untouched. No raccoons in sight.

The sound came from further in the distance. Taking another hit off the joint, I squinted in that direction.

Headlights? Were those headlights glowing behind the cluster of pine trees?

Then, clear as day, "Stop!"

Simone. That was Simone's voice.

Why was she so close to the exit? It was eleven p.m. She and Junie, her daughter, were usually in bed by ten.

I set the joint in the ashtray atop the railing and took off. No matter what I wanted, I couldn't move like lightning down the icy flagstone path.

Her voice was louder as I approached the gravel road. With the stability of the stones beneath me, my careful steps morphed into a steady jog.

I still couldn't make out every word, but there was someone else's too. Someone was yelling at her. They were yelling at each other.

Was there an animal? Had someone reported it, and Simone was sent to check it out? Was that voice Axel's?

That voice was deep enough. It could've been Axel. I couldn't make it out with perfect clarity, but it was definitely a man's voice.

If it was an animal, I needed to be prepared. Jogging still, I fingered the blade inside my hoodie pocket. I'd gotten into the habit of carrying a pocketknife over the last year. Although I had yet to confront a wild animal who wouldn't back down when I yelled at them, it didn't hurt to be prepared.

My heart pounded faster, harder, as I jogged down the gravel road. The shaking of my hands, the pounding in my chest, had me wondering if I was still asleep. Was this even real? I'd had worse dreams, stranger ones.

That question only got louder in my mind when I rounded the bend, closer to the gate, and my suspicion was confirmed. There were headlights.

Before them stood two figures. Nothing more than silhouettes. One had to be Simone. She was my best friend. I'd recognize her voice in a choir.

The other was a man. He was a few inches taller, nearly a foot broader, with a voice that boomed like thunder. I still couldn't make out every word he was saying, until I caught Simone say, ". . . allowed to be here, David."

*David.*

That was her ex-husband's name. A man that made my ex look like a saint.

That monster was *here*.

He stood in front of the open gate.

The gate was open.

I was atop the hill, coming down to them, with at least a few more hundred feet to go. But I wasn't fast enough, because he said something, and she said something, then she was up against the car. Only his silhouette was visible. He was yelling, but I couldn't make out the words. It was an incoherent jumble, just as it always had been with Troy. Syllables mashed together, barely forming sentences—but they weren't what mattered.

The tone was. The deep, husky growl. It wasn't different from that of a wolf's. In therapy, they told us not to look at men as predators, because when we did, we removed their accountability from their actions. They were not predators. They were people who chose to exploit their power, just as David was doing now.

Simone was invisible, hidden behind his frame, and she was silent.

Simone was never silent.

His fist rose, and it fell, and it rose, and it fell, and I screamed, "Stop!"

Only then did he turn.

Sooner. I should've spoken sooner.

"Leave her alone," I said, winded, still half a dozen strides away. "I don't know what you're doing here, but you've got to go."

Releasing Simone, he spun around. She dropped to the ground like a bomb, a thundering thwack echoing through the cold winter night. "You people have my kid. And I'm not going anywhere until I see her—"

"You're leaving before I call the cops and they lock you up for another domestic violence charge, David," I snapped.

The balls he had to mention Junie. After what he'd done to her, after the story Simone told at group tonight, I had to grit my teeth to keep from screaming.

This wasn't about Junie. Just as it wasn't about Honey when I'd left Troy. Men like David used those who mattered most to us as leverage to weasel their way back into our lives, to continue controlling us, to force us into their arms. If I knew nothing about this bastard, I would feel bad that he hadn't seen his daughter in four years.

But I did know. I knew what he'd done to that little girl.

I knew why Simone had run from him. It was the best thing she could've done for Junie. I'd use myself as a human shield to protect that sweet child from this monster if it came to that.

"Bullshit." His face was still disguised by the headlights behind him, all distinguishing features a mere dark shadow. "She hit me first. It doesn't matter anyway. We have a custody agreement. My kid's behind this gate, and I'm gonna—"

"You're gonna leave," I repeated, stepping closer. We were only a few feet apart now. "You're never gonna see Junie again. Get that through your head. I know what you did. I know everything you did, you sick son of a bitch, and you're never going to hurt either of them again."

"I don't know who the hell you think you are," he said, taking another step in. "But I have rights. She has warrants." A wave at Simone, still lying on the ground, barely conscious—if she was still breathing at all. "This bitch stole my kid. That's kidnapping. And you think you can—" Another step in. He shoved his chest into mine.

I pushed back.

Then it was a blur.

He shoved me, I pushed him. His hand came at my face, made contact. I jammed my knee toward his groin, then, somehow, his hand was around my throat.

His hand was around my throat, and I didn't see his face. I didn't see his eyes.

I saw Troy. I saw the nightmare I had just woken from twenty minutes ago.

I wasn't surrounded by knee-high snow. I was standing in my kitchen, and the coffee pot was whizzing past my head, and Troy was screaming, then he was in front of me, those blue eyes so cold, so dead, but I had a blade this time.

I had a blade in my hoodie pocket.

Before I realized what I was doing, my hand was on it, switching it open. Before I realized what I was doing, it was in his gut. Before I realized what I was doing, I stabbed again.

And again.

And again.

Blood trickled from Troy's lips.

I stabbed again.

He released my throat.

He fell to the ground, steam wafting from his blood, a cloud gathering between us, floating from each wound like smoke from the engine of a train.

There, lying atop the snow, covered in crimson, his blue eyes turned brown. His nose got bigger, his lips thicker. Rather than a balding blonde, he had a mop of brown hair covered by a black beanie. Instead of sweatpants and a band T-shirt, he wore baggie jeans. Beneath his black jacket, his white tank top was bright red.

He wasn't Troy anymore.

He was David.

He was dead.

I couldn't move.

Hands trembling at my sides, I dropped the blade. "Shit. Shit, shit, shit."

# CHAPTER 5

## *Gwen*

The cloud of steam forming in the air told me I was breathing, but my hands were as frozen as the snow on the ground. My legs, paralyzed.

I'd just killed a man.

How the hell had I just killed a man?

A cough.

Simone coughed.

The paralysis snapped.

Tripping over David's body, I darted to Simone. She still lay on the snow-covered gravel, unusually still. I collapsed to my knees and took her face in my hands. The headlights behind her were my only illumination. Her left eye had swelled shut. Her always thick lips had ballooned to twice their size. Even as I lifted her head from the ground, she still lay limp.

"Simone," I said, tapping her cheek.

No response.

"Simone, wake up," I said, shaking her shoulder.

A groan. Only a groan in response. It was better than nothing, but not enough.

I lowered her head to my lap. I looked at her, and a fear I couldn't bear enveloped my mind.

*What if she dies too?*

Who would take Junie in? Would the state return her to Simone's family? The people who'd done nothing when David had traded his toddler like cattle to get out of his debt to a drug dealer? The people who'd let their daughter run from shelter to shelter instead of opening their door to her?

What would I do without my best friend?

"Damn it, Simone!" I shook her again, and her right eye opened. "Thank God. Stay with me, okay?"

"I—I'm alright," she said, eyes drifting shut again.

"Can you move?" I shook her shoulders once more. "Shit, we gotta get you to a hospital."

"No." Her one good eye opened wide. "No hospital."

"If you could see your face right now—"

"No one can know." Her words slurred, gargling on all the blood, but she enunciated enough for me to understand. "Can't let this hurt the—" A cough quaked her frame. Eyes falling shut, she shook her head. "We can't."

*Can't let this hurt the ranch.* That's what she was trying to say.

Thousands of women lived within these gates. Thousands of women relied on the anonymity of Rhiannon's Ranch. Thousands of women followed the same rule when we'd signed the NDA required to live here.

*Don't endanger the ranch.*

I ran my fingers through my hair, grabbing two fistfuls at the back.

Would the police believe me if I said it'd been self-defense? The police hadn't believed me when I'd told them Troy hit me first. The scratches on his arms, the red splotch across his face, were signs that I was the aggressor. Not that I had defended myself when he shoved me into a wall with his hands around my throat.

If the cops came, even if they did believe me this time, what about Simone? David had been right about something. The two of them had a court ordered custody agreement.

Simone had violated it when she moved here. She'd done so again when she'd taken on a new identity. Just as we all had. Not a single soul inside this ranch was innocent in the eyes of the law.

It was the only way we could escape our abusers. I'd taken Honey, who legally belonged to Troy. At the very least, I had committed theft. Many women here had done much worse.

But I didn't give a shit what the law said. Simone had broken it for a good reason.

The law was not always just. The law did not always protect the innocent. The law often protected the oppressor.

No. I would not do that to everyone behind these gates.

Carefully, I lay Simone back onto the gravel.

And some foreign entity floated into my body. It seeped up from my feet, moving them from my seat on the ground until I found myself standing. Then I was walking. I stood over David's body, staring down at the pond of maroon beneath him, freezing against the snow-covered rocks.

His frozen, dead eyes stared back.

A shudder coursed up my spine. My stomach retched, and I had to swallow down vomit.

I pulled his lids down.

The entity possessed me again.

My sticky, blood-coated fingers grabbed each of his hands. And they yanked. They pulled. I felt none of his weight. No tension in my wrists or biceps.

Nothing. I felt absolutely nothing.

It was like I was in the eyes of someone else. I saw what was happening. I knew what she was doing. But she wasn't me. This was a movie playing out before my eyes. I was a viewer, not a participant.

My mind? My thoughts, my feelings? I didn't have those anymore. I was just a viewer.

Whatever possessed me decided to drop him at the conifer bushes along the fence line. They didn't cover him, not entirely.

Then I watched as I scooped mounds of snow into the stomach of my hoodie. Like I'd forgotten a hamper and had nothing to dump my fresh laundry into.

*Scoop some snow, dump it onto his body. Scoop some snow, dump it onto his body.*

Over and over until he was a mound of pink, frozen water.

Now on my knees, I did the same thing to the trail of blood. Swept and swept snow on top of it until it covered the crimson.

Then I caught sight of Simone, and the entity released me again.

Slumped into a ball before David's car, her teeth chattered so loud, I could hear it from here. I ran to her and dropped to my knees. Shaking her shoulders, I fought the cold that bit away at every inch of exposed, damp skin. "Simone. Simone, can you walk?"

A low grumble.

I reached under both armpits. "Come on. At least try."

Another grumble. Simone tugged back.

I released an audible groan of my own, dropping her. Dragging David's dead weight was easier.

If she wasn't going to walk, I needed my car.

The run back to my cabin was as blurry as the fight with David. I knew I'd done it. But I couldn't recall how.

All I knew was that my cabin was right there, a dozen strides away, and I ripped off my shoes. Why? Because they were covered in blood, I guessed.

I stripped off my sweatpants and my hoodie for the same reason. Blood tainted every surface of them.

Bundling the clothes close to my chest, I burst through the door. Honey barked and howled, rushing toward me, but I couldn't greet her. The entity wouldn't let me.

First stop, fireplace. Still burning from the fire I'd lit before going to sleep, I dropped the clothes inside.

Then I was a tornado. Raincoat, gloves, bleach, duct tape, a tarp, and other items I can't recall. They were in my bag, and I ran out the door. Then I was in my car, a cloud of snow floating over my taillights. Before I knew it, I was beside David's car, jamming mine into park.

I jumped out and ran to Simone. Grabbing her beneath her armpits and sliding her across the gravel wasn't much more difficult than hauling lumber up the steps for my fireplace. In heartbeats, I had her inside my car. Her head and torso draped over the center console, feet jutting out the door. But a quick, forceful yank had her nestled neatly in the passenger seat. I slammed the door shut. The heat blasted through the vents. Hopefully, she'd wake up soon.

The entity returned as soon as Simone was safe beside me.

The car whipped a one-eighty. I don't remember the drive back to my cabin. I vaguely recall dragging her inside like a drunken college girl. Up the steps, through the threshold, and laying her on the floor. I tucked a pillow beneath her head and draped a blanket over her frame, before rushing back out the door.

The entity stayed with me as I unloaded my bag by David's trunk. It took over while I flipped him onto the tarp from the mound of snow and wrapped him in the thick blue plastic. It rolled duct tape around the tarp. But it didn't do a good job, because when it dragged him across the snow, his feet slipped out, and all I could think of was refried beans slipping out of my burrito at lunch today. That's what his feet looked like. Refried beans slipping out of a burrito.

Thinking about it that way made swallowing my bile bearable as I shoved them back into the plastic.

The entity didn't return until I was hauling him into the trunk. Attempting to, anyway. I couldn't deadlift a two-hundred-pound man.

But the entity could. It was smart enough, too, to lay out the other tarp in the trunk first.

It was smart enough to return to the field it had dragged him through and churn it up. It dropped my body to the ground, making snow angels to disguise the drag marks. It even allowed a few tears to run from my eyes, a few anxious gasps and pants to float through my lungs, as I stared up at the star-speckled cerulean sky.

It drenched bleach over the pool of maroon, diluting it to a pale shade of pink.

It was smart enough to put on my raincoat and tuck my hair into the hood and slip a fresh pair of gloves over my fingers before opening the driver's side door of David's car. It drove me to my cabin and led me inside.

For a heartbeat, only a heartbeat, it left me. For that single instant, I was in my home, and I was safe.

Until I locked eyes on Simone. She still lay on the floor, Honey curled up beside her, and her chest rose and fell with deep breaths. But I hardly believed it was her. Blood painted her face. The swelling had ballooned her cheeks to twice their size.

She was alive, but she was not safe.

Neither of us were safe.

Then I was in the shower. Then I was drying off. I was stepping into a pair of inconspicuous black sweats. A gray, indiscernible T-shirt. The two-inch thick puffer snow suit. Also black. As unnoticeable in the Montana mountains as jeans and a hoodie. All my hair, slicked into a bun and covered with a beanie. A pair of sunglasses over my eyes. New gloves lined my fingers. A paper mask tucked in place around my ears.

The entity did it all.

It led me out the door and behind the wheel of David's car. And it drove.

# CHAPTER 6

## *Gwen*

This wasn't my first encounter with the entity.

I'd been a kid the first time I remembered it showing up. Mom had gotten into a fight with her boyfriend at the time. He'd shoved her through a glass partition in our living room. I heard it, and by the time I got there, he was gone. Mom was conscious, but bleeding profusely from her arm and another wound at the back of her head. I'd left my body, and the entity called 911 and applied pressure to both wounds with a dishcloth while we'd waited for the ambulance.

My next encounter with it had been during my first fight with Troy. Couldn't say what the fight had been about—we'd had so many of them—but he grabbed ahold of my face and squeezed my cheeks so hard that I tasted iron. The moment that blood touched my tongue, the entity took over. It slammed one of my fists into his shoulder, it shoved him off me, and it moved my legs. Moved them so fast I hadn't realized what was happening until I turned over the car's engine and tore off down the road.

I didn't know what it was, not exactly, but I wasn't crazy. I knew no one else climbed into my body. My brain just segmented. Thought escaped me, and my body did what it needed to survive.

It did what needed done.

The entity stopped outside the gates of Rhiannon's Ranch and slid them shut. It returned to the vehicle and took over the wheel. I didn't know, or care, where we were going.

While it manned the road, images flashed through my mind. First, a river five or so miles from the ranch. An overpass, nestled deep in the mountains, that less than a thousand people probably knew about. Far fewer would drive it at this hour.

That's where the entity was taking me.

The next image was a big yellow box tucked behind a chain-link fence. Almost like an eighteen-wheeler. But not quite. Yellow taxis drove the cement on the other side of that chain-link fence.

The last images were little white tags plastered all over a vehicle. On the dashboard, driver side door jamb, even the engine block. The front of the frame, under the passenger seat, trunk floor, and inside the engine compartment.

When that overpass became visible, I knew what came next. Where we were going. What that big yellow box was. How to find those yellow taxis. Why those little white tags mattered so much.

It was straight ahead, connecting two mountains. Six streetlights shone against the concrete, illuminating only those two yellow lines, the white ones off to the edges, the small walkway flush with it, and the four-foot stone banister.

Every time I'd driven past here, I'd admired the gargoyles lining those light posts. Today, rather than watching them, they watched me.

I shifted the car into park in the center of the bridge, idling between two of the gargoyles. There, I stepped from the vehicle and stood on the asphalt.

It would take at least a minute to yank David from the trunk and toss him over the ledge. But sound carried through these mountains. So long as I listened closely, I would hear a car coming well before they saw me.

Once my ears adjusted, hearing the trickle of the water below, an owl hooting in the distance, but nothing else. I pulled in a deep breath.

Careful, cautious, I walked to the trunk. My head stayed on a swivel. Watching. Anticipating. Prepared for someone or something to throw me off.

Nothing did.

I popped open the trunk, grabbed the burrito by the bigger end, and hoisted it to the ground. The beans tumbled out behind.

With all my might, I grabbed hold of David's feet and dragged him over the curb and onto the sidewalk. A small stream of blood leaked from the edge.

Adrenaline pumped to my frozen limbs.

Now at the banister, I grabbed the bigger half of the burrito again in a bear hug. The banister came to my belly button. As long as I got him vertical, I could tip him over it.

I did just that.

It took longer than I expected to hear the splash of his body hitting the water. Only then did I look over the edge.

Gone. He was gone.

In my backpack, the entity had packed me another bottle of bleach. I opened it up, dumped it onto the stream of blood I had left, and watched the red dilute into a barely there pink. When it looked like nothing more than a spilled bottle of water on the sidewalk, I walked back to the car and hopped into the driver's seat.

The entity took over again for the drive. It pulled off on the side of the road, roughly fifty miles from the overpass. It took the pocketknife from the bag it'd packed me and scraped the VIN off the dashboard. Then the door jamb and engine block. It checked the front of the frame, passenger seat, and trunk floor, but no VIN in any of those spots. At the trunk still, it lifted the second tarp, careful to keep the drops of blood inside, and folded it into a perfect square. Back inside the vehicle, it placed the square in my bag, nice and tidy.

It dug inside the glove compartment and center console. Cleared out all the paperwork and laid it carefully in my bag.

The entity resumed control of the wheel and followed signs for Great Falls, Montana. I don't remember the drive. I do remember arriving at the junkyard and stepping outside to pull the plate and place it in my bag as well.

It was on the edge of town. Pine trees to the left, a field of rusted metal ahead, a chain-link, barbed-wire gate before the building, that yellow box I'd seen earlier in my mind, and a McDonald's on the right.

But there were no lights on inside the single floor, red brick building. Only a sign that said CLOSED.

The twilight sky told me why. Only tiny yellow rays of sun trickled at the edge of the horizon.

That was okay. I had work later, but there was enough time to make it back and pretend none of this had happened.

The entity had put all seven thousand dollars of my savings into my bag. I wanted to open a bakery in a few years, and this was every penny I'd saved since getting to the ranch. But staying out of prison mattered more than the bakery.

Unzipping my bag, I gazed down at the array of twenties and fifties. After an exasperated exhale, I began counting. When I made it to a thousand, I laid the sum in my lap. I counted out another thousand and laid it on the dashboard. The other five thousand? I zipped up.

Into each of my jacket pockets, I tucked a thousand.

Now, to find someone as desperate for money as I was to get away with this.

It didn't take long. I made it two blocks down the street before someone caught my eye. A middle-aged man with a scruffy, unkempt beard, a black zip-up hoodie, and a heavy-duty puffer coat over top. He sat on a red flannel blanket. Beside him was an old, even scruffier mutt. His fur was long, white close to the skin and varying shades of brown at the ends. Crust caked up the corners of his eyes. At the edge of the flannel blanket, a cardboard sign read, JUST TRYING TO EAT, MAN. GOD BLESS.

Shame sat like a ten-pound weight in the center of my chest. I didn't want to use this guy. Life had already chewed him up and spit him out.

But he could help me, and I could help him. At the end of it, even if the authorities ever questioned him, there was no way they would charge him with David's murder. David had no connection to this city. He and Simone were from Wyoming. No connection to the city meant no connection to this man.

If they ever questioned him for what he was about to do for me, he could tell them the truth. I wouldn't blame him if he did.

Slowing at the street corner, I rolled down my window. Twenty-dollar bill in hand, I held it out to him.

The man on the flannel blanket was already standing, walking closer. Fingers outstretched to accept, he said, "Thank you, miss."

Given all my clothing, I was surprised he could tell I was a miss. "I'll give you a thousand if you do me a favor."

Face wrinkling with confusion, he cocked his head to the side. "A thousand?"

"A thousand."

"What's the favor?" He glanced me over, then the backseat. "I don't do no funny business, miss."

"No funny business. I just need to junk this car down the street."

"What—down at Tom's?" The man nodded in the direction of the junkyard. "All you gotta do is run in."

"Yeah, I know," I lied. "I just—Well, it's a long story. I'm not on good terms with the management. I know if I go in there, he's not gonna give me a dime for it. And it's not that I really care about the money, but my landlord doesn't want this sitting outside my apartment anymore. It's untitled, so if I don't get rid of this thing, he'll evict me. I really don't want to see that guy, and I really gotta get rid of this car."

"Wait." He cocked his head to the side. "You want me to go in there, junk the car, and then take whatever money they're going to give you for it? *And* you're gonna pay me?"

"Yes, sir," I said. "But they can't just junk it. They've got to crush it."

The man arched a brow, a half smile tilting the corner of his lips. "And you can't do it yourself because you got beef with the guy who works there?"

He didn't believe me, but I still said, "Mhmm."

The man snorted. "Alright. I'll do it. But I'm freezing, so can I have a seat with you in there? And my dog?"

Maybe it wasn't the most responsible decision, but it wasn't like I'd made many of those tonight. "Sure. Come on. We'll go wait for them to open."

# CHAPTER 7

## *Gwen*

Jeff.

The man who agreed to junk the car for me. His name was Jeff. He asked for mine a handful of times, but when I refused to answer, he said, "Yeah, yeah, miss. I get it."

He probably did.

The exact reason why I was so careful to conceal my identity, he would never know. But he knew one thing. I was breaking the law. And he was okay with that, so long as he got some cash.

They always said, 'There is no honor among thieves.' I never agreed with that. Some of the best people I'd ever met were the ones who had the least, who'd gotten a hold of the little they did have through nefarious means and used those little scraps for survival.

The worst people I'd ever met were the ones who came from normal, happy, and healthy families.

Jeff though? Jeff was just a guy trying to survive. He didn't want the details for the same reasons I didn't want the details about how the ranch was run. Plausible deniability.

The two of us sat together outside the junkyard until they opened. At that point, he said he would do the job. But he wanted a down payment.

I passed him two hundred bucks and the car keys. It wasn't until that moment that I realized he could've driven off with the car. Which wouldn't have been ideal. Jeff didn't do that though. He and Felix, his dog, drove up to the gate. After a couple of honks, someone came to the passenger window, exchanged a few words with Jeff, then rolled the barbed-wire-wrapped, chain-link gate open.

Jeff drove through. Once inside, he stepped out of the vehicle and talked to that same man for a few minutes. After an exchange of cash,

Jeff and Felix stood beside the gate. Eventually, the man Jeff had spoken to got into the vehicle and drove it into a big yellow box.

I tiptoed around the fence to see inside. Sure enough, the tractor attached to the big yellow box rumbled to a start. The top of the box descended slowly. Metal crunched, glass shattered, and in a few heartbeats, the evidence that could one day be used to convict me was nothing more than a crushed-up square of metal and debris.

Jeff came out a few minutes later. I gave him the remaining eight hundred and asked where I might find a cab.

It had to have been at least five city blocks before I caught sight of one. The entity must've come back, because I don't remember that walk. I recall cutting through a few alleys and stripping off a couple of my layers and shoving them into my backpack, but not much else.

Eventually, I made it to a busy street. People were walking nearly shoulder to shoulder, probably for an event of some kind. Yellow cabs, several of them, lined up against the curb, waiting for customers.

I hopped in one and entered an address. Not for the ranch. It was a little country store a few miles down the road from the ranch's private drive. Still, at least a three-hour venture for the cabby. He said something about how that was far. I would've been better off renting a car.

In silence, I passed him a thousand in cash. He didn't complain after that.

While I have no recollection of falling asleep in the cab, I may have.

Eventually, I recognized where I was again. The yellow cab dropped me at the old general store, and I walked.

When I got to the private driveway that led to the ranch, I didn't walk along it. I followed the trails through the woods alongside it. One wrapped all the way around the property, including my backyard.

With my cabin finally in sight, a burst of adrenaline coursed through me. I tore up that hill like a monster was chasing me.

In a way, one was.

Because if Simone lay dead in there, all of this would've been for nothing.

Last night, I had locked the door on the way out. Didn't bring my keys either. As I bent for the spare stashed under the flowerpot at the back entrance, the rear door swung open.

Simone stood in the threshold. Her one good eye wide, the other swollen shut. She no longer had on a bloody blouse. Instead, she wore my gray sweatshirt and a pair of my black sweatpants.

As I straightened, our eyes met. Neither of us spoke. For a few silent heartbeats, we only stared at one another. Her eyes flicked over me, mine over her, until tears consumed us both.

"You okay?" she asked, voice cracking.

A few steps up the stairs, I nodded. "Are you?"

Nostrils flaring, a stream of tears leaked from the corner of her good eye. She gritted her teeth and exhaled slowly. A quick nod. Because if she said anything more, that small stream would become a river.

I tossed my arms around her before it could. She did the same.

There, standing just past the threshold of the rear door in the hallway that connected my bedroom and kitchen, we held one another as tightly as our bodies would allow. I don't know who started crying first, but one of us did, and the other joined in, and it took holding my breath to make it stop.

The sorrow was like a vacuum in the center of my chest, ripping me into it and shredding all the scars that had healed over the last year.

We'd run like our lives depended on it, because they had. Simone had left David, and I'd left Troy, because even if we'd managed to survive their violence, we were dead in their company. They had taken our sense of self, sense of confidence, even our sanity. They had taken it all, and Rhiannon's Ranch had given it back.

Last night, we were faced with the harsh reality that all this could be gone in an instant. Each of us here was a domino. If one of us fell, we all could.

When I killed David, I thought that I caught Simone in her rapid descent. In a way, I had. And yet, the two of us were weeping in one another's arms, toppling to the ground, comforting each other in crumpled balls on the floor, yet again, through the chaos of a man's violence.

It took us a while to get up off the floor. Not long after, with a couple cups of coffee in hand, we settled in on the sofa. Honey jumped up between us and cuddled against my thigh. Stroking my fingers through her fur served as the tether to reality I had lost in Great Falls.

We sat in silence for a while. I looked around the room for some signs of what had happened last night. There were none. Any of Simone's blood that had spilled on the floor, she'd cleaned up. I'd left my bloody boots on the floor by the door last night, dripping with crimson and melting snow. Now, they rested on the kitchen table, sparkling as if they were brand new.

I wasn't sure what Simone remembered, but she'd known enough to clean the blood off my boots.

I looked at my friend, her face still swollen, and broke the silence. "How did he find you?"

Tucking herself deeper into the corner of the sofa, Simone eased out a breath. "I'm an idiot. That's how."

"You did open the gate for him," I said, "so I'm not going to disagree with you there."

She shot me the bird.

"Junie," Simone said. "Junie got sick at school the day before yesterday. Her fever was 103. I was in the middle of an appointment with a client who had hair down to her ass and wanted to go platinum." In other words, a very long appointment. "I missed the school's call. She didn't even seem sick when I'd dropped her off that morning. But they asked Junie if there was another number they could reach me at, and I guess she remembered David's. She must've given it to them.

"When I called the school back an hour later, they told me to come pick her up. I did. And the nurse said something about how she talked to Junie's dad on the phone." She shut her eyes, her breath shaking. "She said he would've come to get her, but he wasn't on the list of people who could. She must've told him where I worked, because yesterday, he was outside the salon."

Simone reached up to rub her eyes, wincing when she touched the black and blue one. "We argued outside. It was messy, and stupid, and embarrassing. But some bystanders saw it going down and threatened to call the cops on him. He hauled ass. I figured that would be enough to scare him off. Last time I googled him, he had a mile-long list of warrants. And it's not like he knew where I lived.

"He must've called the salon and asked to set up an appointment or something to get my number, because he started blowing up my phone. Literally, every five minutes from five o'clock on he was calling me.

"Finally, I answered at eleven thirty. I was going to tell him to go to hell, but he said he was at the gate. Must've followed me home." She gritted her teeth and shook her head. "I thought I could go talk to him. Just get him to leave, you know? At least until I figured out how to tell Rhiannon about it. But there's no talking to guys like him. He started saying that I was keeping his kid from him, and he was gonna send me to jail for violating the court order, which I don't even think they would do. But maybe they would. I guess, technically, when I brought Junie here, that was kidnapping. Either way though." With shaking fingers, she rubbed her forehead. "We were fighting, and then you were there."

"If he followed you, wouldn't he have caught up to you on the road?" I stroked my fingers through Honey's fur, hoping it would ease the tremble in them that hadn't stopped all night. "I mean, when you come up the driveway to the ranch, you're pretty much on top of whoever is nearby."

"I don't know how else he would've found it," she said.

"What about an AirTag or something? Did he see you get out of your car at work? Could he have planted a tracker under it?"

Simone shook her head. "He's a paranoid drug dealer, Gwen. All he uses are burner phones. You have to connect accounts to credit cards and shit for trackers and air tags. He followed me here. I guarantee it."

Chewing my lip, I nodded. His car had been too old to have any type of navigation built into it. It wasn't traceable. If he only used burner phones, if I'd missed one inside the car, that was untraceable, too.

"But everything after that," Simone said, voice barely above a whisper, "after you showed up, it's all a blur."

I nodded. If she didn't remember anything after the violence, if this ever got back to the police, she could say she hadn't seen anything. This way, she had plausible deniability.

"That's it?" she asked. "You're not gonna say anything?"

I met her gaze.

"Like, I don't know, explain the blood on your shoes?" Simone asked. "Or how the hell I got back here?"

"What do you want me to say, Simone?"

"Telling me what the hell happened would be a good start," she said. "Discussing what story we're gonna tell everybody might be a good idea. Figuring out how I'm gonna hide these bruises from Rhiannon would be nice, too."

Another moment of silence.

"Damn it, Gwen. I'm not gonna tell anyone. But I think we're kind of in this together now, aren't we?"

"Kinda felt like I was in it alone when you were knocked out, and I was dragging you into the car, and then into the house, and then going back there to grab—" A sharp inhale cut me off. I shook my head and looked away.

"What—do you expect me to apologize for being unconscious? It's not like I intentionally left you to fend for yourself, Gwen."

"Plausible deniability," I said. "I'm being careful with how much I say so *you* have plausible deniability, Simone. I know it's not your fault. *None* of this is your fault. I'm not upset with you. I'm really damn happy that you're alive, though." My throat tightened. "All night long, I have been scrambling. I think I'm at about thirty hours without sleep now. My shift starts in an hour and a half, and I can't miss it, because I need today to look like a normal day to everyone else. I haven't had time to think of a plan for anything else."

A long moment of silence stretched on. We stared at one another.

Eventually, tears gathered in her good eye again. "Plausible deniability?"

I nodded. "Plausible deniability."

A few tears beaded over. She wiped them away and swallowed hard. "Okay. That's good. I mean, it's not good, but it is. That sounds horrible; but this is good."

Now it was me with a lump in my throat and tears in my eyes. "Is it?"

"He would've exposed the ranch," she said, wrapping her arms around her torso. Like giving herself a hug. "The loan I just got for the salon would be gone. I might be in jail right now for kidnapping. At least a couple hundred other women here would be too. He either would've won custody of Junie, or his batshit crazy mother would've, or she would've wound up in the system. Troy would be on his way here to pick Honey up, and we would all be at risk."

The same thoughts I'd had all night. The same rationale.

So why did I still feel like I was going to vomit?

"David was from Wyoming." Simone nodded, her gaze on the floor. "He's not connected to this town. Those couple witnesses might've seen him yesterday, but they probably wouldn't be able to identify him." She paused. "You got rid of everything, right?"

"Plausible deniability, Simone."

"I'll take that as a yes," she murmured, eyes scanning the ground. She hunched forward, rubbing her hands down her cheeks. "Okay. Okay, so I left Junie with Margaret last night. I told her that I was having a bad PTSD day and was coming up here to hang out with you. So we're each other's alibis, right?"

"Kind of evades the purpose of plausible deniability."

She waved me off. "I walked down to the gate this morning. Whatever you did, you did well. It didn't look like anything happened there."

I rubbed a hand over my mouth, my other still buried in Honey's fur. "Tried my best."

"And because I opened the gate from inside, there shouldn't be a log of it in the roster. You didn't come back in through the gate this morning, did you? That's why you came in through the back, right? Because you walked through the woods?"

I said nothing in response. Only nodded, my lips pressed tight together and eyes clenched shut.

"Alright, cut the shit, Gwen."

Simone's tone had me looking up, her own gaze snapped back to mine. She barely looked like herself. Her lips, eye, even cheeks were so swollen, so red and bruised, that the fire inside me ignited again. A glance at her reminded me that I'd done what I had to.

"I know you killed him," she said, her eyes glittering. "Thank you. But if this ever comes back around, I'm not letting you go to prison for it. You saved my life, but this is my cross to bear."

I was the one who killed him. If it came back around, she wasn't the one who would go to prison for it. She had a little girl who needed looked after.

She leaned back and drained her coffee mug, then slammed it back on the coffee table. "So just answer the damn question. You didn't use your key card to get back in, did you?"

I answered honestly. "No. I didn't use my key card."

"And there are no cameras up front," she said, tucking a knee to her chest. "So there's no proof that either of us were outside the gates last night."

"After I got rid of the car, a cab driver brought me back," I told her. "He shouldn't be able to recognize me though. I changed clothes and wore a mask."

Confusion pinched her swollen face. She grimaced at the pain it caused. "Where the hell did you find a cab?"

"At what point will you acknowledge that you knowing too much could be just as dangerous as you not knowing enough?"

Simone took a sharp breath in and folded her knee down. "Fine. I don't need every detail. But, you know this is gonna screw your head up, don't you? You don't kill someone and walk away like nothing happened."

"I think after I get a full night's sleep, I'll be just fine."

Simone leveled me a look laced with concern and exasperation. "I think if you bottle up however this is making you feel, you're gonna lose your shit."

"Most of my shit is bottled up. I've yet to lose it," I said. "We're working on a plan right now. Let's stay on topic."

Grunting her annoyance, she stood and began to pace the room. "Alright. Here's our story. I came here last night because I needed a friend. We were both inside all night long."

That would work. If at any point we were connected to the murder, I would say that Simone had gotten drunk and passed out on my sofa. David showed up, and I'd been the one to confront him.

"Only problem is your face." I waved over her. "Rhiannon's gonna know that David found you."

"So I leave." She propped her hands on her hips. "I text Rhiannon, tell her I got invited to a lash extension class last minute a few towns over, and I'll be gone for a few days. That should give me enough time to get the swelling under control. A shit ton of frozen peas should do the trick. Makeup will cover the bruises."

"Do you think Margaret will watch Junie for a few days?"

"If she can't, will you?"

I nodded. "Just let the school know that I'll be the one picking her up."

"Then I think we've got it." Pacing still, Simone rubbed a hand down her jaw and winced. An annoyed grunt escaped her before she plopped back down on the couch. Honey jumped a little and lifted her head.

"This'll work," she said. "We're gonna get away with murder."

# CHAPTER 8

## *Angela*

"Your call has been forwarded to an automatic voice message—"

Angela slammed the phone onto the glass coffee tabletop. Half-drunk cans of soda toppled over. Liquid doused her pack of cigarettes, melting loose tobacco and the ashes from joints onto its top.

"Son of a bitch!" She tossed the pack of cigarettes to the sunken suede sofa. The plastic casing was damp, but they survived the debacle.

On the edge of the table, fast food packaging still lay from this morning's breakfast, a few crumpled napkins beside them. Angela tossed them onto the mess. As soon as they touched the liquid, they molded into the chaos. Napkins? No. Soggy, useless lumps.

Hands balled to fists, brain sloshing against her ears, Angela headed for the kitchen area of her studio apartment. The washrag drawer was empty. Hanging over the faucet, though, was a crusted, dried-out hand towel. She returned to the coffee table with it.

The job was haphazard, sticky residue remaining on the glass top, but she mopped up most of it.

With gritted teeth, she picked up her phone again, praying that it would light up with his name.

It didn't.

She went back to her call log.

*David (21 outgoing) 9:34 a.m.*

*Work (3 minutes, 52 seconds) 7:06 a.m.*

*PCP (12 minutes, 18 seconds) 4:38 p.m. Yesterday*

*David (32 minutes, 43 seconds) 3:25 p.m. Yesterday*

That was the last time they'd spoken. 3:25 p.m. yesterday.

She had called him twenty-one times this morning. He'd answered none of them.

To hell with it. She dialed again.

This time, she made it to the voicemail. After the generic message played, she rubbed her eyes. "Hey, honey. It's me again. You said that after you talked to Jess and found out about Junie, you were going to call me back. That was at three o'clock yesterday. Now it's nine the next day, and I still haven't heard from you. You didn't get picked up, did you? I know you would've called me by now if you did." Jaw tight, she imagined him, again, sitting in a jail cell, waiting for her to bail him out. "Damn it, boy. If you're not in cuffs right now, I'm gonna beat your ass whenever I get a hold of you. Scaring the shit out of me like this. Call me back, kid."

Angela ended the call.

For a few heartbeats, she stared at that call log. Then she went to her contacts.

*David 1*

*David 2*

*David 3*

*David 4*

All the way up to *David 15*.

She called each number. She got the same automated voice message each time.

This never happened. Never for this long. David always called her back. It may have taken him an hour, or two, or three, but never more than twelve. Even if he was on a bender, he called her back well before twelve hours passed.

Something was wrong. Something was terribly wrong. A mother knew. It was a sixth sense, an instinct.

Angela scrolled through her contacts again, checking to make sure she wasn't missing one of his other phone numbers. When she made it to David 15, another name caught her eye.

*Denise*. A woman she hadn't talked to in three years.

But a woman who may know something now.

Angela dialed, and she waited. On the fourth ring, the woman's voice came through the speaker. "Hello."

Not a question. Not a friendly greeting. A blank, unsure-why-she-had-even-picked-up sort of voice.

Still, Angela needed answers. "Hey, Denise. Long time, no talk. How have you been?"

"Living the dream." Short. Abrupt. As was always Denise's nature. "Do you need something?"

"Yeah, actually." Angela fought the urge to use the same tone Denise had. "I was wondering if you'd heard from Jess."

A moment of silence. "If I had, you're the last person I would tell."

Angela rolled her eyes. "Look, I know you and I haven't always gotten along. But our kids loved each other once. We share a granddaughter. And—"

"And your junkie son is the reason I lost them both," Denise snapped. "We're not friends, Angela. We never will be."

Angela was all but grinding her teeth now. "I never asked to be. But that ain't the point. Point is, David got a lead on her yesterday. But I haven't heard from him since, and—"

"Good. Now you get a taste of what it's like." Every word that left Denise's mouth carried the sharpness of a blade. "The last time I heard from Jess was a week after she disappeared. She told me she was safe, so was Junie, and they were happy. They were going to build a better life. She didn't want me in it, or you, or your son. And let's just be honest with ourselves, Angela. For good reason. I hope he didn't find her, because all he did was make her life a living hell. Fingers crossed one of his drug buddies got hold of him and he's rotting away in a storm drain right now."

Angela's stomach tightened. She clenched her fists so hard that her fingernails left bloodied crescents in her palms. "What the hell is the matter with you? No matter how hard it's been for me, I would never wish something like that on your slut daughter—"

"Because you know the same thing I do. All those problems boil down to your son. How many times did he put her in the god-damned hospital, Angela?" Flames licked each word. "She was a great mother. The only mistake she ever made was getting in bed with David. Don't call me again."

The line went dead.

Angela dropped the phone with shaking hands.

She stared at the mess on the table. She reran the phone call she'd had with David yesterday in her mind. She thought back to that look on Jess's face when she'd lain in a hospital bed, holding newborn Junie in her arms, with a busted lip. She remembered the ice, the emptiness in that child's eyes when Junie had looked at her father only days before they left.

A droplet of tobacco and ash-laced liquid dripped onto her toe beneath the table. And she couldn't take it anymore.

She took hold of that glass table as she stood. A shove toppled it onto the stained beige carpet. Glass shattered. Soda spilled. Ashes and tobacco fluttered through the air, falling to the ground like rain.

For a moment, she just stood there, staring at it. Deep breaths lifted and collapsed her chest and shoulders.

This was the mess she'd made. She didn't even know where to begin cleaning it up.

# CHAPTER 9

## Gwen

As I drove to work, the windows rolled down, I focused on the cool Montana wind biting my cheeks. Rather than the memories, I flicked my eyes over pine trees and the yellow lines through the center of the asphalt and the blue sky.

If it got warm enough, any blood I had missed in the snow would melt. Once it dissolved into the soil, there'd be less evidence to—

*No. Stop that.*

*Pretty blue sky. Look at the pretty blue sky.*

If I didn't shove it all away, I wouldn't be able to work. I wouldn't be able to function. I had to think about the trees or the sky or anything else. Anything that *wasn't* what I'd done beneath it last night.

I made it to my usual parking spot in the rear of the bakery at 1:54 p.m. Six minutes to spare. Six minutes I did not *want* to spare. If I stared at the sky any longer, my neck was going to get stuck like that.

Keys in my pocket, I stepped from the car and pushed the door shut with my hip. My legs still felt like gelatin and my stomach rumbled as I continued down the sidewalk. A bit of snow stood in a mound at the street corner, but the cobblestone sidewalks were clear.

Black Pines wasn't much of a town really. Just a strip of small businesses in the middle of nowhere. Still, all the buildings on each side were unique. The first one on the left was comprised of red brick with a green awning and housed Maple & Thyme. In the spring, a dozen potted plants accompanied the handful of wrought-iron dinette tables we carted out there.

Straight ahead stood a stone structure topped with pretty gargoyles. The fire escape on the right was the entrance for the tenants who lived above the butcher shop. It had a classic, 1950s feel with a red retro sign overhead that read BOB'S BUTCHERY.

The other dozen businesses that lined the street were just as quaint and cozy. The flower shop at the end by the gazebo, the church Sebastian had remodeled into his veterinary office, the diner across the street from it. Even the tavern at the end of the line.

Usually, walking down this street made me feel alive. I could see myself growing old in a place like this. The kind my kids would trick-or-treat at on Halloween and catch sweets and trinkets from the firefighters during the Christmas parade. It was somewhere I wanted to call home.

Today, it was just another pretty sight.

At the entrance to Maple & Thyme, I pounded my snow-covered tennis shoes on the rug before stepping inside, the bell jingling when I opened the door. Beyond the glass, only a few customers sat inside. One stood at the counter, chatting with Molly who rang up their order at the register. She wore her usual uniform: black slacks, a black shirt embroidered with her name, and sneakers.

I closed the door behind me and unzipped my jacket. The usual scent of yeast and cinnamon filled my nose, floating from the pastry cases at the checkout counter and the length of them against the right wall. One step off the entry rug had me slipping across the mahogany laminate underfoot. I grabbed the corner of one of the white Formica tabletops to keep from falling.

"We need a wet floor sign up here," I said, carefully continuing toward the checkout counter. "Someone's gonna bust their head open."

"Get the mop and clean it up." Andrew's voice carried from beyond the swinging stainless steel door. "Then I need you on this cake. I gotta do payroll."

Neither task was all that difficult or daunting. But I would've preferred to be up front today. Working on a cake alone in the back gave my mind too much time to wander. At the register, I'd be too busy talking to customers to think.

I'd be off at six. Just needed to make it through four hours.

"On it, boss," I said under my breath.

As I clocked in at the register, Molly leaned against the counter. She spoke barely above a whisper. "He's in a mood today."

"Isn't he always?"

She snorted, tucking a blonde tendril behind her ear. "Usually. But this is so much heavier."

I stopped tapping the keys. "Do I smell drama?"

"Julia left him." A devious smile tilted the corners of her cherry red lips. "Engagement's off. My sister drove past their house last night, and Julia was screaming bloody murder. She was throwing all his clothes into the yard. I don't know what happened, but I know it's juicy."

"Probably got tired of him looking down our tops all the time," I said under my breath.

"Had to have been bad," Molly said. "You know why they were engaged, right?"

I'd only met Julia the handful of times she'd come into the bakery. She and Andrew were about even on the attractive scale. If anything, she was a few points higher. She was sweet though. Andrew was anything but.

"Because they loved each other and wanted to spend the rest of their lives together?" I shrugged off my jacket and tucked it into the shelf beneath the register. "Or used to, rather."

"Nope," Molly said, eyes gleaming. "She's pregnant. I don't know what she's going to do now."

"Hopefully talk to a lawyer about child support."

Mouth dropping open, laughing, Molly shoved my shoulder. "You're horrible."

"That's not horrible. It's just the logical thing to do." Raising my hands in surrender, I walked backward toward the closet. "Tell me you weren't thinking the same thing."

"Actually, I wasn't." Molly said over her shoulder, lowering her voice. "Because the owner was here when I got in this morning. They were in Andrew's office, and the tone didn't sound good."

With a huff, I grabbed the wet floor sign. "Like he was in trouble?"

"Like he was in *big* trouble."

"I guess karma's finally coming for him." I nudged the mop bucket with my foot. "Wait, isn't it Julia's grandpa who owns this place?"

The stainless steel swung inward. If Molly had taken two steps back, Andrew would've smacked her in the head with it.

Arms open at his sides, his bushy brows dropped deep into his gaze. The dark beard over his jaw and chin covered their roundness, making his tiny nose and big lips look a bit less feminine. Andrew was a stocky guy, just a few inches taller than my five foot five, but heavyset in the structure of his body. His face, while pleasant enough to look at, was nothing special.

In another life, I would have found him attractive. In this one, he was just my asshole boss.

"Last I checked, I wasn't paying you to gossip," he said. "I told you I need you back here on cakes, Gwen."

I held up the wet floor sign. "Also told me to mop first."

He glared. "Molly, you handle the floor. Gwen, in the kitchen."

Passing Molly the wet floor sign along the way, I gave a joyless smile. "Yes, sir."

As I rounded the bend into the kitchen, my shoulders slumped. At least a dozen crumb-coated cakes waited for me on the twelve-foot-long steel table. A note card with customer's requests accompanied each of them. A hundred sticks of softening butter sat out on the white countertops along the walls. One of the stand mixers whirred with buttercream. Powdered sugar coated the countertop beside it.

It wasn't unusual for crumb-coated cakes to greet me when I came in. Andrew often had the cakes baked, filled, and stacked. My job was anywhere he wanted me, but often back here. I was the best decorator on staff.

What *was* unusual was the quantity. Approaching the table, I counted eighteen. Eighteen cakes. On a four-hour shift.

Suffice it to say, I was not getting out of here at six.

By four p.m., I was seven cakes down and had eleven more to go. Thankfully, Andrew came in and got a few batches of buttercream ready for me. I would still need a couple more before I was done, but it was helpful. For as long as it lasted, anyway. His shift ended at four. He told me to—didn't *ask* me to—stay until I had all the cakes done. Just clock out when I'd finished. The overtime was approved.

As I decorated the cakes, sculpting each individual flower, writing happy birthday wishes or congratulations on each top, I didn't have time to think about my night. My eyes were heavy, neck aching from bending over for so long, and my stomach still growled. But at least I wasn't thinking about last night.

At ten 'til five, now with nine cakes under my belt, Molly walked into the kitchen. Gazing down at the table of unfinished cakes, she swallowed hard. "Andrew left already?"

"At four, yep." Focused on the drop lines on the side of the heart-shaped cake in front of me, I only spared her a glance. "Why? What's up?"

"He was supposed to work the counter," she said. "My shift ends at five and I have a class that starts at six."

Molly was nineteen, in her sophomore year at the local community college. On Thursdays, she always got off at five. Not like it was my job to remember, since I wasn't the manager, but Molly was a friend. Unlike me, this was just a part-time job to her. Getting her degree was more important.

Grunting my annoyance, I laid my piping bag on the table. "Get outta here."

She frowned. "I can't leave you with all this. Don't these all have to be finished tonight?"

"*You* aren't leaving me with anything." Arms stretched overhead, I rolled my neck from side to side. "Andrew did. But it's fine. I'm getting overtime. I'll finish the cakes after I close up."

"Are you sure?" Her voice was soft, expression timid. "If you need me to stay a little bit longer—"

"I don't." I smiled. "I need a break anyway. I'll drink some water and eat a pepperoni roll between customers." I gestured to the ones I'd finished. "Just do me a favor and pop these in the cooler before you clock out."

She returned the smile. "You have no idea how much I love you."

Waving her off, I walked past her through the stainless-steel door. No one waited in line at the checkout. In one of the booths, a man sat with his laptop on the table and a cup of coffee in hand. At another in the center of the room, a woman was at the edge of her seat, scrolling social media. A couple teenagers were around one of the other booths, a woman with a toddler in another.

I had a moment to catch my breath and get something to eat.

I grabbed a pepperoni roll from the pastry case, then a cold brew coffee from the fridge. I topped it off with some cream and cold foam.

I doubted it would cure my exhaustion, but hopefully it would get me through the remaining nine cakes. After a big gulp, I chomped into the pepperoni roll. Then winced as it went down my throat. Not the best flavor combination.

My phone buzzed in my pocket.

Fishing it out, a dozen notifications bombarded me. A voicemail, a few texts, judging by the message emblem in the top left corner, but flashing across the screen now was Simone.

I answered it with, "Everything okay?"

"Yeah, everything's fine," she said. "I'm gonna try to talk carefully, because I'm pretty sure you're at work."

"I am indeed." Another bite of pepperoni roll. "What's up? Did Margaret get Junie from school?"

"She did, yeah. She's gonna watch her for the next few days," Simone said. "Do you think you could pick me up when your shift's over? I thought about renting a hotel somewhere, but then I thought maybe it was best if I just stay at your place until my face heals up. Going to a hotel might look suspicious if anything comes out later."

While she wasn't wrong, if anything did come back to us and someone looked into the lash extension class Simone claimed she was taking right now, that wouldn't look good either. But I couldn't say that at the moment. That, we could discuss later.

"Sounds like a good call," I told her. "What did Rhiannon say?"

"That it was probably best for me to get away for a couple days if I was having a hard time. Apparently, it seemed like I was last night."

"I can't disagree with that."

"It sucks." A long sigh echoed through the speaker. "Staying away from Junie these next couple of days sucks. Everything that happened last night, that sucks a lot more. Everything just . . ."

"Sucks?" I washed down the bread and pepperoni with a gulp of coffee. "Yeah. Tell me about it."

I could practically hear her frown. "I'm sure it sucks a lot more for you. I'm sorry you got wrapped up in all this, Gwen. That wasn't how it was supposed to go, you know? I was just—"

"I know."

As unfortunate as it all was, I didn't blame Simone for any of it. Except for maybe my sore back. If she'd woken her ass up, she could have helped me lift his body. But everything else?

"Shit happens," I said. "We're dealing with it. When I get to you though, I need you to drive, because I'll probably fall asleep at the wheel."

"Yeah, of course," she said. "Least I can do."

"I'd say so," I said, tone teasing.

She laughed. "We're going to hell, aren't we?"

A gust of cold wind blew in from the double glass doors. Through them walked two familiar faces. Sebastian, in his usual jeans and T-shirt, and Lizzie at his side.

Just the sight of him brought those flapping wings back to my belly.

Why the hell did my mind even travel there right now? There were bigger fish that needed frying.

Lizzie stood just around five feet tall, long blonde hair wound into a high pony at the back of her head. Her facial features were soft, delicate. A tiny ski slope nose, two big innocent blue eyes, and the widest, most joyful smile.

"Hey, I think I'd like the heat better than the knee-high snow," I told Simone. "But I've got customers. I gotta let you go. We'll talk later."

"Sure. Let me know when you're on your way."

"Will do." I shuttered the phone and shoved it into my pocket. Sebastian and Lizzie were only a few steps from the counter now. "Sorry. Haven't had much time for a break today."

"I can tell," Sebastian said. "You look like shit."

Yeah. I was getting way too far ahead of myself thinking this man had any romantic interest in me.

Lizzie gasped. Shoving her elbow into her uncle's ribs, she shot him a look. "She looks beautiful. Watch your mouth."

Laughing, I headed to the espresso machine for their usuals. "Tell him, Liz."

"I didn't mean that you literally look like shit," Sebastian said quickly. "You look good. You always look good. But you look tired."

"You'd be tired too if you were working on eighteen cakes in a four-hour shift." As his java brewed, I propped my hands on my hips. "And managing the front at the same time."

"You deserve a raise." Lizzie leaned against the counter, trying her best to get a better view inside the pastry case. "Are those eclairs any good?"

"Delicious," I said, starting that way. "How many do you want?"

"Three, please," she said. "Sebastian told me we were rehearsing together tomorrow. Right?"

I had completely forgotten about that. But like Simone said, it was best not to alter our schedules right now.

"That's the plan," I told her. "What are we working on again?"

"That's the thing. I don't know. I have to decide on a song, classic or current, and prepare a performance. How do you decide that sort of thing? Like, when you're preparing a set and choosing which songs to play, what are the deciding factors?"

Collecting all her eclairs into a pastry bag, I raised my shoulders. "It depends."

"On what, exactly?"

"What style are you going for?" I handed her the bag of eclairs over the pastry case. "What do you enjoy the most? Is there any particular song you can't get out of your head? Something that means a lot to you that you want to show to other people?"

She nibbled her lower lip. "I could probably think of a couple."

"Pick three, and we'll learn them all." I returned to the espresso machine and finished up Sebastian's Americano. As I passed it to him over the register, I smiled at Lizzie. "Once you have them nailed, then you'll have a few to choose from for your recital. How's that sound?"

Light shined in those big blue eyes. It reminded me of her uncle, but his had a shroud of something over top. A subtle gauze of darkness that I doubted he would ever share with the rest of the world.

Smiling wider, Lizzie nodded. "That sounds perfect. I'm excited."

"She really is," Sebastian said, laying a twenty on the counter. "Hasn't shut up about it since I told her."

Lizzie narrowed her gaze. "You're annoying."

"Must be where you get it from."

A roll of her eyes. "Whatever. I'm going to wait in the car." A smile for me. "See you tomorrow, Gwen."

Returning the smile, I waved. I went back to counting out Sebastian's change, and he cleared his throat.

Was I the one making this interaction weird? Or was it him? To distinguish, I said, "You good?"

"Uh. I wasn't trying to be an asshole," he said. "You really don't look bad. I just—You look great. I mean it. You always look great."

This was what they meant when they said *mixed signals*, wasn't it? "Thanks?"

Judging by the slump of his shoulders and the tight line he pressed his lips to, that wasn't the response he was hoping for. "I just meant you look like you're having a hard day. I was trying to give you an opportunity to vent about it."

Usually, Sebastian and I talked about my dog, or one of Rhiannon's sick cows, or a piece of art, or current events, or whatever drama there was at the ranch this week. From time to time, we would bitch about my broken-down car or that he was in a rush to pick Lizzie up from school.

But we didn't talk about ourselves all that much. Our feelings. Maybe that was a good thing about our friendship. Maybe it wasn't.

One way or the other, though, I couldn't tell him about the man I'd killed last night.

"Andrew left early. Molly had to get to class. My shift was supposed to end at six, but I still have almost a dozen cakes to finish decorating." I rubbed my eyes with my thumb and forefinger. "I'm just in a mood."

That must've been the response he was looking for, because his shoulders softened just a bit. "Why did he leave?"

"Probably has to figure out where he's gonna live now that Julia kicked him out."

"No shit." His hazel eyes widened. "What happened there?"

"No idea. Molly's sister saw her throwing his shit onto the lawn though, so can't be good." Taking a big gulp from my iced coffee, I sat on the stool behind the register. A sigh of relief escaped me. "Damn, that's nice."

"The coffee? Or the seat?"

"Both. Can't really sit when you're decorating a cake," I said. "But enough about me. Anything going on with you?"

"Same shit, different day," he said. "I better stop holding you up. I gotta get Lizzie to her dance class by six. But thanks again for helping her out. She's really looking forward to it."

"So am I. It'll be fun."

"As long as she's nicer to you than she is to me."

Coffee in hand, turning to head for the door, he gave a smile, but it was different than usual. Rather than his smart ass, crooked grin, his cheeks were warmer, and he had a hard time holding my gaze for too long.

The pepperoni roll roiled in my stomach. I had been trying to get past the nausea that romance brought. Rhiannon said I needed to. That dwelling on the past held me back from my future.

Once, I had craved love and companionship. A best friend to share my life with. That's why I'd gotten married at nineteen. But Troy wasn't my best friend or a partner to walk through life with. He'd never loved me. Not really. Not in the way I needed.

That didn't mean a partner like I'd wanted, like I'd thought I was getting then, didn't exist. Just that now I knew what red flags to look for.

She kept saying, *You can have a partner and a best friend who loves you more than anything, Gwen. But you have to open yourself up to it.*

It wasn't that I disagreed with her.

But I couldn't tell what was happening here.

Clearing my throat, I just said, "She's always nice to me."

"So far," he said, continuing to the door. His smile was a bit more genuine now that there was more distance between us. Maybe I was wrong. Maybe it wasn't a date. "Good luck with those cakes."

"Good luck with the dance moms."

"Oh, and I take it back." He stood outside the door now, holding it open with his hip. "'Heart'. That's my favorite. Not 'All's Well That Ends.'"

Damn those butterflies and that jaw-aching smile.

"Heart" by Rainbow Kitten Surprise was a love song. A beautiful, bouncy, almost jazzy ballad that spoke purely, simply, about two people madly in love.

Was that his way of confirming where this was headed?

There was no stopping the skip in my chest. "It's a good one."

"Made me think of you." His eyes twinkled. A wave accompanied it as the door floated shut. Through the windows, we smiled at each other until he was out of sight.

My heart all but stopped.

And I had to get it together, because I was at work, my feet were killing me, and I had literally killed a man last night. I didn't have enough emotional bandwidth for all of this right now.

Like anyone else in the modern era on a break at work, I swiped open my phone. A few texts from Simone, discussing what she had mentioned on the call. Another from Molly, thanking me for being so understanding, and then three from a number I didn't recognize.

It was a 406 area code number. Not unusual. Girls at the ranch passed each other's numbers around frequently. Maybe someone had given mine to the new girl, Delilah.

I clicked the message.

**Unknown**

What did you do with the car?

Left the wallet and phone in his pocket.

If you're gonna do it, do it right.

# CHAPTER 10

## *Gwen*

I bolted to the bathroom.

Only once I'd dropped to my knees and hurled all that coffee and pepperoni roll into the toilet did I begin to process those texts.

For half a second, I thought it could have been Simone. She understood what I'd done, how dangerous it was. It wasn't out of the realm of imagination that she could've gotten a burner to message me about it.

That half second was nice. Then reality set in.

If it were Simone on a burner, she would've called. She would've called on her regular phone, told me she'd gotten a burner, then instructed *me* to get one. Otherwise, this one-sided anonymity would be useless.

It wasn't Simone.

Someone had to have seen me.

No, they hadn't just seen. They'd found the body. And the personal effects I had been too stupid to remove.

*Shit. Shit, shit, shit.*

What the hell had I been thinking? Why hadn't I checked his pockets?

At that thought, my stomach tightened, and I retched again.

I sat up and wiped my mouth, breaths coming in ragged. They couldn't have just found the body. There had been nothing to connect me to it. Sure, maybe a bit of my DNA. No matter how careful I'd been to conceal it, a hair follicle or two could have slipped out, but it wasn't like I'd pinned a picture of myself to his chest.

Either they'd seen me wrapping him in the tarp and loading him into his car, or they'd seen me dumping him into the river. But I would've known if anyone had followed me to the bridge. That road had been so quiet, no one could've been close enough behind to identify me without me seeing them.

Not unless they'd been in the woods around the bridge. That was possible. Not only possible, but probable. Another thing I should've thought about this morning. Hunting season had just begun.

I shut my eyes and placed a hand on my forehead, running it through my hair to the back of my neck. My hands were like icepacks against my clammy skin.

*Son of a bitch.*

Holy shit, how had I screwed up this badly?

Not unless it was someone from the ranch. How would they have found the body and known to connect me? Unless I had been tailed. But I would've seen headlights behind me, right?

Dazed, lightheaded, and almost certain I wasn't going to puke again, I dropped onto my ass. The cool linoleum caressed my spine through my sweat-dampened T-shirt. Resting my head against the blue-tiled wall behind me, panting, I grasped my chest. My heart threatened to pound its way out of my body.

*Breathe, Gwen. Just breathe.*

They hadn't turned me in. Did they even have proof I'd done it? I'd been bundled up like an infant on their first venture into the winter world. Even if they had taken photos of me, there was no way to *prove* it was me. That, I was sure of.

But why had they sent me a message?

I wouldn't know, couldn't know, until I asked.

With shaking fingers, I typed back.

**Gwen**

Who is this?

*Ding.*

Instant reply.

**Unknown**

A friend.

*Ding.*

**Unknown**

What did you do with the car? Can anyone find it?

My heart sank to my stomach. What the hell did that even mean? A friend. A friend wouldn't message me about this anonymously. They would either turn me in or ask me directly what happened, without the shield of anonymity.

**Gwen**

I don't know what you're talking about. Who is this?

Were they blackmailing me? Was that the plan?

Who the hell would blackmail me? The only person I could imagine doing that was Troy. He was a vindictive bastard. I could see him doing this just to torture me.

But he would've shown by now. Either here at the bakery, the ranch, or at the local bar I performed at on the weekends. He would've shown up and begged me to take him back. When I told him no, *then* he would torture me.

Regardless, there was no way he could've found me here. I'd had no contact with anyone from my hometown, including him, in almost a year. I hadn't used social media in the same amount of time. Lacey Montgomery was dead for all intents and purposes. It wasn't possible—

*Ding.*

**Unknown**

Cut the shit. We both know. I googled him. Bastard probably deserved it. I just want to make sure you were smart about it.

Were they . . . helping me?

I shouldn't have even been having this conversation. While I also used a burner phone, that was only because it was the rule at Rhiannon's Ranch. Every single one of us used a contract-free, pay-by-month, cash-only phone plan. We could only get a regular phone through a main provider once we moved out.

That didn't mean this phone couldn't trace back to me. I used it to talk to everyone at the ranch, my coworkers here at the bakery, and the managers of the bars I performed at.

How the hell could I even know that whoever was on the other side of this line *was* trying to help me? For all I knew, they were a cop with a theory. They didn't have enough proof, and they were planning on using this conversation to get me to confess.

**Gwen**

I don't know what you're talking about. Please stop texting me.

A long stretch of silence. Each passing second had my heart beating faster, harder. My hands were still shaking, stomach swirling, sweat covered every inch of me, and black started edging around my vision.

Nope. No way in hell was I passing out in the bathroom at work.

I lowered myself flat to the ground, lifted my knees toward the ceiling, and shut my eyes. Calming breaths. At least fifty calming breaths before that spinning sensation slowed.

*Ding.*

**Unknown**

Look, I get that you're freaked out. I would be too. But I'm trying to help.

Anxiety lessened, I harrumphed.

**Gwen**

I don't need your help. Stop texting me.

*Ding.*

**Unknown**

Too bad I already did.

**Gwen**

You already did what?

*Ding.*

**Unknown**
Helped you.

**Gwen**
I literally have no idea what you're talking about.

**Unknown**
Get a burner phone. Text me on it instead. That way, you don't have to be afraid someone's going to see this.

**Gwen**
I'm not afraid of anything. I just don't know who you are or what you're talking about.

**Unknown**
Bullshit and we both know it.

**Gwen**
If you don't tell me who you are and wtf this is about, I'm blocking you.

**Unknown**
Look. The only thing I want to know is if the car is taken care of.

It was. I hoped. But no way in hell was I confessing to that over text.

**Gwen**
Didn't tell me who you are or what this is about. Blocking you.

Except, I didn't.

Whoever this person was, they knew what I'd done. Blackmailers would've shown proof by now. Either they didn't have any or they were telling the truth.

They were covering for me.

But why would they do that for a stranger? And how would a stranger have gotten my number?

They called themselves a friend. I had too many of those to count.

My close friends would've confronted me by now. Just like Simone had this morning.

Just as it would've made sense for anyone else close to me to confront me. Or, hell, if they'd been watching from the sidelines, they could've lent a damn hand.

No one did.

Whoever this person was, we couldn't have been all that close.

*Ding.*

**Unknown**
I'll take that as a yes then.

The bell at the checkout counter rang three times, the shrill sound passing through the bakery like the yard alarm in a prison.

I got to my feet, steadying myself with the porcelain sink. My legs shook beneath me, and they threatened to topple over once I let go of the sink's edges. I didn't dare look at myself in the mirror. With one last breath, I strode out of the bathroom.

Nine more cakes to go.

Telling Simone about the mystery messages might've been a good idea.

But she already knew too much. Last night, I'd put her in the line of fire. In a way, I guessed she did that to herself, but I fired a machine gun in her direction.

Everything was at risk. Her budding business. Custody of her child. Before, she may have gotten off with fines for the identity fraud, but now? Now, she had aided and abetted.

I told her nothing when I picked her up from work. As we drove back to the ranch—her in the driver's seat because of my exhaustion—she tried to start conversations about anything, everything. I quickly shut down every attempt. Not with rudeness. Just short replies that wrapped up the conversation before it could start.

When we got close to the ranch, I took the wheel and she climbed into the backseat. She squatted on the floorboards and covered herself up with my mounds of spare hoodies. Why did I keep so many of those back there? Laziness. It was cold when I left in the mornings, but then I got hot and tore the extra layer off during the drive and tossed it in the backseat, where I inevitably forgot it.

Supposed they came in handy right about now.

Simone's reasoning was simple. If anyone saw her in the passenger seat, they may mention it to Rhiannon, and she would know Simone lied about the conference.

Seemed logical enough to me.

A few yards from the gate, we did pass another car. I recognized the woman behind the windshield, but I didn't know her name. We exchanged a wave and honk regardless.

"What was that?" Simone asked.

"One of the girls from the apartments," I said, pulling off to the shoulder to give her room. As I watched her taillights in my rearview, I readjusted the wheel and got back on the gravel road. "I was just letting her pass."

"Gonna give me a heart attack back here."

"It's not like you're trespassing." Gassing up the hill, I glanced at her in my rearview. Still just a blob of cotton. "You're allowed to be here."

"Yeah, and if anyone sees my face, Rhiannon's gonna know, and then we're both screwed."

"You're not screwed." I squinted at the glow of headlights in the distance. "I'll be screwed, but you'll be fine."

"In case you haven't noticed, bitch, I don't want you to be screwed," Simone said. "I want my face to heal, and then I want to forget this ever happened."

"You and me both." Those headlights were getting closer, meaning our paths would probably cross before we made it to the cabin. "But, hey, worst-case scenario, if she does see you here, tell her you fell down the stairs or some shit."

"In the average place, that would work," Simone said. "But we all know the stupid lies we told everybody back then. Rhiannon will see right through, 'I fell down the stairs.'"

That she would.

"It's bullshit you're in a position where you even have to think about that again," I said under my breath.

"Makes it more real, I guess. But I don't know. I've never stopped thinking about it. Have you?"

Almost a year since I'd left. Not a day had passed when I didn't think about it.

My phone dinged from my hoodie pocket in the back seat.

Some shuffling sounded. Simone said, "Sebastian says that he thinks you'd like this song."

Through the speakers, the background music I'd had on changed. And I immediately recognized it. *The Warmth* by Paris Paloma.

There came that damn smile.

He listened to Paris Paloma? I guess it checked out for an artsy guy associated so closely with a radical feminist like Rhiannon. Still not what I'd expected.

"Tell him this is one of my favorite albums in modern music history," I said.

A moment or two of silence passed. "Done. Is this what you guys talk about?"

"Mostly. And obscure painters we find online." Those headlights were brighter now, closer. But they were stationary.

"Why don't you tell *me* about obscure artists you find online?" Simone's voice had a whiny, yet playful twinge to the edge.

"I send you music all the time." Rounding the bend carefully, noting how icy it was, I watched those headlights like my life depended on it. "You just don't send any back."

"Touché."

A big black Range Rover was parked in my driveway.

"Shit," I said.

"What?" Simone asked.

"Stay down, and be quiet," I said. "Axel's outside my place."

"Shit," she said in the same tone. "Just lock your doors when you get out. I'll wait a few minutes and leave after you."

"If I lock the doors, it'll set the alarm."

"Lock the doors, set the alarm, get him out of here, and then unlock the car once he's gone."

Not the worst plan I'd ever heard. "Fine. But seriously. Shut up."

Silence.

I pulled into my driveway.

As I stepped from my vehicle, Axel jumped from his. Little brown curls snuck out from beneath his red beanie, all covered by his thick, black puffer coat. As beautiful as Axel was with his angled jaw covered with a five o'clock shadow, strong nose, and big brown eyes, his cinched brows always made him look angry. They weren't all that thick. Simone waxed them weekly. His forehead just crunched them down into his eyes.

Now more than ever.

Axel charged at me like a wolf after a bunny. "Have you talked to Simone?"

"Earlier," I said, tossing my purse over my shoulder. "She said she got invited to a last-minute conference in the city or something?"

"She told me that too." He crossed his arms against his chest, squinting me over. "But she didn't tell me shit else. No one did."

Cocking my head to the side, my stomach did that spinning thing again. "I don't know what you mean."

"Bullshit," he said, in the same tone I had read that text in earlier. Could it have been Axel? Had he seen something last night? "Something's up, and you know it."

It took everything I had not to swallow hard and swat at the bead of sweat forming above my brow. "What?"

"Margaret told me she came here last night," he said. "Rhiannon told me about her meltdown at group, but she didn't come to me to talk about it. She came to you."

Did he know? Was he dancing around the whole truth for the same reason I was? Because neither of us wanted to admit it?

I loved Axel, but he was a smart, abrasive man. Any stereotypes that said gay men were sweet and feminine were laughable where Axel was involved.

Thinking back on those texts, I couldn't hear his deep, raspy voice saying any of them. Admitting to his involvement, whatever that involvement was with the body, was something he would take to his grave. He and I had that in common.

"She did," I said. "She came over, and we talked. Had a few drinks, passed out, and went on to work in the morning."

Axel crossed his arms against his chest. "What did you talk about?"

"I mean, if you were upset, and you came to me to talk about it, I wouldn't run my mouth about it to someone else." I crossed my arms against my chest too. "But you could call her and—"

"Something happened," he snapped, stepping closer.

Now he looked more like a mom confiding in her best friend

about her child being bullied at school. His brows were still furrowed, but his eyes were soft beneath them. "If she threw a bitch fit at group and insulted everyone there, then decided to leave town for a week without telling Junie goodbye first, *something happened.*"

"I wouldn't say she threw a bitch fit," I said, stalking toward my cabin. "And she didn't just abandon her kid. Junie was already at school when she got the offer. It was a good opportunity, so she—"

"Stop lying, Gwen. You're not good at it."

"And you're not good at salting the road." I gestured behind me. "I slid, like, half a dozen times on my way up here."

"Quit diverting."

"Quit asking me to betray my friend's confidence."

"I just want to know if something happened to her. If it did, that's what she told you about last night. So is that—"

"Fine." I threw my hands in the air. "Fine, I'll tell you. But don't tell her I told you."

Primarily because I knew he wasn't going to back off, and I needed a few milliseconds to come up with a good lie.

Leaning back, he glanced me over, waiting for me to continue.

"Promise," I said. "Promise you won't tell her I betrayed her confidence."

"I promise."

"Because, she was really upset, and if she had wanted to talk to you about it, she would have, but she came to me for some reason, and—"

"I get it. She asked you not to tell anyone. I won't tell her you did. Just get to the damn point, Gwen."

"Something happened at work," I blurted. "When she was outside on her smoke break, she saw a couple fighting. She got really triggered by it, and it just blew up. She couldn't get it out of her head all day, and she had a few panic attacks, and it was just a mess. It was the first time since she got here that she really broke down, and she was embarrassed, and upset, and angry, and she just wanted to talk to someone who got it. Someone who's been there. Then she got that opportunity to leave town for a week, and she figured it would be a good place to get her head on straight. She doesn't want Junie to see her like that."

His expression didn't change. Neither did mine.

There were three possibilities.

1. Axel was the anonymous texter, and he knew I was lying. The point of this discussion was to see if I would confess. Doing so would endanger us both. He was relieved that I continued to lie.

2. He was not the anonymous texter, but he was worried about our mutual friend. He came to me hoping for more context. Now that I'd given it to him, he believed me and was relieved.

3. He was not the anonymous texter, he was worried about our mutual friend, he came to me for more context, but he didn't believe a word that came out of my mouth.

I hoped it was the second possibility.

"She was okay though?" he asked. "When she left this morning, she was okay?"

"Yeah," I said. "She was alright."

"You know she has really bad depression, right?" His expression and tone remained the same. Blunt, assertive. "I don't think she would do anything crazy. She wouldn't abandon Junie. But depression is a screwed-up disease."

Was he worried she was going to kill herself? I didn't see that happening.

"She needed a girls' night," I said. "But yes, she seemed better this morning. I'm sure she's gonna be alright. She just needed a couple days away to get her head on straight."

No change in his demeanor. I couldn't tell which of those possibilities was the case.

He rolled his eyes and sighed. "Whatever. I'll talk to her about it when she gets back. You coming down to town tonight? Rhiannon wanted to talk to you. Said she stopped by earlier, but you weren't here."

"I don't think so. I'm exhausted. My four hour, easy shift wound up taking seven. My back's killing me, and I still need to cook something for dinner."

"I'll let her know." Walking to his car, he spoke over his shoulder. "She'll probably want to talk to you at breakfast."

Or she would show at my door in the next few hours, only to find Simone sleeping on my couch.

# CHAPTER 11

## *Gwen*

Rhiannon had a key. If it took me too long to answer the door when she inevitably came knocking, there was a good chance she would use it. We wouldn't have enough time to get Simone in my closet or under the bed before she made it inside. Rhiannon would see Simone's face, freak the hell out, and a few things could happen from there. The worst of them would be her finding out about the murder. Not much better would be Simone getting kicked out of the ranch for endangering it.

Our best bet was keeping Rhiannon from seeing Simone until her face healed. That meant either I slept on the couch, or we shared the bed.

My back was killing me. I wasn't taking the couch. Nor was I going to make my best friend sleep on the floor when her face looked like a human punching bag.

Sharing a bed for the night wouldn't kill us.

Getting comfortable was a bit inconvenient, given the fact that neither of us were extraordinarily small women. My chunky dog who always slept where Simone now lay wasn't happy about the arrangement either.

But the stress and chaos of the day, paired with the fact that I'd hardly slept in nearly forty-eight hours, made falling asleep a simple task. As soon as my head hit the pillow, I was out cold.

To my surprise, a dreamless sleep followed. Considering the nightmare I'd had the night before, tacked onto the nightmare I'd lived through afterward, I expected to have one tonight. Then again, I had responded to violence with violence. Not only had I survived, but I'd defeated my opponent.

Was that to say that I was proud of what I'd done? Not exactly.

Simone was at risk. The entire ranch was at risk. My freedom was at risk.

But that was my only regret. The possibility of losing the freedom we'd left our lives behind for.

I'd experienced a host of trauma in my life. Troy's relentless psychological and physical abuse had lasted through most of my adolescence and adult life until the last year. The sexual assault I had endured from a boyfriend I'd had before Troy. The drug and alcohol abuse I'd seen growing up, living in poverty—those had kept me up at night.

But killing David? That didn't.

While I wasn't proud of what I'd done, I wasn't ashamed of it either. It'd been self-defense. If I hadn't killed him, he may have killed me. Simone too. Soon after, his daughter could've been on the chopping block.

No, it wasn't pride. It was relief.

I was relieved he couldn't hurt anyone else, that justice had been served.

Because of that, I slept like a baby all through the night. Only to be awoken by a tap on my cheek.

Tilting back, I blinked hard. For a heartbeat, only a heartbeat, I didn't recognize the person beside me. Her left eye was still swollen shut. Those thick lips were still twice their normal size. But her smile was the same as it'd always been, reminding me of where I was and why she was here.

"Morning, sleepyhead," Simone said. "Did you know you snore?"

Yawning, I rubbed the crust from my eyes. "I also talk in my sleep."

"Yeah, you said something about stars and ladybugs." She reached past me to the side table, coming back with a big silver tray with a plate. Steam floated from the hot waffles, scrambled eggs, and mug of coffee at the corner. "Your alarm went off an hour ago, but I turned it off for you since you don't have work today."

Perplexed, I stifled another yawn and sat forward. "And made me breakfast in bed?"

"Well, I made breakfast, and you were in bed, so I figured why not."

I situated the tray on my lap, avoiding Honey at my side, sniffing away. "Is it our anniversary or something?"

She narrowed her eyes. "Don't make it weird."

"I don't think there's a way to interpret anything that's happened in the last forty-eight hours as not weird."

"Which is why I made you breakfast in bed." She snatched a blueberry from the fruit bowl on the edge of the tray. "You saved my life. You very well may have saved the ranch. You offered to take care of my kid, went out of your way to help me make sure Rhiannon doesn't find out about any of this, and you got rid of the guy who has made my life a living hell since I was sixteen years old. I owe you one." She gestured to the tray in my lap. "I figured I could start with breakfast."

"If this is the treatment I get for killing abusive husbands"—I bit into my waffle —"maybe I should do it more often."

"Open an agency." She lifted her hands in the air, as if gesturing to a sign in neon lights. "Assassin Guinevere: Husband hit you? Call now to get a free quote for his murder."

I snorted.

She laughed.

"In all seriousness," I said, "you don't owe me anything. If the roles were reversed, you would've done the same for me."

"I like to think I would, but I don't really know." Frowning, she raised her shoulders. "That last time before I left David was the first time I'd ever hit him back. My trauma response isn't fight. Most of the time, it's freeze. Just like I did the other night."

The first few times I'd frozen, as well. Eventually, I developed the flight response. I ran from my ex if he threatened to escalate violence. The fight response came further down the line.

"I just—I'll never tell anyone, Gwen. I'm a little ashamed to admit how grateful I am. And embarrassed. I had a knife in my pocket, but I didn't grab it. I should have. I shouldn't have let him do this to me again. I should've fought back."

"It doesn't matter now, does it?" Sipping my coffee, I stroked Honey's head. She eyed my plate. "All that matters now is getting through the next week or so. Once your face heals up, we move the hell on from this."

"Yeah, I know." Biting her lip, she shook her head. "And we will. But I'd be lying if I said I didn't have questions."

"Like?"

"Like, are you sure he was dead?"

"Hundred and ten percent."

"But how can you know? What the hell happened anyway?"

A sigh escaped my nostrils. "Plausible deniability, Simone."

"I slept in your bed last night to keep anyone from seeing my face," she said. "I'm already an accomplice. All night, I just kept imagining him rising from a shallow grave with an arrow through his chest, coming back here, and slitting my throat."

Guilt pinched my chest. "I didn't get him with an arrow."

I understood why she would've thought that though. Part of our self-defense course included becoming proficient with a weapon. Rhiannon said it was about building confidence. Guns weren't allowed on the ranch, so I'd chosen a bow. Figured it'd work against a coyote if one ever charged me and Honey.

Simone stared me down, her good eye watering. "What was it then?"

If it would help her sleep better at night, fine. "He got in my face when I told him to leave. He shoved me, I shoved him, and at some point, fists started flying. His hand was around my throat, and I had a knife in my pocket, so I stabbed him."

Brows raising, she cocked her head to the side. "Like, once? That's all it took?"

"Definitely more than once."

"Damn," she murmured. "What was going through your head?"

"'Shit. Shit, shit, shit.'" I nibbled my waffle. "'What the hell did I just do?'"

"No, I mean, before you did it. *While* you did it. Did instinct just kick in, or was it something else?"

"I didn't think about doing it before I did, if that's what you're asking."

"Not really."

"Then what?"

"Like, were you afraid for your life, and you couldn't break free, so you just—"

"No." Shaking my head, I slid the platter from my lap onto the bed. Honey rushed toward it, ready to devour the whole plate. With a grunt, I grabbed it and set it on the nightstand. Honey whined and laid her head back down on her paws. "Nope. I'm not doing this."

"You're not doing what?"

I stepped to the hardwoods and grabbed my robe off the hook on the wall. After I tossed it over my shoulders, I grabbed the platter. "You know what."

"I literally don't."

Already halfway down the hall, I only shook my head. "I don't need you to do the psychotherapy shit on me, Simone. I'm fine."

"I wasn't trying to do any psycho—"

"That's a crock of shit." Setting the tray down on the table, I met her gaze in the hallway. "You want me to talk about my feelings, how it affected me, how I endured another trauma, and I don't need to do that. I'm fine."

"You killed a man yesterday, and you expect me to believe you're just *fine*?" She propped her hands on her round hips. "*That's* the crock of shit, Gwen. We both know some heavy shit was going through your brain when you did that, and that's exactly why you don't want to talk about it."

"I don't want to talk about it because I'm not the victim here. I'm fine." My voice was steady, if not a bit annoyed. "I'm *better* than fine."

Simone's expression twitched to something like amusement. She crossed her arms against her chest. "You're *better* than fine?"

"I am. I feel great. I got a full night's sleep, a waffle in bed, and I know that bastard is not out there in the world anymore. He's not going to hurt anyone else. He's not going to come back for you, or for Junie, or for the ranch to get us all thrown into prison. I slept like a baby knowing the world's a better place without him in it."

"I'm sure you slept like a baby after Troy nearly killed you too," she said. "Because when the brain can't process trauma, it shuts down. It lets you fall into a deep sleep where you can pretend that it didn't happen."

"Out there, I *am* pretending it didn't happen. Because I have to." I pointed at the door. "But I just told you I'm not ashamed of it. That I slept like a baby, that I feel—"

"Fine, I know." Simone raised her hands in surrender. "Just like you told yourself you were fine after your husband nearly killed you."

"What does Troy have to do with this?"

"Because we both know that's what was going through your head when you killed David. His hand was around your throat, but you felt Troy's. That's what the root—"

"No shit that's the root, Simone!" I threw my hands in the air. "Our ex-husbands are the root of all our god damn problems. That's how we all wound up here. But that's irrelevant."

"It's not though." She stepped toward me, her voice softening. "Because you haven't processed it. You still haven't processed all the trauma Troy put you through. That's why we're constantly asking you to speak up in group, because you need to talk about it."

Shaking my head, I yanked in a deep breath. "I'm literally fine."

"Okay. Fine. You feel fine. But we both know how PTSD works. Two people can endure the exact same trauma, and the one who doesn't talk about it, who doesn't work through it, is the one who develops nightmares and flashbacks. You have no one else to talk to about this. I'm the only other person who knows. If you don't talk—"

Honey erupted in a choir of barks.

She ran to the front door.

Simone and I both whipped our heads in that direction.

I followed Honey to the window and pulled back the white, sunflower speckled curtains. Rhiannon's Jeep. A couple dozen yards away, slowly pulling into my driveway.

And I was grateful for it. A long, drawn out conversation about my feelings was the least of my concerns.

Over my shoulder, Simone said, "Knew that was coming. In the closet, or under the bed?"

"If you go in the closet, Honey's gonna stand outside it and bark at you," I said. "Under the bed, she'll just follow you."

"Under the bed it is. But this conversation isn't over."

I waved her off.

She ventured down the hall, and I glanced around. Simone wasn't a messy cook, but the kitchen could use a quick wipe down. Plus it'd look natural when Rhiannon walked in.

Rag in hand, I scrubbed at the clumps of waffle batter on the Formica. It took longer than I expected for the knock to come. I called, "Come in."

The doorknob jiggled. "It's locked."

Still holding the rag, I walked to the door. Opening it, I stepped aside to let her in. "Sorry about that. I thought I left it unlocked last night."

"No worries, kid." As Honey rushed to greet her, tail wagging wildly, Rhiannon laughed. She squatted down, told her a few sweet nothings, and straightened up with her hands on her hips. "You didn't come to the kids' concert last night?"

"Ah, shit."

Until she mentioned it, I'd forgotten all about it. It wasn't a recital—those were scarce. Every Thursday, though, the kids who sang or played instruments gathered in the rec hall to show off what they were working on. Usually, I was there. As a musician myself, I normally showed up to watch the next generation develop their skills and guide them when they needed help.

"I completely forgot," I said. "Andrew stuck me at the bakery 'til almost nine with a million cakes to decorate. Just completely slipped my mind."

"Eh, it happens." Giving a smile, Rhiannon lowered herself to the sofa. "Just wanted to check in and make sure you were okay. Axel said you seemed a little agitated last night. But I guess I would be too if I decorated a million cakes."

"Eighteen during what was supposed to be a four-hour shift, but close enough." Chuckling, I joined her. Honey hopped up between us, and I gave her silky ears a scratch. "Yeah, I was just exhausted. Passed right out when I came in."

"I bet. That Andrew's a piece of work." She made a *tsk, tsk, tsk* sound. "Did you hear Julia kicked him out?"

"Molly told me yesterday, but I still don't have the details."

"She found some text messages." A shit-eating grin lined Rhiannon's slim features. "You won't guess who with."

I propped my elbow on the back of the sofa, swiveling to face her better. "Don't tease."

"The Lamaze instructor." Eyes widening, she shook her head. "Can you imagine? Cheating on your fiancée while she's pregnant with your kid is awful enough. But also, being that instructor? Meeting a guy at a birthing class, where he's with his fiancée, and thinking 'hmm, that's the one for me.'"

Surely my expression showed my disdain. "I wish I could say I'm surprised."

"You and me both." Rhiannon ran her fingers through Honey's fur. "Anyhow, that's not what I came up here for. I was wondering if you'd talked to Simone?"

"I did, yeah. Something about a lash extension class? Or conference? I think?"

"Something like that." Her eyes lingered on my face a bit too long. Like she was watching for a signal that I knew more than I was saying. "She's been here for almost four years now. I've never seen her act like she did Wednesday night."

"Neither have I."

"But I know you guys are close, and it's not that I'm asking you to gossip."

Smirking, I shook my head. "You would never."

Another laugh, but it seemed forced. Like she already knew something, or a whole lot of things, and she was waiting for me to fess up. "Do you know what happened? Why she got so worked up, I mean?"

To the best of my ability, I gave her the same spiel I'd given Axel. I couldn't tell if Rhiannon believed me.

She nibbled the inside of her cheek. "Triggers are strange. I could see it."

Could she? Or did she know I was lying? According to Axel, I wasn't very good at it.

"Well, I could use her right now. Simone, I mean," Rhiannon said. "She always does a good job with the new girls. Showing them around, telling them how the ranch works, all that stuff. I don't know what it is, but she makes them feel right at home.

"The new girl, Delilah, really needs someone to introduce her to everything. I've got a lot on my plate, and with Simone at her class, I was wondering if you could give her a tour? You two seemed to get along pretty well."

"I can," I said. "But I'm not Simone. I can't guarantee I'll make her feel at home the way Simone would."

"I think you don't give yourself enough credit. You know how it is those first few days. It's a ripe time for bonding." Another smile, but she still watched my expression carefully. "Delilah asked about you yesterday. She liked you."

I stifled a yawn. "Sure. It's no problem."

"Thanks, kid." She stood. As she headed for the door, she gave me another smile over her shoulder. "I hope you have a good time tonight. Seems like Sebastian's really looking forward to it."

A hard swallow. "Yeah. Yeah, I hope so too."

Hand on her hip again, she arched her brow. "Are you *not* looking forward to it?"

I opened my mouth to speak, but something between a harrumph and a laugh escaped instead. "No, yeah. I am. I'm looking forward to it."

"'No, yeah?'" Confusion pinched her forehead amid amusement. "Sounds like you're unsure about it?"

"I am, I guess." My cheeks got hot. "I don't know. He just wasn't clear. He asked if I wanted to get dinner after I help Lizzie, but we get meals together all the time. He seemed really awkward and uncomfortable when he asked, and then he was awkward yesterday when he stopped by the bakery, so I'm just a little confused."

"You don't know if it's a date or not."

Pressing my lips together, I shrugged again. "It's cool if it is. It's cool if it isn't. But now I'm not sure if he was awkward and uncomfortable because he thought *I* thought it was a date, and he didn't want to hurt my feelings? Or if he was weird because he wasn't sure if I thought it wasn't a date, and I was going to hurt *his* feelings."

Rhiannon laughed. "I see the way he looks at you. Pretty sure it's a date, kid."

"Pretty sure, as in, he told you it was?"

Another laugh. "Ask him."

I grunted my annoyance.

"Okay, now hear me out for a second." Rhiannon's tone became as soft as her volume. "You've only been with two guys, right?"

An inarguable fact. "Yeah, I guess."

"And both of those relationships were bad." She lifted her shoulders, speaking that almost as a question. When I nodded, she continued. "Those guys were super affectionate in the beginning. They told you how beautiful you were, all the things they liked about you, they treated you like a goddess at the start of the relationship."

"Pretty much." I wasn't sure where she was going with this, but it sounded like data analysis, and I liked facts. "I knew for sure they were interested."

"Because they were love bombing you. It's an abuse tactic. They give you so much at the start, and then they slowly give you less. A healthy relationship starts out a little more ambiguous. It strengthens over time, those declarations of love come later." Another shrug. "So is it possible that your uncertainty comes from that? And not because of anything Sebastian's doing?"

Damn. As the dots connected, I shifted my weight from one foot to the other. "Hadn't thought about it that way."

"Just something to consider," she said, reaching for the door handle. "Anyway, Delilah'll be down at the cafeteria whenever you're ready. And if I don't see you before you head out, I hope you two have a good time."

To that, all I did was sigh. "Drive safe. The snow's a mess out there."

Saying a few more pleasantries, Rhiannon continued outside. I peeked out the curtains behind her. She was in the car and turning it over in heartbeats. As she backed out of the driveway, I called to Simone, "She's—"

"Date?" I jumped at her voice and turned around to see her already in the hallway. "You're going on a date, and you didn't tell me?"

"When would I have had time?"

"Um, I don't know, last night on our drive home?" She narrowed her gaze. "This is a huge deal. Something you're supposed to tell your best friend about, bitch."

Exhaling, I headed past her to my bedroom. "I don't even know if it's a date."

"Rhiannon's known Sebastian since he was a little kid," Simone said, trailing behind me. "If she says it's a date, it's a date."

"She didn't say it's a date." I started digging in my drawers. "And sorry. Kinda had to deal with covering up a murder before I got to gush to my best friend about getting dinner with another friend."

"But you don't want to talk about that either." She trailed behind me as I walked to the bathroom. "You don't want to talk about your date, you don't want to talk about the murder—"

"Repeat that sentence." I laid my clothes on the bathroom counter and stared Simone in the eyes. "Repeat it and then tell me why it's possible I haven't wanted to talk about everything right now, Simone."

Frowning, she crossed her arms against her chest. "Fine. I'll back off. But we're gonna have to talk about everything eventually."

"Eventually," I agreed. "Right now, I need to take a shower, do my makeup, and go show Delilah around. So." I made a pushing motion with my hands. "If you don't mind."

# CHAPTER 12

## *Gwen*

Delilah was waiting for me, so I tried to get ready as quickly as possible.

I could've asked Simone to do my makeup, since the night would end with mine and Sebastian's maybe-date. She would've done a much better job. Also would've pestered me to talk about my feelings. Which I had no interest in.

After scurrying past Simone in the living room, I clipped on Honey's leash. She hadn't gotten her walk yesterday. I knew she was craving it.

Once I broke through the pine trees after a half hour, the view of town had my heart rate softer, my mind quieter, and my body warm with comfort. No matter the icy wind that slithered past my balaclava and leather gloves.

Even if I didn't get away with what I'd done, this place was worth it.

A quarter mile ahead, tucked between conifers and snow-doused mountains, a dozen buildings perched with pride. The ones in the heart of town matched the natural aesthetic of the ranch. Only a story high, two log domes crouched low in the valley. The rec center and the cafeteria, built to feed well over a thousand residents. There was something poetic about those log structures next to the new buildings. The roots of the ranch that had watched so many women come, heal, and go to lay down roots of their own.

At a glance, the stone apartments, the new builds, lacked the character and charm of the original structures. But a careful eye would catch the fairy lights that twinkled around one apartment balcony and the Edison bulbs that illuminated another.

All the hand-painted suncatchers that dangled from the windows of the daycare, and the paper flyers that fluttered on the gym doors, saying, *Volunteers needed for Light Up Night Decorations!* compensated for the boring brick. The women of Rhiannon's Ranch, the community, gave this place charm a construction crew could only dream of.

The buildings were only that. Buildings.

We were the warmth that brought them to life.

But we were dominoes.

Simone had nearly fallen the other night. I'd caught her before we all crashed down.

It was the right thing. I had done the right thing.

Once inside the cafeteria, I scanned for Delilah. At a little past noon, half the damn town was in here for lunch. Delilah may have been swallowed in the crowd somewhere.

This was one of my favorite parts of the ranch. The ceiling came to a point in the center of the room, a circle of windows framing it. During the warmer months, they let in more light than the white hanging globe lights, spaced every few feet apart.

Cafeteria tables, like those used in a school, took up most of the floor space. Buffet bars framed the exterior walls, featuring soda fountains on either end. To feed over a thousand people at a time, buffets were a necessity.

"Gwen, right?" Someone said behind me, tapping my shoulder.

I turned around. Delilah looked better today. The dusting of foundation over her blue eyes covered the bruise. Her dark circles were still visible if I squinted, but a light smile brightened the rest of her features.

"Right," I said. "Rhiannon told me I'd find you here."

"She told me the same." Glancing past me at the buffets, she tucked her arms against her chest. "Are you hungry? Did you come to eat?"

"No, actually, I'm supposed to show you around." I gestured to the buffet. "What about you? Have you eaten?"

"I did, yeah. Surprisingly good for cafeteria food."

"Except for meatloaf day," I said, wincing. "Always skip meatloaf day."

She chuckled. "Noted."

"You ready for the tour, then?"

"Excited for it. I almost got lost walking here from the apartment this morning."

Together, we started for the double glass doors. I held one open for her. "Which one are you in?"

"B, I think." She tugged her jacket in closer as we stepped out into the cold. After two feet forward, Honey sidestepped her, spinning to look at her. Delilah gasped, pressing her hand over her heart. She laughed and squatted to greet her. "Where did you come from?"

"She's short," I said. "Easily overlooked."

"Sweet as pie, though." After giving Honey one more scratch on the head, Delilah straightened. "You're allowed to bring your dog into the cafeteria?"

"As long as she's not being a nuisance, I'm allowed to bring her anywhere on the ranch. A few girls have phobias. Rhiannon encourages exposure therapy, but if anyone's having too hard a time, I just take her somewhere else."

"Wow," Delilah murmured, gazing down at Honey.

There was a certain kindness in her eyes, an affection for animals. But some distance as well. Like it was hard for her to be around one, not because she was afraid, but because she was sad.

"Do you have any pets?" I asked.

"I did, yeah. When I left, I couldn't—" A deep breath. "I don't have them anymore."

Maybe her ex wouldn't let her take them. "If you ever wanted to get one again, just let Rhiannon know. They all have to be up to date on vaccinations, but as long as you clean up after them, you're allowed one."

"Maybe I will." She glanced out over the street. "Where do we begin?"

"How about we start at the farthest end and work our way down?"

"Sounds like a plan."

There were a total of five streets on Rhiannon's Ranch. First, Second, Third, Main, and Hilltop.

We started at the intersection of Second and Main at the gate and ended at First Street. First was still nearly a mile walk from the café, separated only by two fields.

"Most of the other stuff in town is close together," I explained, watching Honey hop through the snow on the left of the gravel road.

"This area through here is spread out because of the types of buildings. If you're in the apartments, you probably won't hang out around this area too much."

Delilah squinted around, eyeing the road toward the mountain peak on our right, the building at the hill beneath it, then the stone building on the far left corner. "What are these places?"

I pointed to the stone building. "That right there, with the green metal roof, is the meat-packing plant. That's where Rhiannon processes cattle, venison, and chickens."

"*Processes?*" Delilah's nose scrunched up in disgust. "She kills them back there?"

"Oh, no." I shook my head. "That happens at the farm in the back. This is just where they get butchered."

Her eyes bulged.

I laughed. "Are you a vegan?"

"No, but it's still gross."

"If it helps, the animals we eat around here are well taken care of before they die. But yeah, I couldn't kill one either."

The irony of that statement was not lost on me.

"That"—I pointed to the glass building on the far right of First—"is the greenhouse. That's how we get a chunk of our produce through the winter. Some of the girls like to hang out in there and take care of plants."

Delilah eyed me as we walked. "No green thumb?"

"Dirt and bugs just aren't my thing," I said. "You?"

"I like to grow a garden in the summer." Squinting at the greenhouse, she pointed past it to the gravel path that snaked up the mountain. "Is that an access road to the farm?"

"That's Hilltop Road," I said. "There's a trailer park up there. On the other side of it is one of Rhiannon's farm areas. I think that's where she keeps the horses. It's part of the ranch, but I don't go back there much."

"The trailer park is part of the ranch too?" she asked, still squinting at the mountaintop.

"It is. It's one of the earliest parts of the ranch, actually." I spun around to head back down Main. Delilah followed. "Rhiannon started this place, like, fifteen years ago? She just had the campground then. So Main Street, the cabins, the cafeteria, and the rec center. All the other buildings came later. But then she bought more of the land, including the trailer park. Now, some of the women with children stay up there. Gives them a bit more space than the apartments."

A moment of silence, followed by a bewildered, "Wow."

Halfway back to Second Street, I gestured to the cafeteria on the right. "Obviously, you know what that is."

"And a little bit down that road"—she gestured the rest of the way down Second—"that's the legal building?"

I glanced at the little wooden cabin, no different from my own, and nodded. "Yep. You go all the way to the end of that street, and you'll get to Rhiannon's house. It's tucked back in the woods a little, so you can't see it from here, but if you ever need her after hours, that's where to knock."

"Is that okay though?" Her voice was timid. "She seems nice and everything, but she has a lot of responsibility here. I don't want to be a bother or anything."

That was a tightrope to walk. Rhiannon gave us a chance no one else in our lives ever had. A free place to live, a community out of a fairytale, a fresh start.

"I don't know many people who are comfortable begging for help at someone's door," I said. "Especially when they've already given so much. But Rhiannon would open hers at any time of the day and make you feel like you just came home."

"I guess she would have to be that kind of person to run this place like she does." Delilah's eyes caught on the circular log building across the street from the cafeteria. "That's the rec center, right?"

"It is," I said.

Eve, the girl who'd told her story on Wednesday night at group, stepped from its entrance. When she saw the two of us, she gave a smile and a big wave. I returned it.

"What's it for?" Delilah asked.

"I go down to play the grand piano when I'm bored, as long as no one else has signed up for a specific event that day. The kids do chorus concerts once a week. Every couple months, they put on a play of some kind for us. During the holidays, we throw big parties there. Dances once in a while. And downstairs we have the community closet."

I stopped walking for a moment and looked at Delilah, keeping my voice soft. "Did you bring any clothes? Or did you get out in a hurry?"

"I've got a few things." Her throat bobbed with a hard swallow. "But I didn't have time to grab much."

"Then we'll circle back here and get you a couple bags full."

Crossing the intersection, I gestured down the left of Second, past the rec center. There was another building down there. More like an insulated aluminum garage, really.

"On the right up there, we have the clinic. It's not a hospital by any means, but if you ever go on a hike and take a nasty fall, that's where you'll want to go. We always have a nurse on staff, but she mostly just gives advice. Tells us whether or not we need to go to the hospital."

"Yeah, Rhiannon showed me," she said, quieter than anything else she had said so far. Before I could question why that might be, she gestured to the end of the street. A similar building stood tall across from the clinic. Also an aluminum building, but this one had a blue roof. "What's that one?"

"That would be the garage," I said. "Rhiannon and some of the maintenance guys store equipment in there. If you ever need to work on a car or something, Rhiannon will let you in. Let you borrow tools too."

"No car yet, and no idea how to work on one," Delilah said, a teasing edge to her voice. "But that's cool. My dad always complained about having to work on cars out on the road. We never had a garage."

Neither had I. "There's an automotive class once a month at the rec center. They taught me how to change my oil and brake pads."

Nibbling her bottom lip, tilted at the corner with a smile, she shook her head. "I'm still trying to wrap my head around everything here."

"Give it a couple months, and you'll never want to leave." I gestured to the stone buildings on the left and right of Main Street. "No kids, right?"

"No. No kids."

"Irrelevant to you then, but that's the daycare." I pointed to the building on the left.

It was one of the newer additions, constructed in the last ten years. It was only two stories high, roughly the size of a small apartment building on the edge of a suburb. Nothing special there either. Just stone block, a dozen or so windows wrapping around the front and sides, and an aluminum roof on the top.

"There's a playground in the back too. On the edge of it, a nice walking trail takes you through the woods. If you follow it the whole way, you'll come out by my cabin at the edge of the ranch."

"You're in one of those cabins at the front?"

"Closest one to the gate. Don't be afraid to come knocking if you need something." I hooked a thumb in gesture to the building we were passing on the right. "Any idea what that place is?"

It stood three stories tall, half the width of the daycare across the street. However, they were decorated the same way. A green aluminum roof, gray stone blocks, and a few dozen windows. Rather than the daycare's metal door for the entrance, it had a set of double glass doors.

"Nope, but I bet you're going to tell me."

"That's our gym," I said. "Once you have your key card, you can go in or out whenever you'd like. There's everything in there. Treadmills, ellipticals, bikes, stepping machines. Nights are my favorite time, because mostly everyone's in bed by then. The only thing is that you can't go into the pool unless there's a lifeguard on duty. Safety issue, you know?"

Blinking hard, Delilah huffed. "There's an indoor pool?"

"No use in having an outdoor pool in Montana." A few hundred strides ahead, a small gravel road led to the apartments on the left. "And back there is where you live. Do you need me to show you around that area too, or are you ready to head back to the closet?"

"I think I know how to get back home from here."

That warmed my heart. The way she called it home. "Then to the closet we go."

I tapped my thigh to get Honey's attention. She spun around with me, romping through the snow in the field between the gym and the cafeteria.

"And I can just grab clothes?" Delilah asked. "I don't have to pay for them or anything?"

"Clothes, shoes, household items. It's basically a thrift store. We all donate to it, and we all take from it. You don't have to pay for anything."

"Crazy," she said under her breath. "All of this is so beautiful, but so crazy."

"It won't always feel that way," I said, veering closer to the right side of the road, to head toward the rec center. "I don't know about you, but I grew up poor. My ex made more than me, so the money was always more his than mine. I had a couple hundred bucks to my name when I left, and even renting an apartment somewhere was just about out of the question. I just didn't make enough money. But all of us, over a thousand of us, live on this ranch because of the way Rhiannon set up a hell of an inheritance. And that's all it took."

Delilah cocked her head to the side. "What do you mean?"

"Some donor inherited a couple billion dollars, and they gave it to her. It's been enough to keep this place running for a decade. And to help a lot of other charitable organizations. It just goes to show how far money can stretch when it's in the right hands."

"I didn't think a billion could do all this."

"A billion is a lot more than you might think," I said. "A thousand million—that's a billion."

"Yeah, I guess. It's just crazy to think about how hard I used to work for not even half of what everyone has here," she said. "You know what I still don't understand, though?"

Now at the rec center's entrance, I held the door open for her. "What's that?"

She stepped through, and I followed.

"How everybody just gets along," she said.

Delilah glanced out the window, watching all the women walk past. Some were hand-in-hand, others pushed strollers beside one another. One thing in common among them all, though, was the energy that radiated from them. Everyone looked comfortable. Some happier than others, but no one would watch these women walk down the street and worry for them.

They were why the other night hadn't been a mistake.

"With any group of girls I've been around," she said, "there's always so much drama."

"There's drama sometimes," I replied. "Just like there is any time you put a large number of people together. But no one is fighting over each other's man around here."

She laughed. "I guess that's fair."

"And there's just a different energy on the ranch." Turning to face her, I raised my shoulders. "Out in the world, there's so much stress. Here, we all know we're safe."

At least, we had been. Until the other night.

"No one's worried about losing the roof over their head. There's always food at the cafeteria if you're hungry. We have access to therapy and doctors. There's no other place like this. Maybe when everyone's basic needs are met, there's less to fight about."

Ever so slightly, Delilah's shoulders loosened, and she tilted her head to the side. I could practically see the light bulb flick on over her crown.

Still glancing out the window, she gave a slow nod. "Yeah. Maybe."

# CHAPTER 13

## *Gwen*

After our little chat in the entryway of the rec center, Delilah and I ventured around all 5000 square feet of the place. I showed her the auditorium, which took up most of the area. Just like an auditorium in an old high school. A few hundred, maybe a thousand, subpar stadium chairs looking upon a large wooden stage, framed in red curtains.

Everything was old, a bit dingy, but of course it was. Why would Rhiannon waste money renovating auditorium chairs or outdated carpet when she could build another apartment complex? This place wasn't about glitz and glam. It was about saving people.

I showed Delilah the back rooms we used for therapy. One was decked out in children's toys for child sessions. Another was where we sat each Wednesday night for group. There were a few more for private therapy.

From there, we ventured down the stairs on the edge of the building to the community closet. We called it a closet, as if it didn't encase a warehouse's worth of clothing and home essentials. There was nothing special about it either. At some point, Rhiannon had put up drywall and laid sheet vinyl, but otherwise, it was just a room that looked never-ending, filled with clothing, furniture, and other necessities.

Delilah hesitated to take anything. On my first day, I had too. Simone pressured me to grab a few more pairs of pants, a couple extra pairs of shoes, and an espresso machine, after having learned how much I loved coffee.

I wasn't sure what Delilah was passionate about just yet, but I filled the cart with jeans and shirts to fill the closet in her apartment and enough hygiene items to last a month. She didn't need the teakettle and makeup I put in her basket, but she was excited to brew herself a pot when we got back to her apartment later. Before we headed back into town, she asked if I minded waiting a few minutes while she covered up the bruise around her eye with the new makeup.

Obviously, I didn't. Honey enjoyed scoping out a new territory as well.

By then, it was pushing four o'clock. That meant that I had my lesson with Lizzie in an hour. Still some time to kill.

Delilah had seemed interested in the greenhouse, so that's where I took her next. A good trip, too. The smile on her face when I told her to pick some hydroponic-grown strawberries warmed my heart. She'd even tossed on some gloves and tended to every wilted limb she came across. I couldn't relate to her green thumb, but I started to understand why Simone liked introducing the newbies. Watching Delilah question everything she'd been taught about life, seeing her relax into a world that made her feel safe, and simply watching her smile, burned my eyes with tears.

Were they tears of joy? Or were they remnants of what I'd done?

And why I felt justified in it?

That feeling lasted well past Rhiannon's call, letting me know that Lizzie waited for me in the rec center. Delilah asked to come along, and I didn't object. Just said we'd have to make sure Lizzie didn't mind her sitting in.

Couldn't say I was a mind reader but judging by the way Lizzie bellowed out *Ocean Eyes* by Billie Eilish, she had no problem with a crowd. She played it damn near perfect each time. Damn near, because she added a few artistic flares. A rubato in the opening verse, followed by some pedal nuance, and some interpretative tempo swells. All things a novice wouldn't dare attempt in a lesson.

Lizzie wasn't just a good pianist. She was excellent.

For a moment, I questioned why I was even here. I would've paid to see the kid perform. Delilah applauded after every set.

As our lesson wrapped up, Sebastian walked in, stuttering and stammering like he had the other day.

And those damn butterflies flapped heat across my cheeks.

Damn it, I had to address it. I had to ask what we were doing here. Not right now, but after I felt it out a bit more. By the end of the night, I would know for certain what the hell this was.

Lizzie smirked at the two of us together before hopping off the stage. She locked Delilah's elbow with her own, and said, "I'm meeting my friend Aubrey at the dining hall for dinner. How about we walk together? You're hungry, aren't you?"

Delilah agreed, and the two all but skipped off. Not before Lizzie gave us a shit-eating grin over her shoulder.

Was she playing little miss matchmaker? Had it all been a setup because she was tired of her uncle being single?

Or had she noticed tension between the two of us and knew Sebastian needed a good excuse to ask me out? Was that language she used with her teacher a short-tempered moment of teenage angst, or had she intentionally thrown the tantrum so she could beg Sebastian to ask me to teach her, then walk him through exactly how to make a move from there?

If so, I respected her conniving nature.

If not, I was doing what I always was. Overthinking.

# CHAPTER 14

## *Sebastian*

The forty-five-minute drive to the hibachi restaurant was awkward.

Just after we got in the car, and I started the engine with trembling hands, Gwen asked how my day at work was. I said, "Good." And nothing else. Not even the same question in response. Just silence. Because apparently, I was fifteen years old and had forgotten how to talk to a pretty girl.

We were at the stop sign between the ranch and the main road, the humming radio still the only sound, when I saw her shiver in my peripheral. "Shit, are you cold?"

"Little bit." Her tone was playful, a smirk across her cherry lips.

Which I should not have paid any mind to, because the second I took the smallest glance at those lips, my stomach flipped, blood pumped, and I knew I should've looked away. So I did. To the dashboard, where I spun the dial to increase the temperature and pressed the button for her heated seat.

"Whoa, whoa!" Gwen yelled.

The truck coasted forward.

I slammed the brake.

We both jarred toward the dash.

I stared ahead at the pine trees on the other side of the yellow lines.

Why? Why was I acting like I had never seen a girl in my life? My hands were shaking and my heart rate was through the roof. Had I forgotten the last year the two of us had spent as friends?

She laughed. Not a little chuckle, but a deep belly laugh that filled all the empty space in the truck's cabin. I swear, those pine trees laughed at me too.

"Okay, it wasn't that funny." Spoken as if I wasn't also warring with the smile that played at the edges of my lips.

"No." She made out between giggles. "Not at all funny. We could've died."

I lost the battle, and a laugh escaped me too. "We could've. That wouldn't have been funny."

"Not at all." And yet, she hadn't stopped laughing.

Neither had I.

Still holding the brake, I laughed harder and harder with her, holding her gaze. And I remembered why I was here. I remembered why we were doing this. Because even at the worst moments, here we were. We laughed and looked at one another and something I'd never felt before spread through my chest. Something worth stepping out of my comfort zone for.

Giggles finally slowing, she playfully swatted my shoulder. "Come on. It's a Friday night. The place is gonna be packed."

I released the brake, and we were on the road again. But our little laughing fit hadn't done enough to break the ice because a mile or two down the road, my hands were still shaking, and my heart was still fluttering. Music would help. Gwen liked music.

I spun the dial on the dash. Johnny Cash's *Walk the Line* pulsed through the speakers.

Now my stomach was turning again. I fumbled for my phone in its holder on the windshield. "Shit, you hate country. Here, you pick." I freed it from the clips and held it out to her between sweaty fingers while the front right tire dropped into a pothole. It left us both swaying side to side. And my phone flying in her direction.

She dodged it just before it hit her in the face.

It fell through the crack between her thigh and the door.

For half a second, I considered reaching over to grab it for her. Only to realize that would look like I was feeling her up.

Giving me a crooked smile, clearly trying not to burst into obnoxious laughter once more, Gwen stretched a hand under the seat. "You know," she grunted, craning awkwardly to reach, "I don't hate country."

"I clearly remember you mentioning that you hate country on at least five occasions."

"I hate *tractor* country." Coming out from under the seat with a crunched up fast food wrapper, her nose curled in disgust. "Songs about beer and good ole' American values." She added a southern twang for that last bit, still digging for my phone. "But Johnny Cash? Dolly Parton? Tanya Tucker? Oh, and Reba McEntire. They're classic."

Which I agreed with entirely. I could go on hours-long tangents about what the country music industry had become. About how far country had evolved from its roots. I didn't even have any "tractor country" on my playlist. Habitually, I listened to Garth Brooks, Willie Nelson, and Loretta Lynn.

But did I say that? No, of course not, because I had no idea how to act like a functioning human being tonight. Instead I said, "Oh."

A long moment of silence passed. Eventually, with a smack of her lips, Gwen said, "Yep."

*Get it together, man. What the hell are you doing?*

I cleared my throat, eyes on the two yellow lines descending the tarmac. "What do you listen to anyway?" Somehow, I mustered a smirk. "Aside from Surprise Rainbow Kittens."

She scoffed. "Get it right, pal. *Rainbow Kitten Surprise*."

"Of course." Now the words were flowing. "Rainbow Kitten Surprise. Sorry."

"To answer your question, everything." Gaze out the passenger window, her breath turned the glass white. "I love jazz. Not elevator music, but soulful jazz. Miles Davis, Louis Armstrong, Charlie Parker. I like a lot of newer stuff too. Underground indie artists. But I've also got a big thing for metal."

There was no stopping my snort. "Metal?"

Smile so sweet, so soft, she nodded. "Black Sabbath. Iron Maiden. Metallica, Pantera, Korn. Which is terribly ironic, considering that if I ever met any of those musicians in real life, I would probably fight them in the street for being the type of men they are." I huffed, and she continued. "My mom listened to them when I was growing up. I listen to a lot of smaller punk bands now. They're usually better people. Melodramatic, maybe, but they write good lyrics. And I like the screaming."

"You know, I can't say that surprises me."

"No?" She arched a brow. "I seem like the angry type?"

*Yes. I know you're angry. That's what I like about you.*

But that seemed like the wrong thing to say. It didn't feel like there was a right thing to say. So I opened my mouth, waiting for the right words to spill out, only to choke on the silence.

Gwen chuckled again, fiddling some more under the seat. "Okay, I think your phone is lost in the ether. And by ether, I mean months old, molding garbage."

"Yeah, probably. I'll get it later. Sorry I almost hit you in the face with it."

"As long as you've got wet wipes in here, I'll forgive you." She held up her finger, covered in some mysterious clear liquid. "Please tell me you have wet wipes."

"Glove compartment."

We arrived at the hibachi steakhouse just after seven.

The line was out the door. Our wait was going to be three hours.

I told the hostess that it was no problem and reached for my phone to call Lizzie.

Standing there in the entryway of the restaurant, shoulder to shoulder with everyone in a fifty-mile radius who had heard about the new spot and was excited to spend Friday night here, I patted my pockets. But my phone was still somewhere in the ether of the passenger seat. With a deep exhale, I turned to Gwen "Would I be able to borrow your phone?"

"You would." She reached into her pocket and held it out to me. "Or we could just go get takeout somewhere. Eat in the car?"

"No. This was supposed to be nice." I frowned. "All that time you spent with Liz this afternoon, the least I can do is get you a nice dinner."

"Take out sounds nice to me."

My frown deepened.

Damn it, I should've just called this what it was. A date. That's what I'd wanted this to be from the beginning. Hell, for months. Maybe since the moment I'd met her. I wanted to get to know her, really *know* her, while we ate delicious food and people-watched and shared a bottle of wine.

"I mean, unless you have an issue with eating in your car," Gwen said. "Can't really blame you. All the mud on your floorboards, it is a work of art, but I think a little dash of rice and beans from that

Mexican place down the street would really be the cherry on top. Like the final brushstroke."

I glared. "I've seen the inside of your car. You've got no right to judge."

"Okay, I have coffee cups and hoodies all over the place. You've got a half inch of literal dirt down there. And decaying food, Sebastian. It's practically compost. If I dropped some flower seeds, it'd be a garden in a week."

"It's an eighth of an inch max."

"Wow." She pressed a hand over her chest, nodding slowly. "A man who accurately depicts an inch. That's humble of you."

My eyes were still narrowed, but I couldn't help the half smile across my lips. "Fine. We'll get Mexican. But I don't eat it often, so I can't guarantee what the aroma on the drive home is going to be."

"You sure know how to charm a lady," she said, gesturing to the door.

Under my breath, I muttered, "Says the one who emasculates men for sport."

# CHAPTER 15

## *Gwen*

The Mexican place was only half a block down the road, so we were in there and had our order placed within ten minutes. We considered eating in, but their wait time was an hour and a half, so we waited the fifteen minutes it took for my enchiladas and Sebastian's tacos. The walk back to Sebastian's truck was only another five. Steam wafted from the food as we laid our dinners on our laps, chips and drinks on the center console, and dips on the dashboard.

A few bites into my enchilada, I eyed Sebastian in the driver's seat, struggling with all his might to keep the contents of his taco from spilling out the other end. I snorted at him.

He shot me a look. "What?"

"You knew we were eating in a car," I said. "Tacos seemed like the easiest thing on the menu?"

"I know I like tacos." Glowering, he laid it out on his lap and tucked the end of the tortilla closer to the meat and toppings. "I didn't know if I'd like anything else."

I arched a brow. "Tacos are the only Mexican food you've ever eaten?"

"No." Another glare. "But I'm picky, and it's hard to screw up tacos."

"So you're the expert on quality Mexican food?"

"I went to college in California," he said. "Which is rich with Mexican culture, if you didn't know."

"Wow, I had no idea." I teased. "Tell me more about this foreign land."

"My roommate was second-generation. He made some bomb ass authentic Mexican food." Covering his mouth between chews, he shrugged. "Shoot me if I'm a little hesitant to expect that quality at a Mexican restaurant run by white people."

"Touché. This is bland." I dipped a chip in the guacamole on the dashboard. "College in California, huh?"

"Four years of university, anyway. Came back here for vet school."

"What was that like? Never been to Cali."

"Pretty much exactly what you'd expect," he said through bites of taco. "Culturally diverse. Way more interesting than Black Pines. There's always something to do. And so much sun." He swallowed. "I miss that damn sun."

"We could use some of that right about now." I glanced at the snow falling out the window onto the busy street. "I don't know though. I don't think I could ever live somewhere that doesn't get snow."

"It was nice for a couple years, but I wouldn't want to deal with that heat twenty-four seven." He angled to face me. "What about you? Did you go to college?"

"No college. I did go to tech in high school," I said. "That's where I learned cake decorating."

"Is that where you got *your* knowledge of Mexican cuisine?"

"No, that came from Diego. One of my mom's boyfriends." Using the side of my fork as a knife, I chopped off another bite of enchilada.

"Ah." Holding one hand beneath his queso-covered tortilla, he carefully brought it to his lips. When he finished chewing, he said, "Just always felt drawn to cakes?"

"Pastries more than cakes. But I'm good at decorating. And they're just easier to make money on. Which I don't understand, because I don't think I've ever heard someone say, 'God, I could really go for a cake right now.'"

"I've never understood that either. Ice cream cake, I get. But sponge cake with sweetened butter all over it? I swear, people only like it because it looks pretty in pictures."

"And it feeds a lot of people cheaply," I said. "So how long does it take to become a vet?"

"Eight years. Four of university and four of veterinary medicine."

"So that would make you . . . ?"

"Thirty-one." A half smile. "I don't think I know how old you are either."

"Twenty-six." I took another bite of enchilada and braced myself to ask what'd been on my mind for months. "If you're only thirty-one, when did you get custody of Lizzie?"

The hazel eyes that had been fixed on me throughout this conversation fell to the food in his lap. He chewed on his lip instead of a taco.

"Shit, I'm sorry. That's probably a sensitive topic—"

"No, it's fine." He cleared his throat. "It was in 2013. I was almost twenty-two."

Twenty-two, in college, and raising a toddler. Holy shit, I couldn't even imagine. "That must've been hard. Taking care of her while you were in school, I mean."

"It would've been," he said. "But I had Rhiannon. She'd let me bring Lizzie to the daycare anytime I had class. It was good for her, actually. So many people at the ranch, all that community, they helped me raise Lizzie. She pretty much sees Rhiannon as a surrogate mom."

"I think we all do." Shifting in the passenger seat to face him better, I leaned against the door behind me. "How do you know Rhiannon, anyway?"

"She worked at the ranch back when it was my summer camp." He bundled the foil from his tacos, laid it on the dashboard, and swiveled in the driver seat to face me. "Then when the camp shut down during the winter, and later when she started turning it into what it is now, I came down to ride horses. My parents wouldn't let me have pets, but I loved coming to the ranch and visiting them."

"No shit. No one ever talks about how the ranch started."

"Yeah, just a summer camp. When the owner passed, she willed it to Rhiannon. It wasn't making much money by then anyway. So she turned it into what she was most passionate about."

"That woman's a saint."

"That, she is." He grabbed his soda from the center console and took a few gulps. "She was basically a second mom to me growing up."

"Even though she was just your camp counselor?"

He opened his mouth to speak, but no words came out. After a few hard swallows, he shrugged. "Things weren't great at home. But I spent a lot of time at the ranch. The bus dropped me off at the gate after school most days, and I'd walk in, and Rhiannon would take me down to the animals, or have me sit down with some of the girls for dinner. Then she'd drive me home at the end of the night. Went on like that through most of my adolescence."

"I wish I'd had someone like that when I was a kid."

"Things weren't great at your house either?"

"Yeah, not really." I forced a laugh. "I never met my dad. I loved my mom, and she loved me. But she loved crack more."

His brows raised. "Damn."

"Not gonna lie, I figured if I dumped some of my trauma, you'd dump some of yours."

A genuine laugh escaped him, widening that crooked smile. "I don't know. My dad had a temper when he drank. And he drank a lot."

"You get it then."

"I get what, exactly?"

"What it's like to love an addict."

"Never said I loved him." Sebastian chewed the inside of his cheek. "I know you're not supposed to say that. Everybody's supposed to love their parents. But mine was a prick. I hated the bastard. He's why I left for college and didn't move back until he died."

I understood that, but I couldn't relate. It wasn't that I inherently loved my mom either. I loved her because she was a good person. She liked getting high, but at her core, she had a kind heart and an open mind. My memories of her weren't all bad. Many were, but not because she was ever cruel to me. If she hadn't been an addict, she would've been a great mom.

Some of her boyfriends, on the other hand, were more like Sebastian's father.

"What about your mom?" Another chip in hand, I scooped up some salsa from the Styrofoam cup. "Did you guys have a good relationship?"

"Wouldn't say it was as bad as my relationship with my dad. But couldn't say we were close either."

"And she wasn't jealous of you looking at Rhiannon as a mom?"

He flapped his lips together in a trill. "I don't know. Maybe? We weren't a very talkative family."

"Mine was. Well, my mom was. Crack has that effect on people. Kinda makes them talk a mile a minute."

"So she talked, and you listened?"

"Listened, and played along when she'd let me get a word in." He laughed, and so did I. As it faded, still smiling, I shook my head. "Look, one of us has gotta say it. What is this?"

"What is what?"

"You know what." I gestured to the food, then between the two of us. "Are we just hanging out? Or was this supposed to be a date?"

Joy in his expression dissipating, he pressed his lips together. "Did you want it to be a date?"

"I asked you first."

"You asked if it was *supposed* to be a date."

"Aw, now you're embarrassed to say it was?"

"You know that emasculating thing? You're really good at it."

"It is something I pride myself in." He rolled his eyes, and I laughed. "If it *was* supposed to be a date, I'd say it's been a good one."

His eyes met mine. They looked warmer than usual. Happier. "Yeah?"

"Yeah. I mean, we're both really bad at it, but I'm having fun."

"Mocking me over an array of Mexican food—that's fun to you?"

After the week I'd had? "That is my idea of a good Friday night."

Something between a harrumph and a laugh escaped him. "Happy to be of service."

"What, are you *not* having fun?"

"I never said that." He frowned. "I'm just really bad at it."

"Bad at having fun?"

"Bad at dating. But yeah. Bad at having fun too."

"If it helps, I have no idea what I'm doing," I said. "I haven't done this since I was a kid."

"Had fun?"

"Who's giving shit now?"

"You started it."

I tossed my balled-up straw wrapper at him.

He chuckled and tossed it back. "Last time you went on a date was when you were a kid?"

"Last time I went on a first date," I said, reverting my attention to another chip. "I met my ex when I was fourteen. Was with him until I came here."

Sebastian's eyes softened. "I haven't really dated since I got Lizzie."

Cocking my head to the side, I squinted him over. "You haven't dated in a decade?"

"I've gone on a couple," he said. "But there aren't that many people in Black Pines. I grew up here, so I know everyone, and everyone knows me, and we're not big fans of each other. Dating someone from another town is a pain in the ass logistically, so I kinda just gave up. With Lizzie and work, I haven't had time to devote to a relationship."

I made a noncommittal noise. "People in town don't like you?"

"You work in the heart of it." He tossed another chip into his mouth. "I thought you would've heard the lore by now."

"Ooh." I leaned forward with my hands under my chin. "You gotta tell me all about it."

"Not much to tell, really. I was the weird horse kid. Smart and scrawny with thick black glasses. Never fit in with the jocks, no matter how badly my dad wanted me to. Sarah did, and she tried to bring me into that crowd, but I just never got along with them."

I'd never heard that name before. "Sarah?"

"Lizzie's mom. My sister. She was Black Pines' little sweetheart. I was her weird little brother. My parents were always well-liked. Did the whole PTA thing. Took part in all the town celebrations, donated to help build the school stadium and all that shit. Then they all died. My perfect family didn't fit into their pretty little box anymore."

Heart throbbing harder in my chest, my brows raised.

When I didn't say anything else, he grabbed another chip. "What's that face for?"

"That was just a very blunt way to tell me your whole family is dead," I said. "I'm sorry. I didn't know."

"Not my *whole* family. I've still got Liz." He chewed the chip and swallowed. "I don't know. It sucks. But it's history."

Maybe that was true. I still got choked up about my mom's death, but for the most part, I had to keep on living.

But I also had a community behind me now. I guessed Sebastian did too. It was just hard to imagine a young single guy, raising a little girl on his own after his whole family died. Especially because the only person he seemed close with at the ranch was Rhiannon. And me now, I supposed. Sacrificing his dating life and all his free time on top of that gave me a new sense of respect for him.

"So, no serious relationships then?" I asked.

"Not since I got Liz, no."

"And before Liz?"

"A couple, yeah." Another slurp from his soda. "Three. Two in college, and one at the end of high school."

"Well, you can't leave me hanging like that," I said. "What happened?"

He set his drink down and eyed me. "If I tell you about my failed relationships, are you going to tell me about yours?"

# CHAPTER 16

## Sebastian

Gwen squinted and leaned back in her seat.

When she didn't say anything, I did the same. "What? What's that face about?"

"You know what the ranch is."

"I do."

"Then you know why my past relationships failed."

I knew she'd been abused in some way. That it'd been bad enough that she'd felt the only way out was to erase her identity and start over. He had to have been one sick son of a bitch.

But I didn't know what made her who she was. It wasn't my place to insist she tell me every detail, but wasn't it my place to know what she had been through? To be sensitive to the specific topics or issues? So that I didn't accidentally say or do something that'd trigger her PTSD?

"Vaguely," I said.

Still, she said nothing.

Cocking my head to the side, my eyes flicked over her, surveying for a signal of discomfort or pain. This was supposed to be fun for both of us. I wasn't trying to turn our first date into trauma porn. If she wasn't ready to talk about it, or if she never wanted to, that was okay.

I made sure to soften my voice when I said, "You don't want to talk about it?"

Gwen scratched the side of her head. She opened her mouth and shut it a few times. Eventually, quietly, she said, "I don't want you to pity me for it."

"What does pity mean to you?"

Her open mouth stayed silent a moment longer. Eventually, she shrugged. "I don't know. Whiny, I guess. Pathetic. They're all synonyms."

"That's what's wrong with the world," I said under my breath. After grabbing a chip from the center console, I dipped it in the queso. "Pity, by definition, means compassion and sorrow on someone else's behalf. Why the hell is having compassion and sorrow for someone viewed as whiny or pathetic?"

She arched a brow at that, and I saw the wheels turning behind her eyes.

"Not saying that you're wrong for viewing it that way," I told her. "I mean, if you don't actually look up the word, it does sound like an insult. But I think we should all pity each other a little more. Life might be a little less grim if we did."

Gwen's eyes sparkled. Not with tears, but consideration. Like my words made her think. Eventually, she said, "Yeah. It might."

"The rest of the world can go on making fun of us, and we can have our pity party." I smiled. "Only if you wanna talk about it. You don't have to."

A breathy laugh escaped her. "Well, I don't really *want* to talk about it. But I feel like you have the right to know?"

"I'd consider it more of an honor than a right."

Her expression softened. An unusual start to the night, maybe, but it seemed to have broken all the ice. She was only an octave or two above a whisper when she continued.

"It's probably the same story you've heard a thousand times. We were together until last year, when I left. Mostly, anyway. I don't know. I tried to leave many times before I finally did. And it didn't go the way it does in movies. He didn't wear a wife beater and come home each day and scream at me about the dishes.

"I guess he did, a couple times. Scream at me about the dishes, I mean." She scratched her head. "I don't know. I was young. I was dumb. My mom thought he was great, mostly because I didn't tell her everything. By the time I was eighteen, he wasn't really interested in me anymore. Not romantically, not physically. But he didn't want to lose the other things I gave him. A clean house. An assistant to arrange his life. A therapist to vent to.

"Every time I tried to leave, it was chaos. Most of the relationship wasn't, though. I guess because, somewhere along the way, I realized that if I didn't bring up how I felt or the problems we had, there wasn't a fight, so I stopped talking. Gradually stopped caring. The only thing that was hard about leaving were the logistics. Hence, the ranch." Pressing her lips together, Gwen looked out the windshield for a moment, watching the snowflakes. When she turned back, the melancholy tone was gone, and a smile spread across her lips. "But he never wore the wife beaters. Wasn't half bad at it, but he never dressed the part."

A half laugh escaped me, not because I found it funny. Because that's what she needed. The only way she could manage spitting that out was if she knew I wouldn't look at her like she was pathetic for having put up with it.

And I wouldn't. I would never.

To show some semblance of solidarity, understanding, I said, "Yeah, my dad never dressed the part either."

She didn't shudder. No wince either. Just a frown of the same solidarity. Understanding. "They usually don't."

"So, did you have any other romantic relationships?" I dug around in the paper bag for a napkin. When I found one, I wiped my mouth with it. "Outside of him."

"A couple. But it's your turn." Gwen grabbed her soda and tucked herself against the door. Legs crossed lotus style in the passenger seat, she slurped away. "Go on. Tell me about your dating history."

I chuckled. "Not much to tell, really. Had my first girlfriend during my senior year of high school. I was still the weird, dorky kid, but I got contacts and gained a little weight. We were too young to understand what love was." I swiveled in my seat as well, propping one knee against the steering wheel and tucking the other underneath me. "We thought we were going to stay together when we went to college. Over winter break, she let me know she'd cheated, so that was the end of that."

"Ouch."

"Second girlfriend was a rebound, right after I broke up with the first. She was cool? Edgy, exciting. We painted together, she had blue hair and a vinyl collection—you know the type."

Air lighter now, Gwen's smile returned. "Sounds like my kind of people. What happened there?"

"She was just a little too eccentric. Asked to open the relationship, and I had to duck out."

"As a monogamist myself, I can respect it."

"We stayed friends though." I took a sip from my paper cup. "We still wish each other happy birthday on Facebook."

"Amicable."

"I think so."

"So, anyone after her?" She took the last air-filled slurp of her soda.

I passed her the rest of mine, chest warm when she grinned her thanks. "One more. But I think it's your turn again."

There went the joy in her eyes. Slowly returning the soda to its holder, she nibbled on her bottom lip. "Your relationship stories are all so normal and suburban. Mine are a lot messier."

I gestured to the disaster that was my truck. "I don't mind a mess."

The tilt at the corner of her lips didn't come close to reaching her eyes. Eventually, she exhaled. "I was twelve when I met my only other boyfriend. He was sixteen, I want to say?"

My stomach turned, and I did my damnedest to school my expression.

I remembered being sixteen. Twelve and sixteen were very different numbers. Sure, in ten years, a four-year age gap wasn't a huge stretch. Gwen and I were five years apart, but mentally, we were in the same headspace. We were both adults. Our development had reached a certain plateau.

Twelve-year-olds had barely hit puberty, if they had at all. Sixteen-year-olds were deciding between college and the job force.

That was why I didn't allow Lizzie to date anyone older than her.

"I know." Gwen cupped a hand over her face. There was no hiding the shudder that coursed down her spine. "I know how bad that is now. How gross he was for even looking at me. But he did a lot worse than that, so." Another shudder, followed by a harsh clearing of her throat. "Anyway, that was a really bad relationship too. Just in a different way. Some of the same ways, I guess? But it doesn't matter. It was a long time ago. I've blocked out most of it. I only remember bits and pieces."

I wished that my brain's defense mechanism worked like that. I hadn't forgotten a single thing my dad did. Every fight, every broken piece of furniture, every mark on my mom's, my sister's, or my skin, was forever etched into my memory.

Not to say that made it easier for Gwen. But maybe it would've made it easier for me.

"Anyway." A big smile, this one playful. "Tell me about your other failed relationship."

I snorted and rubbed the bridge of my nose between my thumb and forefinger. "Her name was Ashley."

"Ashley." Gwen wiggled her brows. "Sexy."

Unsure if I should laugh or grimace at that, I did some combination of the two. "Yeah, I don't know. I was in a really bad place when we met. Sarah had just died. My parents were raising Lizzie, and they wanted me to come home. I wanted to, to be there for my niece, but it was midsemester. I couldn't just leave. And then Ashley asked me out, and we fell hard, and we fell fast.

"Year or two later, I got a call. The doctors were vague. Just said that my parents were in an accident. Made sure to tell me to get on the first flight out. It was early December, and Ashley and I were already planning on coming up here for Christmas. But she couldn't move her flight up. Which was understandable. Then I was here, at my parents' deathbeds, and she decided to go to her family's for Christmas instead."

Gwen's face screwed up in confusion, head cocked to the side. "Wait, she just completely bailed on you?"

"I wouldn't put it like that." I rubbed a hand over my beard. "I'd only ever told her the bad things about my parents. She knew that I hated my dad, that I didn't have that great of a relationship with my mom, so she hadn't wanted to come to Black Pines to begin with. But the bigger issue was Lizzie."

Face still scrunched up, Gwen blinked a few times. "Are you saying you guys broke up because your already orphaned niece was orphaned a second time, and you didn't dump her into the system?"

Sure did paint a bad picture of Ashley when she framed it like that. "We were young. It was a lot of pressure. And yeah, it was shitty. But she didn't want the life I was headed into. Honestly, it was my bad. I had talked about taking Lizzie after I graduated, and Ashley always changed the subject or made a comment suggesting that might not be the best idea. It's not like she completely blindsided me. I knew she didn't want kids. I respected her decision to go on with her own life and let me go on with mine."

Gwen made a *tsk* sound. "You're a better man than me."

Not really. Ashley and I had been college sweethearts, but not much else. It never would've lasted, and it was for the best that it hadn't. If we had met at a different time, I would've recognized that too. We'd only lasted as long as we did because my grief for my sister had been so fresh.

To Ashley, I was a fun way to pass the time. To me, she was a distraction from the worst pain I'd ever felt.

"We were together for a couple years, but it was never that serious." I shrugged. "And it's ancient history now. Lizzie was three when that went down."

"Fair enough." Gwen raised a hand in surrender. "So Ashley wasn't the one who got away, huh?"

"I don't believe in that." I rolled my neck from left to right, more annoyed than I had been about our lack of reservation at the hibachi restaurant. "People say that when they're unhappy in their current relationship or they fumbled a good one."

Nodding, she wagged a finger. "I like the way you think, Mr. Everett."

Interesting. She knew my last name. Had she googled me?

"Agree or disagree with the way I think?"

"Agree," she said. "That sort of philosophy, 'the one that got away,' reeks of 'peaked in high school.'"

The laugh I let out further fogged the window behind her. "So I've told you about my parents. What are yours like? Or were?"

"Were, yeah." Gwen wet her lips, then clicked her tongue. "I don't know my dad. Never have. But my mom was great. Aside from the crack."

"That checks out." When Gwen chuckled, I took a small sip from the soda that sat between us, mindful to leave enough for her. "How did she pass?"

"Also a car accident," she said. "Luckily, I wasn't in the same position you were in. She died at the scene. Probably easier than watching someone you love waste away in a hospital bed."

So many times growing up, I had prayed for that night to happen. I would fantasize about my dad speeding on an icy backroad, or on one of his many business trips to the beach, and his car flipping over a guardrail. I wished I felt sorry for that, but my only sorrow was that my mom had been in the car with him.

She hadn't been a great mom. My big sister had given me most of the affection I'd gotten growing up. The meals I ate were from a maid. The only adult that had ever come to any of my talent shows or school competitions was Rhiannon.

My mom never stood up to him. She never protected us. She allowed him to make all our lives a living hell.

Older now, with a better understanding of how those dynamics worked, I had more empathy for her than I used to. Doubted I would ever completely forgive her, but I would've never wished her ill.

Yet, she'd been the first one to die in the hospital.

"I don't think it's ever easy to lose someone," I said. Even if my dad's death had brought me peace. "Sarah's death was a lot harder on me. With my parents, at least I got to say goodbye. I didn't get that with Sarah."

Gwen studied me for a moment, mouth ajar. Like she was debating asking the question.

*What happened to her?*

Relief loosened my shoulders when she said instead, "Yeah, I get that. I bet it was hard having to plan their funerals on your own too. You don't have any other family around, do you?"

"Distant cousins, but no one nearby. The funerals were mostly planned in the wills anyway. I just had to sign off on some documents." I stretched an arm overhead and hooked it at the back of my neck. "What about you? Was anyone around to help you with your mom's?"

"We didn't have an actual funeral," Gwen said. "She always wanted to be buried, but it cost too much. My savings would only cover cremation. A friend of hers had a nice house though. She let us hold the wake there."

My heart ached, and guilt turned my stomach. "Weren't you with your ex then? He wouldn't chip in for your mom's funeral?"

"He did. I only had a couple grand in savings, and it was three for the cremation." Ever so slightly, she squinted. "Would've been closer to fifteen for the formal ceremony and burial."

"Oh. Right." I nodded, hoping that didn't come off as rude. "That makes sense."

Another heartbeat of silence passed. Maybe more than a heartbeat, because now all the windows were foggy, and I couldn't see the snow falling behind Gwen anymore. I did see her cock her head to the side, eyes like that of a hawk.

I was just about to change the subject, to say that was enough about grief and trauma for the night.

But Gwen cut in with, "You've got money, don't you?"

My stomach ached. "What?"

"Your parents arranged their funerals in advance. They had wills and the whole nine."

"Lots of everyday people have wills."

"Middle-class people are also one hospital stay away from bankruptcy, and somehow, you survived two." Still squinting, her jaw dropped all the way into her lap. "Holy shit. It's you. You're the donor. You're the billionaire donor who funded the ranch."

*Damn it.* "Look, I don't—"

"Don't lie to me. The ranch grew from a couple cabins to a city about ten years ago. That's when Rhiannon got the donation. That's when your parents died. You went to some good school in California. You raised Lizzie while you were in college, presumably without much income." Her grin stretched almost up to her eyes. She'd figured it out. "Rhiannon told me you wanted to stay anonymous, so your secret's safe with me. But that's crazy. I would've never thought that you had money. Not driving this clunker around." She tapped her hand against the dashboard.

I almost defended my twenty-year-old truck but decided against it. "I'm not rich."

"Clearly. You gave your inheritance to Rhiannon."

"Most of it." A fund that could only be accessed for college had paid for all my tuitions. Some of it sat in an emergency fund on the insistence of a financial advisor. Which I agreed wasn't too bad of an idea. "Lizzie has about ten million waiting for her when she's twenty-five. Obviously, she can use it for college before then. And reasonable housing. I still felt like that was too much but given what my parents were worth, and how much of that would've gone to my sister, then to Lizzie, it seemed like the right thing to do. I have the feeling she'll be donating a lot of it when she's twenty-five, too. Just didn't want to leave her without the option."

"Ten million." Gwen let out the words in a near whisper. "Damn. I mean, you don't have to justify how you spent it, but—"

"I do." Trailing my fingers through my beard, I searched for the words. "That kind of money. Billions of dollars . . . No one needs it.

No one can spend it in a lifetime. They just hoard it. That's what my parents did, and their parents before them, and so on. They used that money to exploit people and hurt people, and I didn't want any part of it. The things I have, I like to earn."

Doe-eyed, I almost thought I saw a tear trickle over. "I get that," Gwen said, "and I agree, but you didn't have to, and you still chose to do an amazing thing. You saved so many people's lives with that money. On behalf of everyone, thank—"

I held up my hand. "Don't thank me. Please. It wasn't my money. And even if it had been, it was blood money. My however-many-greats grandpa was already rich when he came over here on the boat. He took advantage of so many people to get it. With money like that, you have the power to make real change in the world. All any of the men in my family ever did with it was hurt. Money was their weapon. I just had to do what they all should've done. Get the hell rid of it. But like I said, I didn't donate every penny, it paid for my college, and I don't pay a mortgage on my house. So please, don't thank me, Gwen."

She didn't.

She reached across the center console, grabbed my cheeks in both hands, and tugged me in. Our lips met, and the world stopped spinning.

I had wondered what this would feel like since the moment we'd met, but no fantasy did it justice. Her lips were as soft as flower petals, and the gloss over top of them, the taste of watermelon. We'd never been so close before. It was the first time I got to fully appreciate her perfume, like honey and sugar.

My fingers started in those soft red curls and traveled to that beautiful curve in her waist. I had always wondered how it would feel to slide my hands across it, to feel the heat of her body against mine, and there were no words for it. There was a desperate need in me to pull her closer, to shelter her frame with my own. To never let her go.

Never had I kissed someone and felt all of this. The pathetic ache to stay within this moment where we were together, where we were safe, for the rest of my life.

Inching back, resting her forehead on mine, she breathed hard. "Was that okay?"

I pulled her back in.

# CHAPTER 17

## *Gwen*

We kissed a little more, and we talked a lot more.

Some of the girls at the ranch described Sebastian as a man of few words. They probably described me the same way. But Sebastian and I just talked in a language they couldn't speak. We didn't like simple conversations. If it wasn't deep, if it wasn't about something that was bigger than us, we got bored.

I supposed that was contradictory, given how elusive we both were about the details of our pasts. But it wasn't that we were shallow about our pains, our traumas. We'd just buried them deep beneath the surfaces of ourselves. The things we discussed tonight were only topsoil, yet deeper and more vulnerable than I had gotten with anyone in ages. I imagined Sebastian could say the same.

It was almost eleven when Lizzie texted Sebastian to ask when he was coming to pick her up. I agreed it was time to get home.

The drive home couldn't have been more different from the drive earlier, filled with laughter and the comfortability we had found in the last year of friendship. Neither of us knew how to make that switch from friendship to romance. But we ended the night laughing, teasing one another, and with one more kiss.

Simone, who must've been peeking through the blinds, gushed about it. And even though I walked out of that truck with a smile on my face, chest fuzzy and warm with hope and excitement, the moment she wanted to gossip about it, the rest of this week came back.

I'd almost forgotten about David.

It only took a glance at Simone's face, her swollen eye, her busted lip, for the memories to slam through my mind like a semitruck hitting a wall. The warm, cozy feeling vanished.

I put on my poker face and told Simone about the date. That we sat in his truck, ate subpar Mexican food and talked about our pasts, how we both wound up here. All I left out was the promise I made to keep Sebastian's secret.

Only for her face to screw up in confusion. "That's what you call a date?"

It was everything I wanted in a date.

Roses, candlelit dinners, ties and tuxedos—those were a performance. One I'd fallen for before. Troy got me flowers every time he hit me. He took me out to a nice dinner every time we made up.

If I was going to do this again, if I was going to love someone again, I wanted it to be real.

By the end of the conversation, Simone's conclusion was, "I'm happy if you're happy."

I couldn't remember the last time I was this happy.

This was the first time in years I had been excited for the future.

Excited, then terrified when I remembered what I'd done.

What if Sebastian found out? Would he understand? *Could* he?

What if someone else found the body? What if the cops tied it back to me? What if I had to decide to tell the truth and lose the little bit of a life I'd built since I came to the ranch, or run and start all over?

Sebastian wouldn't join me. He couldn't. He had Lizzie, and a business, and a life.

Where would I run to anyway?

How could I get comfortable in all this hope, all this joy, if I could lose it all?

I retired to my room, and Simone got comfy on the couch since we didn't expect Rhiannon to show tomorrow morning. Sleep didn't come. Not without the help of a joint.

Just before I dozed off, my phone dinged with a text from Sebastian.

**Sebastian**
I had a lot of fun tonight. We should do it again.

**Gwen**
So did I. Just say when.

The next morning, I woke to a text.

**Sebastian**
What are you doing Sunday? And good morning, by the way. Hope you have a good day.

Which had my belly fluttering.

The butterflies weren't as scary as they'd been. Now, part of me wanted to run headfirst to him, and the other part wanted to run as far and fast away from him as I could get.

Not for my benefit. For his.

In this relationship, I was the one keeping secrets. I was the liar.

But maybe I could do what Simone and I had said we would. Maybe I could pretend it'd never happened.

**Gwen**
Probably just hanging around the ranch. And good morning to you too. I also hope you have a good day.

When I read it back, it sounded like an email to a work colleague. Emojis may have helped, but I didn't have a therapist to guide me through every text interaction I had, so it would have to do.

I went about my usual morning routine. Showered, took Honey out to do her business, fed her, made a cup of coffee to go, tiptoed around Simone, and made sure to lock the door behind me. Today's drive to work was much more peaceful than the last.

Did my stomach still turn when I drove over the bridge I'd dropped David off? Yes. Was I going to push that memory to the very back of my mind? Also yes.

I made it to work with fifteen minutes to spare. Good thing, because my homemade coffee tasted like garbage. I had just enough time to go behind the counter, make myself a nice latte—with pumpkin spice, since that was back on the menu heading into the holidays—and maybe a breakfast sandwich.

As I hung my coat on the hook, I eyed the pastry case to see if we had any croissants left over. Plenty of English muffins on the bottom shelf, half a dozen bagels, but no croissants. That was fine. A bagel would do.

I walked around the counter and grabbed a parchment paper to put it on. As I reached into the pastry case, Molly said, "Behind you," and brushed past me. "That's for you, by the way."

Bagel in hand, I straightened back up. She stood in front of the espresso machine at the far end of the counter. As she fiddled with it, I looked around. Nothing caught my eye. "What's for me?"

"That." She pointed to a red gift bag by the checkout.

It was small, roughly four-by-six. Red tissue paper peeked out of the top. Sparkles covered every inch of it. I knew as soon as I picked it up, I would find pieces of glitter all over my clothing, car, and cabin for the next six months.

"Andrew said someone left it at the door yesterday. The tag has your name on it."

I flipped over the tag on the ribbon handle. There it was. *Gwen*, in pretty calligraphy. "It doesn't say who it's from."

"Probably one of the customers you made a cake for." She shrugged and headed through the swinging, stainless steel door. "They start giving out Christmas presents at this time of year."

Made sense. Some of the patients at my old job did that too.

I peeled back the tissue paper. Inside was a small box, covered in wrapping paper the same color as the gift bag.

I grabbed the whole bag and walked around the counter to sit at the booth in the corner. Wrapped gift in my lap, I pulled the paper back.

A pay-as-you-go phone.

My stomach sank.

I flipped it over and found a typed note on a plain white sheet of printer paper.

*Your friend.*

# CHAPTER 18

*Gwen*

*A Couple of Weeks Later*

Sitting in the group room at the rec center, I had to fight the urge to kick my feet like a little girl.

**Sebastian**

Those jeans you were wearing at the café today. You should wear them more often.

**Gwen**

Oh, is that right?

His response was instant. As it tended to be in the evening after he'd finished working.

**Sebastian**

Mhm. Wear them again this weekend?

Cheeks hot, tingles spreading through my lower stomach, I texted back.

**Gwen**

Only if you wear those gray sweatpants.

And at my side on the floral sofa in the meeting room of the rec center, Simone said, "Bow-chick-a-wow-wow."

"Shut up." I shut my phone and slid it into my hoodie pocket.

"Wait, what's going on?" Delilah dropped onto the sofa on my other side, a plate of cookies from the table by the door in hand. "What did I miss?"

"Sebastian flirting with Gwen." Simone reached over me and snatched a cookie. "And Gwen blushing like a little girl."

I shot her a look. "Can you just not?"

"'Can you just not?'" Simone mocked.

"Aw, what did he say?" Delilah asked, glancing around for my phone.

It dinged again. I fumbled around in my pocket, clicking the switch for silence. "Ya know, I don't think that my private text messages are something that I have to share at group therapy." I grabbed a cookie off Delilah's plate. "But maybe I would if Simone didn't have to make fun of me every chance she got."

"I'm not making fun of you." Simone waved me off. "It just makes me happy to see you happy."

Was I happy? With Sebastian, I had no complaints. What I was happiest for was that David was dead, and no one had figured it out yet.

Simone's face was looking much better. Aside from the ten pounds of makeup she was wearing to hide the bruising, all the swelling had receded.

So far, it looked like mine and Simone's plan had worked. A week or so after David's attack, she'd returned to her apartment. Of course there were questions, but everyone believed her story.

"How's that going, Gwen?" Rhiannon asked, voice carrying from somewhere in the room.

There were a couple dozen of us in here, some sitting, some still standing, waiting for the clock to hit six thirty and our session to start. She appeared through the crowd, settling into a sofa across from me.

"Seeing someone for the first time after you left, I mean." Rhiannon took a sip from the steaming tea in her hand. "We haven't talked much about it."

"It's going." I forced a smile. "How does Sebastian think it's going?"

"Alright, alright. I won't pry." Chuckling, she wagged a finger at me. "But that *was* a topic I thought we could address tonight." She gestured around the room and raised her voice over the roaring crowd. "Come on, everybody. Let's have a seat."

"What was a topic you thought we could address tonight?" I asked her.

"Dating after what we've all been through." She took another gulp. "But don't worry. I won't single you out."

A shudder coursed through me. Because even if she didn't directly address me and Sebastian, she would find some way to make this a lecture about me and Sebastian.

The room quieted as everyone found a couch or beanbag. Once everyone was seated, Rhiannon glanced around the room. "How many of us have tried dating after we left?"

She, along with about half of the room, raised their hands.

Reluctantly, I did the same.

"Now, has anyone been in a relationship for longer than six months after leaving their abuser?" Rhiannon asked.

Roughly half the hands went down, mine included.

"Haley," Rhiannon said to a girl on one of the beanbags. "What's your boyfriend's name again?"

"Tyler," Haley said, chomping into a cookie.

"And how long have you and Tyler been together?"

"Almost two years now." Squinting, Haley cocked her head to the side. After a second of silence, she laughed. "I didn't realize it'd been that long."

Rhiannon propped her chin in her hand, elbow on the arm rest of the sofa. "Where do you see your relationship going at this point?"

"We're talking about moving in together soon," she said. "Not gonna lie though, that freaks me the hell out. I told him I can't yet. Not until I have a decent enough nest egg to fall back on if something goes wrong."

"That's not a bad idea," Rhiannon said. "It's one of the primary objectives of this place, actually. Teaching you girls the importance of independence."

"I'll never lose my independence again, that's for damn sure," Haley said.

"Anyone who wants you to isn't someone you should have in your life. How big do you want your nest egg to be?"

"Ten grand. I've saved up about seven so far, but I'm not giving up my apartment until I have ten."

"That's a good number." Rhiannon cozied up with a throw blanket from the back of the sofa. "If you're thinking about moving in together, stands to reason you might be thinking about getting married again."

Grinning, Haley plucked her cookie in half. "That does stand to reason."

"I'm sure you've already thought about a prenup and all that. But I'm curious what you think of the word *inter*dependence."

Haley's tilted head told me she didn't know what that word meant.

I tucked myself further into the corner of the sofa.

"Interdependence is the goal of a healthy relationship," Rhiannon explained, stifling a yawn. "By definition, it's holding onto your identity while still supporting your partner and them supporting you. Would you say that label describes you and Tyler's relationship?"

"Honestly, yeah." Haley covered her mouth between nibbles on her cookie. "But I dated a couple of guys before he and I got together, post leaving. And I definitely didn't feel that way with them."

"Can you explain that a little bit more?"

"It just came naturally with Tyler. From the get-go, there was no drama. Sure, we had the honeymoon period, but to this day, we've never really fought about anything. There's conflict from time to time, but we just work through it."

"And it wasn't like that with those other guys?" Rhiannon asked, chin in her hand again.

"Nah, something always came up early that told me to dip." Haley wiped her mouth using a balled-up napkin from her lap and went to throw it away. "First guy sulked when I offered to split the check. Second one lived on bikini feeds." She veered our way to return to her beanbag, holding a cup of water and a fresh plate of cookies. "I read a study that says men who do that literally process women like objects. It activates the same brain regions as when they look at power tools. I'm all for women posting whatever they want. I'm just not dating a guy who treats us like scenery—"

Haley's foot caught on the area rug at the edge of our sofa.

She dropped forward, paper cup full of water and plate of cookies flying.

Water splashed us all.

I rushed forward to help her up. "Are you okay?"

"Physically, fine." Laughing as she took my hand, Haley shook her head. "Mentally, mortified."

More laughter sounded throughout the room. Once she was back on her feet, a few other girls came over with napkins, offering them to all four of us.

It didn't even compute in my brain until Simone said, "Ow."

Rhiannon's voice. "What's . . ."

I turned around, just in time to see her dab some water from Simone's face.

Water and makeup? Not a good mix.

A splotch of black and blue took up most of Simone's chin and spread across her lower lip.

Still standing there, holding the napkin covered in makeup and water, Rhiannon's mouth fell open. She stared at Simone. Probably waiting for her to say something. For her to explain.

Simone's eyes were wide, and her breaths came in fast and hard. She glanced at me, then back at Rhiannon, then back to me, then back to Rhiannon.

Rhiannon looked at me too. Her eyes narrowed.

The rest of the room was loud, still joking about Haley's fall, becoming a background noise to our silent conversation.

It was like being a kid all over again. Mom just walked in on me and my best friend trying the cigarettes she had stolen off her dad. She caught us red-handed, and neither of us could think of how to lie our way out of this.

"Both of you," Rhiannon said, voice firm. "Legal building. *Now.*"

When we first got to legal, Simone attempted a quick blanket lie. She fell down the stairs.

Rhiannon cut her off with, "Lie to me again, little girl. I dare you."

She paced the hardwoods behind the large, cherry desk, hands on her hips. Her eyes flicked between the two of us. They stayed on me a moment too long, and I turned my gaze to the floor.

"What—you're not gonna ask why you're here?" Rhiannon snapped. "You knew something happened, and you lied to everybody about it."

Couldn't argue with that. Not that I would try to. I had too much respect for Rhiannon to argue with her.

My heart spun in my stomach. Simone and I hadn't had the chance to work out a plan in case something like this happened. Once the swelling had gone down, we thought we were in the clear.

Of course, we were idiots. After committing murder, you were never in the clear.

Rhiannon reached into her desk drawer and came out with a packet of makeup wipes. She tossed them at Simone. "Take it off."

Simone looked down at them, then up at Rhiannon. With tears in her eyes, she opened her mouth to speak.

Before she could, Rhiannon gritted her teeth and spoke between them. "No, we're not playing this game. I need to know how bad it is. Take it off. Now."

Simone peeled the label back with trembling fingers and pulled out a wipe. As she touched it to her face, tears mixed with the makeup remover. Little by little, she wiped it away, wincing as she uncovered each bruise like an archaeologist dusting off individual artifacts.

Rhiannon watched each swipe, eyes softening with tears. As more of the black and blue became visible, covering almost every inch of Simone's face, a quiet gasp dropped into Rhiannon's lungs. So much sympathy, so much pain like she wore each bruise herself.

She cupped a hand over her mouth and whispered, "My God."

"I'm sorry," Simone began through quivering lips. "I'm—"

"You're sorry?" Rhiannon said. "What are you sorry for? Did you miss him? Did you call him?"

"Of course not," Simone said.

Rhiannon waited for her to go on, but only silence sounded.

"Then what? What the hell happened here?" Never had I heard Rhiannon's voice so deep, so strong. "And don't you dare tell me 'nothing.' It was David, wasn't it? I know you're not seeing anyone new."

A hard swallow bobbed Simone's throat. All she gave in response was a short nod.

"You need to tell me right now if you reached out to him." Rhiannon's brown eyes widened. "I need to know if you're leaving the program—"

"No!" Simone shook her head. Tears came down her face in rivers. A quiet sob escaped. "No. It was Junie. I was at work, and my phone was on silent, and Junie got sick at school. When I didn't answer, they asked her if she knew any other numbers to reach me at. I guess she remembered David's."

Rhiannon's shoulders released. Her brows were still furrowed. "How did he track you down?"

"I don't know." Simone sniffled. She used the dirty makeup wipe to dab up her tears. "Junie said she talked to him. That the nurse handed her the phone. I think she told him that I worked at a salon in Black Pines. There are only two, so it wouldn't have been hard for him to call around and figure it out."

Rhiannon leaned against the desk in front of us. "That's where this happened? At the salon?"

"That's where he confronted me first," Simone said. "I was out on my smoke break, and he came walking down the street, and he started yelling at me, and some people standing around told him that he needed to leave. Apparently, he didn't go far. He was waiting at my car for me when I got off."

While I was no good at thinking of lies on the spot, I had to assume that Simone had practiced. Her cadence, the terror in it, even the way her face scrunched up in fear was perfect. And judging by the look on Rhiannon's face, she was believing it.

"That's where he did this to you?" Rhiannon looked her over, surveying every inch of her face. "In the parking lot when you got off work?"

I looked over at her, panic gripping at my chest. *No. Say no.*

That timeline wouldn't match up. Simone's meltdown at group therapy happened just after she had gotten off work. Her face hadn't been screwed up at that point. The following morning was when she sent the text to Rhiannon about the lash extension class.

"No, it was later that night," Simone said, voice quivering. She held Rhiannon's gaze. "I went up to Gwen's after group to talk about it. He wouldn't stop blowing up my phone the whole time we were hanging out. Gwen told me not to, but I said I would be fine. I figured I could meet up with him, tell him to leave me alone, threaten him with harassment charges, and he would leave. And he did. But not until after this. Not until I threatened to go to the cops. He had warrants, and he knew he would go to jail again.

"So he left, and I haven't heard from him since." Gesturing over her face, Simone's shoulders sank. "I was in really bad shape, but I made it back to the ranch. Gwen took care of me. She wanted to tell you what happened, but I told her we couldn't."

A moment of silence as Rhiannon looked between us. "Is that true, Gwen?"

Doing my best not to swallow the lump in my throat, I nodded.

Rhiannon shook her head. "Why the hell couldn't you tell me?"

"Because I thought that you would kick me out." Nostrils flared, more tears escaped the corners of Simone's eyes. "I know the number one rule. Don't endanger the ranch. And I did. He didn't find the ranch, not exactly, but I knew this would be too close for comfort. I knew you'd kick me out, and I–I don't know what to do without this place. I don't know how I'll survive. I just spent all of my money on my car, and then the salon, and it's not making much yet, and—and—" She let out a sob. "I'm sorry. I'm so sorry. I didn't mean to do this. I really didn't. I just—I just—"

And that was all it took for Rhiannon's eyes to water. Without hesitation, she said, "Come here, kid. Come here," and opened her arms. Simone stood and collapsed into her.

For a while, they just stood there, holding one another.

Relief loosened my shoulders, but it didn't do much for that spinning in my stomach. Rhiannon didn't hate us for this. Not that I ever believed she was capable of such a thing.

But maybe everything would be okay. The lie was well constructed enough that it sounded believable. More than believable. Probable. Knowing Rhiannon, she wasn't going to kick Simone out for it. So long as she never found out the truth, the two of us were both safe.

Until Rhiannon pulled back and said, "I know it's not your fault. You can't help what Junie did. I'm not upset with you for all this." She stroked the tears from Simone's face, thumbs grazing the bruises. "But you can't lie to me." She looked at me. "You either." Eyes shifting between us both, she shook her head. "Something like this happens, we find a solution. You don't hide it. Judging by the looks of it, you should've gone to the hospital."

"That's what I told her too," I said under my breath.

"I just didn't want to go through all this again." Simone's voice was hardly above a whisper. "Being back there again, all the chaos . . . I just wanted to move on."

"And we will." Stroking some hair behind Simone's ear, Rhiannon leaned in and kissed her forehead. "Normally, in a situation like this—because, yes, there have been situations like this—I move you to a different facility." Simone opened her mouth to protest, but Rhiannon continued before she could. "But considering how close you are to starting a real life of your own here, I'm not going to do that to you."

An audible sigh of relief left me. Holding her heart, Simone did the same.

"But that's not where this stops. We don't move on from something by acting like it didn't happen." Rhiannon pulled away and walked to the back of her desk. "I'm gonna have Edwards come down and take a statement from you. At the very least, the local cops gotta be aware this guy showed."

My stomach lurched. The mention of police had me back on that bridge for a split second, struggling to tip David over the handrail. "What?"

"No, I can't," Simone said, shaking her head. "He's gone. It's not gonna help anything for them to know. He—"

"He beat the living hell out of one of *my* girls." Hand over her heart, Rhiannon tapped her chest. "He thinks he can come to my town and act a damn fool? I'm gonna make sure every cop in a fifty-mile radius knows that he was nearby. He's got warrants. They can pick him up on them."

"But—"

"No buts," Rhiannon said, fire burning in her voice. This time, not at us, but at David. "No, this is what we do. We report. We have a paper trail. In case anything ever comes up again, we need a damn paper trail, Simone. And it ain't up to you. This is my ranch, these are my girls to protect, and the law doesn't always do what's right, but sometimes, we gotta work within it.

"With something like this, we *have* to report it. This is how we keep the ranch safe. I'm sorry if you don't want to relive it, but it's not just about you. It's about everyone here. And I'm not fighting with either of you about it."

# CHAPTER 19

## Gwen

Rhiannon had us wait in the front of the cabin while she made the call to the local police department. Colleen, "the head of legal," sat behind the desk up front. She was the grouchiest person I had met at the ranch. Middle-aged, with gray hair and thick black glasses that always hung halfway down her nose.

All I knew about Colleen was that she'd gotten me my new identity. She'd sat behind a computer, typing away, and told me that a few days later, I would receive my key card.

Simone and I exchanged a glance that said, *Guess we can't talk about this now.*

We sat in the two metal chairs by the door, waiting. This cabin had the exact same dimensions as mine. Only difference was instead of a couch, TV, and coffee table, there was Colleen's desk and a few metal chairs.

Given the hour, there wasn't much to see outside the window, aside from some snowflakes and bluish moonlight behind thick clouds. Our only entertainment was the music of Colleen's fingers on the keyboard.

My mind raced a mile a minute. Primarily over the same few sentences.

*Now, the cops are going to know David was here, in Black Pines. They're going to be looking for him. If they look hard enough, will they find his body?*

Someone else sure as hell had.

What had they done with it?

It was the dead of winter. The ground had already frozen. Whoever had found it couldn't have buried it.

Where the hell was his body?

Only one way to find out.

But I couldn't send a message with Simone beside me. She would read it over my shoulder, then know that someone else was involved, possibly panic, and tell Edwards what I had done. No. She couldn't know. Plausible deniability.

Eventually, Edwards arrived. I hadn't met him before, but he was a decent-looking guy with a dark complexion and medium build. One look at Simone had his eyes softening. Rhiannon greeted him, then ushered him and Simone into her office in the back.

As soon as they were out of sight, I whipped out my phone.

**Gwen**

Where did you put it?

Their response came a few minutes later.

**Unknown**

Somewhere safe. Why aren't you using the phone I gave you?

**Gwen**

Same reason you haven't told me who you are or what the hell you did with it.

**Unknown**

That doesn't even make sense. You think I bugged the phone? It was still sealed. I didn't even open the package.

**Gwen**

I have no proof of that. But you've got lots of it.

Their responses came quick.

**Unknown**

Not really.

**Gwen**
Wtf do you mean not really? You've got the biggest piece of the puzzle.

**Unknown**
Really wish you would use the burner so I could give you more details.

**Gwen**
Can't exactly get to it at the moment. Shit's hitting the fan.

**Unknown**
Wdym

**Gwen**
Thought we weren't giving away too many details.

**Unknown**
Then text me on the damn burner when you can.

The door to Rhiannon's office clicked open. She walked closer and glanced back at Colleen. "Would you mind running over to the cafeteria and getting me a cup of coffee?"

Colleen glanced at Rhiannon, then at me. Rolling her eyes, she stood. "Will do."

Rhiannon's eyes stayed on me as Colleen walked out the door. Another deep breath eased through her as she sat beside me. For a heartbeat or two, neither of us spoke. The only sound was my heart pounding in my ears. I prayed she couldn't hear it.

Rarely was Rhiannon silent. The fact that she was now made my stomach turn. My throat swelled, too.

I couldn't tell what she thought or felt. Was there a risk of me getting kicked out of the ranch too? I didn't know what I would do without this place. I had some money, but not enough. It was barely enough for a deposit, let alone first and last month's rent somewhere.

But I wouldn't blame her if she did kick me out. Rhiannon had integrity. She didn't like liars.

Maybe that's why I felt so sick. Not just because I didn't know what she was thinking, but because I had been lying to her for weeks.

Unable to take the silence anymore, I said, "Does it normally take this long to make a statement?"

"Statement's over with." Rhiannon crossed her legs and leaned back in the seat. "Simone is just giving him some background. Hopefully she remembers something that will lead Edwards to David."

Biting my lip, I gave a nod. Because that was all I could think to do. Even spitting out those words tasted like vinegar on my tongue.

"I'm not angry with you." That should've eased my mind, but Rhiannon spoke like she was ordering a coffee. Casual. Blunt. "This place is all about sisterhood. Women supporting women. That's what you did. You were there for your friend when she needed you. Just like I know you'd be there for any of these girls. I don't just respect that. I appreciate it."

My eyes burned with unshed tears. All I could manage was a glance her way. She wasn't looking at me either. Her eyes were on the fireplace in the corner.

"I really didn't want to lie to you," I told her.

"Then why did you?" Her voice was gentle as she turned my way. Confusion overtook her expression. Like a mother disappointed with her child.

I kept my gaze on my feet and shook my head. "I don't know."

"Sure you do. You're a lot of things, Gwen, but thoughtless isn't one of them. All you ever do is think. And usually, you come to a good decision at the end."

I could feel those dark brown eyes surveying every inch of my soul, maybe even my mind. Rhiannon had that gift. She understood people just by looking at them.

"So, what made you think hiding this from me was the right decision?" she asked.

Rhiannon would know if I lied. My shaking hands and quiet voice would give me away. I landed on a version of the truth. "The same reason you don't tell us how you get our fake identities. Plausible deniability."

She cocked her head to the side. "What do you mean?"

*Shit.* Not the best way to say it. If she was the anonymous friend who was texting me a moment ago, would she have wanted that answer?

"You keep things from us to protect us," I said, voice hardly above a whisper. "I figured that if this came out at the ranch, it would make everyone feel unsafe. You would be the one to deal with the fallout. Everyone would be scared, and you'd have to assure them that everything was okay, and I didn't want to put that responsibility on your shoulders."

She squinted at me, but a frown tugged at the edge of her lips now. "It's not your job to protect everyone, you know."

"It wasn't yours either," I said. "Until you made it yours."

She gave a half smile, shaking her head. "I've met my match with you, haven't I?"

"I don't think I'll ever be half the woman you are."

"We gotta work on that." She tossed an arm around my shoulders and kissed my forehead. "Because you already are, kid."

How badly I wished that were true.

"But we've got a lot to work on," Rhiannon said, still holding me close. "Group therapy doesn't seem to be doing much for you. You just listen."

"I thought that was the idea of group." I tugged at a frayed hem on my jeans. "We listen and we support one another. It's about community building."

"It is. But you're surface level with everyone, Gwen. Even your closest friends, you don't open up to." She frowned. "And I get it. I was the same way. Group therapy was good at helping me understand everyone else, but not at helping anyone understand me. So I think you and I are going to start weekly sessions. One hour of your time, you are gonna share with me, and we'll try to get to the root of some stuff."

Considering I already saw Rhiannon several times a week, for several hours a day, that wouldn't be a problem.

"Alright."

"And I want a poem."

"You want a what?"

"A poem." She stood and propped her hands on her hips. "You used to write songs. I've heard you sing them down at the rec center. Those are deep. They talk about the things you've gone through and how you felt."

I cringed. "I wrote those when I was an angsty teen."

"Yeah, before you shut yourself off from anything vulnerable." The door to her office clicked open. "I've heard about writer's block, so I won't give you a deadline. But I want you working on it."

Edwards held the door for Simone. She came out first, shoulders curled inward, head hung toward the floor. Edwards stayed at her rear, his expression blank. Probably saw things like this every day.

"Report all taken care of?" Rhiannon asked.

"Yes, ma'am." Edwards hooked his thumbs through the straps of his bulletproof vest. "Honestly, I agree with Simone. From what she said about this guy, he's probably long gone."

"In my experience," Rhiannon said, "guys like this are persistent."

"Sure. That's why he came back." Edwards shook his head. "But the whole street saw him talking to Simone the way he did. After that, he stuck around for another shot. Then he beat the living hell out of her, and she got away. No way in hell he doesn't know that she filed a report. I don't see him coming back. But if he does, call us. We'll take him in. Get you a restraining order too, if we gotta."

Everything I had done to conceal David's murder was because I feared the police. But had I needed to? Clearly, they had some understanding of what the ranch was. It stood to reason they knew Simone was living under a false identity. If they hadn't run David's record already, but they did soon, they would learn that Simone had violated a custody order. Would they be back for her then?

"Alright." Rhiannon raised her hands in surrender. "Thanks, kid."

They exchanged a few more pleasantries before he headed out.

Rhiannon looked at Simone. "Do you want the ranch to know? Or do you want to keep this quiet?"

"Between us, preferably?" Simone's tone was as meek as her stance. I had never seen her like this before. "I don't want anyone else to worry about an ex coming back for them."

"Got to figure out what we're going to tell them then," Rhiannon said. "How about something happened at work? You had to file a report about an angry customer who didn't pay."

"That should work."

"Wait," I said, standing. "Wait, are we sure Simone's not going to get in trouble for violating her custody order? If the cops know she did that, they could arrest her, couldn't they? Surely she has warrants by now."

Rhiannon's shoulders, her eyes, everything about her demeanor was so casual. Like she had been here before. "Don't worry about it."

"The local cops are in on the ranch?" I asked.

"If they weren't, the ranch wouldn't be running." Rhiannon gestured outside. "It's late. We should all turn in. I'm sure Margaret's waiting for you to pick up Junie, Simone."

"Probably." Simone headed for the door. Over her shoulder, she said to me, "Call me when you're back up to your cabin."

I had already planned on it. I needed to know the exact story she gave Edwards. But since the day I'd gotten here, I had wondered how this place ran. Simone had mentioned once that the billionaire's backing covered more than just fees at the ranch. Now, I had to wonder . . .

I caught up to Rhiannon as she started outside. "Are you saying you own them?"

Rhiannon scoffed. "Excuse me?"

"The local cops," I said. "You pay them to look the other way, don't you?"

She pulled the door shut. "I do."

For a few heartbeats, I just looked at her.

"Are you judging me for that?" She propped her hands on her hips. "Do you find it hypocritical or something?"

"No," I said. "Not at all."

"Then what the hell is that face for?"

"Respect." I shrugged. "Mobs and gangs have been buying local cops for decades, maybe centuries. It's about time a good person does it for good reason."

A half smile. "Goodnight, Gwen."

Maybe it would've been a better night a few weeks ago if I had just told Rhiannon the truth. Maybe no one would've worried about going to jail for David's murder, and I wouldn't have thrown out my back lifting him into the damn trunk.

"The exact same story," I said into the phone. I propped it between my shoulder and ear, prying open the burner phone from its box. "You gave Edwards the exact same story as Rhiannon?"

"Didn't miss a beat," Simone said on the other end. "It's fine, Gwen. I know Edwards. He didn't suspect anything."

"Why would he? No one's going to suspect I killed the guy."

Still tearing at the plastic that lined the burner phone, to no avail, I tossed it onto the couch. This job would require scissors. I padded to the kitchen and grabbed a pair from a drawer.

"That's not what I'm worried about," I continued, returning to the living room.

"What the hell else is there to worry about then?"

"If his family filed a missing persons report, then no one would have connected him to Black Pines yet."

Shoving the scissors around the plastic wrapping, I chopped at the case until it peeled open. "But now, he's been connected to this place. They could be looking for him. God only knows what they'll find if they look hard enough."

"What *could* they find?" Simone lowered her voice. "I thought you said you took care of everything."

The cardboard box emerged from the open plastic casing, which I tossed on the couch. "I did. I think."

"What the hell does that mean?" Terror tinged Simone's voice. "You *think*? This isn't something you just *think* about, Gwen. If you were gonna think about it, maybe you should have just called the cops."

"Maybe *you* should have told Rhiannon in the first place. Then neither of us would be dealing with this right now. Should've, could've, would've."

"I'm sorry." I could hear her pout through the phone. "I'm not trying to point fingers."

Running my hands through my hair, I let out a deep breath and lowered myself to the sofa. Honey hopped up beside me. Stroking my fingers through her fur slowed my racing heart.

"I'm sorry, too. I know why you didn't. I'm just stressed."

"And I get it." Her tone sounded softer now, calmer. "But I don't think we have to worry. We're so close to the Canadian border, Gwen. I'm pretty sure if you walk through the woods around the property long enough, you'll end up in Canada. That's probably the assumption. David was a bad dude. It makes complete sense that he would've made a run for it."

Was that common? American criminals running to Canada? Everyone had heard of them running to Mexico or Colombia, but Canada wasn't known for harboring American fugitives.

"Alright." Prying the cell phone from the plastic innards, I re-situated mine between my shoulder and ear. "Alright, until further notice, we go back to what we've been doing. Pretending it never happened."

"You don't sound eager about that."

"I'm not *eager* for any of this." I rubbed my eyes with my thumb and forefinger. "It's just—I thought we were in the clear. Now, I'm worried we're not. But you're right. There's a good chance no one will ever suspect a thing."

So long as they didn't find a body, they would never be able to convict me anyway.

"I think we're fine," Simone insisted. "Just relax. Have a drink, read a book, and go lie down. You'll feel better in the morning."

"Sure do hope so," I said. "And I know that was the polite way of telling me you need to get Junie ready for bed, so I'll let you go."

"I do, but if anything comes up, or if you start to panic, call me, alright?"

"Will do. Sleep tight."

I set my phone on the coffee table and turned my attention to the burner. Straight from one phone to the other. I went through the setup process. Made a fake account, with a fake email address, and a fake name. Jane Doe was taken, so I became Jane Dobe.

It looked ridiculous across the screen, but all that mattered was that I had a way to contact this 'friend' anonymously.

Once the thing was up and running, I headed to the text messaging app.

**Gwen**
On the burner now. What did you do with it?

The response came in heartbeats.

**Unknown**
Burned his personal effects and buried the body.

**Gwen**
So you have a Ripper attachment on an excavator, a hydraulic hammer, and a Hydra back truck?

**Unknown**
Guessing you have no idea what

any of that is, so I'm assuming you googled what it takes to dig a hole through frozen ground.

I had done exactly that. But what was their point?

**Gwen**
I'm just having a hard time believing that you went through all that effort for a stranger. But you knew it was me, so we can't be strangers. You call yourself a friend, and you hide behind an anonymous number.

They read it. They began typing. They stopped. Then they began again. When that went on for a while, I took Simone's advice. Maybe a drink would ease my racing mind. Just as I was finishing pouring a glass, the burner phone dinged again.

**Unknown**
You're right. I didn't go to all this effort for a stranger. We are friends. But I have shit to lose, too. Sorry I'm not willing to throw my whole life away.

**Gwen**
Yet you buried a body for me.

**Unknown**
Yeah, and made sure no one knew it was me.

**Gwen**
How did YOU even know it was me?

**Unknown**
Recognized the raincoat and tennis shoes while you were dumping him over the bridge.

So, furthering my theory. It could've been someone from the ranch or from town. But it had to be a woman. Men didn't pay so much attention to shoes and raincoats.

Gay men did, though. More times than I could count, Axel had complimented or condemned an outfit choice of mine. Those very tennis shoes once, in fact. They were Hokas. The most comfortable shoes I'd ever worn, purchased because long hours at the bakery were killing my feet, but they were bulky and big. Axel had said it looked like I had clown feet.

Could this be Axel?

**Gwen**
Why would you even be in the woods at that hour?

**Unknown**
Who said I was in the woods?

**Gwen**
You weren't on the bridge and you weren't on the road. I would've seen you. So you had to be in the woods.

**Unknown**
Fine. I was in the woods.

**Gwen**
Again, why?

**Unknown**
It clears my head.

**Gwen**
So you're not a hunter, then?

**Unknown**
I'm not telling you who I am.

I rolled my eyes.

**Gwen**
How did you bury it?

**Unknown**
Built a fire. Let the ground thaw. Put the fire out. Dug until I hit frozen ground. Lit another fire. Rinse repeat.

Damn. Why the hell hadn't I thought of that?

**Gwen**
That had to have taken hours.

**Unknown**
A couple.

**Gwen**
Why so much effort?

**Unknown**
I googled the guy. Took me all of two minutes to figure out why you did it.

**Gwen**
And why did I do it?

**Unknown**
Simone. He showed up, either threatened or hurt her, and you defended her. I respect it. Probably would've done the same thing in your position. But you didn't know what you were doing, and you screwed up. It looked like you were coming from the ranch. If I were you, I would've just incinerated it there. There's one at the meatpacking plant, you know.

No. I sure as hell did not know. And even if I had, I wouldn't have known how to get inside the meatpacking plant. Could I have figured out a way? Sure. If I told Rhiannon I was curious about how to process meat, gave her a spiel about my desire to live off the land, she would have given me a job at the plant. But I wouldn't have had time for all that while hiding a decomposing body.

Still, something about their attitude put me off.

**Gwen**
You're too calm about this.

**Unknown**
You're too panicked. That's what could get you caught.

Maybe they were right.

**Gwen**
The only way your reaction makes any sense is if you've done this before.

**Unknown**
I assure you, I have never seen a friend drop a body off an overpass, then drug it out of the creek myself, only to spend my entire day burying the damn thing.

**Gwen**
Maybe not. But you're too calm about a murder to have never been involved in something similar.

**Unknown**
Could've been manslaughter for all I know.

In the eyes of the law, that may have been what I did. I didn't know, and it didn't matter.

What mattered was how comfortable they were with all this.

If it were Rhiannon, was it possible that she'd killed a man like David before? I could see her capable of it. Most people, under the right circumstances, were capable of killing.

But Rhiannon had looked genuinely shocked by Simone's bruises. Whoever this was wouldn't have been.

Unless that had been a ruse too.

Axel still seemed more likely. A man his size would have an easier time moving the body than Rhiannon or I would have.

While Axel and I weren't the best of friends, I knew a thing or two. Like how he'd gotten this job. His mom had left his dad and came to live at the ranch. I'd never met her, so I wasn't sure if she had passed or moved away after getting back on her feet.

But was it possible that she had killed her husband? And that coming to the ranch was about escaping more than just her trauma?

**Gwen**

Fine, I won't pry. But I need to know where he is.

**Unknown**

You really don't. You do need to tell me what you meant earlier though. What shit hit the fan?

**Gwen**

Rhiannon saw bruises on Simone's face. She knew it was David. We didn't tell her exactly what happened, but she made Simone file a report. The cops are gonna be looking for him.

**Unknown**

Oh. That's fine. They won't find him. As long as you did a good job of getting rid of the car.

**Gwen**

I did.

**Unknown**

Not gonna give me any more context there?

**Gwen**

Nope.

**Unknown**
Why not?

**Gwen**
Why won't you tell me where the body is?

**Unknown**
Because it's handled. And it's safer for both of us if neither of us know. Then we can't incriminate one another.

**Gwen**
Then you better accept my answer too.

**Unknown**
Which wouldn't be a problem, if you hadn't dropped a body over an overpass without so much as weighing it down.

**Gwen**
I was in a bit of a hurry.

**Unknown**
Were you in a hurry to get rid of the car?

**Gwen**
No, that took me all morning.

**Unknown**
Then I have faith you didn't screw it up.

I jumped at the loud knock on my front door.

# CHAPTER 20

## *Angela*

"Yes, ma'am, I know that David was last seen here in Black Pines," the cop on the other end of the line said. Edwards? Was that his name? Angela couldn't remember. "Like I reported to his PO—"

"He was last seen with *her*." Angela spat that word like it tasted acidic and dirty. "My son was last seen with the woman he fought with daily for half a decade. And now I haven't heard a word from him in a month. You're going to tell me you don't see a connection there?"

A breath vibrated the speaker. Silence followed for a moment too long.

"Given his history and the charges he was facing, I have to assume the obvious here, ma'am. And I'm sorry—"

"Sorry my ass!"

Pacing her apartment, Angela snapped her arm against the wall. All it left her with was a throbbing wrist. No relief.

"The obvious? The obvious is that she knows where he is. Either she threatened him or she—" Angela's chest tightened, and she couldn't even think the words. "Officer Edwards? That's your name, right?"

"Yes, ma'am."

"Look, Officer Edwards. I know my son."

The good, the bad, and the outright despicable. Angela knew it all. She knew the police in Cheyenne, Wyoming weren't wrong. David was a dealer. Sometimes, deals went bad. And yes, he'd killed a man. With tears in his eyes, breaths nearly impossible to find, lying his head in her lap as he wept, he'd confessed it to his mother. He hadn't meant to kill that man.

It was a mistake. An awful, horrible mistake. But a mistake. Just because the mother of the man he killed lost her son didn't mean Angela should lose hers. Not really. Not forever.

So she had helped him. She'd found everything he would need to start over on the other side of the border.

The murder had happened only days before he got the call from Junie. That timing? It was meant to be. It had to be.

Together, they'd packed his bag: clothes, freeze-dried food, a tent, fire starter, and a few thick blankets. They secured his false identification. They mapped the route he would take.

First stop? Black Pines. Collect Junie. Then back in the car, farther north, until he made it to the border. There, he would hike with Junie on his back for as long as it took to make it to Canada.

He had enough cash to stay in a hotel for a few weeks while he arranged flights to the Yukon. Friends of David's friends had connections. One of them was a rich old man who owned property there. For a few years—until things died down in Cheyenne—David and Junie would stay in the cabin. She would get virtual schooling.

And, to boot, he would be away from the drugs. He'd have no choice but to stay clean.

It would be good. It would be good for everyone.

David, who could finally get his life on track.

Junie, who desperately needed her father, whether she realized it or not.

And Angela, of course. She would make trips every few months to see them both. She would regain contact with her granddaughter and maintain her relationship with her son.

It was supposed to be good. It was supposed to be good for everyone.

"He was going to call me," Angela said into the phone, heart heavy as she replayed the perfect plan. "He was gonna call me when he got to where he was going. My boy, he calls me every day. Every single day, Officer. And I haven't heard from him in over a month. He didn't just run to Canada."

"Where was he planning on going?" Edwards asked.

"I don't know exactly." Angela hoped her lie sounded believable. "But I know he would've called—"

"Not after what he did, ma'am," Edwards said. "He beat S—Jess within an inch of her life. He was already wanted for questioning in

Cheyenne, then he came here and committed battery. If anybody gets a hold of him, he's not going anywhere for a long time. We're talking years. Decades. Maybe the rest of his life."

"Please," Angela said under her breath. "Were you there? Because I know Jess. That girl can hold her own just fine. I wouldn't be surprised if she hit herself just to make him look bad."

"A crowd of civilians witnessed him harassing her at her job." There was a bite to Edwards's voice now. "I took the testimony myself, and I saw her face. She didn't do it herself, and I won't be commenting any further on her condition or her recollection of the events."

Angela snorted, gritting her teeth. "Fine. We don't have to talk about Jess. But we do have to talk about the fact that you're not doing your damn job. My kid went missing, and—"

"Your kid made himself disappear, because if he didn't, he would spend the rest of his life in prison. As he damn well should. I know the stories. I've read his records. I know why Jess left him. As any decent mother would, after her partner tried to sell their daughter. I've already talked to my supervisors and all the detectives in our department, and we all agree about what happened here. You can keep calling, but I'm gonna keep telling you the same damn thing, Miss Burke."

Hands trembling at her sides, teeth clenched so tightly she was sure they were going to break, Angela snapped, "Rot in hell, pig."

She shuttered the phone and tossed it across the room.

How dare he? What gave him the right?

David wasn't perfect. He was so far from perfect. Angela would never deny that. But god damn it, he didn't deserve whatever that bitch did to him.

She stared at her keys hanging on a hook by the door.

Eight hours wasn't too far of a drive.

Angela was going to get answers.

Once she had them? She was gonna make what David did to Jess look like a tantrum.

# CHAPTER 21

## *Gwen*

My heart dropped into my stomach.

Honey ran to the door, barking and howling. Her tail wagged, making her whole body wiggle. She knew whoever waited on the other side.

I still looked at the set of butcher knives on the counter.

I fumbled with the burner phone to shut it down and shove it in my hoodie pocket.

On the tips of my toes, careful to remain quiet if it was someone I didn't want to talk to— or someone dangerous, no matter how paranoid that may have sounded—I made it to the window on the left of the door.

Delilah stood behind it.

My shoulders loosened, deep breath parting my lips. I unlatched the deadbolt and swung it open. "Are you okay?"

She nodded, smiling, her nose bright pink from the cold wind. At least an inch of snow piled on top the hood of her coat. "Yeah, I'm fine. I'm sorry for just showing up. I was walking around, and I wound up on this trail, I remembered you saying that you lived here, and—I don't know. Your lights were on."

My heart swelled. She needed someone to talk to.

Stepping aside, I held the door open for her. "Come on in."

"Are you sure?" She glanced me over, likely noting my silly pink pajamas covered in doughnuts. "If you were getting ready for bed, I don't want to—"

"Please. Insomnia keeps me up half the night anyway." I gestured toward the couch. "Seriously. Have a seat."

Eyes softened, she thanked me, shook the snow off her jacket onto the porch, and did just that.

"Do you want a drink?" Out of instinct, I reached for the whiskey on the table. Then I looked at Delilah again. Her round, supple cheeks, her small stature. "Wait, how old are you? I don't know if I've asked."

"Eighteen." She tugged off her coat, a teasing smile curving the edges of her lips. "But I won't tell if you don't."

"Of all the things, that won't be what I go to prison for." A similar smile in response. "How about tea? Or hot chocolate?"

"Oh, you don't have to go to all that trouble for me."

"It's no trouble. I could go for some hot chocolate." I grabbed some heavy cream from the fridge and started for the stovetop. "It mixes well with whiskey. In a couple years, I'll make you some."

While the cocoa and cream melted together in the pot, Delilah let out a halfhearted, almost ironic chuckle. "I probably shouldn't drink it anyway. I'm not sure how it works. Is it dangerous to drink while you're pregnant because of the baby? Or does it hurt you?"

I stopped stirring, replaying that over in my mind. Delilah didn't clarify, she didn't say more, so I had to assume that I had heard correctly.

It wasn't uncommon around here. As a woman without children, I was the minority at Rhiannon's Ranch.

Slowly, I spun to face her. "You're pregnant?"

With tears in her eyes, she pressed her lips together and gave a nod. "But I won't be for long."

Frown tugging at the edge of my lips, I debated how to respond. That explained why she asked the way she had. Certainly had me considering corrupting the minor.

"Rhiannon took me to my appointment in Black Pines." Delilah stayed only an octave above a whisper. "She told me before that if I didn't want this, we could find a way to make that work, but I did. I wanted to keep it. But today at my ultrasound, they said something wasn't right. The baby, it's on my tube? Or something like that. And when it gets bigger, it's gonna kill me. I still don't understand it all, but . . ."

"It's ectopic." I left the ingredients to simmer and returned to the sofa beside Delilah. "I'm so sorry. How are you doing?"

She tried to smile, but the tears started falling. It took a few hard swallows and tissue dabs before she continued. "I don't know.

I wanted her. I really did. She's the reason I left. But I don't understand why they can't just move her. I get that she is on my tube, and when she gets bigger, the tube will burst and I'll bleed out. But if there's nothing wrong with her, and it's just where she's at, I don't understand."

"Science hasn't gotten that far yet." I reached out for her hand. "I'm *so* sorry."

Delilah squeezed my fingers. "Maybe it's for the best. I'm sad, but I'm relieved too. But when I think that, I feel horrible. I was excited, and I was happy, and—" A sharp breath. "I don't know if that makes any sense."

"It makes perfect sense." I grabbed another tissue off the coffee table and held it out to her. She accepted and wiped her eyes. "I can't say that it was for the best, or that it was meant to be, because no one can know. That's not how life works. Sometimes, things just go wrong. And it sucks, and it's hard, but if it helps, when I was in a position like yours, it *was* for the best. My life would be a lot different if that baby had made it. I can't say I'm happy it didn't, but things did work out for me."

Cocking her head to the side, Delilah's eyes softened. Like the two of us were standing together against the same common threat. "You had an ectopic pregnancy?"

"No. They call it a chemical pregnancy. A couple positive tests, but then I started bleeding before they could do an ultrasound or bloodwork. It was very early, so I didn't really form a bond with it or anything. Still hurt though. Sometimes it still does."

Teary-eyed, Delilah pressed her lips together. Probably to stave off a sob. After a moment, she said, "But, in a way, are you happy about it?"

Chewing my cheek, a deep breath lifted my chest. "I wouldn't say happy, no. At the same time, I made sure to always use protection with my ex after that. When I got the positive test, I was happy. I was depressed when they told me that it was gone. But I kind of thought about it in a weird, spiritual sense? Which is strange, because I'm not religious."

"I am," she said quietly. "Born and raised Irish Catholic."

That surely made all of this a lot harder for her. "I thought maybe my body saw something in my husband that I didn't. Like it rejected his DNA because it knew we weren't right together. Maybe God knew your ex wasn't right for you either. Maybe this was his way of setting you free from him."

I didn't believe that. Biology was strange. Things went awry. Statistically, one in four confirmed pregnancies ended in miscarriage. But when I'd gone through it, I found comfort in thinking there was something ethereal about it all. A sense of destiny, that it wasn't supposed to happen like this. A deeper meaning that gave some kind of merit to my pain.

Maybe this logic would help Delilah too.

"That's what I keep saying to myself," Delilah whispered. "It does make me feel better for a minute. But then I feel so guilty because I think about Evan, and I think about how much this would hurt him." She swatted a few more tears away. "He wasn't all bad. He really wasn't."

At the sound of quiet boiling on the stove, I stood and headed that way. "Of course he wasn't. If he was all bad, you wouldn't have been with him."

"Is that okay to say around here?"

I spun the spoon through the sizzling cocoa. "You can say whatever you want around here."

"Yeah, I know. In theory." Delilah wiped up the rest of her tears. "But in group, it's all about everything we hate about them. That's what's so hard. So much of me *is* Evan. I became who I am with him. It's weird trying to come to grips with a version of me that isn't so tightly wound around him."

This wasn't about Evan. It was about Delilah. Her sense of self, and the lack thereof. She didn't want to talk about what he'd done to her. She wanted to converse about how impossible it was to unthread herself from him.

"Do you want to talk about him?" A spoonful of cocoa landed on my tongue. The texture was creamy, almost as thick as ganache, but the bitter taste had me grimacing. I added some more sugar. "We can. I don't mind."

"Kind of? If that's okay?" Soft, almost confused at first. It didn't match the strength in her tone when she said, "But only under one condition."

"And what's that?"

"You don't accuse me of wanting him back." Those blue eyes were wide, unblinking. "Because I don't. I *really* don't."

"I believe you. You just want to talk it through. Get your head on straight." I grabbed a few mugs from the cabinet above the sink. "How did you two meet?"

My phone rang in my pocket.

I rushed to silence it, but Delilah stopped me before I could. "It's okay. You can take that."

I frowned. "This matters more right now."

"It'll matter just as much after you talk to whoever that is." Sniffling still, dabbing her cheeks, she chuckled. "I'm fine. Seriously, answer it."

Judging by her heavy exhales, the forced laugh, and all the wiping of her eyes, she wasn't saying that for my benefit. She wanted a moment to find her composure.

That was the only reason I lifted the phone from my pocket and noted the incoming call. Sebastian.

"Hey, I'm sorry I didn't get back to you earlier," I answered in a hurry. "And I'm sorry for what I'm about to say now."

He laughed. "Well, hello to you, too."

"I know, I'm sorry." It was hard to ignore the warmth that rose in my chest. "Delilah stopped by. Can I call you back before I go to sleep?"

"Actually, I have an early surgery in the morning, so I'm heading to bed now," he said. "But it's alright. See you for lunch tomorrow?"

So smooth. Everything with him was so smooth, so easy. Simple, like Haley had said in group today. "Yeah, that's perfect. Sleep tight."

"You too, pretty girl," he said. "And hey, don't forget about those jeans."

I only let out a half laugh, doing my damnedest to be sensitive to Delilah in her state. With my face toward the stove, she couldn't see my blushing cheeks. "Hold up your end, and I'll hold up mine."

"Oh, I will." He laughed, and I chuckled, and we got off the call.

"Was that Sebastian?" Delilah's puffy eyes still glistened, but the redness receded.

"It was, and I'm sor—"

"Don't be." She sniffled again, smiling. "Maybe one day, I'll have what you guys do."

I snorted. Not because there was anything wrong with him or our relationship. There was just a whole hell of a lot wrong with me.

"It's all fresh. But yeah. Things do get better. You wouldn't recognize the girl I was when I got here. But back on topic. How did you guys meet?"

"His dad was friends with my dad. We kinda grew up together, I guess," she said. "He's older though. When I was in third grade, he left for college. He came back when I was fifteen. We just reconnected, you know? I was older and more mature. He didn't see me as a little kid anymore."

If he left for college when she was in third grade, he was nine or ten years older than her. It worried me that she saw herself as mature at fifteen.

Then again, when I was fifteen, so did I.

"That must've made leaving harder." Full mugs in hand, I returned to the sofa. "If your families were close, I mean."

"It did, yeah. That was the crazy thing." She closed both hands around her mug, staring at the contents for a few heartbeats. "It was early on in our relationship when he hit me for the first time. And I didn't tell anyone, because I didn't want anyone to think poorly of him. But when I couldn't take it anymore, and I finally told my dad, he didn't really care."

"It wasn't that he didn't believe you?"

"No, he believed me. He just didn't think it was all that big of a deal. He said he thought I could defend myself."

"A few of my friends said the same thing when I told them. Wasn't a good feeling." Juggling my cocoa, I cozied up beneath a throw blanket. "It's so funny, because in society, one of the worst things you can be is a woman beater. But when you actually tell someone that your man is beating you, they think there's no way you can be a part of the statistic."

"He wasn't entirely wrong though. I did defend myself a lot of the time." Delilah lifted her legs onto the sofa, crossed them lotus style, and tucked her cup in the center. "He was a big guy, but he usually backed down after I hit him too. That's probably why I took it for as long as I did."

Like Rhiannon had said on Delilah's first day, that's why we were all here. None of us were perfect victims. Very few perfect victims existed. Almost everyone who experienced domestic violence defended themselves eventually. That's why it took so many of us so long to even acknowledge we were in that situation.

"Why did you decide to leave?" I asked.

A hard swallow. Delilah had a hard time meeting my gaze. "He didn't back down that last time. He shoved me so hard that my head went through the wall. That was the worst pain I ever felt. I danced ballet for years. I know what pain feels like. But it was just so different. I couldn't see straight, I was sick to my stomach, I couldn't even *think*, and then I had to lie in bed beside him afterward because I had nowhere else to go."

I knew that pain too. "The disorientation of a concussion can be terrifying. Especially if you don't go to a hospital to get assurance that you're gonna be okay."

"And I definitely didn't," she murmured, still staring at the cocoa. The snow out the window behind her fell heavier and harder now. "I went to my dad's the next day and asked him if I could stay with him, and he said no. That I needed to work it out with Evan."

"That's when you called the shelter?"

A nod. "All the local ones were full, so they got me in touch with Rhiannon. I feel a lot better here."

I could tell. It sure was ironic that this conversation started with her saying that there were good times, yet she'd only spoken about the bad.

"But?" I asked.

"But . . . I guess I'm just lonely. And I feel like he has the right to know about the pregnancy. If the roles were reversed, I would want to know. Not because I want to go back to him, but . . ." Gritting her teeth, Delilah shook her head. "I don't know."

That cold look in her eyes told me more than her words. "Because you want this to hurt him the way it's hurting you."

Slumping her shoulders, she met my gaze. "Does that make me a horrible person?"

There was a good chance I wasn't the right person to ask.

"No," I said. "It makes you a fair one. You wish you could balance an uneven scale."

She let out a breath and wiped at her nose, sniffling. "Thank God. I felt so guilty."

"Shame is something you feel when you've done something wrong," I said. "Guilt is empathy we've been taught to feel for any and everyone, even when they don't deserve it. Evan doesn't deserve your guilt."

She chewed her lower lip. "I really haven't done anything to feel guilty for. I left, but that's not something I should be ashamed of. It was just about protecting myself. And, I thought, protecting my baby."

"If anything, you should be proud. It took me eleven years to leave my ex. It only took you three."

"I don't know about that." Delilah finally lifted her mug to her lips. She blew on it but still didn't take a sip. "I mean, I know that I did what I had to. But this wasn't where I saw my life going, you know? Me and my dad, we had a good relationship. Until all this, we really did. I wanted to be who *he* wanted me to be. The sweet, innocent little flower. The good girl."

My heart beat a little harder, and the same fire I had felt when I'd killed David burned in my chest. "No, Delilah. That's not who you want to be."

"It kind of is though," she said. "Or it was, I guess. That's what I always wanted. Marry my high school sweetheart, have a couple kids, buy a little house in the suburbs, and live happily ever after."

"But now you know." Setting my mug on the coffee table, I shook my head. "Now you know that the happily ever after is just that. The rolling credits at the end of a fairytale. That's not real life.

"In real life, women fit in two boxes. We're either the delicate flower or the violent storm. The victim or the villain. One harsh storm is gonna break the flower's neck. All victims get are thoughts and prayers. At least villains get justice. If you've gotta be the flower or the storm, be the damn storm. And be proud of it. Because if you were the flower, you wouldn't have survived. You *had* to be the storm. And I'm glad you were."

A smile quirked the edge of Delilah's lips. "Yeah?"

"Yeah. Because you're here to tell the story," I said. "Because he could've killed you, and you got away before he had the chance. Because we're sitting here, drinking hot cocoa, and snow is falling outside, and a fluffy dog is curled up under your legs, and everyone in this room knows that they're safe, and that we have a future ahead of us.

"We wouldn't be sitting here right now if we hadn't fought back. If we hadn't chosen to be the villain when we could have been the victim. You and I, we get to be friends. We get to have lives. One day, maybe we'll marry better men, and we'll have kids, and they'll be friends too, and they'll never go through what we went through, because we won't teach them to be flowers. We'll teach them to be storms."

A few seconds passed, and she just looked at me. Her eyes crinkled at the edges, and that touch of joy at the corner of her mouth climbed higher.

"What?" I asked, eyes creasing with confusion. "Why're you looking at me like that?"

The smile climbed. "We're friends, huh?"

I laughed. "I think soon, we'll be best friends."

Smiling wider, she shook her head. "I haven't had any of those in a while."

"Well, now you've got a whole hell of a lot. And friends drink each other's cocoa." I gestured to it. "C'mon. Tell me that's not better than store bought."

Chuckling, Delilah took a sip. Eyes wide, she gulped down another. "I need this recipe. Like, yesterday."

"I'll jot it down for—"

*Crack-cra—Thump!*

We jumped to look out the window behind the sofa.

Half a dozen yards from my cabin, a tree limb, white with snow, lay half on the ground. A few streaks of wood still bound it to the conifer's trunk, holding it at an angle. Somehow, it looked like it'd always been there. Like it'd grown that way to lend support to the entire tree's structure.

Delilah chuckled, and so did I. She said, "You know what?"

"What's that?"

"Storms are prettier than flowers anyway."

# CHAPTER 22

## *Gwen*

Delilah and I talked a bit more, but before long, she was dozing off. I got her a blanket and shut out the light.

I wasn't so lucky. After lying in bed for close to an hour, almost certain I wouldn't fall asleep on my own, I stepped out the rear door and took a few puffs. Like magic, I drifted to a dreamless sleep as soon as I went back to bed.

Delilah was gone in the morning. She texted me saying she had a job interview in town, but she was grateful for the conversation. As was I.

She was so young, with so much life ahead of her. What would my life have looked like if I had been smart enough to leave my ex at the age she had?

By nine, I was at work, decorating cakes. At one, I took my lunch. Sebastian met me as planned. In my mind, it was a nice respite. A break from the anxiety of what Edwards could find when he dug deeper into David's case.

More than once, however, Sebastian asked me if I was okay. I kept telling him I was. And that was true. Sitting across the table from him, sipping coffee and eating sandwiches together, eased my racing mind. I felt perfectly fine. Perfectly myself.

With Sebastian, life was easy. I didn't need to think and stress and obsess in his presence. Sitting with him was like popping a pill whose effects read: peace, quiet, comfort, simplicity.

Even if I wanted to, I couldn't worry. Everything was just okay. Any time we sat across from each other in this café, or beside each other in his truck, or his name lit up my screen, peace washed over me.

More and more often, I craved that feeling. I was becoming addicted to it.

I was no longer afraid of it. Those butterfly wings were more like a massage now.

A blanket apology seemed to do its job. "Yeah, I'm sorry," I said. "Just didn't sleep well last night."

Apparently accepting that as answer enough, the conversation progressed. The one today wrapped up with him reminding me of my lesson with Lizzie tomorrow.

Of course, I told him I would be there.

"Maybe we can do something after?" he asked.

No way I'd turn that down. I told him I couldn't wait, and I meant every word.

But life resumed. He had work, so did I, and unfortunately, that was the rest of my afternoon.

When I got home, I shot Delilah another text. Usually, I wasn't the greatest at reaching out to friends. Sure, I'd killed for one of them, but suggesting spending time together? As though I was the one who needed *their* support? I would never.

But Delilah had needed a friend last night. Maybe she needed one now too.

She responded, asking if she could come by. I agreed. When she arrived, she was in much better shape than she had been the night before. Cheerful, giddy, maybe even a bit silly.

This place was starting to feel like home to her. Which was exactly what the ranch was founded on. Delilah and I had formed a bond of some kind, and as an unspoken rule, it was my responsibility to welcome her into our community.

While we were cooking dinner, Simone called. Her tone was casual, only asking if I had plans for dinner yet. When I told her that Delilah and I were already cooking it, she asked if she could come over as well. Obviously, I said she could.

She arrived a little while later with Junie at her side. As Simone and Delilah worked on the spaghetti, Junie and I got down to business with some cookie dough. She was a sweet kid, with brown pigtails that reached her shoulders. Today, her full cheeks were covered in two blue and purple butterflies. Normally I struggled to get more than a few words out of her, so I was surprised when she raved about how Mommy did them this morning for some event at school. Since Simone was so bubbly and energetic, one might have thought that her daughter would be similar. She was not.

After we ate, Junie cuddled up on the couch with her chocolate chip cookies and a book from the library at school.

I wondered if she knew. Simone had mentioned that she was careful to take her makeup off after Junie was in bed and to apply it before she woke up. She had also made the decision not to bring up the phone call Junie had made in the nurse's office at school.

But did Junie have any idea? Was there some small part of her that knew her father had come back?

Did a part of her know he was gone for good?

Did she live each day fearing that her father would find her again? She'd been young when they'd left him, but Simone said Junie still had nightmares about him from time to time. That little girl had not forgotten the monster who'd donated his DNA to her existence.

Would it give her comfort to know he was dead? Would those nightmares cease?

I couldn't say.

But I knew one thing for damn sure.

My home was filled with girls who were laughing, smiling, gossiping, reading—simply living. Not one out of the four of us was afraid in this moment. Each of us were happy. At the very least, safe.

If this was the aftermath of an abusive man's death, how could it have been a bad thing?

After they left, that question helped me fall into a fast sleep.

No weed was needed to get there. No nightmares after the fact, either.

I awoke rejuvenated for my nine to six shift. When I arrived at work, Andrew was in a mood again. Molly and I ignored him, decorated our cakes, and served our customers.

Just as I was untying my apron to take my lunch, the front door swung open.

Face flushed, sweat dribbling down his brow, Sebastian all but ran to the counter. Luckily, we were slowing down from the lunch rush, so he didn't have a line to wait behind. Given how quickly he got to the other end, I wouldn't have been shocked if he'd knocked a few people over to get to me.

Before I could greet him with my usual, "Hey, how's your day going?" he spoke a mile a minute.

"I'm sorry, I can't stay," he said. "Shit, I'm not gonna be able to bring Lizzie to the ranch tonight for her lesson either. Damn it. I'm sorry. I'm really sorry."

If he was just stopping by to tell me that he couldn't make it for our usual lunch, he would've texted. He was here for a quick bite to go.

"Don't be sorry." Reaching into the pastry case, I came out with his usual. A ham and cheese that Molly and I had prepped this morning. "Is everything okay? Is Lizzie alright?"

"Yeah. Yeah, I'm sorry." He dropped a ten on the counter and shook his head. "I'm fine, Lizzie's fine. But a patient of mine is on his way. It's bad. I don't know how bad yet, and I won't for about"—he glanced at his watch—"nine minutes. But judging by the screaming, it's bad."

"Cat, dog, or something else?"

"Dog." He shook his head in disbelief, eyes wide as they scanned the counter. "Six-year-old golden retriever. His mom's one of my patients too. First time I saw him was on an ultrasound. Been with him through every checkup, a bowel obstruction from chewing on toys, regular health visits. And ten minutes ago, his mom called. The human one, I mean. His leash malfunctioned while they were on a walk, and he got hit by a car."

Tears bubbled in my eyes. "Poor thing. How bad is it?"

"She said his nose and back leg are bleeding, a wound in his stomach from the fender, and he's just crying and whimpering." With his thumb and forefinger, he rubbed his eyes. "Nearest emergency vet is an hour away, and I don't think he'll make it there. So I told her to bring him in. I'll probably be in surgery for hours."

I passed him the sandwich. "You're going to need your strength then."

"To say the least." Accepting, he gave a half smile. "Thanks. I just wanted to let you know. Figured it was best to stop by so you weren't wondering why I bailed."

Not once in my life had a partner shown so much consideration for my feelings. In the grand scheme, I guessed it was a small thing. It felt big to me though. If he hadn't shown, I wasn't sure what I would've done. Probably sat at the booth in the corner, wondering what I did wrong and already imagining my life without him. Rhiannon called that catastrophizing.

"I really appreciate that." Propping my hands on my hips, I cocked my head to the side. "But why wouldn't I be able to have the lesson with Lizzie tonight?"

"She gets off the bus around three-thirty, and you have your lesson at seven, but I'm not sure if I'll be done by then. I don't know if I'll be able to drive her to you."

"The bus drops her off right down the street," I said, squinting with confusion. "If she doesn't mind sitting here a few hours while I finish up my shift, I can just bring her back to the ranch with me. I can drive her home too, if you want."

Eyes softening, stiff shoulders doing the same, he shook his head. "I can't ask that of you."

"You're not." I stretched over the counter and touched my lips to his. He cradled my jaw for the short while that it lasted. As I pulled back, I smiled. "I'm offering."

"Are you sure?" Those big hazel eyes scanned mine, waiting for some sign that I didn't want to do this. "Because you don't have to babysit her or anything."

"She's not a baby." I laughed. "She'll scroll on her phone, I'll get her something to eat, then we'll go on with our night. Don't worry about it. Just take care of that puppy."

There was still a bit of hesitancy in his eyes, a bit of fear, but the relief outweighed all that. He grabbed my face, pulled me back in, and kissed me again. This time harder, deeper, probably too deeply for public.

When he pulled back, between hard breaths, he just said, "Thank you."

"You're welcome." Another smile. "Good luck."

# CHAPTER 23

## *Gwen*

After Sebastian left, Molly offered to cover the last hour or two of my shift. So when Lizzie arrived at three thirty, she only had to wait half an hour for me to wrap things up. I packed us some sandwiches to go, and we were on our way to the ranch around four.

Of course, we didn't make it there until almost five, but the drive was nice. She talked about the geography test she had taken today, her plans to spend the night at Aubrey's after our lesson, and how much fun they would have snow tubing tomorrow afternoon. She talked most of the time, and I listened.

Once we were through the gates, we stopped at my cabin. I fed Honey her dinner, clipped on her leash, and the three of us walked to the rec center. Honey pranced through the snow off to the side of the gravel path, her tongue lolling out of her mouth.

Lizzie continued chattering about anything and everything. How fascinating it was that the pine trees didn't lose their greenery in the winter. The bluish moonlight reflecting off the snow. How much she enjoyed walking after dark, even though it was cold, because of how quiet everything got.

Lizzie always talked a lot, but tonight, more than usual. Was it because Sebastian and I were progressing? Was I stepping into a new role for her?

At the rec center, Honey cozied up on the carpet beneath the stage. For the most part, I sat in one of the auditorium chairs next to her. But when Lizzie had a question, or needed help with nailing a particular finger placement, I hopped up beside her. My thighs sure did get a workout as I hopped on and off that stage for the next two hours. Around seven thirty, Sebastian texted that he was on his way.

When I relayed that to Lizzie, she asked if I wouldn't mind going through the song *Ocean Eyes* with her a couple more times. I agreed.

On the third try, she hit every note with perfection. It sounded identical to the studio recording. Then she added her flares again that, dare I say, leveled it up from the original. When she hit that last note, a smile tilted the edges of my lips.

I started a slow clap that gradually progressed. When I ended a clap or two with a "Woo!" Lizzie laughed with blushing cheeks.

"It's *almost* perfect," she said, pushing a blonde tendril behind her ear. "I think my tempo was a little off. Like I was half a second too fast."

"Your tempo was perfect. Every note, every chord, was perfect, Lizzie." I propped my hands on my hips. "Keep practicing at home, but I really don't think we have much more work to do on this one. I think you're ready for your recital."

"Can you help me learn something new then?" She spoke quickly, eyes wide, nervous. "I mean, I'm supposed to perform at least one song. But I can do more. Up to three, I think. And some of the classical ballads, they're really hard. Pop is so much easier. But I want to get better. I want to get into intricate, fast-paced, expert level piano."

"You might need an expert to teach you expert level. But we can work on whatever you want to, whenever you want to."

Her shoulders softened. "Cool. I'll brainstorm the next song I want to learn."

"And I'll find the sheet music once you do."

"Awesome." A big smile, followed by a tilt of her head. "But why did you say it like that?"

"Say what like what?"

"Something about how you're not an expert. That's crazy. You play better than any of my teachers ever have."

Doubtful. I played music she *liked*. "It wasn't meant to be self-deprecating. Just a fact. I've never been really into classical music. That's not my area of expertise."

"Maybe not classical music, but you can play any sheet music that's in front of you," she said.

"I guess. But that's generally how it goes for most experienced pianists. Even you. You've been practicing this song for a couple weeks, and you're flawless at it now. We can add our own artistic flares, but if we know the basics, we can all play just about anything. That doesn't make me an expert."

"Fine, fine." She waved me off. "But you *are* really good. There's something about the way you play. It's like you've been doing it since you were in the womb."

"Hardly." Laughing, I shook my head. "My mom couldn't hold a tune if her life depended on it."

"She didn't teach you how to play?"

"Nope. Couldn't play any instruments. Could barely hum a melody." Honey's gaze met mine from the floor, so I squatted to scratch her ears. "She loved music though."

"So did my mom." Lizzie tossed one of her legs over the bench so she could face me better. "That's what everyone tells me, anyway. When I was little, I used to fall asleep to videos of her playing. That's why I wanted to learn."

My eyes burned, but I didn't let any tears gather. "That's the most beautiful thing about music. It has a way of bringing people together."

"That's how I see it. Every time I play, it makes me think of her. I don't remember her, but I think she'd have liked to see me on stage."

My chest tightened.

Lizzie didn't want me to teach her because I was an expert. Not even because she needed help with her recital.

She wanted a feminine figure to share her passions with, the way she would've with her mom. We both knew I would never, *could* never, be that. But maybe I was the closest she'd ever get to one.

"I'm sure she would," I said. "You know, I'm really enjoying these lessons together."

Lizzie's smile came back, eyes a little wide. For a girl so blatant, so headstrong, she looked all too sweet and timid now. "Really?"

"Hell yeah. I get a free concert every other Friday." She laughed, and I returned the smile. "And I love our talks."

Cheeks rosy, her eyes glassed. "So do I."

"We could do that more often." Standing, I stretched my arms out at my sides, then my neck left and right. "Just talk. On the phone, or out in the world. I've been in the market for some new clothes. Maybe we could go shopping. The post-holiday sales are gonna be crazy in a couple weeks."

"I need some stuff too, and Seabass sucks to shop with." She stood too, eyes aglow with excitement. "I'd love that."

"We'll have to set a date then."

The auditorium door clicked open.

Sebastian walked through it. Honey erupted in barks. When she realized it was him, she ran at full speed and jumped all over his legs.

As he squatted to greet her, Lizzie stood and said, "I'm gonna go grab my bag. Thanks again for the lesson."

My chest warmed. "There's nothing to thank me for."

As she disappeared behind the stage's curtain, Sebastian moved closer to me. "Where's she going?"

"Getting her stuff in the back." Now that he was only a foot or two away, I softened my voice. "How was your surgery?"

His expression reminded me of a wilted flower field after heavy rainfall. "Hard. Hard as hell. But he's okay. I have a vet tech staying with them twenty-four seven this weekend, which means I'm on call, but I really think he's gonna pull through. It was dicey there in the beginning, but the little guy has a lot of life left in him."

Chest warm with hope, I had to fight the tears that burned my eyes. "That's amazing. *You're* amazing."

"I'm just relieved." Smiling, he leaned in and touched his lips to mine. When he tugged back, that gentle glee still twinkled in his eyes. "How was the lesson?"

"Fine," Lizzie said, returning onto the stage behind me. "Gwen says that I've nailed the song and need to start working on a new one. So that's the plan for next week. But it's the weekend, and I got all my homework done in my free period this afternoon, so is it okay if I stay at Aubrey's tonight? Her mom's going to take us snow tubing on the ridge tomorrow."

"Well, hello to you too." Sebastian leaned against the stage beside me, facing her. "As long as that's okay with her mom, sure."

Grinning ear to ear, Lizzie raced down the stairs of the stage. "You're the best!"

"But I want her to call me!" Sebastian called after her as she galloped toward the exit doors. "I'll find you if I don't hear from her within the hour!"

"You will, calm down," Lizzie yelled back, waving at him over her shoulder.

Turning back to me, he narrowed his eyes, but a half smile tilted the corners of his lips. "Looks like I just got a free night. What're your plans?"

"Is that your way of asking me out?" I returned the half smile. "Because you could've just asked. You already did yesterday, if memory serves."

His eyes creased, then widened. Confirming that he'd forgotten we did, in fact, have plans. "Is that a yes then?"

"It's a probably not, actually." I gripped the edge of the stage and hopped down. "I also forgot I already had plans tonight."

He crossed his arms against his chest, scanning me over. "What does that mean?"

"That you're on-call, so I doubt you'll want to sit at a dive bar all evening." The watch on my wrist read 8:36. "I have a show at The Pour House at ten-thirty. If I want to make it on time, I need to go get ready, like, five minutes ago."

"I can enjoy sitting at a bar and watching you perform without drinking." Still scanning me for my true meaning, he uncrossed his arms. "Unless you don't want me to watch you perform."

"I'm perfectly fine with you watching me perform." Gently, I grasped hold of his shirt and craned onto my tiptoes for another kiss. "But if you make fun of my costume, I will never play in front of you again."

"Guess I'll have to resist the urge."

Scoffing, I playfully smacked his chest. "You owe me a ride back to my cabin for that."

A chuckle, followed by, "A request I'm happy to oblige."

# CHAPTER 24

## *Sebastian*

Every thought left my head when Gwen stepped out of her bedroom. Why would she ever think I'd mock her costume? She looked beautiful.

Always, she looked beautiful. Not a moment passed where I found her any less than perfect. Especially tonight.

Her makeup was nothing out of the ordinary. The usual dark wings that rimmed her eyes, accentuated with a bold red lip. The cherry red locks that dangled around her face were curlier than normal, half of it held up with a pretty flower-shaped clip.

The outfit was new, though. I had only seen Gwen in sweatpants and jeans. This was the first time I'd seen her in a dress. The black sleeves were long, the neckline low, hugging and flowing in all the right places. The skirt rested in just the right spot between her thighs and knees. Classy, elegant, with the perfect edge of sex appeal.

On the car ride to the bar, I talked more about my day, and Gwen about hers. I told her about the Cardigan Corgi puppy who'd come in for her twelve-week vaccinations. That had Gwen grinning ear to ear, talking about how, even though she preferred the Pembroke's demeanor from what she'd read, she had always wanted to meet a Cardigan.

A tangent started there about my desire to get a puppy. My office was running well now, and Lizzie was old enough that I didn't have to worry so much about her safety. Gwen suggested a corgi, and I howled with laughter. As much as I adored Honey, I wanted no part in the feisty breed.

The rest of the car ride, we bickered and laughed about which breeds were the best, which were the worst, and concluded that a golden retriever would be the perfect pick for me.

As we drove the winding back roads, teasing one another, laughing at each other, my chest was warm with fantasies. The two of us sitting on a porch somewhere, watching the dogs frolic through knee-high grass. A couple glasses of wine, laughter filling the air, and infectious smiles we passed back and forth.

A future. A life together. Something I'd never let myself imagine before.

Over the last decade, people would ask why I didn't date. I'd always said it was because my niece needed stability. It was bad enough she didn't have parents. I didn't want her to struggle with getting to know someone who may not have stuck around.

That hadn't been a lie. It hadn't been the truth either.

I just couldn't see it.

The only positive influence I'd had growing up was Rhiannon. She did everything on her own, and she did it all right.

I didn't know what a healthy couple looked like. How could I want something I'd only ever seen on TV? That wasn't real. Real relationships sucked. People lied. They hurt each other. Married couples gripped so tightly to what they wanted to be that they lost any semblance of the love they'd once had.

But maybe our relationship was different. Maybe me and Gwen, with all our baggage and scars, could be different. Not a fairytale with a happily ever after, but something positive. Something simple and safe.

When we arrived at a pub on the edge of town, one I had never once entered, we found two seats at the bar. It was a Friday night, meaning all the small tables and booths were already taken. The place reeked of cigarette smoke and cheap liquor. In the low light, we could hardly see one another. The stage in the corner took up half of the square footage.

Still, there was something sensual about this place. Specifically, about Gwen inside it. Not because Gwen belonged in shady dive bars. She was anything but comparable to the hillbillies chugging and spilling beer all over the place.

It was like her presence atop the tearing, worn-in leather barstool dressed the place up. Simply her existence here livened the atmosphere. When I'd walked in, it was only a bar. With Gwen seated inside it, it was a cabaret.

There was something about Gwen's aura that I couldn't quite put into words. If I painted her, I doubted I could capture it. As we sat there, Gwen sipping her vodka cranberry and me nursing my Pepsi, I tried to put my finger on it.

She listened so closely, admiring the country singer on stage, then made comments to me about how beautiful her inflection was, or how skilled she was with the fiddle to pull off the song that vibrated through the speakers.

A heartbeat later, when a drunk man shoulder-checked her, she not-so-subtly snapped an "Excuse you."

Such a fascinating dichotomy of a woman.

When ten thirty hit, and the bartender told her to go ahead up, I leaned back in my chair and studied every move she made. What made her so different? What was it in her demeanor that made me see a future together?

Just before she walked on stage, she fastened something around her head. It wasn't until she sat at the piano that I got a good look at it.

Across her eyes, obscuring the top half of her face, she wore a masquerade mask. The base was black, trimmed with red lace, topped with a few black feathers on the right side that wrapped into her hair.

Not so much as sparing me a glance, she started on the keys.

On many occasions now, I had witnessed her perform. Mostly at the ranch. Gwen always played the piano while the kids on stage sang holiday songs or silly musicals. Then, she had smiled and watched with pride at all the little ones who had worked so hard for their big show.

But this? This was different.

That grand piano was to Gwen what sand was to ocean waves. I didn't recognize the songs she played. But I didn't need to. This wasn't about singing along.

Watching her lips move, knowing she was singing despite the muted mic, had thoughts connecting in my mind for the first time.

Nearly a year, we had known each other. Nearly a year, we had been friends. But it wasn't until this moment that I understood her.

The way she played brought all attention to the stage, every hair on every arm to its end, and every buried tear to the corner of each eye. Like each tap of the keys was a laced lasso cast out into the crowd. It twirled around my body, around the frame of everyone else, and held us captive. What she created, what she breathed into the world, silently took hold and demanded you feel it as deeply as she did. It wasn't a plea or a request, but an insistence. Even if I wanted to, I couldn't look away. I couldn't ignore the heat that rose in my chest or the burn in my eyes.

Gwen Kane was an artist, sure. But this went deeper. She didn't just create art. She *was* art.

Art captivated. It caught the eye, and it held you in place.

A beautiful, tortured being filled to the brim with sensibilities and suffering who could only ever relay such things this way because no words in any language could capture the broad scope of who she was.

She'd wrapped me up in ribbons long ago, ready at any moment to be what she wanted, what she needed. But now, I could see the threads. I saw who she was beneath the masked, guarded exterior. I saw all the vulnerability inside her that had roped me in, and I loved her even more for it.

I was her captive, and I wanted to stay in her chains for the rest of my days.

After complimenting Gwen's performance, my stomach rumbled, and I asked if she was hungry. Her eyes lit up at the mention of food. The only place open at this time was a diner off a nearby highway. Half an hour later, just before midnight, that's where we were.

While we sipped our drinks, waiting on our meals, I got the conversation going with, "It was amazing. *You're* amazing."

Rather than brushing me off with a passive wave of her hand, Gwen propped both hands beneath her chin and gave a big smile. "Why, thank you."

Returning the smile, a quiet laugh escaped me. "But I gotta ask."

"About?"

"The mask."

Confusion pinched her brows. "Isn't it obvious?"

"It may be, but I had a seven-hour surgery today, so." I sipped my coffee. "My head's not all here at the moment."

"Anonymity." A casual shrug. "It's the same reason I sing with my mic off. Before I came to the ranch, I performed at a couple bars. Even opened for some D-list musicians. If someone were to record me singing here and put it online, someone could put together who I am. That would blow my cover and endanger the ranch."

Her answer only led to more questions. Who would find her? Her ex? Someone else? Who was she before? What did her voice sound like? Was it as magical as her piano?

But it was only curiosity. She found safety and comfort in her anonymity. What did the past matter anyway? Wasn't it a future we were after?

"See," I said, "you could've told me that it was just a part of the stage persona. That you were going for a classy meets goth vibe, and I would've believed you."

She laughed. "Guess it's a good disguise then."

"A damn good one." Leaning back in the red leather booth, I squinted her over. "So you were a singer, too?"

"I still sing," she said. "Just not on a stage."

"Are you any good?"

Narrowing her eyes, she gave a half smile. "I'm about as good at singing as you are at painting frogs smoking cigarettes."

"Whew." I clicked my tongue. "That's a shame."

She laughed. "Stop it. You're an amazing artist."

Was I skilled at duplicating an object's likeness in paint on a canvas? Sure. Was that why I did it? No.

"I told you before, I'm a painter. Not an artist."

"What's the difference to you?" She propped her elbows on the table and came closer, squinting me over. "What makes someone an artist versus a painter or a musician?"

"The product," I said. "I paint because I like painting. It's funny to make weird shit. But when you play, there's passion and fury and heartache behind it. When you're up there, you're like a piece of art yourself. When I'm painting, I'm just thinking, 'how can I make this the weirdest, coolest thing anyone has ever seen?'"

"Humor might not be an emotion, but the joy it provokes is." She laid her arms on the Formica and interlocked her fingers, smiling. "We have different styles with our art, but that doesn't make yours any less legitimate than mine. Just like a screamo band, or a country band, or a pop singer. They aren't any less of artists just because we produce different kinds of music."

"We're gonna have to agree to disagree." Raising my arms at my sides in surrender, I shrugged. "When art becomes nothing more than a product like it is for pop singers, I don't see it as art anymore."

"Now the commercialization of art, that's another story. One that I can talk about for hours." Gwen sat up, tucking one of her legs under the other. "But that's not the conversation we're having. You don't even sell your art. It's for fun, for entertainment, and for laughs. Mine is for relaxation and peace. Both are art."

I just waved her off.

"Don't dismiss me." Mouth falling open, a smile played at the corners of her lips. "You know what? I don't even think it's about your definition of what art is and isn't."

"No?"

"Nope."

"And what is it then?"

"Self-esteem issues," she said, nodding quickly. "It's typical among men like you, you know."

"Alright." I reached for a napkin at the edge of the table and patted it against the corners of my eyes. "I'm ready for your daily dose of emasculation."

"Actually, I'm trying to do the opposite." She studied me carefully. "You were the weird kid in school. You outgrew it, but in your head, you're still the awkward nerd. So now, you have chronically low confidence."

That wasn't where my self-loathing came from. But I'd entertain it. "Do I?"

"You do." A curt nod. "You disguise it with sarcasm, but I guess as your . . . I don't know, whatever I am, it's my job to compliment you. So don't argue with me when I tell you that you're an amazing artist, because you are."

Her admiration had my chest warming more than the coffee in my hands ever could. Of course, I would never say that aloud. Why? Well, I didn't know. Rhiannon would probably have a good answer if I asked.

"That sure was a bossy way to give a compliment," I said.

"Never claimed to be passive."

"I could say the same thing about you." I narrowed my gaze the same way she had hers. "Maybe your sarcasm is a disguise for your low self-esteem."

"Oh, no. It's not my low self-esteem." Gwen shook her head, tone still playful. "It's a defense mechanism because I'm afraid of letting anyone in. In Rhiannon's expert opinion, anyway."

I had said it to poke fun. Because that was how the two of us communicated. We teased and bickered. It was the root of our friendship. But I didn't believe her self-esteem was low. Gwen had a robust sense of confidence. I envied it.

"That one checks out," I said.

But she had nothing to be afraid of.

I would cut off my own hand before I dared raise it at any woman, let alone Gwen. If that was what she was afraid of, if she feared that I was putting on a show, and one day, my true colors would too closely resemble her ex-husband's, she didn't need to be afraid. This brash, sarcastic asshole was me.

I was no sheep in wolf's clothing. What you saw with me was what you got. Beneath the rough exterior, yes, I was a humanitarian. But I was, in fact, the brash, sarcastic asshole I showed to the world. That was me. I was more than that, just as everyone was more than one thing, but this was no façade.

Maybe that wasn't what she feared.

"Why do you think that is?" I asked.

Confused, Gwen asked, "Why do I think what is?"

"Why are you afraid of letting anyone in?"

Something between a scoff and a laugh escaped her. "Why is anyone afraid of letting people in?"

"Because they're afraid of getting hurt." Resting my elbows and forearms on the table, I leaned in. "I think we have that in common, actually."

"Considering you've been single for the last decade, I'd have to agree."

Always so witty, so teasing. Someone else may have found that offensive, but not me. I knew it was just Gwen's way of leveling the playing field. How could she be vulnerable when I wasn't?

"Fair enough," I said. "In my defense, I do have Lizzie to worry about. But lots of people date when they have kids, so I think you make a valid point."

"Technically, it was the point you made. I was just agreeing." She, too, rested her forearms on the table and leaned closer. "What are you afraid of?"

I couldn't say it. It'd scare her. And it should've. She should've, on some level, been afraid of a future with me. With genes like mine, everyone should've been afraid to get too close to me.

But she deserved some version of the truth. "The American dream. A white picket fence that seems oh-so-perfect to the rest of the world but looks more like iron bars from the inside looking out."

She arched her brows at that, eyes softening. "Deep."

A crooked half smile. "Your turn."

With a quiet sigh, she returned the expression. Only for a moment. Then her gaze fell to the table, around the room, and she nibbled on her lower lip. Supposed this wasn't the question Rhiannon had asked in therapy. It took longer than expected for her to look me in the eyes again.

When she did, they were the gentlest I had ever seen them. "Betrayal."

"Being betrayed by what, exactly?"

"Anything. Everything." The wall stayed down. Her voice, her eyes, everything about her stayed soft. "Infidelity, sure. That would suck. Violence, obviously. Promises that we're in this together, that we want this to work, but not showing up for the hard conversations that will inevitably arise. Stonewalling or gaslighting when I'm upset about something and want to work through it. Swearing that you're in this, that you want this, and then abandoning me when things aren't easy."

Without thought, I said, "I'm not going anywhere."

Her eyes sparkled for half a second, then her cheeks turned red. An awkward smile pulled at the corners of her lips as she leaned back.

"What?" I studied her. "What was wrong with that answer?"

"Nothing. Nothing at all." Smiling, she shook her head. "It's just—I don't know."

I slid my hand across the table and onto hers. As our fingers twined together, I said, "I think you do. And hey, you're the one who said it. You want someone who's going to show up for the hard conversations, don't you?"

"Well, yeah, but—"

"But you're gonna be the one who ducks out?"

She traced her tongue along her teeth, a smile still resting over it. A deep inhale dropped between her barely parted lips. "We haven't been doing this for very long. It's not that I don't believe you, but words are words."

I understood. She needed time to believe me. I didn't blame her for that. It's not like I was in any rush either. "That's alright. Eventually, you'll believe me."

She gave my hand a squeeze. "And eventually, you'll believe me."

The only problem was me. That I wasn't sure if I believed myself.

So, I changed the subject. "You know, I like seeing you perform."

"Yeah?"

"Yeah. There's something different about you afterward."

"It's the poor folks' high."

I snorted. "The what?"

"That's what my mom used to call it. That feeling after a live performance. Even if I'm not the one performing, when I leave a concert, if the music's good, I just feel this rush. Like nothing could go wrong. Like everything makes sense for once. Like my brain has finally shut off."

It seemed to me that, for the first time, her mind was fully open. Maybe the music dulled the racing thoughts, her worries and anxieties, but she was more available and vulnerable than ever before. That was what I liked about it. How honest it made her.

"But why phrase it like that?" I asked. "Anyone can listen to music. It's not class dependent."

"She always said because it was similar to coke. The rich man's high." Laughing, Gwen shook her head. "It's strong, it comes on fast, and it's gone in heartbeats."

I laughed too. "I guess I can see that."

"Does painting give you that same rush?"

"Not really. I get more of a rush when I successfully finish a surgery," I said. "Knowing I saved a life, knowing I helped someone, that's what I get a rush from. Art is just fun for me."

The smile that spread across her lips made my heart skip a beat. "I think that's my favorite thing about you."

"What's that?"

"How much you care." Her eyes twinkled, perhaps with tears, but she didn't let them escape. "That's what I meant earlier. You act like you're so apathetic, but you're so gentle. The way you are with Honey. How great of a job you're doing with Lizzie. The fact that you could have been a billionaire, but you chose to fund the ranch . . . I don't know. Your heart's just so big."

I tried my best not to cringe, but inside, I did just that.

Gwen was an intelligent woman. Surely she wasn't so naïve. After all the time she'd spent with Rhiannon, all she had learned at the ranch, why did she keep her rose-tinted glasses on?

I knew what a bad man was. My father had been. I was not that. Yes, I was a half decent man. But only half decent.

"I don't think I've ever pretended to be apathetic," I said, surprised at how timid my voice came out. "That's just how I am sometimes."

She laughed again. "Can you just take a damn compliment?"

It wasn't the compliment that made me uncomfortable. It was what that compliment implied.

The dark exterior was not an act. It was a part of myself I wished I could lock away. I could be cold. I could shut myself off from everyone and everything when I had to.

I wasn't my father. But I was my father's son. I kept a noose around my temper, but it was there. It could break the rope I had around its neck if it tried hard enough, if it needed to escape.

It had before.

It wasn't a ticking nuke, sure to explode again. More like an idle bomb lost in rubble after a war. Years could go by, decades even. Then someone would step on it.

And boom.

Off it'd go.

I was not a passive man. I could be, and had been, violent.

But not to Gwen. I would never hurt her. No matter how dark, how cruel I could be, I would never direct it at her.

There was no way to say that, to make her understand that complexity without scaring her away. Her paranoia and distrust would send her running if she knew it all.

I couldn't risk that. I wanted this. I wanted *her*.

But I didn't know how to explain it all.

So I said, "I don't deserve a pedestal, Gwen. Don't put me on one."

"Please." Waving me off with one hand, she squeezed mine with the other. "I don't have anyone on a pedestal."

"I'm just saying. I've seen what happens when women put barely decent men on pedestals. It's not good for anyone."

"You're not 'barely decent.'" Her eye contact was still soft, but intense. "I see you for who you are, and that's what I like so much. Most people try to hide the bad. But you do the opposite. You hide the best parts of yourself. You pretend you're not as soft as you are."

"Maybe they're not the best parts. Maybe softness gets you hurt."

She huffed, eyes falling to our hands, still twined together. "And is that what you like about me? That I'm never soft?"

"That's what I adore about you."

Gwen rested her chin in her hands again. She flashed a grin. "Then we have a perfect understanding of one another."

Me, more than her.

# CHAPTER 25

## *Gwen*

### *A Few Weeks Later*

This was my first major holiday at the ranch.

I'd arrived just after the new year. So grateful to be out of the position I was in, I'd never given much thought to what the festivities here would look like. Now that I was witnessing it, only one word could describe it: magical.

So many women filled the cafeteria, our Thanksgiving was like a concert for the world's biggest pop star. Sebastian and Lizzie met me at the doors. Simone saved a table big enough for all of us—Delilah, Rhiannon, Axel, Junie, Sebastian, Lizzie, and me. Once Sebastian, Lizzie, and I filled plates with the basics for the table—turkey, mac & cheese, green bean casserole, cranberry sauce, and pumpkin pie—we weaved through the crowd to join the rest of them.

Honey sat at Simone's feet, giving her a look I knew well. One that said, *See? I'm waiting patiently for my next snack.*

"Aw, no drinks?" Junie asked, surveying our smorgasbord.

Sebastian grumbled something under his breath, barely able to juggle the mound of turkey and mac & cheese he already held.

Laughing, I sat across from her. "Didn't you bring your juice boxes?"

"Yeah, but Mommy shared them with everybody." She crossed her arms against her chest. "And mine's empty."

"Everybody else shares with you." Simone tugged her in and planted a kiss above her braided pigtails. "It's not empty yet anyway. Finish it off, then we'll go and find another drink."

Junie pouted some more, picking at the mac & cheese Sebastian laid before her.

"Hey, Rhiannon?" Delilah poked her head around Axel, looking for her at the head of the table. "Is it okay if I brought a dish? I wasn't sure if that was allowed. It's not enough for everyone, but I eat it every Thanksgiving, and I wanted you guys to try it."

"Of course it's okay." Rhiannon propped her elbows on the table, lined with a paper cloth decorated in hand turkeys and cornucopias. I hoped they were cornucopias, anyway. The kids at the daycare had created the masterpiece. "What is it, honey?"

Grinning ear to ear, Delilah stretched below her into an insulated shopping bag. She came back up with an aluminum dish covered in a plastic lid. "Just my grandma's pecan pie. It's nothing special, really."

"I'll be the judge of that." Lizzie stretched across the table for it.

As Lizzie cut into it with a plastic knife, Rhiannon said, "I'm sure it's amazing, sweetheart. Thanks for bringing it."

Cheeks bright red, Delilah waved her off. "It's the least I can do. I'm just so grateful to be here. Thank you again. For everything."

"I think the point of today is to thank any and everyone." Simone swayed around Axel to meet Delilah's gaze. "So thank you for the pie and thank you for joining us."

Delilah's blush stayed in place, but she smiled as she rubbed her hands over her arms.

"I could go for a beer," Sebastian said, spooning some mashed potatoes onto his plate.

"You and me both." Axel covered his mouth between chews. "If you're getting up, mind getting me one?"

"And some extra plates," Lizzie said, struggling to cut through the pecan crust. "Maybe a real knife too. Oh, and a couple of napkins? Preferably some wet ones?"

Shoulders sinking, Sebastian grunted with annoyance. "Anything else, your highness?"

I laughed and started to stand. "Come on. Four hands are better than two."

He ushered me back down. "No, no. You sit. I'll just grab one of those carts from the back." Standing, he looked around the table. "Anybody else need anything?"

"Well, if you're getting a cart . . ." Smiling, I batted my eyelashes. Already defeated, he smiled and waited for me to go on. "Glass of wine, please?"

"Red or white?"

"Red. And sweet."

"Can you get my drink too?" Junie asked.

"Guessing that's not wine, huh?" Sebastian asked Simone.

Now it was Simone's shoulders sinking. Sighing, she stood. "Come on, kid. Let's get your drink."

"The kitchen's chaos right now," Rhiannon said, standing as well. "I'll get you the cart, but you're loading it, and you're pushing it."

"Yes, ma'am." Sebastian planted a kiss on the top of my head. "I'll be back."

"I'll be here." We exchanged another one of those sweet expressions as he headed into the sea of people with Rhiannon.

That left me, Delilah, Lizzie, and Axel. I said, "And then there were four."

Axel glanced at Delilah, then Lizzie. "Shit, would one of you mind doing me another favor?"

"What do you need?" Delilah asked.

"I've got to head out in a couple of minutes to plow Main Street." He reached into his pocket and held out his keys. "Mind starting the truck for me?"

"Yeah, sure." Delilah gave him a pat on the back as she stood. "Where's it at?"

"The back alley," Axel said.

Smiling awkwardly, Delilah's cheeks got red again. "And where might that be?"

"I'm waiting on a good knife anyway." Lizzie stood, waving in a come-here motion over her shoulder. "Come on. I'll show you."

"You're the best," Delilah said, holding on to Lizzie's shoulders so they wouldn't get separated in the crowd.

And then there were two.

"Probably shouldn't be drinking on the job," I said to Axel.

"I'll drink it when I get back." He wiped some food from his lip, gaze unusually heavy against me. "Simone healed up nicely."

My stomach twisted. I cleared my throat. "Yeah, she looks good."

"Didn't look too good that day though." He took a sip from his water on the table. "I imagine, anyway. Since that's the day you lied to me."

Shit. I figured this moment would come eventually. Honestly, I'd been dodging him ever since it happened, because Axel wasn't the type of guy to drop a grudge.

"Look, I just did what she asked me to. She didn't want anyone to know, so—"

"You did it really well. The lying, I mean." Elbows on the table, leaning in, Axel lowered his voice. "You did what you had to. To protect your friend. I respect that."

Not where I thought this was going.

He posed those words so carefully. As if he'd rehearsed them. There was something in his inflection that sounded familiar. The blunt nature of it. How poised and blank his face was.

Like the texts had been.

Was this his way of confirming my suspicion? Was he saying, in so many words, that he was the anonymous friend who helped me get rid of David's body?

"Well, like you said." I crossed my arms and laid them on the table as well. "I did what I had to."

"Right." His eyes flicked between mine. "We've all done things we aren't proud of, but we had to. That's the nature of this place, isn't it?"

That tightness in my stomach softened. This was it, wasn't it? The texter was obsessed with their anonymity. If the roles were reversed, I would be too. If I was the one who'd gotten rid of the body, if I only wanted to make sure the tracks I covered weren't *un*covered by the person who did it, this was how I would address it. I would dance around the point I was trying to make, hoping they understood.

Maybe this was the closest I would ever get to confirmation that the anonymous texter was on my side.

"I guess so," I said. "Have you ever done anything like that? Lied about something huge because you had no other choice?"

"I've done worse than lied." A crooked half smile. "I mean, I know Simone didn't tell you where David was after that went down. But he couldn't have made it very far. If I would've shown in that moment, that prick would've never walked again."

There it was.

For a few heartbeats, we just stared at one another. Knowing. Understanding.

He wouldn't admit to his part, and I wouldn't admit to mine.

But we both loved Simone. We would do anything to protect her or anyone else in this place. That was Axel's job title, after all. Security.

I would never know beyond any doubt, but sitting here, holding his gaze, was the most secure I had felt since that first text had appeared on my screen.

"Good thing we all have each other's backs around here," was what I managed in response.

"I'll drink to that." Standing, Axel nodded to someone behind me. "I'm gonna go clear Main. Don't drink that by the time I get back."

"I'll grab you another if I do." Sebastian looked over the overflowing lunch-lady cart he pushed. "Where the hell did Lizzie go?"

"Just started up the truck for Axel." Clearing my throat, I forced a smile. "Where is that wine?"

I couldn't express my relief.

It was Axel. And we agreed—everyone at the ranch had each other's backs. If I had to guess, he'd seen me in David's car—or followed me to the creek to be certain it was handled—saw the body float, and brought it back to the ranch. There, he put all those tools in the garage to use.

No body, no crime.

I was gonna get away with this, Axel was why, and I could finally breathe.

Finally, I could bask in all the good things I had going now. Like Simone and Junie's safety. Like my new friendship with Delilah. Like Sebastian.

I'd been so afraid to fall, for him to learn who I was, for everything we were building to crash down around me. But maybe I was finally safe, too. Maybe I could relax my shoulders and let out a deep breath.

Life felt so good after that chat with Axel, days passed when I forgot what I had even done to David.

It only resurfaced at group.

Whenever I heard a woman tell her story, or watched her cry at the memories, that torment lit a familiar fire in me. Simone had asked to talk about it a couple times. Some of the time, she just wanted to talk about her own feelings. Her frustration that he had shown. Her regret over not having gone to Rhiannon with it to begin with. The fear of one day having to explain any of it to Junie.

As well as her relief that he was gone, and that he would never come back.

Then she'd ask me about my own feelings.

I could never answer, because I feared the way she would look at me if I told her the truth.

It'd been the right thing to do. That was my truth. If I were in that situation again, I still would have killed him. And I felt no remorse for it.

I knew how that sounded. Like I was some type of sick psychopath with no empathy or compassion.

But just looking at Simone and Junie made my eyes water with compassion and my throat thick with empathy. I had it for those who were hurt, not those who did the hurting.

How many women at the ranch would be safe if the men who put us here got a real punishment for what they'd done? What if they got what I'd done to David? After all, these men had already killed us once. Our hearts may have still been beating, but part of us had died at their hands. Was a life for a life truly cruel?

In a perfect world, it may have been. The world we lived in, though, was far from perfect. Wednesday group sessions were a reminder of that. Each week, I remembered just how screwed up the world was outside of the ranch.

But I wasn't sure I could get anyone else to understand. I wasn't sure someone who hadn't been in a position like Simone and I had *could* understand. I wasn't even sure she did.

I listened to all the other women, all their pain, and tried to forget what I had done. Not because I was ashamed, but because if I spoke up too loudly, or too quickly, I would go on tirades about how much I hated men like David. How angry I was that they got to go on living while so many of these women had to leave their lives, even their voices, behind.

And I would end up telling the truth.

I'd killed a man, and I wanted to kill so many more.

So far, I had gotten away with it.

Then Light Up Night came around.

Most towns held their Light Up Night in early- to mid-November. We were almost halfway into December now and tonight would be the first night we lit the tree.

Over the last month, everyone chipped in hanging lights, tinsel, and wreaths. Each door down Second Street was wrapped in some variation of wrapping paper, all featuring a big red, green, silver, or golden bow in the center. Nearly every inch of the café and rec center was covered in twinkling golden lights.

Christmas music pulsed from speakers in the corners. Fold-up tables covered in snowflake or Christmas present cloths lined both sides of the road, stretching from the garage at the end of the street to the fifteen-foot-tall pine tree just outside the rec center doors. Each was filled with cookies or hot chocolate or games.

Looking around at it all had my heart fluttering. No one could call me a grinch, but I had never been all that excited over holidays. But maybe that was because I had no one to be excited with.

Now, Simone had her forearm tucked into mine. Delilah walked beside her. Sebastian curled his fingers into my other hand. Lizzie and Junie had been walking alongside us, until they caught sight of the spinning wheel game by the cafeteria. Now, the two of them were standing in line while we scoped out the cookie table a dozen feet from the rec center doors.

I didn't want this day to end.

"God, she is so sweet with her." Simone gestured to Lizzie, squatting to say something to Junie that had them both laughing. "If she ever wants to make some extra cash babysitting, you've got my number."

"Don't you have, like, a thousand babysitters around here?" Sebastian arched a brow at her. "There's a whole daycare down the street."

Simone covered her mouth to keep the thumb drop cookie crumbs inside. "When I was Lizzie's age, I liked babysitting. It taught me a lot of life skills. And the cash wasn't bad either."

"I don't know if I would call child-rearing a life skill," Sebastian said, "and I don't know if it's one I particularly want her learning. I'll be happy if she remains child-free her entire life. But babysitting Junie is a lot safer than working at a fast-food chain, so that's alright by me. You pass it along to her though."

"Speaking of children," I said to Delilah, "how are you liking the new job?"

A smile stretched across her bright red lips. Her full cheeks scrunched up into her eyes, obscuring the pretty brown shadows and mascara she had surely worked hard on. "Oh my God, I love it."

A couple weeks ago, Delilah had spoken to Rhiannon about what sort of job she could take on at the ranch. They'd decided the daycare was a good fit. She'd agreed to take any shift, doing any duties.

"I've always loved kids," she said, "but I can't even describe it. Being around so many of them, playing games all day—I just love it so much. My dream job is being a preschool or daycare teacher full-time. I really think that's the path I want to take."

"Aw," Simone said, dabbing at cookie crumbs along her smiling lips.

There weren't enough words in the English language to describe how beautiful and wondrous it was when all the work at the ranch paid off. A young girl had a life, a real, marvelous life ahead of her because she'd chosen to start over.

I snatched one of the Russian tea cookies I had brought for the festival. "Have you talked to anyone about how that would work? Getting started in college, I mean."

"Yeah, one of the girls at the nursery explained it to me. I have a meeting with Colleen next week and she'll get me started with a counselor at a local college. I might even be able to do it online."

"That's convenient," Simone said. "My schooling was all hands-on. It was a bitch driving all the way to the closest beauty school."

"I bet," Delilah said. "Part of me wants the whole college experience, but I think I'll be okay with just the degree."

"The college experience isn't all it's cracked up to be anyway." Sebastian sipped his hot cocoa and smacked his lips. "I enjoyed it, and I'm grateful for it, but the degree is what you're really after."

"Seabass!" Lizzie called, barely visible on the other side of Main Street through all the bustling heads. "Come here!"

A heavy sigh lifted and softened his shoulders. Despite the drama, the hint of a smile told me he wasn't all that mad. "Duty calls."

He pecked my cheek before weaseling into the crowd.

"I can't." Simone shook her head, smiling as her eyes flicked between me and him. "I can't with how cute you guys are."

"Ew." With a wrinkled nose, I took another bite of my cookie. "Can you not refer to our relationship the way you might refer to a puppy?"

"How in the hell is being called cute a bad thing?" Delilah laughed. "You guys *are* cute."

"Cute is what you call teenagers in puppy love."

"Cute is what you call people who look happy and healthy and normal," Simone said. "When I look at you two, all I can see is a picket fence."

"Again, I say, *ew*." Quite literally, I had to fight a gag. "Been there. Done that. And I don't think either of us are cut out for picket fences. Maybe a cottage in the woods though."

"Aw!" Delilah clapped her hands together before her chest. "That's what it's looking like? Like you guys are gonna, you know, be together? Long term?"

"I don't know." My cheeks must've been bright red, because they felt like fires on my face despite the snow and chill nipping at my nose. "We haven't talked about it. But it's not like we're just hooking up or anything. Usually dating has the intention of a relationship."

"Obviously." Simone's tone was the slightest bit annoyed. "It's just a little shocking. Opening yourself up is a huge accomplishment."

I made no attempt to disguise my eye roll.

"It's not a bad thing." Delilah stretched out to rub her hand up and down my arm. "It's a great thing. I know for girls like me, who haven't been here for very long, it's just beautiful to see you two so happy."

"I guess," I agreed. "But don't get too excited. We're taking things slow."

"And that's amazing." Not a touchy-feely person myself, I was still adjusting to all of Delilah's mannerisms. This time, she grabbed my hand with a big smile and squeezed with all her might. "I'm so happy for you."

"Thanks." When she released my hand, I tried to sound as enthusiastic as she did. "I'm sure one day, you're gonna have the happily ever after you're waiting on too."

"Oh, I know I will." Still wearing that massive smile, she shimmied her shoulders with excitement. "But I'm gonna do it the right way. I'm going to go to school, I'm going to get a degree, I'm gonna make sure that I have my own money and my own life to fall back on, and I'm not going to wind up where I did before. That's for sure."

"Ha, that rhymed," Simone giggled.

To Delilah, I said, "I can't think of a better plan."

"Me neither," Delilah agreed. "It's funny though, because I have as many fantasies about this happy, independent life that I want to live as I do about telling my ex off."

"Yeah," I said. "I fantasize about that sometimes too. Also watching him cry, for some reason?" Simone choked on a laugh, and Delilah snickered. "I mean, I watched him cry many times. He always did when I told him I was gonna leave. But I would have loved to see him realize that I wasn't coming back."

"That's exactly what I mean," Delilah said. "And I know it sounds cruel, but damn it, after everything he did to me, I feel like I'm entitled to a little karma."

"Not gonna lie," Simone said, sipping on her cocoa, eyes dark, "closure's nice."

"Closure." Delilah snapped her fingers and pointed at Simone. "That's what I want. Closure, and maybe a little bit of nonviolent revenge."

Simone muttered, "Violence isn't so bad either."

"What was that?" Delilah asked, clearly not having heard.

Light returned to Simone's eyes. "At the end of the day, you have your whole life going for you. A plan for the future, the community you're building here. All that outweighs revenge."

"I know that rationally," Delilah said. "Just a nice little fantasy that helps me fall asleep."

Rhiannon's voice carried from somewhere behind me. "Simone."

When I found her in the crowd, I waved. It was far from unusual for Rhiannon to be nearby and call for one of us. The look in her eyes made my heartbeat quicken.

Then a navy blue uniform approached from behind her.

Edwards.

My stomach dropped into my ass.

Rhiannon brushed past half a dozen people in the crowd. "I've been looking for you everywhere."

"We've been here." Simone managed to keep her tone flat, normal. Even her smile looked legitimate as she said, "Merry Christmas. Or Happy Holidays. Whichever floats your boat, officer."

"Merry Christmas to you too." His cadence, posture, even his smile looked just as natural. "How you ladies doing tonight?"

"Can't complain. Just enjoying all the festivities." As Simone grabbed a cookie for herself, she got an extra for him. "You're not gluten-free, are you? Because you have to try these. Gwen is a goddess behind an oven."

"Not gluten-free, but I am in a cut right now—"

"Wait 'til the new year." Simone extended the cookie. "They're worth every calorie."

Lips plastered together, he accepted. "Thanks."

Delilah glanced between the four of us. "Is everything alright?"

"Everything's just fine," Rhiannon said, tone as kind and casual as usual. "It's just about that report Simone had to file a couple of weeks ago."

"What report?" Sebastian's voice came from behind just as his warm fingertips brushed my lower back. His free hand outstretched for Edwards. "How've you been, man?"

"Same shit, different day." Edwards accepted the shake, then looked over the two of us. "What about you? What's up with you lately?"

"Too much." Sebastian chuckled, his voice a touch deeper.

Now that I thought about it, in the last year I'd known Sebastian, I hadn't seen him interact with another man. Aside from Axel, anyway. His voice remained a few octaves higher for my friends and me. Did he intentionally deepen it around other men?

"We should get coffee sometime and catch up," he told Edwards.

"I'm sure we can make that work."

Turning to Delilah, Sebastian said, "Junie wanted your help with something over there. A friendship bracelet you guys made last night at the daycare? I don't know, she's having problems with it."

"I swear, if that latch broke again," Delilah said under her breath. "I'll be right back. Save me some cookies, Simone!"

"No promises," Simone said, grabbing another. "Anywho. What's going on?"

Edwards glanced at Sebastian, then at me, then back to Simone. "Do you want to go somewhere private?"

"She's my best friend. I'm going to tell her anyway." Simone sipped her cocoa to wash down the cookie. "And he's her boyfriend, so she's probably gonna tell him too. It's okay."

"Alright. If you insist." Edwards raised a hand in surrender. "Look, after you filed a report, and we knew David had been nearby, I reached out to his PO, who connected me to the PD in your hometown. Turns out he was already on the run when he showed here and did what he did to you."

"Wait, here?" Sebastian asked, glancing between Simone and me. He looked at Rhiannon too. "Who is this? What the hell did he do?"

"My husband," Simone said, tone casual. "My *ex*-husband. He didn't show up here, at the ranch. He showed up at my work, harassed me, and messed me up a bit." Her attention went back to Edwards. "But that doesn't surprise me. David's always on the run. He owes somebody money, or he has a warrant, or whatever the case is, that guy lives under the radar."

"That was my first thought. Especially when I had a look at his record. What wasn't expunged anyway." Edward's jaw tightened at that. "He's gotten a bigger rap sheet since you left him. A real big rap sheet. This latest charge, what he's running from, might be the worst one yet."

"I don't know about that. He's done a lot of bad things that the cops never got wind of," Simone said. "But what is it this time?"

"Primary suspect in a gang-related murder," Edwards said. "I can't get into the specifics, but the evidence they have against him is compelling." He leaned in and lowered his voice. "Off the record, he definitely did it."

Simone didn't even flinch. "That doesn't surprise me either."

"Problem is, he was living under the radar for a couple months back in Wyoming. And no one's heard from him since he came here."

"Probably because we're so close to the border." Rhiannon crossed her arms against her chest, tone defensive. "We're only a couple hours' drive from Regina, Canada."

"That's true," Simone said. "He always said that if things went to shit here, he'd run to the Yukon. Said there's so much land up there, nobody would ever find him."

"Nobody's ruling that out," Edwards said. "But after I talked to that PD, I got a call from a woman. Angela Burke? Does that ring any bells?"

"David's mom." Simone rolled her eyes. "Yeah, I know her."

"Right." Edwards rubbed a hand down his jaw. "Look, I don't want to stir anything up here. I didn't give her your name or nothing like that. But I guess he'd talked to her before he came here. Even though he was off grid, they were in contact."

*Shit. Holy shit.*

"Oh yeah, they talk every day," Simone said. "Always was a mama's boy."

"My point here is, somebody knew where he was before he came here. And now, no one does."

"Okay, I get that." Rhiannon took the slightest step inward, slightly in front of Simone. "But I don't get how that's her problem. Or mine. Or anyone else's here."

"I guess it's not, ma'am." Edwards raised his hands at his sides. "And I'm not saying I disagree with you. Considering the charges he was facing, and everything he's done to Simone, it wouldn't surprise me one bit if you're right, and he did run to Canada. Ain't like there's service in the deep parts of the Yukon."

"Then what's your point here, kid?"

At Rhiannon's voice, his grew timid. "Angela's poking. She's asking questions. It wouldn't surprise me if she made a trip up here."

"If she does, tough shit." Rhiannon's posture stiffened. "She ain't welcome through my gates."

"As is your right." Edwards raised his hands in surrender once more. "And look, I know what this place is. I know how important it is. So does the sheriff. We know all the women here are victims, and we're not gonna hurt you any more than your pasts already have. But because we care about each other, we wanted you to know that someone's asking questions. So it might not be a bad idea to lock up and keep things secure for the time being."

*Shit.*

# CHAPTER 26

## *Angela*

She didn't look the same as she used to.

Five years had passed. It made sense that she wouldn't look identical. Still, each time Angela watched her walk into the coffee shop—Maple & Thyme—she had to do a double take.

Jess had always been pretty. That's what David saw in her, Angela had always known. It's not like the girl had that great of a personality.

When they'd met as teenagers, Jess already had a womanly figure. Full chest, wide hips, narrow waist. Her midsection was the only place she didn't carry weight. Tack her height onto that, and the girl could pass for a model. Youthful in the face, not a stretch mark in sight.

Angela smiled at the fact that life had caught up with her. Now, she wore those trendy high-waisted jeans that—yeah, showed off her round hips and big ass—but made that mound around her stomach all the more obvious.

This was who Jess had become, and she thought she could do better than David?

Aside from Jess's figure, which she was rapidly losing with age, what did she even bring to a relationship? One thing was for sure. She would never again land a man as beautiful as Angela's son.

Through the glass windows, she watched Jess exchange a few words with another young woman. Mid-twenties, maybe? She stood behind the counter, her cherry red hair swept into a curly bun.

She was pretty too, but in a different way. That woman had a cuteness about her. She looked soft. Sweet. Angela would never understand the girls these days and their need to dye their hair such obnoxious colors, but even with it, she still looked normal. Approachable.

Jess didn't.

That jet-black hair with hints of blue throughout looked absurd. At least red hair was something you could be born with. No one came out with blue hair.

Trashy. That was the only word Angela could use for it.

She flicked her cigarette into the ashtray and pulled in another deep draw. Jess and that girl kept talking. Laughing. Over the last three days since Angela had arrived in Black Pines, she had watched Jess walk into this building each morning. Those two girls always shared some pleasantries, but today was different.

Jess reached across the counter to adjust the other woman's apron. That girl, the redheaded one, shooed her away with a wave of her hand and splashed some water at her. Jess laughed in response.

That was not the way a typical customer and employee relationship worked. Those two were friends.

Maybe Angela would stop in for coffee. Build a rapport. Then ask the other woman questions.

But she could do that later.

She had just sat outside the salon all day, waiting for the place to clear out. There was no use in confronting Jess in a crowd. She would do what she'd always done. Play the victim. Call the cops. Kick Angela out.

No, no, no. Angela had to time this just right. She needed a private moment with Jess.

Maybe she'd have more luck finding a private moment with Junie instead.

Jess walked out of the restaurant, iced coffee in hand.

Angela hated that look on her face. So smiley, so smug.

How dare she smile? How dare she be happy when Angela spent every waking moment worrying about her son?

Hands clenched tight around the steering wheel, Angela watched Jess walk down the street, and click her car alarm. Further down, the lights flickered.

The other days this week, Jess had gotten a ride with someone else to work. Angela assumed it was because Jess was too broke for a car. She always had been before.

Now, she watched her step into a shiny Toyota Corolla. Nothing fancy, but brand spanking new. Couldn't have been more than a year old.

Jess took a moment to turn over the engine, but the moment she pulled out of the parking spot, Angela was on her tail. At least a hundred feet behind. She made sure to let others pass as they started onto the winding mountain trail. That way, there were a few car lengths between them. If Jess saw her, she would do that victim bullshit again. She'd call the cops and then pursue charges and blah blah blah.

It wasn't like Angela was stalking her. Not really. She was just watching. Learning.

She kept her eyes on Jess's flank. Followed every turn she took. Even snapped a quick photo of her license plate. In TV shows, they were always able to find people that way. Angela would too.

If she couldn't find her address first.

Angela followed her deeper and deeper into the mountains. More than half an hour driving onto the darkest and dimmest of roads. The sun was still shining, but the snow-covered tree canopy hardly let anything through. Her stomach curled and coiled the farther they got from civilization.

Bile burned up her throat when Jess turned onto a gravel road.

Did she know? Had she realized Angela was following her? Was Jess leading Angela to her son in the worst way she could imagine?

Angela pulled over.

She waited on the side of the road. She checked where they were on a map, but all it mentioned was some forest.

Why had Jess driven into a forest, alone, not long before nightfall?

Her fingers trembled and her heart slammed harder. Time passed, but she couldn't say how much. She just had an odd, sinking sensation that she was in danger. That Jess knew, and Jess would do to her what she had done to David.

Whatever that may have been.

Cars drove past. One woman even rolled down her window and asked if Angela needed any help. Angela only shook her head, forcing a smile.

Then, that very woman, in an old beat-up van, turned down the gravel road.

Angela waited. She waited until that van was out of sight, then shifted into drive.

She kept a distance. The other woman couldn't have seen her, not through the cloud of snow that floated from her van's rooftop.

The moment Angela saw her taillights, she tapped her brakes. She stayed practically frozen between the conifer trees, waiting for the dust to settle behind that woman's vehicle.

When it did, other shapes became clear. A tall metal fence, wrapped in barbed wire. A small metal box—the kind the correction officers talked through when Angela had visited David or her late husband in jail.

A security measure of some kind.

But there were only trees behind the fence. Trees and a gravel road stretching uphill.

That fence. The longer Angela stared at it, the sicker she felt.

Something was wrong here. Something had happened. Angela couldn't put words to it, but a mother knew. A mother *always* knew.

*What the hell is this place?*

# CHAPTER 27

### *Gwen*

### *A Few Weeks Later*

Rhiannon faced me from her armchair. I sat cross-legged on the floral sofa Simone, Delilah, and I claimed each Wednesday night for group. For the fourth week in a row now, only Rhiannon and I sat here, mostly in silence, aside from an occasional question from Rhiannon.

We'd gotten past the "How are you?" and "Anything new going on?" before we moved onto "How have the nightmares been?"

"I haven't had any," I told her today. "As long as I smoke before bed, I sleep like a baby."

"That's a good thing," Rhiannon replied. "Did you always smoke weed?"

Was that her way of asking if I had a problem? "I liked it when I was a teenager. It started giving me anxiety in my early twenties, so I quit. Insomnia and nightmares kicked in after I came here, so I took Simone's advice and started again."

"If the nightmares and insomnia improved, would you quit again?"

"Probably." Chewing the inside of my cheek, I squinted at her. "What does that matter?"

"I guess it doesn't." She lifted her legs and crossed them beneath her, doing her best to make me feel like this was a casual hangout. Her next question was proof that it wasn't.

"Did your mom smoke?"

"Probably."

"Probably?"

"Yeah. Probably."

"So you don't know?"

I blew a raspberry. "I didn't know what she was smoking when I was a kid, but in hindsight, it smelled like weed. Sometimes smelled like burnt plastic too, which was probably the crack. Maybe meth? I don't know. But is that what you wanted to hear? That my mom was a crackhead? She was a horrible mother, and that's why I wound up where I did?"

"I never said that." Rhiannon's eyes and voice softened. She tilted her head, her long braids falling over one shoulder. "Is that how you feel?"

"Is what how I feel?"

"Like she was, in your words, a crackhead and a horrible mother who's to blame for your relationship with Troy."

My scoff was involuntary. "No. That is not how I feel."

"How do you feel, then?"

"For my mom?"

"Yes. For your mom."

"I don't know." I clenched my teeth together. "Like she did the best she could."

"That may be true." Rhiannon nodded, eyes still gentle. "But that wasn't what I asked."

"Yes, it was. You asked how I felt about my mom."

"Everything you just said was a rationalization of her behavior." Rhiannon frowned. "Not a feeling. So how do you feel for your mom?"

"How do I feel about the way she raised me? Or how do I feel for her as a human being?"

"Either. Both."

"Sorry," I said. "I feel sorry for her."

"Why is that?"

"Because her life sucked. Her dad was abusive, and her mom did nothing to stop it. She ran away from home when she was fifteen. Then she got pregnant with me, by a man who wasn't much different than her dad." My tone was sharp, abrupt. "And that sucks. It sucks her life was as hard as it was."

"That does suck." Rhiannon propped her elbow on the armrest, cupping her chin in her palm. "Do you feel the same way about the way she raised you? Sorry?"

This time, it was more of an annoyed huff. "I feel like she did the best she could."

"Not a feeling, Gwen."

"I don't resent her for it. She wasn't a perfect mother, but she loved me, and she did everything she could for me."

"I believe that."

"Then what's the point here?" I threw my arms in the air. "I don't blame my mom for my marriage. I made my own choices. The trauma from it, having to leave it behind, that's on me."

"You're right," she said. "Those were your choices."

"Then what, Rhiannon? How does talking about my mom help me with anything?"

"I didn't say it would help you." Rhiannon crossed her legs and settled into her seat. "It'd help *me* understand you. But if you don't want to talk about her, we won't. Let's talk about something more recent."

"Like Troy?" His name tasted like vomit on my tongue.

A hint of a smile teased the corner of her lip. "If you want to."

"I'd rather not."

"Nothing in particular you'd like to talk about?"

"Not really, no." Dropping one foot to the ground, I leaned back into the cushions. "I don't really get why I'm in here at all. One-on-one therapy with you is for the girls who are really struggling, and I'm not. I've been here for almost a year. I'm fine. As soon as I got away from that son of a bitch, I was fine."

"I believe that *you* believe that. But to say that you're fine, that you don't need therapy, is to say that your psyche is completely normal. That you're a perfect human being who does no wrong, ever. Is that what you believe?"

My shoulders slumped, voice softening. "No. Of course not."

"Good. We're on the same page." She did her best to contain it, but irritation tinged her voice. "So if you don't have anything in particular that you'd like to talk about, my next question is, how are things going with Sebastian?"

"Perfect. Fine." I shrugged. "No complaints, really."

"What about Sebastian? Does he have any complaints?"

"Not to my knowledge." I pinched my brows. "Has he complained to you about anything?"

"No, he says the same thing you just did. Everything's perfect, everything's fine." Watching me carefully, she raised a shoulder. "That's good. I'm happy for you two."

"Why did you say it like that?"

"How did I say it?"

"Nonchalant. Like you do feel some kind of way about it, but you're trying to cover it up with a nonchalant attitude."

"That's how you talk about it. Is that how you feel about your relationship? Nonchalant?"

"No," I said. "I'm really happy with him. There's nothing I would change, even if I could."

"Nothing at all?"

"Is there something you think I *should* change?"

"I wouldn't say that."

"Then what would you say?"

Tone still nonchalant, expression still blank, she leaned back in her seat. "I might ask a question."

"And what's that?"

"Why didn't you tell him about David?"

At the mention of his name, my stomach sank. But I couldn't show that. "Why would I have?"

"I don't know. Simone thought you would've."

"What?"

"When Edwards came to Light Up Night. Simone said that you could stay while the two of them talked because she was going to tell you anyway, and she figured that you were going to tell Sebastian." She crossed her legs. "Why didn't you?"

*Because I'm terrified that if I talk about David, I'll admit to killing him.*

"Because it wasn't my story to tell," I said. "It's Simone's. She didn't want anyone at the ranch to know, so I didn't think she would want Sebastian to know."

"Consideration for your friend. I respect that." Rhiannon thumbed the journal in her lap. "How did Sebastian feel when you explained it to him afterward?"

"How am I supposed to know how Sebastian felt?"

"If he asked why you hadn't told him, that might tell you that he felt hurt," Rhiannon said. "If he was angry, that may have told you the same thing. Did he express any feelings after the fact?"

"No." Which was what I liked about him. He handled his emotions on his own and didn't make them my problem.

"Did you guys talk about it afterward?"

"Yeah."

"What was said?"

"He asked for the whole story, I gave it to him, and that was it."

"That was it?" She narrowed her eyes. "He didn't have any questions?"

Another sigh. "He asked if I was okay. I told him I was, and that was the end of it."

"Was that the truth?"

Annoyance scrunched up my face. "Are you asking if I lied to him?"

"I think there's a big difference between lying and avoiding," Rhiannon said. "After you saw Simone in the state she was in, were you afraid?"

"No, I was not afraid that Troy would show up and beat the living hell out of me, if that's what you're asking." Although, as soon as the words left my mouth, I wasn't sure if they were true. In my mind, for a moment, they had been.

"Were you afraid at all?" Rhiannon asked.

"Why does it matter?" It came out in a sharp snap. "I had some anxiety over the whole situation. But why does that matter? I got over it, didn't I? I'm fine."

"You know what, Gwen." Rhiannon pulled off her glasses, sat forward, and propped her elbows on her knees. "I care about you, kid. So I'm gonna say this as nicely as I can. What the hell happens to you when you walk into this room?"

"What?"

"Out there"—she gestured out the window, then the door—"me and you are friends. We talk about everything. You laugh, and you smile, and you are a very likable person to be around. But then we come in here, and you're not just resistant. You're combative. Every question I ask, you answer aggressively. And I want to know why. What happens when you walk through that door? Why does just sitting here with me and talking about your feelings make you angry?"

Guilt roiled around in my gut, a familiar sensation I knew like the back of my hand.

There were few people in this world I cared for more than Rhiannon. Even fewer I respected as much as I respected her. The last thing I wanted to do was offend her. "I'm sorry. I'm not trying to be aggressive or combative."

"You don't need to be sorry, but you do need to think about that." Rhiannon studied me. "What do you feel when you sit down here to talk to me? What emotion do you feel?"

Biting my lip, I shook my head. "I don't know."

"Then what does it feel like in your body?" She looked me over, watching every move I made. "What does it remind you of?"

That, I could answer easily. "Like when I was a kid, and I first started performing. Like I can feel everyone's eyes on me, and I don't want to screw it up."

*I don't want you to see how much of a shitshow my head really is.*

Rhiannon's stiff expression softened. "There's no pressure to perform here, Gwen. I'm not judging. I'm just trying to help you."

"I know that," I said. "And I appreciate it. I'm just not good at this. I don't know what's broken in me that I'm supposed to fix."

"Who said you were broken?" Her voice sounded softer now too. "I don't think you're broken."

"Then why do I have to do this? Why do we have to sit here and talk about my feelings if there's nothing wrong with them?"

"Because you need to be able to identify what they are, Gwen." Deep lines etched her forehead, suggesting she was as confused as I was. "You need to be able to have a feeling and name what it is."

"Why?"

"Why what?"

"Why do I need to name my feelings? They come, and they go, and a new one comes, and it goes. It's a never-ending cycle. I feel something, and I fix it, and I move on. What else is there to do with them?"

For a few heartbeats, Rhiannon just stared at me. Confusion dissipated as she nodded. "We might be getting somewhere here."

"And where are we getting, exactly?"

"What you just said there, about *fixing* them. That's the root of a lot of your problems, kid."

Blood sloshed between my ears, throbbing harder and harder. I rubbed my temples. "You're gonna have to explain this to me like I'm two."

"You think that feelings are problems that need solving." The beads in Rhiannon's braids clinked with the shake of her head. "They're not. A feeling might point to a problem, but if you can't feel that feeling, then name that feeling, you're not going to get to the root of the problem."

"I thought you said trying to fix them was the root of my problem."

"It is," Rhiannon said. "Our goal is not to *fix* them. If you don't learn to feel your feelings, name them, and search for the root of them, you're just gonna bury yourself. You've done it before. When you were with Troy, the first time he put his hands on you, he hurt you, and it scared you, but you resolved the issue at hand. You two kissed and made up, because that was easier than dealing with the fear. You solved the simplest problem in front of you instead of the root problem."

"Alright," I said, sinking back in my seat. "A valid point."

"The very first time he hurt you, what was the root of the problem on your end? Not whatever reason he gave to justify it."

The words were sour leaving my lips. "He used violence to control me."

"And what was the healthiest way for you to solve that problem?"

"Leaving." I fought the urge to squirm at the unpleasant chill that ran down my spine. "But I did that, so I don't see what your point here is."

"Just that getting to the root of that problem is how we progress as people." She leaned in again. "That's why I asked about your mom. Not to judge her, but to understand what happened in your life that makes expressing your feelings so hard. Did you ever talk about your feelings with her?"

I went back to chewing my cheek. "Not really."

"What about her feelings?" Rhiannon squinted me over. "Did she talk about hers?"

"I guess, yeah."

"Can you give me an example?"

A deep breath escaped my nostrils. "I don't know. She told me about feeling unloved and unwanted by her boyfriends a lot."

"And what did you think when she told you those things?"

My heart thumped hard, and my chest got tight. "They didn't deserve her anyway. She needed to stop worrying about them."

"How did you know that?"

Raising my shoulders, I shook my head. "Because she could hold a job when she was single. She cooked dinner. She was awake when I was getting ready for school. She functioned better without them. They just made her life harder."

Rhiannon's phone rang on the side table. She silenced it. "And those feelings, you only saw her express them when she was having problems in her relationships?"

"I guess, yeah." I gestured to her phone. "You can answer that."

"It can wait." Her eye contact didn't waver. "Her feelings were catastrophes that *did* need solving, right?"

That wasn't an insult to my mom. It was close to one though. I had to consciously release my tight fists. "Well, she was in a revolving door of abusive relationships, so yeah, I guess so."

"And when she didn't solve them, you had to pick up the slack. You got ready for school by yourself. You had to cook dinner."

"She was overwhelmed," I said, doing my best to keep from coming off aggressive. "I was fine."

"I know. Just like you're fine now," Rhiannon said. "And you are, Gwen. You show up to work each day. You're saving to open your own business. You're opening yourself up to love again, and that's huge. I'm proud of you." Her phone rang again, and she silenced it once more. "But your problem has never been whether you can take care of yourself. It's always been that you think you have to take care of everyone else."

I'd killed a man to protect my best friend. So I couldn't argue with her about that.

"Is it such a bad thing?" I asked. "That's what community's all about. Sacrifice. Give and take."

"No, it's not a bad thing." Eyes big, brows creasing in the middle, she frowned. "But doesn't it get heavy? Carrying around everyone else's pain?"

A chill swept over my arms. All I could do was shrug in response.

"Let me ask you this, Gwen." She rubbed the bridge of her nose. "Have you ever had someone *you* could really lean on? Someone you could tell everything to, and they wouldn't judge you. Someone who would help if you asked."

"Does Simone count?"

"Before Simone."

No. I didn't. Mom was chaos. Her problems were always bigger than mine. Throughout my teens, my friends had relied on me the same way she had. I was who they went to with their problems. When mine were bigger, they were nowhere to be found.

Chewing my cheek, I shrugged again.

"That's why I want you to name your feelings, Gwen. Because I want you to have mutual relationships. I don't want you to carry everyone else's burdens and never lay out your own." Her phone rang. She grunted, ignored it, and muted the ringer. "Closeness, real closeness, is vulnerability on both sides. Are you sure you weren't afraid when David hurt Simone?"

A knot swelled in my throat, and my fingers quivered. I clenched them steady. "I don't know. Maybe I was."

"And you didn't want to tell Simone that because, like your mom, her crisis was bigger. She was the hurt one. Your feelings went to the back burner because they had to in that moment."

A half smile touched my lips. "Are you agreeing with me?"

"I am actually." Rhiannon chuckled, and so did I. "But Sebastian didn't have a crisis, did he?

There went my smile. "No, I guess not."

"And you still didn't open up to him, even though he could've been exactly who you needed right then." The corners of her lips fell. "I have a feeling he would've been."

Yeah. He would've. Just like he had validated my experience that night in the truck. I didn't have to put on a show for him. He didn't judge me. We'd sat in solidarity together.

"That's why, Gwen. That's why we have to talk about our feelings, so we can unload our burdens together." Her phone vibrated again. "Son of a bitch."

I laughed. "Is one breakthrough enough for today? Someone clearly needs you more than I do."

"Is that your way of saying *you* agree with *me*?"

I stood and headed for the door. "It's my way of saying I see the points you're making."

"At least we made it that far." A deep breath loosened her shoulders, but she smiled. "Get outta here, kid. But I still want you working on that poem!"

So far, the poem she wanted was still a blank sheet of paper.

As I left the rec center, it was the last thing on my mind. The heavy snowfall blurred around me and provided a blank canvas for my thoughts.

Why *did* I get angry when I sat alone with Rhiannon? Was it all about the pressure of having to talk?

Whenever she brought up my mom, I braced for an attack. Most my life, when people talked about my mom, it was to attack. I understood why. She was an addict. Her priorities were often skewed. She existed in a realm of moral ambiguity.

Maybe that was why I defended her. Because she had been hurt enough, and I wanted to honor her memory. To me, she was good. To me, she was kind. She wasn't a perfect mother, but who was?

And why didn't I like talking about Troy? Because he was a chapter of my life I wanted to forget. One that made me sick to think back on. The things I'd tolerated, the things I should've reported to the police, the things I should've killed him for. It hurt my stomach and sent bile rising up my throat.

That was what made Rhiannon's Ranch so appealing. Leaving that life behind and starting a new one. I knew we only did that for safety reasons, but—

A police car.

An SUV, to be exact.

A police car rolled past me.

Was this about Simone?

About David?

Until David, I had never seen a cop inside the ranch.

My stomach fell into my ass as they pulled to a stop before the rec center doors. I tried not to look, only sparing a few glances over my shoulder. I still had a twenty-minute walk ahead of me. How long would they be in there, talking to Rhiannon?

If I slowed my speed, maybe I could get Edwards—if it was him—to roll down the window and tell me what was happening on his drive back out of the ranch.

Could I think of some excuse to stay close, so I could ask Rhiannon about it afterward? Maybe if I went to the cafeteria, or the gym, I could kill some time until they left, then find her after and ask what it was about.

But I didn't have to.

I was just passing the daycare when I heard Rhiannon call, "Gwen, are you busy, sweetheart?"

It was so cold, so dark, that no one else was out and about. I had only made it a block away from where Rhiannon now stood.

Now, despite having wanted to know so badly what was going on, I was terrified to head back. What if she was calling for me because they had figured it out? What if they knew I killed David?

"Just heading home to take care of Honey," I called back. "Everything okay?"

"I, um, I could just use your input right now." Her voice was an octave higher than it had been earlier. I couldn't make out her expression through the snow that fell between us. "Would you mind coming back?"

Did I really have a choice? What was my other option? Make a run for? If this was about me, if they believed I had killed David, wouldn't they be the ones chasing me?

This was something else. It had to be something else.

With a hard swallow, I started back in that direction. Once I was at the rec center doors, I opened my mouth to speak, but Rhiannon cut in first. Her voice was low. Quiet enough that Edwards and the suited man beside him on the far side of the entryway couldn't hear.

"Delilah's real name is Alison," she said. "Alison Kennedy."

# CHAPTER 28

## *Gwen*

I didn't understand why that was relevant. Rhiannon and Simone were the only people here who knew my old name. Coming to the ranch meant leaving your old life behind, starting fresh, a blank slate. To me, Alison Kennedy was Delilah and would remain Delilah. It almost felt a bit disrespectful, like a betrayal of Delilah's trust, for Rhiannon to share her old name.

What kind of trouble could Delilah have been in anyway? Her picture was beside *innocent* and *naïve* in the dictionary.

"How you doing, Gwen?" Edwards asked.

I had seen him blunt, I'd seen him casual, but there was something different in his eyes this time. A softness, a kindness.

The same applied for the man who stood beside him in a suit. White, middle-aged, with a full head of graying brown hair. He stood right around six feet tall with a frame just as wide as Edwards's, but on the slender side of bulky.

"You two know each other?" the other man asked.

"She's Sebastian's girlfriend," Edwards said.

This was news to me. Sebastian and I hadn't had that conversation yet.

"Wow, I didn't know he was seeing anyone." Outstretching a hand, the man smiled, a certain sadness still in his eyes. "Detective Robert Mitchell. Most folks call me Mitchell though."

"Nice to meet you, Mitchell," I said, accepting the shake. "And I was doing alright before this." I looked between them. "Can I ask what this is about?"

Edwards and Mitchell both glanced at Rhiannon. She stood on

my right, chewing her nails. Nothing spilled over, but her dark eyes were glassy already.

When she said nothing, Edwards said, "Maybe you should have a seat."

"I'm alright," I said. "I do need to get back to my cabin and let my dog out though, so—"

"They're right." Voice hardly above a whisper, Rhiannon only glanced at me. "You should have a seat, Gwen."

Ice spread through my chest. The cops telling me to sit down awoke a rebellious teenager in me. But Rhiannon? Rhiannon, I trusted.

Edwards grabbed a couple chairs from up against the wall. He sat in one and offered the other to me.

Hesitant I may have been, but I took the seat. "Rhiannon mentioned that this was about D—Alison. She's not in any trouble, is she? Because I just can't see that. She's the biggest sweetheart with the kindest soul, and whatever you think she did—"

"She's not in any trouble." A hard swallow bobbed Edwards's throat. "You guys were close though, right? I saw you together at Light Up Night, and Rhiannon mentioned you kind of took her under your wing here."

"Yeah, we're friends. Really good friends." Shaking my head, I squinted at him, and then at Mitchell who stood behind him. The way I'd grown up, I'd had more interactions with cops than I could count. Never had I seen any who looked so . . . sad.

"If she's not in trouble," I said, "then what's this about?"

Edwards's eyes stayed on mine, expression still gentle, but I could see the hesitancy in the way he opened and shut his mouth. It took a clear of his throat before he said, "She passed away this morning."

I laughed. Obviously, that was a joke. She was eighteen. Healthy. Able-bodied. Completely normal, aside from her circumstances before staying here.

No one else laughed.

When I glanced at Rhiannon, she wiped a tear away.

"Wait, what?" Still certain they were confused, or joking, or lying, I shook my head. "No. No, she didn't. We just had dinner together last night. She was fine. She was completely fine."

"I'm really sorry for your loss." Edwards frowned. "Nobody ever expects something like this."

"No, because you're wrong." I shook my head so hard, I was surprised it didn't fall off. "No, she's at the daycare down the street. That's where she's working now. I'm sure we can walk there and you can see her, and you'll know—"

"She didn't show this morning." Rhiannon's voice came out soft, quiet. "I did a welfare check too, and she wasn't in her apartment. Then I checked the logs, and her key card was used to exit last night. I texted, and I called, but I haven't heard anything. One of the girls at the daycare said she borrowed her car last night."

"We found the car at the scene. I recognized the body," Edwards said, voice soft. "It's her, Gwen. She's gone."

But Rhiannon hadn't seen the body. Edwards only met her once. It wasn't Delilah. It couldn't be.

"Was it a car accident or something?" I asked. "Because there are lots of pretty, young blonde girls. Maybe this girl just looks a lot like D—Alison. It's not—it can't be her."

"At this time, we're suspecting suicide," Mitchell said. "That's why we figured we'd—"

"What? No. No, if it was suicide, it definitely wasn't her. Something's mixed up here. You don't have the right girl. That's not her."

"I'm really sorry, Gwen." Edwards shook his head. "It's her. She had the key card to the ranch in her pocket. I'm sure when Rhiannon scans it, her name is going to pop up."

I stared at him in disbelief for a few heartbeats, but I said nothing.

He did know what Delilah looked like. They had met. They'd spoken, and interacted, and—

"When we spoke with her father," Mitchell began, "he informed us of her mental health issues. Considering her history of depression, and the PTSD Rhiannon mentioned, unfortunately, we understand the situation. We just thought this was news to deliver in p—"

"Her *father*?" I spoke that title with disgust. "Her father let her date a twenty-five-year-old man when she was fifteen. When she showed at his door with a black eye and asked for a place to stay, her *father* told her to go work it out with the guy who abused her. So why should we trust any word out of that man's mouth?"

They both cringed at that.

Edwards said, "She did have a clinical diagnosis for depression, Gwen—"

"She has the same situational depression that every woman has when their partner beats them, and their father doesn't listen to them," I snapped. "PTSD, fine. But she isn't depressed."

Mitchell stepped forward. "Rhiannon mentioned the miscarriage—"

"She was *sad*." My eyes darted to his, unblinking. "She was sad the same way that every woman who's had a miscarriage—at least fifteen percent of us—gets sad. But she wasn't depressed. I have only seen her happy since she's been here. Happy to be away from that bastard. Just last night she was talking about going to college to be a preschool teacher. Depressed people don't plan their lives. People who want to kill themselves don't speak openly about their future."

"Are you saying you don't think it was suicide?" Edwards asked.

Mitchell gave him a look for that. As if to say, *She's just in denial. Don't feed the fantasy.*

"I'm telling you that if she's dead, her ex had something to do with it," I said. "She didn't kill herself. She *wouldn't* kill herself."

A deep breath escaped Mitchell's nostrils.

"I know how my grief works, sir." My voice shook as I continued. "When the doctors told me my mom was dead, I had a moment of disbelief. Then they said she'd been drinking and driving, and it all clicked. This isn't that. I know Alison, and I *know* she didn't kill herself."

"We can do a bit more digging," Edwards said. "But I gotta be honest with you, Gwen. There are no signs of foul play on her body. Right now, it looks like she drove out to the woods, and she did it herself."

"How?" I shook my head again. "How did she do it? Did she take a bottle of pills? Did she jump off a cliff?"

Mitchell said, "I'm not sure the family would be comfortable with us sharing—"

"To hell with her family!" I shot him another look, unable to stop my voice from cracking. "Her dad is friends with her abuser. He didn't just ignore that behavior—he *expected* it. I wouldn't be surprised if he's covering for the guy."

"Let's say you're right." Despite my yelling, Edwards remained calm, expression still compassionate and kind. "Let's say her ex-boyfriend did this. How would he have found her?"

I opened my mouth to respond, but no words formed. My shoulders slumped.

"This place is secure," Mitchell said, softening his voice. "Completely fenced and off the grid. Why would she have run into his arms? And if that was the plan, why didn't she go back home? Why would she meet him half an hour down the road?"

*After everything he did to me, I feel like I'm entitled to a little karma.*

"Revenge," I said. "I can't count how many times she told me that she wanted him to pay. She wanted him to hurt the same way he hurt her. She wanted to tell him about the miscarriage, just because he wanted kids so bad. She wanted him to hurt. Maybe she called him. Did you find her phone? Did you look through it?"

"Not yet, no," Edwards said. "We do have a couple guys sweeping the scene."

"She had her key card in her pocket, but not her phone?" Surely, my face expressed my annoyance. "What eighteen-year-old girl doesn't carry their phone in their pocket? He must've taken it. It was a burner phone. We all use burners. If she did call him, if she did get in touch with him, and they'd met in the woods, he probably got rid of it. It wouldn't be traceable after that."

Edwards pressed his lips together again, as if to say, *Tell me about it.*

"We will look into all of that," Mitchell said. "We really appreciate all your help."

"What—that's it? You're just gonna ignore this? Me and Rhiannon—we're the ones who see her all the time. We would've known if she was depressed. Right, Rhiannon?" I looked at her. "You seem as shocked by all this as I am, so you couldn't have thought this either."

She still nibbled on her nails. "No. I wouldn't've thought this."

"See?" I turned back to Edwards and Mitchell. "Don't listen to her dad. He doesn't know her. He doesn't give a shit about her. If he did, he would've never let her date that grown ass man when she was just a little girl. He would've opened his doors when she showed up with a black eye. You can't just ignore this. You can't just let this asshole get away with murdering her."

"We're definitely going to look into all of the possibilities." Mitchell frowned. "But thank you for all your help. Both of you. I'm sorry to meet under such poor circumstances. We just wanted to make sure you guys were aware."

"No," I said, shaking my head as he took a step toward the door. "No, please. Everyone ignored her. Everyone ignored what Evan was doing to her. Nobody cared. Nobody helped her." My voice cracked. "Please. Please don't let him get away with killing her. Please."

His frown only grew tighter lipped. He gave a curt nod, exchanging a look with Edwards as he approached the door.

Once it shut behind him, and Edwards stood, I stood with him. "I'm not in denial, Edwards. I'm not."

"I believe you," he said, eyes still gentle. "And I'll keep looking. But I'm an officer. I'm not a detective. I barely know Mitchell, so I don't have pull with him. And if we can't find evidence that supports this theory—"

"It's there," I said. "It's gotta be. Delilah wouldn't have killed herself."

He gave my shoulder a squeeze. "I'll keep looking. You just hang in there, alright?"

He said that like I had any other choice.

"I'm sorry again, Rhiannon," Edwards said, heading for the door. "If you find anything that might be important—"

"Yeah, yeah. I have your number." Rubbing a hand down her jaw, she couldn't so much as look at him. "Thank you for letting me know."

When the door clicked shut, I turned her way. "You don't think I'm crazy, do you? Because I just can't see it. I can't. Delilah is happy, and bubbly, and—they're wrong. They've gotta be wrong."

"I don't think you're crazy." She swatted at a tear that escaped her eye. "You're probably right. They're probably wrong."

"Then why are you so calm?" Baffled, I scanned her for some sign that I was misunderstanding her body language. "Why didn't you argue with them?"

A humorless laugh escaped, ending with a clear of her throat. "You did that for me, don't you think?"

"But he didn't believe me," I said. "That detective, he didn't believe me."

"We're used to that, aren't we?" She swallowed hard. "Not being believed."

A deep, visceral pain reverberated through my chest, like a horse had just kicked me.

Rhiannon shook her head and shut her eyes. "I'm sorry. I still need to process this myself and I shouldn't talk about it until I do." She placed a gentle hand on my arm. "Are you okay? Do you need a ride up to your cabin?"

I bit my now quivering lip. "I'm okay."

Before she could respond, I was heading for the door.

"If you need to talk—"

"I have your number," I said under my breath.

I couldn't remember the conversation we'd had last night.

Ever since I walked out the rec center doors, I replayed seeing Delilah at dinner in the cafeteria last night.

Before my eyes, I could see the snow. I recognized that it was cold, that my nose and hands were going numb. I didn't feel it though. I didn't feel much of anything, aside from confusion and a general sense of distortion. The world around me looked as it always did, but it didn't feel right. It was like I was detached from my body, stuck in that memory of last night at dinner while I walked on autopilot.

It had become routine. If I wasn't eating out with Sebastian, then me, Delilah, Simone, and Junie ate dinner at one of our homes or the cafeteria. I saw Delilah every day. She was my friend, quickly becoming my best friend alongside Simone.

Who made distinctive notes of every conversation they'd had with each of their friends? I hadn't realized it would be the last one. Even now, I couldn't believe that it had been the last one.

What the hell had we talked about?

Had she looked sad? No. No, I remembered that we were all happy. We were laughing, and picking off each other's plates, and talking about . . .

What the hell had we talked about?

*Beep-beep!*

Headlights came toward me. Was I walking on the road? Did they have enough room to pass?

I stepped further from the gravel into the snow, but the car slowed. Once it was beside me, it halted.

"I know you like to get your steps in and everything." Simone. Simone was in the car. "But it's, like, eight degrees out here. Do you need a ride?"

It was thoughtless. I yanked open the passenger side door, and I sat.

"You going up to your place?"

All I did was stare ahead. What was I supposed to say? How could I break this to her gently?

"Hello?" Laughing, Simone waved her hand in front of my face. "Anybody in there?"

"Delilah's dead." Why it left my lips that way, I couldn't say.

"What?" The overhead lights in the car began to dim, and Simone smacked them back on.

My eyes started to adjust. Simone gently grabbed my face and turned me toward her.

She whispered, "What did you just say?"

"Delilah's dead." The hot sting of a tear burned down my frozen cheek. "The cops just came to talk to Rhiannon and she had me talk to them too. They say she killed herself, but I know she didn't. I know she didn't kill herself. It was her ex. It had to have been her ex."

Shifting the car into park, Simone's mouth dropped open. She covered it with a shaking hand. "Oh my God."

"I can't remember what we talked about last night." I rubbed my temples. "I didn't think it was gonna be the last time I talked to her. Everything was normal. Everything was fine. But now I can't remember the last thing we said to each other. What did I say to her?"

"College," Simone murmured, eyes falling to her lap. "She was talking about college. How excited she was to start the spring semester."

"See?" Shaking my head furiously, my voice raised, cracking over every word. "She was happy. She was planning for her future. Last night at dinner, we were all happy. She didn't leave that dinner and kill herself. I know she didn't. But he didn't believe me. The detective, Mitchell, I think, he didn't believe me. Edwards said that he would keep looking into it, but the detective didn't believe me, and Edwards is just an officer, and—and—I can't believe this. I can't believe she's gone."

"You're right," Simone murmured. "She wouldn't have killed herself."

"But she kept talking about wanting revenge. Maybe she got in contact with him. Maybe she wanted to tell Evan how much better off she is, and how happy she is that she's going to college, and how much she hates him for all the ways he hurt her, and—and that's all that makes sense. That's the only thing that makes sense."

Headlights shone behind us.

"Shit. I'm blocking the road," Simone said. "Do you want to come back to my place?"

"No, I need to let Honey out. And I think I want to be alone right now." I rubbed a hand down my face. "I can just walk."

"Like hell you can." She shifted the car back into drive, cut the wheel as far as she could to the right, and skirted off to the side of the gravel. Out the window, she waved her arm at the other driver. "I'll take you home."

Maybe that was best. I wasn't sure I could distinguish between up and down at this moment.

I rambled some more, just repeating that same sentiment over and over.

*Delilah didn't kill herself. It had to be her ex.*

Simone kept agreeing with me all the way until we reached my front door. Then, as I reached for the handle, she grabbed my other hand. "Are you okay?"

I nodded out of instinct. But I was not okay.

"If you need me, just call." Eyes filled with tears, she squeezed my hand. "I'll leave Junie with Margaret, and I'll be here. I'll be here in a heartbeat."

Swallowing hard, I nodded. "Thank you. You too."

A nod of understanding. As I stepped from the car, she called, "Love you!"

"Love you too," I said.

She waited until I was in the door to back out of my driveway.

Honey's obnoxious barks filled my ears as I stepped through the threshold, but it sounded hollow. Muffled. I shut the door and collapsed to the hardwoods, my knees numb on the contact.

As I ran my fingers through Honey's fur, more tears escaped my eyes, burning my icy cheeks.

Honey lapped at them.

Holding her helped. Feeling the soft, yet fluffy texture of her hair felt real. Most else didn't, but she did.

The truth was, I didn't want to be alone.

Phone in hand, I scrolled through my contacts. When I made it to his name, I pressed call. He came through on the third ring. "Hey, beautiful."

My voice cracked again when I said, "Hey. Are you busy?"

"I'm never too busy for you," Sebastian said. "Are you alright?"

I tried to breathe slowly, but the words came tumbling out. "Yeah. Yeah, I'm—I don't know. I don't know what I am. But I don't wanna be alone. Can you come over? Shit, no you can't." I grabbed a fistful of hair at the back of my head. "Lizzie's probably in bed. I'm sorry. I shouldn't have called. I'm just—"

"Hey, hey. Slow down, alright?" His voice was smooth, but firm. Grounding, like a stone softened by millennia of erosion. "Lizzie's old enough to be alone for a while. I can come over. Or you can come to my place, if you want? I've been meaning to invite you over anyway."

That sounded nice. Maybe a drive would be nice. "Can I bring Honey?"

"I'd expect nothing less."

# CHAPTER 29

## *Sebastian*

I'd been dozing off on the couch when her call came. She had never sounded like that before. Nasally, erratic, anxious. I'd considered begging her to stay on the phone with me while she drove over. Or hell, getting in my truck and meeting her wherever she was because it didn't seem safe for her to be behind the wheel.

What the hell had happened?

In record time, less than half an hour, the crunch of tires on gravel sounded down the driveway. Before she even parked the car, I was in the threshold. She stepped out, but the first thing visible was the potato covered in fluff that bolted around her front bumper.

"Hey, Honey," I called.

Her big ears pointed toward the deep blue sky speckled with snowflakes and stars. Tongue flapping out of her jaws, she raced toward me and barreled up the stone stairs.

I bent down to greet her but kept my eyes on Gwen. She wore a pair of jeans and a tattered Lynyrd Skynyrd T-shirt, trekking slowly up the steps. Each move she made was weighted by some invisible force. Like something sat heavy on her shoulders.

"I'm sorry," were the first words out of her mouth. "I'm so sorry for bothering you. Showing up like this. I know it's late."

When would she realize that I didn't care what time of day it was? If she needed me, I would be there. For anything, anytime, anyplace.

"Don't be sorry." I straightened up with Honey's leash in hand. "What's going on? Is everything alright?"

Now only a few strides away, she wiggled her brows, but didn't meet my gaze. Her eyes flickered over the estate. The stone walls, the turrets, the fountain in the center of the wraparound driveway.

"I get why you kept this place," she said. "It's really pretty. Has this whole classic, goth vibe to it. Kinda dark, kinda gloomy, but classic and regal and—and it's not you." A half laugh escaped her. "Like, not at all the style I thought you'd be into. But it's nice. Really nice."

"Dark and gloomy is the vibe I get too." I lifted the bag that hung over her shoulder while her gaze wandered. "But yeah, not my taste. Lizzie can decide what she wants to do with it when she's old enough."

Gwen still wouldn't look at me. Too busy admiring the sculpted winged babies around the arched doorway. Gently, I caught her cheek. She jolted at the cold temperature, then relaxed into my touch. Our eyes finally met.

The whites of her blue eyes were red as roses. They were almost as puffy and swollen as her lips. Her pink nose watered, and she sniffled.

Something was wrong.

Something awful.

And I was who she came to.

I traced my thumb along her cheek. "What's the matter, Gwen?"

"I, um—" A sharp breath cut her off. "I'm sorry. I don't even know why I came here. It's late, and you were probably getting ready for bed, and—"

"And I'm here." Keeping my voice soft, I held her face just a little tighter. Enough to make sure she knew I wasn't letting go. "I promised you I wasn't going anywhere, and I meant it. Don't apologize for cashing in a check I gave you. What's going on, Gwen?"

Her eyes softened. For the first time, beyond any doubt, I saw tears form across them. Like that was the greatest thing I could've ever told her.

Had she ever had this? Someone she could count on? Someone who didn't just tell her they were there for her, but proved it?

She spoke, hardly above a whisper. "Delilah. My friend Delilah, she's dead. They think it was a suicide, but I know it wasn't. Someone killed her. And—and I don't know. I thought I wanted to be alone, but my chest is so tight, and my head won't stop pounding, and I can't stop thinking about everything she's not gonna get to experience now. Everything she's missing. All the dreams she had, all the goals she was working toward, it's all gone. She's gone. I'm never going to see her again, and, and—I just wanted to see you. Simone told me I could call her, but I didn't want to be with her right now. I wanted to be with you."

My mouth dropped open, eyes as wide as the fields that stretched on my left and right. It took playing that over a few times in my mind before it registered. I hadn't processed all of it, not that the grief was mine to sit in any way, but I heard the important parts loud and clear.

Gwen was hurting, and she needed me. She wanted me to be the one who held her and comforted her, and for someone who asked so little of everyone else, who never asked for help, that was the greatest honor.

"I'm sorry," I whispered, twisting my arms around her waist. I didn't need to pull her in. She collapsed into me. Her fingers were like vice grips around my back. She grasped me so tight, as if the two of us were hanging off a cliff, and I was the one who held the rope. So long as she didn't let me go, she'd survive. "I'm so sorry, Gwen."

We stayed there for a while, just holding one another in the entryway. Gwen was so disoriented, she didn't seem to notice how cold her hands were becoming.

I ushered her inside and asked if she was okay. She shrugged and shook her head, which I took as answer enough. Not that it would make much of a difference, but I offered her a drink or something to eat, and she declined both. Swallowing hard in the entryway, she glanced around and asked if there was somewhere she could lie down.

"Oh, right. Yeah, we can go to the living room if you want. The couch is better for aesthetics than comfort, but—"

"Could we just go to your room?" Those big doe eyes turned up to mine, almost embarrassed to have asked for the simplest of necessities.

But it was good she asked, because I wouldn't have offered that. There was a certain suggestion that came with inviting a woman into your bed. Now wasn't the time to make that move.

Since she asked though, I gestured up the winding staircase. "Yeah, of course."

I stayed at her flank, guiding her left and right through the mansion's maze. Gwen made lighthearted quips, saying things like, "I'd get lost in this place without you," and I hated that she was right.

This thing was enormous for no good reason. Every ornate detail, no matter its beauty, made me grit my teeth. Aside from the obvious, pretentious display of wealth, there were too many bad memories here. I couldn't wait for Lizzie to grow up and decide to live in it or sell it. I already had a good nest egg in savings to buy or build something else.

But I didn't say that, because I doubted Gwen cared. She just wanted to distract herself from the bigger thing on her mind.

When we made it to my bedroom, a quiet gasp dropped into her chest. Standing between the cherry French doors, she scanned every inch. The twelve-foot coffered ceilings, trimmed in the same stain as the doors and wainscoting. The silk wallpaper above it. She had wanted to lie down, but she practically ran across the hardwoods for the second set of French doors, wrought iron with windows that opened onto a balcony and overlooked the Rocky Mountains.

"You just wake up to this every single day." She cupped a hand over her mouth and stared out at the view. "Like it's no biggie."

Honey was already at her side, wagging her tail, glancing between Gwen and the patio.

"Don't let her out there." I carefully clicked the bedroom doors shut behind me. "I can get a little gate for her, but the gaps between the banister are too big. She'd fall right through."

Gwen bent over, grabbed Honey's leash, and gave me a big grin over her shoulder. "If I hold onto her, can we check it out?"

I laughed and gestured through the glass doors. "Go ahead. The knob's a hundred years old so it might stick."

Her smile reached her eyes.

My God, the things I would do to keep that smile across her lips forever.

With Honey's leash around her wrist, Gwen spun the lock and shimmied the knob. As she pulled the door open, snow spilled onto the wooden floors.

Honey backpedaled. So did Gwen.

Pressing her lips together, she awkwardly scratched her head. "Maybe not the time of year for this. Do you have a towel?"

"Don't worry about it." I walked that way and sat on the ottoman at the foot of the bed. Realizing that was alright, Honey yanked against her lead, bolted to me, and hopped up beside me. "You wanted to lay down, didn't you?"

"Yeah, but I made a mess. I can't just leave it for you to clean up."

I didn't mind cleaning up her messes. "You can. Seriously, just sit down."

"I would, but . . ." She thumped the French door shut with her hip, then propped her hands on them. Taking slow, careful steps through the room, her gaze traveled all over. "This doesn't feel like a relaxing kind of bedroom. This feels like a museum."

"Not exactly my taste either." Stroking my fingers through Honey's fur, I gestured to the Chesterfield by the window, then the bed. "Furniture is comfy though."

"None of it?" She gestured to the canopy bed behind me. "Not even that?"

"I appreciate the craftsmanship." The hand-carved floral details adorning the spindles, swirling upward to the square headers at the top. The brass rings that held the black linen that swayed between them. "But I'm pretty sure this frame is worth twenty grand. That's insane."

Blushing, she did that simultaneous shrug-nod thing again. "I guess."

I squinted her over. "You like it, don't you?"

The blush didn't fade, but a smile touched her lips. "I kinda love it, actually."

"If it'd fit in your cabin, you could have it."

Gwen laughed, strutting across the room to it. As she sat, she shook her head. "No, if you're going to get rid of it, you should sell it and donate the proceeds. But just imagining all the hours that went into this." She trailed a red manicured finger down one of the spindles. "The artist who fed their family for weeks or months from the sale. The stories of all the people who've lain in it. The babies made in it." I laughed, and so did she. "I mean, I see your point. It is wasteful. But past the expense of it, there's beauty here. History and culture. Value."

"I respect that viewpoint." Now that Gwen was settled in on the mattress, Honey leapt over the edge to join her. "But maybe I'd appreciate it more if I was the one who built it."

"Maybe I would too." She smiled at me, then frowned at Honey. "Baby, you're gonna get hair everywhere."

"She's fine." I stood and gave Honey a few scratches on the head.

"I come home from work every day covered in dog hair. A little more isn't going to kill me."

"I still feel bad. We just completely took over your space." Petting the back of Honey's head down to her hips, Gwen gave me those doe eyes again. "At least sit down with us?"

I'd been hoping she would say that. I just didn't want to presume anything.

"If you insist," I said. As I lowered myself to the silky linens, Gwen lay on her side. I joined her against the opposite pillow.

The moment we lay down, the tone shifted. That playful little smile, the banter to distract her from the chaos in her mind, was gone.

Now it was just me, Honey, Gwen, and her thoughts.

I wished I could read them. I wished I could know exactly how she felt about tonight's turn of events. I wished she could relay every recollection and every theory she had for her friend's death.

If for nothing else than to know she was moving through the grieving process. Depression, anger, denial, bargaining, acceptance. Just something. Anything to show me that she was processing this, and that she was going to get through it.

But she didn't so much as utter Delilah's name. Maybe she couldn't yet. She whispered, "This was all she wanted, you know?"

Unsure if I understood the question, I tucked a piece of hair behind her ear. "Hmm?"

"What we have, you and me." Her voice was still so quiet, I could barely hear it. "What we're building here. A good relationship. One where we can count on each other, where we're kind to each other, where we challenge each other, but we never hurt each other. We're just good to each other." The tears welled in her eyes again. "That's all Delilah wanted. Just a normal, healthy relationship. She's never going to have it now."

The memory of that young girl at Light Up Night flashed through my mind. She was only a couple years older than Lizzie. When I looked at her, that was all I saw. A little girl. She may have legally been an adult, but the law didn't know what it was talking about, because that was a *child*.

All evening, she had watched Gwen and me as we did the most basic things. Holding hands. Trading sips of hot cider for hot chocolate. Gwen dabbed some whipped cream from the corner of my mouth, and when I complained about my sore back from a long surgery earlier that day, she rubbed my neck.

Throughout it all, the look in Delilah's eyes had reminded me of Lizzie when I'd taken her to Disneyland. At eight or nine years old, she'd been obsessed with Belle and the Beast. When she met them, it was like magic. The light in her eyes could have illuminated a city.

That evening had been a good one. I enjoyed walking through the ranch and holding hands and sipping hot chocolate and the two-minute massage Gwen had given me. But that was the bare minimum. It wasn't Disneyland. We weren't magic.

That memory burned my eyes with tears. Gwen was right. Delilah had never wanted for much, and even the simplest of desires had been ripped away from her.

All I could manage was, "No. She won't."

"It's not fair," Gwen whispered.

"No. It's not."

Silence snuck in. Gwen inched closer, tucking her head against my chest. I coiled an arm around her waist. Honey chuffed and grumbled before scampering to the edge of the bed.

Gwen broke the silence with the most unexpected question.

"Were you upset about David?"

My stomach sank. "What?"

"Simone's ex. The guy who showed up and beat the shit out of her." She tensed under my grasp. "Did it upset you that I hadn't told you about him?"

Oh. That's where this was going.

"No. Why would it?"

"I don't know. I had a session with Rhiannon earlier, and she mentioned it." The pace of her words was slower, voice softer. "She wants me to open up more. Says it's not good that I'm so closed off from everyone and everything. I see her points. Maybe I should talk about my feelings more. Maybe you have to give some to get some. I don't know why it's so hard for me, but I just . . . I don't want you to think that I keep things because I don't trust you. Or because I don't want to be close to you or something. I do. I do want to be close to you."

I took her hand, squeezed it tight, and kissed her knuckles. "It feels to me like I'm one of the only people you let get close."

Her cheeks warmed. "So you're not mad?"

"I could never be mad at you." I cupped her jaw in my palm, finding comfort in the warmth of her skin. "If you want to talk about it, if you think that'll make you feel closer to me, we can. I just figured it hit too close to home. Probably freaked you out that he managed to find Simone. I'm sure part of you was scared that your ex could do the same. But if you don't want to talk about it, we don't have to."

She shivered, likely trying to trap in a shudder. It took her a moment to whisper, "I wouldn't say scared. Maybe deep down, yeah, but I was just pissed. Still am. That bastard showed up and hurt my friend, and I hate him for that. I was scared for her, but all I've ever felt for that son of a bitch is rage."

The most I could do was validate her. "You have every right to feel that way."

"Does that count?" She gave a half smile. "Talking about that, it was opening up, right?"

A quiet laugh escaped me. "I think it's a start, yeah."

Not like I had the right to judge. I wasn't the most open of books either.

"Good. Because I don't want you to think we can't talk about how we feel," she said, voice still quiet. "I feel a lot for you, and I want to make sure you know that. I want you to know how much you mean to me. When I wake up in the mornings, you're the first person I think about. I go to bed thinking about you. Sometimes I get lost in little fantasies about us together, and . . . I don't know."

I knew that. If she didn't care for me as much as she did, she wouldn't be here right now. There wouldn't have been dates and texts throughout the day checking in on each other. She wouldn't have chosen to take her lunch when I took mine, just so we could sit together for an hour each afternoon.

Still, my chest warmed at hearing those words in her voice. I didn't know what was happening as it left my lips. All the control I kept over the last few months thoughtlessly spilled out.

"I love you too, Gwen."

Slowly, her lips parted. Nothing came out. Her cheeks turned a brighter shade of red.

Just when I was about to tell her that she didn't have to say it back, that I wasn't sure why I said it now of all times, she grabbed hold of my face, and she pulled me in.

Our lips touched, and then our chests, and then every inch of our bodies. Her fingers slid down my neck, then my shoulders, like she was taking in every corner of me. And the timing may not have been right, but her touch was entrancing.

For a heartbeat, maybe two, my body took on a mind of its own. I basked in the beauty of her curves, the heat of her skin. That honey, cake-like perfume that radiated from her chest, her neck, was like dessert against my tongue.

The breathless sigh that parted her lips as her legs spread around my waist, wrapping my back, snapped me back into reality. Into control.

"Gwen," I whispered, pulling back to look at her. I kept one hand around her waist, the other on her cheek, and shook my head. "You have a lot going on right now. We shouldn't—"

"I love you too."

She said it with more confidence than she'd ever said anything. Snarky, bossy, she'd been many times. But this was sincerity. Honesty.

"I've loved you for a long time," she said, inches from my face, "and now it's turned into a different type of love. The kind I've never felt before. I don't think feelings this big, this powerful, come around often. And I think if I get caught up in timing or what every moment is supposed to be, I'll lose out on the ones that are *meant* to be. Life's too short. One second, you're here, avoiding conversations you know you should have, avoiding plans you know you want to make, trying to forget bad things that have happened, stressing and stressing and never slowing down to be grateful, to enjoy where you are. Then the next second, you're gone. It's over. You're dead, and you didn't get what you wanted. I know what I want. And it's you. I want you."

She took hold of my shoulder and pushed me gently onto my back. Her knees opened around me. But her expression wasn't half as confident as her speech had been. I saw the hesitance in her shaking fingers.

"Don't tell me I have too much going on right now," she whispered. "Tell me to stop, if that's what you want."

It only took half a heartbeat to understand what that hesitation was. Fear. She was afraid that she had poured everything out for me, that she did exactly what Rhiannon told her to, and it still wasn't enough. She wanted to find safety in vulnerability together, but if I rejected her, I would confirm that fear she never dared admit aloud.

*I'm not what he wants. I'm not what* anyone *wants.*

But Gwen was everything. If I could paint the woman of my dreams, it would be Gwen Kane.

She wasn't drunk or high. She initiated this. She made the decision to climb on top of me, to profess her love, in a moment of deep vulnerability.

How could I turn her down when this was exactly what I wanted too?

"You know it's not." One hand on her cheek again, the other swept down the side of her torso. I looped an arm around her waist and tugged her down to me. A quiet gasp fell from her parted mouth. I kissed her lips just as her smile formed.

Against them, between brushes of our lips, I whispered, "Whatever you want, if I can give it, it's yours."

# CHAPTER 30

## *Gwen*

It wasn't fair to compare Sebastian to Troy. I wasn't trying to. But everything about this interaction was so different than anything I'd ever experienced.

Troy and Ryan were the only men I'd experienced.

One of them didn't understand what the word "no" meant. The other stopped wanting me this way shortly after I could legally buy a pack of cigarettes. He'd only made advances after I found leaked photos of a teenage girl he'd gotten from some kid in his Discord chat. When I'd been infuriated and disgusted, when he thought I would leave, then he'd give me affection.

That sex was always passionate. Angry and sensual at once. Up against the kitchen counter. In the shower as I washed away my smeared mascara, dodging the skin he'd cracked open when I told him I'd go to the cops. Under the blankets first thing in the morning when I had lain awake all night, debating if I could survive on one income.

It'd been full of apologies. Excuses and rationalizations. Rationalizations that, in those moments—when I'd been so emotionally deprived, so afraid of staying, just as afraid of leaving—I'd convinced myself were true. The emotional torment paired with the physical pleasure had been a spell I couldn't escape.

But this, sex with Sebastian, was intimate in a way I'd never felt. When he was unbuttoning my jeans, he looked up too quickly and head butted me square in the nose. Laughing, apologizing, he asked if I was okay, if I was sure I wanted to do this, and I kissed him in response.

Now wasn't the time to think about Troy, but it was more than the simple things that were different. The way he kissed. Troy's tongue had always felt like a worm crawling into my mouth. Sebastian kissed me deeply, hard, but never invasive. It was like the clouds meeting the moon. Like two things that belonged together touching briefly, then sliding freely to the next touch.

When Troy had trailed his hands down my body, when he held me in his arms, they were like iron locks. Sturdy and strong. Unbreakable. Even in the most intimate of moments, he held me so tightly I wasn't sure if I could ever escape.

But Sebastian's hands on my body felt like the water in a heated pool after a hike through the snow. They were everywhere, cradling me, holding me. But free-flowing. Soft yet powerful. As he peeled off my layers, as his weight came down on me, I didn't even for a second fear that I would never be able to leave. That if I did change my mind, if I didn't want this, I would be stuck beneath him.

People always said that comparison was the thief of joy. In this moment, comparison was salvation.

It didn't have to be the way it had always been. With Sebastian, intimacy, sexuality, wasn't a bargaining tool. It wasn't a manipulation tactic. It wasn't a lock, or a rope, or, worse yet, a noose.

This was something cosmic. Something I'd read about in books, something I heard other women talk about, but I'd never realized existed in the flesh.

Once the clothes were gone, and the heat of his bare chest radiated into mine, it all dulled.

The memory of Troy's hands where Sebastian's were now. The sickness in my stomach at the thought. That sensation of being locked in chains.

It was gone.

Right now, there was heat, and there was touch, and there was pleasure, and there was safety. Those were the only words I could use to describe these feelings, and yet, they didn't even come close to what I felt in this moment. I'd felt heat, I'd been touched, and I knew pleasure, but not like this. Not with him.

With him, everything else vanished. Even our bodies. My eyes were closed, his lips on mine, and at one moment, my knees were in the blankets, legs spread around him, and then cotton sheets cradled my back, and then it all vanished.

Was there flesh at all here? Had I died and made it to the afterlife? Was this heaven?

Because I felt all of this. All of him. The smoothness of his skin, the definition of his muscles. Each of his gravelly groans that floated into my ears or from his open mouth to mine. The salt of his sweat popped on my tongue. That citrusy smell of his cologne mixing with his natural musk filled my lungs. Every rock of his hips, every wondrous place he massaged within me, every grasp of his calloused fingers.

I felt all of it, and I knew each individual sensation. But when they all came together, I couldn't tell where I ended and he began.

We were one within two. Our skin, our flesh, were two streams that opened into the same ocean. For a moment, only a brief moment, that thought had my heart falling and my stomach spinning.

Reality. I needed a tether to reality.

But when my eyes opened, our foreheads were pressed together. His fingers threaded through my hair. He held on to the back of my neck, lips parting to meet mine. The second they did, that falling sensation stopped. Now, the spinning was around me. Rather than nausea, it was the touch of intoxication after a few drinks. A blissful buzz that left all my limbs tingling, heat blossoming at every point where our bodies met.

Those hazel eyes. Only the thinnest rim of brown around the pupil, brightened by the deepest shade of verdant. A pale blue ring encased it all.

Until now, my favorite color had always been red. Not anymore. That thin rim of brown stretching into emerald with a smoky blue edge. That was, and would be from now until forever, the most beautiful collage I'd ever beheld.

They were a portal to another dimension. That cosmic one where our bodies, our spirits, our souls, merged down those free-flowing rivers into an ocean that could never separate us. No matter how hard we tried, bits of him and pieces of me were within one another now, and no schism, no rift, could pull us apart.

One of his hands traveled down my bare back. The other came for my cheek. He held it closely, softly. Like I would break if he wasn't careful. Like I was the most wondrous thing he'd ever had the pleasure of embracing, and he had to handle me like the finest work of art.

"I don't know how I ever lived without you, Gwen Kane."

My name. The name I had chosen. The name that gave me power and a sense of self when I'd had nothing but a garbage bag full of things I'd managed to throw together as I ran in the night.

My name, on his lips, in his voice, brought that blissful buzz to a deep trembling vibration. It took hold of each limb, each finger and toe, every drop of blood in my body. I couldn't even form words. All I could manage was to hold him closer, to wrap my arms tighter around his shoulders, to take in all those bits and pieces of him again. The smoothness of his skin, the salt on my tongue, the scent of him in my lungs.

It was beauty and passion and love and safety in a way I had never felt, and I never wanted to leave. I wanted this to last forever. I wanted to stay in this moment for the rest of my life.

Between heavy breaths, sweat dampening my shoulder, he whispered in my ear, "But I never want to again."

Tingling all over, still enraptured in the heat of this moment, my head collapsed to his shoulder. His arms coiled around my waist, my legs doing the same to his. A quiet laugh escaped me. Another trembled his chest. His lips came to my cheek, then my hair, and together, we sank into the soft linen below.

It felt like I was high. Maybe drunk.

Simple euphoria. The euphoria anyone felt when lying skin to skin with someone they loved. Simple, I called it, but how complex it felt when so much time had passed since having last experienced it.

Then again, I'd never experienced anything quite like this before.

Resting my head on his chest, I glanced around at the curtains, the canopy on the bed, then the intricate woodwork of the frame. "You really don't like this stuff?"

"Hmm?"

I propped my chin on his chest, stroking my fingertips through the hair atop it. "The decor in here. You don't like it at all?"

"Honestly, I don't think I've given it much thought." Sebastian pushed some hair behind my ear. "In college, all my stuff was from IKEA."

"All my stuff at my old house was from IKEA," I said, "but only because I couldn't afford anything better. You could. When you got the inheritance, you could've spent a little bit of it to get furniture you like."

"I guess I'm just not that materialistic a person. The money was better spent elsewhere. This place had everything I needed, so it was fine."

"Well, aren't you just the stoic."

Chuckling, he thumbed a bit of lipstick from the corner of my mouth. "Is this your way of saying you like all this?"

"Practically, no," I said. "It's pretentious and vain to spend this kind of money on furniture. The most responsible decision would be to sell it off and donate the money."

"But if you weren't being practical?"

"Oh my God, I love it." He laughed, and I joined in. "The trim work alone. And the fact that it's all in such great condition. Now, don't get me wrong, I don't like the yellowish cream color of the wallpaper, but the furniture? It's like a dark academia Pinterest board."

"If it would fit in your cabin, I would give it to you." He pecked my forehead and sat up. "I need a drink. Do you want anything? A snack, maybe?"

"I could eat." Draping the sheet around me as I joined him upright, I gave a smile. "Whatever you're getting's fine. Thanks."

"Anything for you." He came back in for another kiss, smiling still when he tugged away.

Once he pulled on his sweats and headed for the door, I found myself smiling at the back end of it.

I hadn't forgotten how this night started out. But for a while, it was nice to focus on something else. It was nice to fall into a life that didn't feel like my own.

This was all I'd wanted since I was a little girl. It was how I'd wound up with my ex. It was all Delilah had wanted, too, and how she'd wound up with hers. The same could be said for Simone. All any of us wanted was to love and be loved by someone.

But each of us had almost identical stories. We'd each thought we had found someone who was kind, caring, to share our life with, to be our partner through the ups and downs. Only for them to ruin it with infidelity or abuse. They'd tainted each of us with their chaos and control.

My stomach sunk at the realization that if something went wrong here, it would be because of my own chaos. Because someone would find out what I had done.

The timing may have seemed silly. For the past few minutes, maybe the last hour, I had been relishing in pure, unadulterated bliss. Now, I was reaching into my purse, scrambling to find the burner phone.

**Gwen**

Are you sure no one will find the body?

I stared at the text for a moment.

*Ding.*

My heart sank, eyebrows furrowing in confusion.

No. No, that couldn't be right.

I copied and pasted the text I had just sent and clicked send.

*Ding.*

No. No, no, no.

With shaking fingers, I clicked the contact at the top of the text message. I pressed the green button. On the far left of the room, in a small mahogany dresser, a phone rang.

Sheet still wrapped around my chest, I stepped from the bed with legs of gelatin.

It was like lead weights were strapped to them, making it damn near impossible to clear the distance between me and that dresser at any reasonable speed.

This couldn't be real. It couldn't be.

This had to be a dream. That would explain why I went from so sad earlier, so heartbroken at the loss of my friend, to so euphoric now. Dreams always worked like that.

As I opened the drawer, I said that to myself again. This had to be a dream.

Beside the ringing flip phone was a small handgun.

I grabbed the phone.

The burner phone number lit up the screen, still ringing in my other hand.

I ended the call.

Missed call from *You Know Who* lit up the screen.

New text from *You Know Who.*

**You Know Who**

Are you sure no one will find the body?

When I scrolled up in the text, they were all familiar. The exact conversations we had had in the past.

It was Sebastian. Sebastian had found the body.

"I wasn't sure if you were being mindful of your caffeine or not, so I got ginger ale and Pepsi," he said, voice somewhere down the hall.

I whirled to face the door. Sebastian was just outside, voice as calm and nonchalant as ever. Struggling with a tray of food, he hadn't so much as looked my way yet. "I wasn't sure if you would want sweet or savory either, so I got—"

"It's you."

He looked up. Mouth falling open, his eyes flicked between the phone in my hand.

And the gun in the other.

"Shit," he murmured.

# CHAPTER 31

## *Gwen*

"Shit?" I snapped. "That's all you have to say. Shit?"

"Okay." He took a step closer toward me. "Okay, let's talk—"

"Don't move." With gritted teeth, I kept the gun aimed at him. But I couldn't do much with the phone in my other hand and still holding the sheet around me in place. I dropped the phone to get a better grip. "Don't you dare move, Sebastian."

"I'm not going to hurt you, Gwen."

"Clearly. I'm the one with the gun."

"What, you're going to shoot me while Lizzie's sleeping down the hall?"

"Do you want to find out?"

His frown only deepened. "Can I at least set the tray down?"

I glanced at the dresser, then the open door behind him. "Put it down and shut the door."

Eyes on me, careful not to move too quickly, he set the tray on the dresser, then clicked the door shut. Once his hands were free, he raised them at his sides. "Just calm down, alright?"

"Don't tell me to calm down." I shook my head in disbelief. "You've been lying to me for months. And for what? So you can hold this over my head? So you could blackmail me—"

"What the hell would I want to blackmail you for, Gwen?" He looked just as confused as I felt. "I told you why I didn't reveal who I was. And now that you know it's me, don't you get it? I made sure to cover all my tracks. I made sure no one would find him. But I don't know that *you* did. I don't know that you made every right call, because dumping him in the river without even weighing him down sure as hell was not the right call—"

"And how the hell do you know that?" My eyes shifted rapidly between his. "Why are you so comfortable with this, Sebastian? No normal person is going to hide a body for their friend, because in case you forgot, that's all we were at the time. We hadn't gone on a date yet, we weren't boyfriend and girlfriend or husband and wife. But you decided to hide a body for me. No, not just *for* me, but *from* me."

"Because you dumped it on my property." Something between a snort and a scoff escaped him. "I'm assuming you didn't know that. I also assume it was a crime of passion. You didn't have time to plan it. You just needed to get rid of the body as quickly as you could, and your first thought was dumping it into the creek. Not realizing that you dumped it straight onto my property, where a cop would see it driving by the next morning, because it had already washed up onto the brush."

Shit.

I hadn't known that.

Okay, so him taking the body made sense. But that didn't make it all okay. That didn't make any of this okay.

I held the sheet with trembling fingers. "Answer the question."

"What question?"

As if answering a question with a question didn't tell me that he was evading. "Who did you kill?"

He tensed. Utter silence sat between us for a moment.

"No, you're not gonna answer that." A snarky half laugh escaped me. "Because this way, you have all the cards in your hand. If you know all my dirty secrets, you can use them against me at any point, but God forbid I know yours, right? Because you have too much to lose, and I have nothing, right? That's the point you're trying to make, isn't it, Sebastian?"

His eyes softened. "No. No, of course not."

"Then explain it to me, God damn it!" My voice raised, shaking over every word. I took a deep breath to soften it, afraid that Lizzie would hear. "You expected me to trust that you weren't going to use this against me, but you *are* the one with all the power, all the control, and I'm sure you can imagine why that is a shitty place for me to stand, Sebastian."

"I was just trying to help," he said, voice soft, eyes sympathetic. "I didn't realize what was going on. I didn't recognize the car stopped on the road until you stepped out of it. And forgive me, but I've spent a lot of time looking at your body. I know your demeanor. I know the way you stand, the way you carry yourself, and then I saw a glimpse of your face."

"That doesn't answer a damn thing. That doesn't explain why at some point, you couldn't have told me it was you."

Those shoulders were so tight a moment ago. They loosened the slightest bit as his hands went to his hair. Grabbing two fistfuls at the back, his mouth opened and closed a few times, like he was searching for the words.

"I thought about it," he said. "But then I figured it was best for everybody if I didn't. If you didn't know, neither of us could incriminate one another. And I don't think it'll get to that point. As long as nobody finds David's body, we're both safe.

"But that's all it was. I was just trying to protect you, Gwen. If I hadn't, someone would've figured it out by now. Simone's already in on it, you're in on it, I was in on it, and the more people who knew, the more dangerous it would become. So I just thought we could all move on. I thought that's what you were trying to do, too. You did your best to get away with it, and you were just going to pretend that it never happened—"

"And I'm just supposed to ignore the fact that my boyfriend is a murderer?" I spoke in a hushed yell. "You know all the shit I've been through, and you think I'm supposed to be comfortable with this, like I'm okay with the fact that you were trying to protect me by getting rid of the body, because apparently you know how to get rid of bodies, because you're oh-so-comfortable with just killing people?"

His eyes softened again. "Do you think that maybe that was part of why I didn't tell you?"

"What, because I'm just so crazy and traumatized? I can handle killing someone, but I can't handle knowing that *you* did?" Playing that sentence over again in my head, a humorless, ironic laugh left me. "This is insane. Every bit of this is insane. How the hell are we standing here acting like this is a normal fight?"

"I can't say it's the worst fight I've ever been in." Arms still up at his sides, he gave a half smile. "I think we're handling it the best that we can, given the circumstances."

"Don't be cute. Don't you dare try to be cute right now. Where's the body, Sebastian?"

"I told you. It's buried somewhere no one will find it."

"Take me to it."

His face screwed up in confusion. "It's buried, Gwen. We only had a couple of inches of snow when I dug the hole. There are at least two feet out there now. That's gonna take all night."

"Then we should put some clothes on, shouldn't we?"

Shoulders dropping, he scoffed. "Why? What are you going to do with it?"

"I guess load it up into my car and take it somewhere no one else will find it." Considering how cold it had been, would he be frozen? That would certainly make transport easier. "Go on. Get some clothes on."

For a few heartbeats, he just stared at me. "It's safe, Gwen. There's nowhere safer you can take it, not unless you got a job at the meat-packing plant, and you can sneak in with the body and incinerate it in the middle of the night."

"It's okay for you to not trust me with your identity, but I'm supposed to trust you after you've lied to me for months?"

"I haven't lied."

I stomped a foot. "You lied by omission. And you're too damn good at it. I thought it was Axel, I-I never even thought it could be you. Not for a second, and . . ."

"You weren't exactly eager to tell me you killed a man, either."

"I'm not doing this." I juggled the sheet under my armpit to keep it in place and held up a hand to silence him. "Get dressed. Then we're going."

A deep breath rose and fell through his chest. With a roll of his eyes, he headed to the walk-in closet in the corner. I followed him there, keeping the gun aimed on him as he sifted between the clothes that hung from floor to ceiling. When he crouched down to grab his boots, he came out with something else.

Black in color, roughly half the size of my forearm. At the top, a copper bullet sparkled in the dim light.

Still crouching on the ground, he held it up to me. "Gun's not gonna do you much good without the clip."

# CHAPTER 32

## *Sebastian*

*Just don't hate me. Please don't hate me.*

It was pathetic. Of all the things running through my mind right now, those three words were the loudest. *Don't hate me.*

How could I whine about the position I'd put myself in? Since the moment this began, I knew this time would come. Maybe in a year, maybe five, maybe twenty. Eventually, she was going to realize it was me.

But I'd hoped we'd build enough rapport by then. I'd hoped she would trust me. That she would understand I hadn't done this to manipulate her or hold it over her.

I was just trying to help.

But you know what they say about intentions and the path to hell.

Gwen wanted the body, so I would take her to it.

It was too cold to go out in what she had worn here. I gave her one of my snowsuits and a winter coat. She stepped into them, all while juggling the now-loaded gun.

Hadn't she realized yet? If I wanted to hurt her, wouldn't I have done it while she was holding an empty, useless weapon?

The moment that thought ran through my mind, my stomach twisted and my head hurt, because of course she would keep the gun aimed at me. An hour ago, the two of us were wrapped in one another's embrace, drunk on the warmth and comfort of each other's skin. She'd professed her love, I'd professed mine, and then I did the very thing I had feared from the beginning.

I'd made her worst fear a reality.

I'd betrayed her.

Not only had I gotten rid of David's body. I'd known how to do so. I'd lied to her, to everyone, too well.

I was too damn good at this, and that scared her.

Keeping the gun on me was smart.

But she didn't understand.

If I wanted to keep her, I had to tell her the truth. I had to tell her everything.

That was the obvious conclusion, but as I led her from the primary suite down the steps and out the rear door, all with Honey at our side, my brain kept spinning.

*What if she takes the body and gets pulled over with it in the trunk? What if she tells them what I'm about to tell her? I shouldn't tell her. I can't. It wasn't the same thing. She won't understand. It won't make anything better. She'll still hate me. She'll hate that I lied, that I was so damn good at it, and she'll hate* me.

*I can't tell her.*

*But she's going to see. There won't be a way to hide it when I bring David's body out of the grave.*

*Don't I need that? Don't I need to tell someone? Isn't it time?*

*All her secrets are on the table. I know the worst things that she's done. She deserves that same transparency, doesn't she?*

*No.*

*No, because she's never going to look at me the same after this.*

*But she's never going to look at me the same anyway.*

*That's why she needs the whole story.*

Sick to my stomach, I led the way to the garage. Gwen's fingers trembled around the gun, and I wanted to puke.

She was afraid. Of me.

Careful to keep my hands visible, I collected the basics. Into the bucket of my tractor, I loaded a couple tarps, a few bundles of firewood, a handful of flashlights, and a shovel.

I gestured to the seat of the tractor. "Do you want to drive? Or—"

"Can't keep the gun on you if I do." She nodded up to it. "Go on. Me and Honey will walk."

"We're going a solid five miles up and down the mountain." Clicking my tongue, I shook my head. "You can't walk that far in the middle of the night in ten-degree weather, Gwen."

"Well, I don't know how to drive one anyway," she snapped. "So any other suggestions?"

"You can sit up here." I patted the metal box behind the driver's seat. "Not as comfy, but better than walking."

Glaring, she gestured to the open walkway on my right. "Move."

Like a blade through my chest.

She wouldn't even walk past me? Why? Because I could reach her? I could grab her? I could . . . what?

Kill her?

She thought I would do that?

I blinked at the sting across my eyes. I moved.

With at least a five-foot berth—one my arms couldn't reach through—she walked with her back to the tractor and her eyes on mine. That blue gaze was cold, lethal, but her fingers still quivered.

Gun still aimed at me, she lifted one foot onto the tractor. She gripped the rollbar for stability and climbed onto the tackle box. Once she was up there, she held a hand out for Honey. "Come here, baby."

Honey did as she was told, but even on her hind legs, she could barely reach the first step. I stepped forward to help her, to give her a boost.

Gwen said, "Don't touch her."

I frowned up at her, only to find the gun inches from my face. "You really think that I would hurt her?"

"I think I have no idea who you are, Sebastian." She spoke between gritted teeth. "Get back."

The knife in my chest twisted.

I stepped back.

Gwen laid the gun on the floor beneath her feet. She kept her eyes on me, as if to remind me she could reach it before I could. Because truly, from the bottom of her heart, she believed I could do it. She believed I could point that gun and pull the trigger.

She was right.

I could use that on a thousand people. I could mercilessly fire that weapon. I was physically and psychologically able to point it at someone's head, someone's heart, and pull the trigger. I could paint my garage in someone's blood, mop the white matter off the ground, neatly pack the skull fragments and tissue into black bags, without so much as a tear escaping.

But not her.

I couldn't even raise my voice at Gwen.

With Honey in her lap, she grabbed the gun and aimed it at me. "Let's go."

Shoulders curling, I grabbed one of the flashlights from the bucket of the tractor and passed it to her.

She took it but said nothing.

I loaded into the seat, turned the engine over, and our trek through the woods began.

Once we were on it, bouncing up and down the mountainous terrain, struggling over mounds of snow, my mind started turning again.

*Tell her the truth and lose her, or lie and lose her. Those are your options.*

Would lying keep me safe? Would it keep the truth from coming out?

No. Not really.

She knew we had all too much in common now.

She had killed. I had killed.

But Gwen had killed in self-defense. I didn't know the whole story, but I could tell from the body. The slices in his knuckles. The scratch marks descending his neck and torso.

She'd done what she had to.

I had done what I wanted to.

She couldn't forgive that, could she?

Maybe she would tell me her story if I asked. I wouldn't be able to hear it over the roar of the tractor, but when we stopped, when we got to the grave, maybe that could start the conversation. Maybe she was as desperate to get it off her chest as I was to get it off mine.

It was almost an hour later when the pine tree became visible. It stood higher than all the others. On a normal day, that's how I remembered this spot. But one time, I came out in the middle of the night, and I couldn't remember which one it was. So I searched and searched, finally found it, and carved an S into the tree.

That S stared back at me now.

Lit only by Gwen's flashlight and the moon above, I stepped from the tractor and started shoveling by hand. The bucket may have moved the snow faster, but I needed to stretch after that ride. I needed the cool air against my skin. The flush of adrenaline as I hit the ice layer was the boost I needed.

Grabbing a bundle of wood from the bucket, I searched for Gwen's eyes behind the blinding flashlight. "I should've told you sooner. I'm sorry I didn't. I just—"

"Shut up and dig the damn hole."

Sucking my teeth, silence resumed. Deep, aching silence. The kind only winter brought.

No bugs hummed in the brush, no birds sang in the trees. A few twinkling snowflakes fell from the sky, but no wind rustled the branches. The only sound for miles was the crackling of my fire and Honey's panting.

When the ground was wet enough, I stomped out the fire, climbed back into the tractor, and dug. An hour must have passed by the time I hit ice again. Rinse, repeat. I hopped out, lit another fire, and let it burn for a while. We stayed silent while it did.

I almost apologized again. But I swallowed it back down, because she didn't want to hear that. She knew why I'd lied. Didn't change that I was so damn good at it. Didn't change that I wasn't who she thought I was.

When the fire had burned a while, I stomped it out again, climbed back into the tractor, and resumed digging. We were close now. One more fire, and I would reach David.

Right now, Gwen was inches behind me, her body heat warming my back. Each breath she took, I felt against the nape of my neck. Her knee was right against my shoulder, and what if this was the last time we sat so close to each other? What if she never wanted to see me again after this?

What if she hated me?

I needed to say something else before she saw the body.

Over the hum of the tractor, I choked out, "What happened?"

"What happened to what?" Each word was as pointed as a sword.

"With David. I know the story you told Edwards was bullshit, but I've been trying to map it out for months." I dipped the bucket down into the hole. Now full of damp dirt, I lifted the arm in the air and dumped it beside the tree. "I have the feeling you were there. Or maybe Simone called you and told you he hurt her, so you hunted him? He had a lot of defensive wounds though, so I'm leaning toward the former. I don't know. I'm just curious how it went down."

A long moment of silence. She broke it with, "I was outside smoking. Saw lights at the gates. I heard Simone. She was screaming." Gwen's voice broke. Another moment of silence passed before she continued. "He was beating the living shit out of her. I told him to leave. He wouldn't. He got in my face, and he was screaming, and then I was screaming, and he pushed me, and I pushed him, and then his hands were around my throat." Her voice cracked, and I swore I felt her tense, even though the only part of our bodies that touched were my shoulder and her knee. "I had a knife in my pocket, so I used it."

Damn it. This would've been so much easier if she had hunted him down. "I figured it was something like that."

"Whoever you killed," she said, almost inaudible over the rumble of the tractor, "was it like that? Self-defense?"

I dipped the bucket into the hole again, now at least three feet deep. As I came back up, I said flatly, plainly, "No. It wasn't."

"Lovely," she said under her breath. "Just lovely."

I dumped the soil onto the pile of dirt beside the pine tree with the S. With a hammer in my heart, I turned the engine off. Holding the rollbar for support, I hopped down. Shovel in hand, I gestured to the hole. "Mind shining me a light?"

She kept her distance, far enough from the shovel's length. As if I would use it against her. Like I would slash it across her throat or slam it over her head.

That visual had me swallowing bile.

Climbing into the hole didn't. I'd moved a body before. No one was around now, so I didn't have anything to be afraid of. The only thing about this that made me sick was knowing she thought I could do this to *her*.

Each dip of my shovel into the soil was as patient and careful as my incisions in a surgery or the stroke of my paintbrush. The bigger mess I made, the more difficult it would be to move the body.

When I hit something soft and meaty, I tossed the shovel into the snow, crouched into the hole, and wrapped my gloved fingers around the slippery tarp.

Grunting, I grasped hold of it, wiggled my feet to the sides of the body, and yanked. I yanked, and yanked, and yanked until the top half of the blue tarp lay atop the dirt beneath the tree with the S.

There was no intense smell. No bugs flying about. I was grateful for that.

Panting, I waved over my shoulder for Gwen to join me. "Come here."

"I'm good." She shone her light on the blue-tarped figure. "Just put the body in the bucket, and—"

"If you want to know who I killed, take a look." I gestured into the grave, hoping she would turn the light this way. Also hoping she wouldn't. "Not much left of him now, but here he is."

I couldn't make out her face in the glow of her flashlight. I wasn't sure I wanted to. It would confirm perhaps my greatest fear.

That I had become my father.

No, worse than him.

He beat his wife, beat his kids, drank himself into oblivion each night, but he'd never killed anyone. Certainly not in cold blood.

I had.

And I'd gotten away with it.

The only sound was that of Gwen's feet sliding through the snow. She stood to my right, light aimed into the grave at my feet.

Another body lay there, wrapped in now-muddied white linen. All that was exposed was his face. His dusty blond hair, his hollowed-out, nearly mummified cheekbones, and the deep caverns beneath his eyelids where bugs had feasted for a decade.

Everything from the nose to the throat was gone.

"Wait, I'm—" Confusion mixed with disgust riddled each word. "You put David in the same grave?"

"I did."

Seemed logical to keep them close. Why taint this land in two places? Better if both pieces of shit laid together for all eternity.

"Where are. . ." She gagged. "Where are his lips? Who is he?"

"In the atmosphere, technically?" Scratching my head, I leaned against the wall of dirt behind me. "I burned his jaw. Every tooth. His hands, too. Did the same thing to David." I nodded to the figure wrapped in the blue tarp. "Those are the two easiest things to trace. Dental records and fingerprints. If there would've been any real investigation into this guy's disappearance, they would've figured out that it was me pretty quickly. But I still tried to check all my boxes."

A long stretch of silence. Gwen flicked the flashlight onto me, and for a moment, it was like I was in an interrogation room. But I wasn't shaking.

"Jason Dickens." The first time I had spoken his name in years, and holy shit, it felt good. Like taking a piss on a road trip. Not a sightly thing, not a fun thing, but god damn, the relief. "He was my best friend. For a while, anyway. In hindsight, I don't think he was ever really a friend. I was a pawn to him. He played with me, shifted me around a little, but it was always to get to the queen. Sarah."

I still couldn't make out Gwen's face, but the flashlight had trembled when she looked into the grave. It was steady now. "Sarah? Your sister?"

Nodding, I planted my gloved fingers on the lip of the hole and hoisted myself onto the edge. "Gwen, meet my brother-in-law."

"What the hell is this, Sebastian?" she snapped. "Are you trying to make a point? Or are you just trying to show me that you're a psychopath?"

"Yeah, I am. Trying to make a point, I mean." I tore off my glove and rubbed my eyes. "He killed her. Sarah was the only friend I ever really had, and Jason killed her. He orphaned my niece. And he would've gotten away with it, and I couldn't let that happen. I couldn't live with myself if, some way, somehow, he got custody of Lizzie. So I killed him. And my only regret is that I didn't do it the moment I realized he was hurting my sister."

Another long stretch of silence.

"This is Lizzie's dad," Gwen whispered.

"Yes," I said. "This is Lizzie's dad."

# CHAPTER 33

## *Sebastian*

"Biologically, anyway. Wasn't much of a dad." Rubbing a hand over my jaw, I raised my shoulders. "He was a lot like mine. Drank a lot. Had a bad temper. Was never much of a partner. And it's kind of my fault, because Sarah didn't like him. Not in the beginning. She turned him down half a dozen times. Then he befriended me, and I was lonely, and dorky, and Sarah felt bad for me, and she liked that the cool, popular guy was nice to me. Because of me, she gave him a chance, and she fell in love with him, and she got knocked up right out of high school, and he killed her when she tried to leave."

Somehow, that was both the long story short and a ramble at once. I didn't know how to explain it all, because there was so much more. Years of friendship, years of signs I'd overlooked, years of red flags I'd ignored because I'd been so desperate for friends. For stupid, external male validation.

"I don't . . ." Gwen began, voice hardly above a whisper. "I don't understand. Are you saying that this guy is what happened to Sarah? That's why you don't talk about it?"

Was she asking if it was hard for me to talk about Sarah's death because Jason had caused it? Or because I'd caused his?

"I don't talk about Sarah because her death was the hardest thing I've ever gone through. I don't talk about Jason because his death was my fault, Gwen." My voice cracked over those words, and I wasn't sure if I was making sense. "His death, yeah. That was all on me. I planned it. But I'm not ashamed of that, just like I don't think you're ashamed of what you did to David." I waved at the blue tarp. "But I hate myself for ignoring the way he treated my sister. That's why I don't talk about him. Because it's my fault they got together, and it's my fault she died, because I should've killed him the first time I saw the signs."

And there'd been many.

One time, we'd all been hanging out in a big group at a football game. Sarah was a cheerleader. Jason had said something about how her uniform looked nice today. Because she had "put on some weight and was finally filling out the spanks."

Everyone laughed. I hadn't. Didn't even understand the joke.

But I'd seen the hurt in my sister's eyes, and I'd said nothing.

Sarah was late to her own eighteenth birthday party. Jason had dropped her off in the driveway, then peeled off down the road. Her lip was swollen, her phone broken, and when I asked what was wrong, she just said that Jason was being a pain in the ass again.

Jason showed up a few hours later. Sarah, me, a couple of her friends, and the only other one I'd had—Edwards—were hanging out on the back patio. Sarah was beside me, Edwards beside her, and his girlfriend at the time next to him. But Jason saw the two of them sitting together, and the look in his eyes was just like my dad's.

Sarah saw it too. She'd chased after him, and we'd all heard arguing from around the side of the house. I followed them. They stood only inches apart. He puffed his chest out, making their height difference far more obvious. I couldn't catch what they were saying, but I hadn't liked the way it looked.

"Is everything okay?" That's all I'd managed, and it hadn't been nearly enough.

Sarah had told me she was fine. She was handling it. She'd be back soon.

A few minutes later, his car rumbled to a start, and I didn't see her again until the next day.

There'd been more. So many more.

But she'd kept acting like everything was fine. Sarah, I could get a moment alone with, but never Jason. If Jason was around, his nose was in Sarah's asshole.

What would I have said anyway? I didn't like the way he talked to my sister? It wouldn't have mattered. I was the silly little brother. I was lucky they even let me hang around. Who was I to open my big mouth?

I should've opened my dad's gun safe.

"What . . . what happened?" Gwen whispered. "To Sarah, I mean."

"They got a house in town right after high school," I told her, ignoring the cool dampness that seeped through my pants to my ass, still planted on the edge of the grave. "She was in college. He was working construction with a friend of his dad's. They weren't far away, not physically, but they kinda closed themselves off." I trailed my fingers through my beard, grabbing at the end. "I thought it was because Sarah finally got away from our parents. That last year, when she was out there with Jason, and I was in my senior year of high school, we didn't see each other much. So I don't know everything that happened.

"I didn't know anything was happening, not really, until my second year of college." A knot stiffened in the back of my throat. "She called me. She was nasally, and upset, and Lizzie was screaming in the background, and she needed me to call Rhiannon. And I knew what that meant."

Gwen was still invisible behind the blinding light, but her silhouette swayed. The tractor bounced as she leaned against it. She laid the flashlight on the seat below Honey, casting the faintest glow across her face. Enough that I could make out her features. Not clearly, but I could tell we were making eye contact now.

She finally lowered the gun. "And you did?"

"Call Rhiannon? Of course." Jason stared back at me from his grave. And I hated that I liked looking down at him like this. I hated even more that I had damn near nothing to show for it. "Jason's dad was the sheriff back then. Sarah called the cops, and no one came. Rhiannon did though. With a couple of her security guys. The ranch was a lot smaller then, but from what everybody's told me in hindsight, Jason was a perfect gentleman when they got there.

"Sarah called an hour later. She said everything was okay. Rhiannon got her and Lizzie set up in a little cabin. And she kept apologizing." Chills rose over my arms at the memory of her voice on that call. "The only thing I was sorry for was that she was going through this for so long by herself. Because it had been going on since high school."

The knot in my throat thickened. Swallowing didn't soothe it. The closest I got was clearing my throat. "Anyway, her last straw was that day. He'd hit her while she was holding Lizzie. Sarah dropped her on her head. And she wasn't going to take it anymore. She gave me this whole spiel about how she didn't want to be our mom. How Lizzie deserved better. Lizzie couldn't grow up the way we grew up.

"I wanted to applaud her for that, but I couldn't. I was so angry." Licking my teeth, I stared at Jason. His hollow, empty eyes. Just as empty now as they'd been when he was alive. "I told her I was going to get on a plane. I was going to kill the son of a bitch. She convinced me not to. Said she was going to talk to our parents and see if they could loan her enough money to get an apartment.

"They wouldn't." At my sides, my hands balled into fists. "Told her to work it out with her husband. So she stayed at the ranch for a while. She was going to graduate from college in a few months, and then she was gonna get a place of her own. But they'd moved past the first stage of the divorce. They were on to working out custody and child support.

"Rhiannon said that Jason wouldn't meet in public." My throat was so thick, so dry, that I was surprised I could still form words. "Rhiannon told Sarah she could send one of her guys over with her when they talked about it all, but Sarah said no. He was just going to hold up the divorce if she did that. He wanted to talk to her alone. So she went to their house." My eyes burned, then clouded over. I swatted the tears away and choked out the words. "And she never walked out."

"Shit," Gwen whispered. "Shit, I'm so sorry."

Pressing my lips together, I raised my shoulders. "They said she killed herself. Never released pictures of the scene. Jason suddenly had big plans to move to New York. He was going to let my parents keep custody of Liz. And I knew. It just wasn't possible. Why the hell would she have gone over there to shoot herself in the head? What would've been the purpose?"

"There wasn't one," Gwen whispered. "She just wanted it to be over. To say her piece."

"Yeah. Well, he got the last word." Jaw tight, I smacked my foot against the linen-wrapped bag of bones. "So I planned it. When I came back home for the funeral, he was there. He was crying, and everybody was pitying him, even my parents, and I knew I had to tread carefully. Nearly bit my tongue off trying to keep my mouth shut.

"After the burial, I got him alone. Said we should take a walk and smoke a joint." I gestured around. "Favorite pastime for the three of us. And while we were walking, he said something. Something about how she never knew when to shut up. And that was the closest I got to a confession.

"My plan had been to strangle him. Easier cleanup that way. Shouldn't have been hard, because he was drunk and stoned, but he said that, and I lost it." The memory of his blood splattering, of his screams, flashed behind my eyes. "I know I started punching him. I don't know when or why I stopped. But eventually, I was sitting in the dirt right there." I pointed to a boulder behind Gwen. "I was covered in his blood, and he wasn't breathing. So I dug the hole, I dumped him in it, got rid of the jaw, the hands, and filled the grave back in. Haven't regretted it since."

A long stretch of silence.

I'd expected her to say something. Ask something, or blurt how despicable I was. Just something, anything.

But Gwen stayed silent, just staring at Jason's body in the soil.

Maybe she did. Maybe she hated me.

I couldn't blame her. Only an animal could do what I had done and feel no remorse for it.

Another tear burned across my eye. I slapped it away.

"Do you?" I asked her. "Regret it?"

She spared David a glance and shook her head. "No," she said. "I don't. I did what I had to."

Biting my lip, my eyes went back to the grave. Snow accumulated against his leathery skin now. "I didn't have to. It wasn't self-defense. But when he said that, I could picture him saying the same thing about Lizzie. Or another woman he'd bring into the picture. He would do to her what he did to Sarah, and maybe he'd get custody of Lizzie, and she'd watch that. She'd experience it, and she would wind up exactly where her mother was. And I couldn't. I couldn't let it happen."

Slowly, Gwen lowered herself to the footrest on the tractor. She didn't comment on what I said, only stared at Jason. "No one questioned his disappearance?"

I shook my head. "Not really, no. He was already planning on leaving, so that's what everyone assumed he did. I think his dad helped him cover it up. After that, I think they came to an understanding. Sheriff never wanted to see Jason in this town again. But I don't know for sure."

Her eyes came back to mine, and I couldn't tell what she was thinking. She didn't look afraid. Didn't look happy either. Just attentive. Like she had a pair of tweezers, and was using them to dissect my every word. "Did you ever talk to him? The sheriff?"

"After it happened?" I asked. She nodded. "No. I got on a plane the next morning. Went back to college. Sheriff retired a few months later. My plan was to get custody of Lizzie once I finished my degree and everything. My mom agreed that was best. She was 'done raising kids.'" I held up air quotes. "I thought that I would run into him when I came back to Black Pines. I did once, when I brought Liz to the grocery store right after my parents died.

"He was sick. I don't know what was wrong with him, don't know if he's alive or dead now, but he could barely look at me. One glance at Liz had him tearing up. It's screwed up, but I smiled at that. Knowing how ashamed he was of the son he'd raised." A deep breath fell from my nostrils, loosening my shoulders and forming a cloud before my face. "But yeah, no one really questioned anything."

"And you're okay with it?" Her voice was quiet. Not accusative, but soft. Curious. "It doesn't keep you up at night?"

"This part has." Shoulders dropping with relief, a half-laugh escaped me. "Bottling all this up. Keeping it quiet. That's been hard. Exhausting. Sometimes, I just stand in the bathroom mirror and rationalize it. Like I talk myself through what I did, why I did it, why it was the right thing. But most of the time, no, it doesn't keep me up at night."

"No one else knows? You never told anyone?"

"Not until right now. Pretty sure that's how I got away with it. People talk. You don't give them anything to talk about, and no one finds the body, then there's no trail for them to follow." But it all fell so effortlessly from my tongue today. My tense shoulders were soft, my turning stomach settled. "Holy shit, though, this feels good. It feels so good to let it all out."

Gwen winced.

Shit, I shouldn't have said that. "Not in a crazy, psychopath kind of way. It didn't feel good to do it. It didn't feel good to pull David's body out of the creek either. I hated it. The cleanup, the mess, the blood, the lying. I didn't do any of it because I liked it. I did it because it needed done. And I hated that it needed done. It was the right thing to do. The world's a better place without these men in it. If I had to do it again, I would, but not because I want to. Just because I'm tired of watching. I'm tired of seeing horrible men ruin good women.

"And when they do stand up for themselves, when they do leave, they're the villains. Like my parents and Sarah. They were so angry at Rhiannon for giving her a place to stay, for giving her a choice, for 'breaking up a family.' But then this bastard killed her. He *killed* her, god damn it." My fingers tightened, and my jaw clenched. "They acted like he was her mess to clean up. Like he just made some mistakes, but if she was good enough, she could fix him. And she tried, but she couldn't, and when she finally threw in the towel, he killed her.

"It was almost like those sons of bitches were in on it too. They wouldn't listen when I said it wasn't a suicide. They thought it made sense. A young girl, already married, already raising a child. Her life was over now. No one else would want her. And I . . ." Massaging my eyes between my thumb and forefinger, I shook my head. "I'm sorry. I know I'm rambling. I've just had so many thoughts and feelings about it all over the years, and I've never been able to tell anyone. So thank you. Thank you for listening."

"Thank you for telling me." Gwen's voice was still soft. "And I don't think you're a psychopath."

Was it a laugh that parted my lips? It must've been, because she let one out too.

We held one another's gaze, and for a few heartbeats, did nothing else.

But maybe we could. Maybe we understood one another now. Maybe this would bring us closer together in some screwed up, twisted way.

"I know this is a lot," I said. "And I'm so sorry. I shouldn't have lied to you. When I got rid of the body, I wasn't trying to hold it over your head or use it to control you. I was just scared. I didn't want to get caught any more than you do."

"I know." For the first time all evening, she squatted and laid the gun on the ground. "But you shouldn't have lied to me. And the anonymous texting shit was a little crazy, Sebastian."

Scratching my head, I shrugged again. "I was just afraid of a digital footprint. I saw you in his car, so I had to make sure that you got rid of it. How did you get rid of it?"

"Drove it down to Great Falls." She crossed her arms against her chest. "Paid a homeless guy to junk it for me after I scraped off all the VINs."

My brows lifted. "Smart."

"Thanks." Swallowing hard, she gestured to the rays of pink and blue that crested the edge of the sky. "Sun's coming up. We should get you home before Lizzie wakes up."

*We should get* you *home.*

She wasn't planning on coming back with me.

"Right." Clearing my throat, I stood up. "Do you still want the body?"

She shook her head. "I just want to go home. Get my head on straight."

That lump swelled in my throat again. All that relief in my shoulders wound back up. Stiffening, I nodded. "Let me clean this, and I'll take you to your car."

# CHAPTER 34

## *Simone*

After Simone wiped down her leather chair and dropped her combs into the blue barbicide on the countertop, the bell above the door at the entrance dinged. She had just finished with her last client, and the next had called ten minutes ago to let her know she would be twenty minutes late. Twenty extra minutes Simone really didn't want to spend at work two days before Christmas. Not after the news she'd gotten last night.

But service with a smile. Prepared to politely explain that her salon didn't accept walk-ins, she opened her mouth to speak, but the words vanished.

His was the last face she expected to see in here.

Rather than his uniform, Edwards wore a pair of excellently fitted jeans. The white V-neck paired with a couple silver chains exposed the beautiful hard lines of his chest. His biceps swelled the fabric around his arms.

Simone's belly flipped.

Silly. Pathetic. How could her mind even drift in that direction with everything else going on right now?

Still, she said, "Hey, you. Do you need an appointment?"

His tone was just as friendly, despite the pinch of grief in his eyes. "I'm sure you would do an excellent job on my head, but it would cause all kinds of family drama with my barber if I switched up on him."

"Well, we don't want that." Simone leaned against the checkout counter, grabbing her broom from behind it. She felt her hip pop out at the side in something of a pose. "Not here to snuff out the competition, are you?"

"I was just telling him, 'Uncle, you hog all the male clients in this town. Don't you think you should refer a few to poor Simone down the street?'" Simone laughed, and he smiled. Only for half a second. Then it fell. "I'm actually here about your friend. Delilah?"

Any playfulness in Simone's expression vanished as well. She found herself leaning on the broom for support instead. "Oh. Right."

"Yeah, I tried to talk to Gwen yesterday, and I shot her a text this morning, but she seems to be taking it really hard."

"She didn't want to talk to me either. I'm pretty sure she was with Sebastian last night if you really need her, though." Frowning, Simone went back to sweeping up the hair trimmings on the black-and-white checkered tile. "But if there's anything I can do to help, I'm all ears."

"I'm not sure yet. Really, I just . . ." He smacked his lips together, lifting and lowering his shoulders. "I don't think Gwen is wrong. From what I saw of Delilah, she seemed really happy. Were you guys close?"

"We're friends." Simone realized she used the present tense a moment too late. So did Edwards, but he didn't correct her. "But kind of casual friends, if that makes sense? We sat together at group, we ate in the dining hall together sometimes, but never just me and her. It was always with Gwen. Gwen and Delilah were way closer."

"That was what it looked like to me too." Edwards leaned over the reception desk, brown eyes somewhere in the distance. "You didn't happen to see Delilah two nights ago, did you?"

"I did, actually." Simone returned to the reception counter, standing on the opposite side to face him. "Me, Junie, Gwen, and Delilah had a dinner get-together. Why do you ask?"

He nibbled on his lower lip for a heartbeat or two. His eyes scanned her, as if surveying for something. "What she was wearing . . . when she was found . . . it seemed odd to me. I'm curious if it's what she wore the last time you saw her. I do have some photos on my phone, but I'm not sure if that's too sensitive."

Simone's stomach clenched. "I mean, is it just her clothes? Or is it . . . you know. Her?"

"Yeah, it's her, but her face isn't in it. But if it's too hard, I can show Rhiannon, and—"

"No, it's okay." It wasn't. Not really. After David, Simone didn't do well with death. But Rhiannon loved all her girls more than the clouds loved the sky. It was better that she see this than Rhiannon. "I can handle it."

Nodding slowly, Edwards dug around in his pocket. He came out with the phone and swiped around on it. He offered it to Simone. "Those pants, and those shoes. Is that the sort of thing Delilah would've worn?"

At first, they looked like only that. With the flash of the photography, the navy-blue sweatpants and black-and-white sneakers were all that was visible. It was only when she zoomed in closer to look at the shoes that she realized—

They weren't flat on the ground. They weren't lying at an angle on a tabletop.

They were floating midair.

She was hanging. Delilah was hanging.

Simone had to swallow the vomit that burned her esophagus. She zoomed in on the photo, studying the emblem on the shoes. "I mean, yeah, she wore tennis shoes all the time. But these don't look familiar to me. Are they brand-name?"

"Nike Air Force Ones." Holding out his hand for the phone, Edwards clicked his tongue against the roof of his mouth. "Expensive. They also seem a little big on her. I know that everybody gets donations at the ranch from the community closet, but Delilah didn't seem to be the type to care about quality sneakers. I doubt she would've taken them just because they were there, especially if they weren't her size."

"You think somebody put different shoes on her? After she—" Simone stopped herself, unable to finish the sentence.

"I think it's weird." He shrugged, jamming the phone back into his jeans pocket. "I don't know if I've come to the same conclusion Gwen did. I don't think that I agree with Detective Mitchell though. But I don't know yet. I just wanted to hear from someone who knew her well. If she had a sneaker obsession or anything."

"Not to my knowledge, no." The nausea from the photo began to dissipate. "I do know that we keep an inventory of everything in the community closet. Delilah showed up at the ranch with the clothes on her back. If she got those at the ranch, there will be a record of it."

"Right. Sure, that's great. I'll give Rhiannon a call and ask her to look over her ledgers." He managed a smile. "Thanks for all your help."

"No worries. And Merry Christmas."

"Yeah, you too."

But he didn't turn around. Didn't head for the door. Just stood there for a minute, eyes locked with Simone's.

She forced a laugh. "Do you need anything else?"

"No. Not really. I guess I just—how have you been?" He scratched the back of his neck. "With everything. Has that guy come back around?"

Her stomach twisted again. "I've been okay. Good, even. Excited for the holiday. And no. Haven't seen him since that day, thank God. Hopefully never see him again."

"Good. That's really good." Another smile, this one just as forced as the last, but a bit sweeter. "If he does, you can call me. Anytime. Day or night. You have my number, don't you?"

"Yeah, you gave it to me when you took my statement." He seemed to flinch at those last couple of words. Simone did her best not to respond with the same anxiety when she continued. "And I definitely will. But hopefully I won't have to. Like you said, he probably ran far and fast from here."

"Right. Of course." Edwards trailed his tongue along his lips, eyes flittering between hers. "You know, with everything considered, this is probably a really bad time. Which is totally understandable. So no pressure at all. But a couple of friends of mine are having a little get-together for New Year's. I'm pretty sure Sebastian's going to be there, he'll probably bring Gwen. So it wouldn't be awkward or anything if you came. If they'll both be there, I mean."

Eyes crinkling, the corners of Simone's lips twitched. "Was that an invitation?"

"A really bad one, yeah." Edwards laughed, and Simone joined in. "Whatever kind of invitation you want it to be."

Propping her elbows on the counter, Simone leaned in, confident her low-cut shirt held his attention as much as his V-neck held hers. "A date? Is that what you're inviting me to?"

"Well, I'd devote a hell of a lot more time and attention to a date." Another one of those little shrugs, accompanied by a smirk. "I'm a bit of a romantic myself. But if you wanted to call it a pre-date, I'd be okay with that."

Laughing, she looked up at him through thick eyelashes. "A pre-date?"

"A pre-date," he confirmed. "We can look at our schedules and get a real one lined up for after the new year, if that works for you?"

"I think I can find a way." Heart fluttering, she straightened. "My schedule is tight right now though. I have a client on the way, and I've still gotta finish wiping down my chair."

"Alright. I'll quit holding you up." He lifted his hands at his sides and backpedaled for the door. "But you have to text me to get the address for the party."

Broom in hand again, she popped out her hip. This time, with intention. "I'll text you."

The sweetest, yet sexiest crooked smile. "I'll be waiting."

She laughed as the bell rang over his head. He waved as he continued down the road.

Simone turned back to the pile of hair on the ground, lightheaded. Yet, she couldn't pull down her smiling lips. They turned up so wide, her cheeks were pushing into her eyes, nearly blinding her.

Had that really just happened?

One of the most beautiful, jaw-dropping men she had ever seen. So kind, so respectable. Most of Simone's adult life had been spent battling the cops to believe her experiences. To throw David behind bars.

Now the best one she had ever met not only gave a damn about what she'd lived through but desired her despite it. Something she'd thought made her unappealing, too damaged, entirely unlovable, ignited a fire with the sort of man she thought only existed in her dreams.

Her instinct was to pick up her phone and call Gwen, but the bell rang above the door again. She cleared her throat and called over her shoulder, "I'll be right with you, Kathy. Just gotta finish cleaning up from my last client."

"Take your time, Jess."

Simone's heart dropped to her torso. All her limbs went numb. Memories flashed.

And when she turned over her shoulder, she had to pinch herself. This had to be a nightmare, because life didn't go from so good to so bad this quickly.

Angela stood at the door.

# CHAPTER 35

## *Gwen*

By the time Sebastian filled the hole and got me back to my car, it was five a.m. The goodbye was awkward. He stammered over his words. I didn't say much of anything. Honey and I loaded in, and I watched him watch us head off down the driveway through my rearview mirror.

I couldn't grasp it all. On a rational level, I understood everything that had happened in the last few hours. But it hadn't settled in.

The only thing about killing David that made my stomach hurt was the fact that I didn't feel anything. How could I be so cold? Why did I care so little about another human life? Shouldn't I have had some empathy for him as well?

But Sebastian had the words for it. Words I'd said and thought but never seemed valid until they came from his lips.

*I hated it. I didn't do any of it because I liked it. I did it because it needed done. And I hated that it needed done.*

There were few people alive who could understand, but he did. Sebastian understood it because he felt it. We had stood in the same shoes.

But they weren't the same. Not really.

Sebastian was someone I'd chosen, someone I loved, because I saw normalcy in him. I saw stability and consistency. There was good, so much good, in him.

Until now, I couldn't imagine Sebastian being a violent man. Until he had hit me, I couldn't have imagined Troy a violent man either. But he was. Clearly, Sebastian could be as well.

To top it all off, he had aided in David's murder at the start of our relationship. We'd gone on our first date only a day after, and he'd disguised it. Not only had he disguised his involvement, but he'd disguised a huge part of himself from me.

Of course, I had done the same thing.

But holy shit, Sebastian was *good* at it.

Then again, was he? When he'd told me I looked like shit in the café that day, he was referencing the fact that I'd been up all night after killing a man. Had he been giving me an opportunity to open up? Had he debated telling me about his involvement?

No, he couldn't have. He'd already had the burner in his pocket. He'd texted me just after we'd exchanged that longing smile as he left the building.

Sebastian had premeditated tormenting me with those texts. He said he was just trying to help, he hadn't intended to terrify me the way those texts had, but intent and impact were separate things.

Then again, he'd done this before. He'd refused to tell me details because that's what had kept him safe after he'd killed Jason.

Holy *shit*, he'd killed Jason.

Not the way I had killed David. Not to defend himself. Sebastian had planned it for the right reasons, but he'd lost control. In a red-doused rage, he'd beaten the man to death with his bare hands.

Then he'd chopped off half his face and hands. The hands and face of a man he'd once called a friend.

Was I supposed to pretend that didn't terrify me?

Sebastian was a surgeon. If blood and guts disgusted him, he couldn't do his job.

But he'd done that before becoming a surgeon, when he was just a college student.

I'd seen the man tear up at roadkill. He was not some lunatic who enjoyed the gory suffering of others.

*It needed done. I hated that it needed done.*

Did it change who he was? No. He was still exactly who he told me he was. He warned me about that damn pedestal, and I still held him up on it. That was my bad.

Knowing this fractured the sculpture I had molded of him in my mind. This was just a new lens to view him through.

Was I seeing him through a lens at all? Or was I looking in a mirror?

It was almost poetic that he'd laid David in the same grave as Jason. Like a way to say, "If you go down, I'm going with you."

I'd been so afraid to fall for him because what if he learned what I'd done? What if it all came out, and I had to run? I'd believed he wouldn't run with me.

But now I knew he would.

Now I knew why he hadn't donated *all* the money he'd inherited. In case he had to leave the country and start over.

Putting David in that same grave was his way of saying, "If you need to run, we can run together."

Those butterfly wings had razor blades on them again.

I was halfway home when I remembered why I had gone to his house in the first place. That deep ache in my chest returned.

When I got back to the ranch, I brought Honey inside and sat on the couch. It was almost six a.m. I didn't have work today, thankfully. Within a few hours, I would be exhausted.

So far, though, I wasn't. My eyes were heavy, and my chest hurt, but I wasn't tired. I was nothing. Everything that had happened in the last twenty-four hours felt like a shot of Novocain over my entire body. Each finger, toe, and limb was numb.

Simone was probably at work by now. She worked early on Saturdays.

Rhiannon was up, I imagined, but I didn't want to bother her with all this. I couldn't tell her about Sebastian anyway.

Delilah was someone I would've liked to go to with this. I could be vague enough in my descriptions. I wouldn't have needed to go into every detail. But she would give me advice. She would smile, and she would make me do the same, and I would make us breakfast, and we would laugh while we ate it.

That wouldn't happen anymore. That would never happen again.

In the past, if I had thought of her while I was home, I would shoot her a text and ask what she was up to. She would say she was getting ready for the day and ask if I wanted to walk with her to the cafeteria, or the rec center, or somewhere else in town. I would say of course, then walk down Main Street, up to her apartment, and wait for her to finish her makeup before we headed out.

Maybe if I did that, if I walked to her apartment, if I sat inside that silent living room where she usually sat at the mirror in the corner, dusting on her blush, it would feel real. Maybe if I was there, while she wasn't, it would sink in.

So that was what I did.

I left Honey at the cabin and walked down Main Street.

As I made it to her apartment building and climbed the steps to the fourth floor, I detached from the world. Like I had last night. This was just the average day. I was walking to my friend's apartment, and we would laugh while she got ready and everything would be okay.

As I made it to her door, for a split second, I thought that the last twenty-four hours had been a dream. Now, I was waking up. Everything looked a bit brighter. Beams of sunlight glowed out the cracks of the apartment door. Because on the other side of it, the shuffle of feet sounded. Someone was walking around in there, and it had to be her. Delilah wasn't dead. She was right there, on the other side of the door, and everything that had happened in the last day was the dream.

I walked in, and the warm beams of sunlight vanished. A dark cloud fell over the studio apartment.

Standing at the window was not Delilah. It was Rhiannon.

She jumped at my entry. One hand, she pressed over her heart. The other, she wiped her face with. A practical, not at all legitimate laugh escaped her. "Acting like I have the right to be startled when I'm standing in somebody else's living room."

Rhiannon had the right to do anything she wanted in this place. It was hers, after all.

But why was she here?

She spoke before I could ask.

"How you doing, kid?" She wiped her glistening cheeks, forcing a smile. "Did you go to Sebastian's last night?"

Squinting, I cocked my head to the side. "How'd you know?"

"Basic deduction skills. I saw your key card was used to leave. That's good. Relying on him a little bit for support when you're struggling with something."

All I could manage was a nod. Maybe if I didn't say much else, she wouldn't ask why I was back so early.

"How are you handling it?" Rhiannon asked. "It's fresh, so I understand if you don't know how you feel, but if you are feeling something, if you need help working through it, I'm here."

"I'm sad. And I'm angry." I didn't realize I was speaking until the words left me. My voice quivered, not with anxiety, but because of the lump forming in my throat. "Mostly, I'm sad I'm never going to see her again. I'm sad that she wasn't here when I opened the door just now. I'm sad we're not going to breakfast together. I'm sad she's gone. But I'm angry. All night, I've been trying to figure out why my chest feels so tight and aches like this, and it's because I'm angry."

Her lips trembled, and she pressed them together. She gave a short nod. "That's normal. Anger is a part of grief."

This was different. But I didn't want to get into that. Clearly, Rhiannon was struggling too.

Clicking the door shut behind me, I took a step into the room. That put us half a dozen feet apart. Rhiannon was in the corner before the closet, right next to that mirror where Delilah sat on the floor and did her makeup.

I considered heading for the sofa, but I leaned against the kitchen counter instead. "How are you handling it?"

Rhiannon glanced around and let out a half laugh. "About the same as you. Sad and angry."

"I guess that's to be expected."

"But confused, too." She rubbed a hand down her face and gestured to some photos taped to the wall. "This one, I'm assuming it's her mom. She looks like Delilah. The rest though? Every photo is of you guys." Rhiannon pointed at each one as she spoke. "You and Delilah. Delilah and Simone. Delilah and Lori, from the nursery. Junie and Simone. Even a picture of Honey."

Laughing dryly, she shook her head. "Everything in here is neat and tidy. Just look at her closet. She has her shirts and pants organized by color, style, cut. And when I was looking through everything, I found this." She grabbed a notebook off the windowsill. With tears in her eyes, she flipped between the pages. "She's been making a list of everyone who's helped her here. Every article of clothing we've given her, every pair of shoes, every bit of makeup Simone loaned her. It's a ledger she was gonna use to pay everybody back or maybe donate to the ranch once she was on her feet. I don't know. But I've been in the apartments of depressed people, and they never look like this.

"This girl wasn't depressed." Rhiannon wiped some snot from her nose with the edge of her sleeve. "She was happy, and she was hopeful. And she was just the sweetest thing. We gave her close to nothing, but it was everything to her, and I just can't believe this. I can't believe any of it."

That lump in my throat got thicker with every word she spoke. Tears finally spilled over. Not in a stream, but a gush. A sharp inhale kept me from sobbing. But the tears weren't stopping.

My voice quivered again when I said, "Is this what Sarah's cabin looked like?"

Rhiannon's face screwed up. Her lips swelled as the tears came down. It took a few calming breaths before she could nod in answer. "Sebastian told you about her, huh?"

I nodded too.

"She was the first person I thought about when Edwards and Mitchell showed yesterday." Rhiannon swatted some tears away. "Similar story, I guess. But at least this town shamed Jason out of it. He got some sort of punishment. Not as much as he deserved, but he didn't get to go on living his life like nothing happened.

"And this son of a bitch, this Evan, or Ethan, or whatever the hell his name is, he's going to get away with it. Jason did too." The tears came down again, and Rhiannon gulped in a breath. As she let it out, she rubbed her eyes. "All these bastards get away with it."

"That's why I'm angry." My lips trembled like the wings of a hummingbird. The tears came down harder, but I didn't stop. I had to say it. "I was angry when my mom died, but not like this. My mom died because she was drinking and driving. I was angry she never got her life together. I was angry that I didn't have time to heal that relationship. I was angry she was gone, and we were never going to fix the things that were broken between us. But this is different." It was a sob this time. "This is different, Rhiannon."

Eyes pinched shut, she cupped a hand over her face to regain her composure. She lowered it with lips in an O, exhaling slowly. "I know it is. I know, kid."

"I don't know how you do this." Breaths were getting harder to find. Even when I told myself to breathe, I couldn't get enough air into my lungs. Not between the tears. "I don't know how you can handle all this pain. We bring you all this, and you help us. You heal us. You were healing her. It was working. She was learning. She had hope, and dreams, and a future. And now it's gone. It's just gone because of him.

"I know he killed her, just like I know David could've killed Simone, but I don't know how you deal with this. I don't know how you can stay so calm. I don't know how you can hear these women tell their stories and not want to kill the bastards who did this to them."

It was either a sob or a laugh that escaped Rhiannon. I couldn't tell. Maybe it was a combination of both. "Moments like this don't make it any easier."

The only way to stop my trembling lip was to bite down on it. But when I opened my mouth, it just started again. "I can't write a poem. I can't write about the way that I feel, because there aren't words for this. Words can't explain how sick this world makes me. How it treats women, how it punishes us for every breath we take, every move we make, but men are rewarded for nothing. It's *our* fault when they hurt us. It's our fault for having bad taste in them. The world thinks so little of us, that even when we're working toward something, when we're doing everything right, everything *they* did will catch up to us, and we can't handle it. They think we'll kill ourselves because we can live *through* what they did, but we can't live without them?

"I just—" A gasping sob cut me off. "I love this ranch, but it shouldn't have to exist. Women shouldn't need to run here because no one else will help us. We shouldn't have to live in fear that an ex is gonna show up and beat the shit out of us like David did to Simone. We shouldn't have to come here at all, because they shouldn't treat us the way they do.

"Then they won't leave us be. Me and Delilah both had to run in the middle of the night, because they wouldn't just *leave us be*. Troy never really wanted me to begin with. He just wanted what I could do for him. Now, I'm the crazy one. I'm the one who can't sleep at night. I'm the one who needs drugs to keep the nightmares at bay. I can't trust any man, can't open up to anyone, and he's fine. He's just fine, and I'm crazy. If he ever shows, if he ever hurts me again, all he has to do is put the gun in my hand, and everybody'll say I did it myself. Just like with Sarah. Just like Delilah."

Lips shaking, head pounding, I gripped the counter for stability.

The image of blood splattering consumed my mind. Delilah in Sarah's place, a bullet ripping through her forehead, crimson shooting out her pretty blonde hair, gray matter sticking to the trees behind her, staining the snow like David's had. "Is that what he did? Did he shoot her, Rhiannon? What did he do to her? Why do they think it was a suicide? *What did he do to her?*"

Rhiannon came across the room to me. Her arms twisted around my shoulders, and mine around hers. I collapsed into her, unsure if anything I just said made sense, unsure if she even heard it through my weeping.

"It's okay, sweetheart," she whispered through tears of her own. "It's okay—"

"It's not okay!" A sob or a scream, I wasn't sure. It bellowed into the crook of Rhiannon's neck as we collapsed to the vinyl floors. "None of this is okay!"

"I know." Sniffling, gasping in breath, she held me tight and ran a hand over the back of my head. "I know, sweetheart."

Rhiannon knew the pain, but she didn't know the fury.

*The world is a better place without these men in it*, Sebastian had said.

He was right. The world was a better place without David and Jason in it.

It would be a better place if only men like Sebastian got to live in it.

Rhiannon and I stayed like that for a while. I cried, and she held me. She cried, and I held her.

When we stopped blubbering, she pulled away, wiped my tears, and told me how proud she was that I'd opened up. For a few moments, I was vulnerable. That would help in my healing journey.

For the average person, maybe that was true.

Rhiannon didn't understand. I locked it all away because crying in her arms wasn't enough. That wouldn't help me. It couldn't heal me.

My vulnerability opened the gates of hell.

She invited me to come to the dining hall for breakfast. The plan was to announce Delilah's death and arrange a vigil in her memory. I told her I'd be back by dinner, but I wanted some time to myself.

I was only by myself for the time it took to get to my house, change my clothes, feed Honey, then drive to Sebastian's.

It was just before eleven a.m. when I finished my trip up the gravel drive. The place looked just like it had this morning. Classic, dark, perhaps a bit eerie.

One of the curtains on the main floor fluttered when I pushed my door shut. I was halfway up the steps when the ones on the mansion pulled open. Sebastian stood in the threshold.

His smile didn't reach his eyes. I doubted mine did either.

Exhaustion had taken its toll, judging by the dark circles and washed-out color of his usual peachy cheeks. Since I was still wearing my makeup from last night, and I had cried most of it off, I was sure I didn't look much better.

"Hey," he said.

"Hey." I was at the top of the steps now, glancing past him into the house. "Mind if I come in?"

He stepped aside and held the door open for me. "I don't think I'll ever tell you no."

Once he heard the request I was about to make, that opinion could change rapidly.

With my feet on the hardwoods, I glanced up at the winding staircase straight ahead. It was one of those fancy foyers I'd only seen in movies. On the left, a cased opening to a formal living room with furniture worth as much as I made in a year, and the same applied to the cased opening on my right into the dining room.

If the circumstances were different, I would spend a while admiring all the architecture, all the attention to detail, the beautiful woodwork.

But the circumstances were what they were.

"I wanted to call," Sebastian began, "but after the way everything went down, I figured you wanted some space—"

"Is Lizzie here?" I asked.

"No, she left with Aubrey a while ago. They're going skiing." He cocked his head to the side. "Why do you ask?"

"No cameras around either?"

His thick brown brows crunched into his eyes. "There are a couple outside, but no, none in here. Why?"

Throughout my drive, I had known exactly what I was going to say. I knew what I had to do. I knew what was right, and I knew what was wrong. So did he. But it was damn near impossible to look into those kind eyes and remember he was the man who'd dug up two bodies last night.

"What's going on, Gwen?" Sebastian reached for me, but hesitated, studying each move I made. "Is it about David? Because if you really want me to dig him up again, I can, but—"

"No. I mean, kind of." Swallowing hard, I shook my head. "No, I don't want you to dig them up again. But yes, this is about him."

He squinted at me. "Okay. I'm ready when you are."

"I'm going to do it again." Only after those words left me did my shoulders release. "I'm going to kill the man who killed Delilah. And I want your help."

L.T. Ryan is the *Wall Street Journal*–, *USA Today*–, and Amazon-bestselling author of the Jack Noble, Rachel Hatch, and Gwen Kane series, among other mysteries and thrillers. More than eight million copies of his books have been sold worldwide. When not penning his next adventure, Ryan enjoys traveling, hiking, riding his Peloton, and spending time with his wife, daughter, and four dogs at home in Charlottesville, Virginia.

C.R. Gray writes gritty, emotionally charged mystery thrillers designed to linger long after the final page. When she's not writing, she's hiking the Appalachian Mountains with her dog, tackling DIY projects, or reading late into the night. She also writes fantasy romance as Charlie Nottingham.

## DISAPPEARING IS JUST THE BEGINNING.

You thought you knew how far someone could be pushed.

Experience the dark, emotional prequel to Gwen Kane's story, brought to life in duet narration that pulls you deeper with every word.

**FIND L.T. RYAN AND C.R. GRAY'S *BREAKING POINT* WHEREVER YOU LISTEN TO AUDIOBOOKS!**